VIPER'S
HEART
CHAOS

BY
DANIELLA.ROUCHY
INSTA; @daniella.g.m.rouchy

Daniella was born prematurely with many complications that required yearly operations, regular dental surgeries, and home recovery from birth to twelve years of age. During surgeries, she had turned to the comfort of creativity and imagination as she aged with each operation; all the surgeries stopped at the age of twelve as she finally settled with her family in England when her father retired from the army. Her passion to become an author increased throughout school and then college as her teachers admired her work and wanted her to continue towards her aim. She worked in and out of jobs when reaching eighteen. She wasn't able to get a simple job right away, not until being guided by job supporters and would gradually be introduced to volunteer work, then temporary and short part-time work. Even with the job complications and short-term work, she would always aspire to be an author. With little to no good grades, her confidence and willpower provided all she needed to be self-driven to success. Whether it was a new job or a new book, she would take any challenge and learn from each mistake and turn it into a learning curve. The only rule she lived by was very simple: have confidence in your abilities and in yourself. She took the confidence to not only write her stories with passion, but she even self-taught herself later on in life on all the skills she needed to edit and release each story, showing pride in each and every book.

Chapter One

Uneven Grounds

Before thinking about going ahead with the plan I turned to Narla as I questioned,
"can you do something for me? I need you to go back to my team",
she glanced at Neon only to see she got the confirmation, she faced me wondering,
"alright, where about are they?",
I turned to the forest stating,
"they are beyond the forest, but I think you will need this",
I pressed the centre of my armour, relieving me of the power suits grasp as Narla swapped places.
She gave me her rifle before stepping to the suit; she looked to her arm only to wonder,
"what do these buttons do?",
the suit closed on her firmly, letting her head be exposed, seeing we were short on time I stated,
"we don't have enough time to go over it, but Alis will talk you through it, she was there when the captain went over it with me",
she looked to her side, seeing the katanas were there as she

persisted,

"if I'm having this off your back you're taking your swords, rather you get a fighting chance",

upon unclipping the katanas from her waists I slotted them behind, where my revolver and dagger were placed, they were firmly behind the two holsters and out of the way ensuring I had easy access for them.

As Narla let the helmet cover her head she raced off into the forest, the glowing suit was dimmer as she left our sight, only to fade as she was further from us, this ensured me the very least that we couldn't be seen from the view of the crash site, upon looking back at the dim glowing city I stated,

"let's keep moving",

Neon kept to my right as we proceeded south, towards the city, curving left as we glanced to the crash site far from us to our right, the green glowing ship was smoking and caught on fire, I just hope the people are okay.

As we gained ground upon Rhovis Crater, the radius was growing darker, the night sky was rising, and the stars were muffled behind the thick layer of clouds above us, the first time I've seen the place cloudy for once.

I kept my left hand on my short katana hilt, ensuring my body could react to any sudden trouble.

Neon scouted the area only to warn,

"quick over here, we got a patrol of two, we can take cover by the edge of the crater",

we hurried to the edge of the crater ahead of us to our right, laying flat against the ground that had dents and dips within it.

We laid firmly facing away from the crater as the patrol was making their way to us, they couldn't quite see us not unless we gave them a reason to step closer to the edge of the dark crater.

Neon made a small movement, causing rocks to dust behind us, bouncing off the walls of the crater below, with a whisper, he cursed,

4

"shit, sorry",

the two patrol-men were in light white armour, dusty and coated in bloodstains. They wore thickly armoured jackets, zipped up and kept together with a dark grey bulletproof vest over it; they wore white murky combat trousers padded with black over armour, knee pads and shin pads, the white parts of the armour had blooded hand-prints smeared all over it, like as though they had come out of an arena.

Their rugged black boots were straying to a stop when hearing the rocks fall into the crater, it made little noise but noticeable from a few feet away.

The two silhouettes stopped far ahead of us, only to hear one question,

"did you hear that?",

the woman responded,

"yeah, sounded like it came from the crater",

I glanced right, seeing Neon was climbing down from the ledge of the crater, he persisted,

"just do it, before we get caught",

with haste I copied him, moving further from the ledge, hanging off the crater with him as the voices grew louder. We had our feet grasping the smallest cracks or ledges we could find within the crater wall before our arms gave way, my breaths went quiet as the torchlight grew brighter as the man pointed,

"the sound came from here, I saw something move",

I looked to Neon, only for him to let go of the edge of the crater with his left hand, showing me a green glow that came from his hand, forming a layer of green glowing serum over his hand, seeing the glow brighten small orbs floated from it, resembling like a swarm of fireflies.

The light gave us away, but his hand stopped glowing when the serum went back into his system, the swarm of fireflies raised as the man questioned,

"the hell is that?",

the woman pointed,

"turn the torch off",
as they did the light no longer was going to give us away as they walked closer to the edge, soon seeing Neon's plan come into motion.

He quickly used his left hand again, reaching the man's foot, as the man stepped on the ledge of the cliff to look at the fake fireflies. He pulled the man off the cliff, causing him to scream as he flung past us. With haste I grasped the woman's foot as she went to look over the edge, causing her to fall forward, hitting her head on the rocky ground before being dragged past the crater wall, falling past us in silence, as her unconscious body tumbled and hit against the rocks of the crater that peaked upon the sides of the wall, causing her bones to crack and deform along with blood splattering and painting the rocks of the crater.

Neon lifted himself from the edge of the crater with ease as I grasped the sides with both hands before losing the grip. Neon took my hands, helping me up as I used my feet to walk up the wall, gradually touching the flat ground again as I thanked him. We looked down the crater only to take note of the bridge a few feet ahead of us; we set course to the concrete framed bridge, it was very well made, and I could see each part sectioned, but how did they build it so well? No doubt they had the help from Free Liberty, their Chinooks, and the stolen aircraft.

The bridge's rails were made of thick rugged rope and wooden poles, around five inches wide per pole and a metre gap between them, most likely to ensure security for whoever walks across the bridge.

With haste we proceeded to the bridge, walking towards the city finally, seeing the rising buildings that cluttered upon a solid metal platform, held by a solid metal pillar, yet it was rusting, it looked almost as though they didn't bother to keep up with the repairs, some of the tiles were coming off, I could even hear the occasional creaks, I'm starting to wonder why none of the dead have bothered to show up, perhaps the crater is their way of dealing with the undying, traps them at the bottom, but even then it can't hold up forever.

The city was made up of shacks, they had built a city around an old hotel, they even painted the buildings a white colour, matching their armour like we previously saw.

The buildings lit up with bright lights, some of the windows were covered over with rugged sewed together rags, and even then, the light was still visible. The buildings around it were perfectly squared, a perfect one-floor apartment for four people, they all looked the same but different shades of white, some were murky white, deep grey, a bright white as if most was freshly painted.

The city was large enough to hold hundreds of people in it, the crater to think of it was larger than anticipated, I looked down upon the bridges wooden floor, seeing the dark black gap of the crater.

When looking over the edge to my right it confirmed my fears that there was nothing down there, or too dark to see how deep it really went, but when focusing deeply upon the noises coming from far below, it sounded as though hundreds of the dead were feasting, presumably the people we killed earlier…not the best way to go in my opinion.

We were closing in only to see guards were waiting upon the other side, Neon reassured,

"don't worry, they will let us pass",

I walked in front of him as he motioned me to do so, only to see him put my hands behind my back. He took out a set of rugged and rusty handcuffs from the back of his holster, something I failed to notice as it blended in with his clothes.

He tightly put them on as he remarked,

"you made this too easy",

with a frown I questioned,

"what do you mean?",

he continued,

"pretending to be your friend, I knew what was going to happen when we didn't shoot the ship down, so I ensured we didn't, and my team was wiped out, they were useless to me anyway.",

we got closer to the guards who wore the same get-up as the patrols, they had their spears crossed, ensuring we didn't enter as I remarked,

"when I get out of these",

he mocked,

"what you'll kill me? see what I did back there, I can do worse than that, not some shitty light show",

he hooked his left arm around my right side as the guard to my right questioned,

"state your business, Neon?",

the woman pierced her eyes to me, only to face Neon as he introduced,

"I just caught us the Commander of Zion city, she can get us a free pass out of here",

I observed their spears, which I then was focused on getting to the hotel, seeing a commotion of a sort.

The spears were tipped with a sharp cone-shaped tip, they had spikes crowned below it, curving upwards to ensure it tore flesh out of anyone they penetrated the spear into, the spear's body was a slim pointed metal stick, making it usable from both sides.

Gradually the spears were out of my sight, letting me see the open lit pathway ahead and the crowd that was forming by the front of the hotel, the guards took over as she stated,

"we'll take it from here",

whatever Neon had in mind it didn't go to plan as he refused,

"no I need to stay, see what happens to her",

the other guard stopped him from entering the city, seeing his plan of trying to act like the bad guy failed, I could see through his acts, trying to make me angry at him, make it more convincing that I was his capture, he tried but he can only do so much.

As we passed each shack the pathway was getting more cluttered with people, they didn't take note of me but were taking note of a woman who was arguing with someone.

The guard stopped the movement as we were at the edge of the crowd, seeing the two people at each other's throats. The woman wore the patrol-man's armour, but it had no blood upon it; her blonde hair was flowing to her left side of her head as the right was shaved off, a braid was planted where the hair met the shaven part, giving it a sharper look as her rugged face finished off the appeal she was emitting, the tough look.

She had a little boy behind him as she defended,

"you can't stop a kid from wanting to talk to me are you stupid?",

the man she was arguing with was broad in shape and toned on the arms. The man wore a rugged bronze crown, it pressed against his forehead as his dark black hair showed at the top, spiked and oiled back; his broad body was exposed from the top, showing the scars that brushed against his body, on his right side that faced us had an armband, tightly clamped on his upper arm, decorated with dozens of silver pyramid spikes, lined up perfectly within the centre.

He wore rugged white combat trousers, deep grey boots, and a thick black leather belt. His slightly tanned body was dripping with sweat that dropped from his head; his cleanly cut beard squared around his jaw, he clearly cared about his facial hair, just not what slashes at his body, he looked like he was in many fights. His left hand firmly held a unique spear, different from the rest, the tip was the same in form of the pyramid but on the edges, there was three thin thorn looking spikes, curving upwards, the bottom of the tip was sloped back into the rugged copper body of the spear.

The body of the spear had a shimmering vine twirling downwards reaching the foot of the spear that touched the ground, it was chilling to look at, he was angry at the guard for some reason, but we will find out soon enough, as the guard escorting me wanted to see the argument.

The boy stayed behind her, seeing he was afraid of the man,

the boy wore the same appeal as the guards, with less blood like the woman but lighter for the kid to be able to wear it without breaking a sweat. His hair matched his attire, it was was oiled, flattened down. He waited to see what happened. The man raged,

"you believe that because you are my royal guard, you have right of way, the child is not to be spoken with and yet you talked to him, that's not protecting me",

the woman shoved the boy back as she persisted,

"get the hell out of here kid before I kill you for this too",

the boy ran back to his parents in the crowd, they were disappointed in the boy but were worried about the woman. She challenged,

"to hell you think I will be your royal guard anymore, you want me dead, then you'll have to fight me for it, you should have been dead long ago",

the crowd were cheering as the woman approached me, the guard didn't stop her as she remarked,

"you don't stand a chance, Zetori",

Zetori unsheathed my katanas from my holsters before moving back to the fight circle. The man was waiting, it was as though he knew who was going to win. He had the spear aimed at her as she was ready to fight him with the swords; he remarked,

"you think because you have two swords, I will be taken down?",

they were in the musk of it all, slashing, striking at one another.

Every time he missed he just grew angrier, and vigilant, as he would block her attacks. Each time he did, the blades would spark green, causing confusion between them both but they kept on fighting. The man hit the back of her leg, causing her to fall upon the floor.

He kept trying to stab her on the ground, but she dodged each attack, rolling from side to side, only to swipe his leg with the sword, causing him to move backwards, letting her gain

10

ground as he grunted,

"you bitch",

the crowd was cheering, and taunting both, encouraging the fight to grow into a fury as he charged at her, she dodged the attack, causing the man to impale the boy he was threatening to kill earlier.

His parents were in shock, tears, fury, they didn't know what to show first. The young boy was on the end of the spear as the man showed the body to the woman, dragging the body against the floor as he chuckled,

"see that, you killed the boy, all you had to do was let me kill you stationary. All well, guess it's going to have to be you next",

with a force he dug the spear into the dirt layered ground, pinning his body to the ground as the man went to finish the fight with his hands.

My eyes watched with disbelief as I tried to interfere with the fight, the guard held me back along with a second pair of hands, keeping me in place as the guard covered my mouth, the second pair of hands got a firm grip upon my left side as my shouts to stop were muffled by the roars of the peoples' cheers.

The man was fighting with his fists, making swings at Zetori as she made hasty slashes to him as she raged,

"you made this, you created this city and you're destroying it",

the man grasped her hand, snapping her arm in half, causing her to drop one weapon as she hunched in pain, seeing that her right arm had fallen limp, hanging there as her elbow was like flexible rubber.

She kept the katana within her left hand, making clumsy strikes, which the man to hit her hard across the face, causing her to fall on her front.

She was grunting as she was persistent to keep fighting, she used her left hand to crawl upon the floor, digging her fingers into the dirt as she reached for my katana, the man laughed as

---

he mocked,

"let's hear what the public have to say, should she die for this betrayal? Stepping out from her post as a royal guard, putting my life in danger?",

the crowd cheered, causing the man to drag her by her feet.

My eyes filled with fury and upset, not being able to say or do anything to stop him, end this torture as he stomped forcefully upon her joints, breaking her arms and legs as she cried in agonising pain. Tears rolled down her eyes as she helplessly laid on the ground, every time she tried to move, she was only in more pain as her knees were dislocated, and fractured from the repetitive stomping. But if that wasn't enough to send her into despair, what he was going to do next would end it.

He moved down to her head, he scorned,

"you had your chances of being the best you could be, but you failed me",

her cries turned to muffled shrieks as he dug his fingers into her eyes, moving her head up, causing her cries to choke as she soon fell to gargles. Her head was torn off from her body, he ripped her head off by forcing his foot down upon her neck, then using the strength of his broad body to do the rest.

Every emotion from upset, discomfort, and anger filled me as I looked at the man with disgust, seeing his crazed eyes scour the crowd as his bloodied hands held the skull of the eyeless woman, he held the head high as he stated,

"if you are a royal guard, and you betray me, this will happen, no matter who you are, you're heads are coming off, but not the old way, the brutal way, the Free Liberty way",

the head was dripping with blood, as her torn flesh and skin hung from where her neck once was.

He dropped the body on the floor as the cheers quietened as his words were going to continue.

He announced,

"we may be Free Liberty's property, but we are our own, make ourselves different from them, their technology won't save us, it's our strength and brutality that gets us to strike fear",

he picked up my katanas, holding it firmly in his bloodied hands as he remarked,

"see, our new prisoner over there, and ones on the ship we shot down, they see the fear",

he pointed one of the swords to me as he mocked,

"see that, she's afraid, she sees the way it has to be",

with a snarl I snapped,

"the way this is? All I saw was an untamed debate, and you killed someone for no reason",

he stood firmly in front of me, looking to the guards as they let go of me, letting myself not be restricted.

He smiled sinisterly as he stated,

"see the thing is that was more of a result, the problem was dealt with, both of them and best of all I get a prize at the end",

with a frown I mocked,

"you're crazy, the hell do you live with yourself",

I tried backing off as he moved closer but the guards kept me from moving, using their spears to balance on my back, showing if I made another step I will be finished.

He put my short swords by my side as he pointed,

"you killed people before, how is that fair? You're just as crazy as me",

he put his hands on my waist, moving his grasp to the front of the belt as he continued,

"but I'm not afraid of the monster in me…",

he moved closer, moving my body to his by tugging my belt.

He moved his head to my ear as he firmly stated,

"it gets me what I want, and if being crazy, as you call me, gets me to where I need to be, then I will",

he moved away from me as he ordered,

"get her inside the throne room, my wife would like to meet her, she would like the mouth on her, it's even starting to get me into another fight", the guards forced me past him, letting him eye me up as he commented,

"oh, and don't worry, I'm sure your friends will love their punishment too. You've just made things worse for yourself, and for them",

the parents of the kid looked to me, seeing sorrow filled their eyes, they watched me walk past only to walk away from the crowd.

The leader announced,

"be prepared for midnight, it's the festival of bloodshed, the favourite time of the year, so be sure you have those blunt swords with you, you don't want to make it quick, you want it bloody",

these people were crazy, mad and deluded, my consideration of trying to join us with them are restricted, these people follow the leader, but even so, will they get out of the cycle of carnage? I can't be sure of it, some people can change yet some of them are too far gone…I need to end this before the festival.

Before things get out of hand and more people die.

Chapter Two
Bloodshed Festival

The guards escorted me past Rhovis, entering his brightly lit throne room; the wide room had a set of elevators to the left, to be precise there were two, spread apart ensuring the deep crimson red walls could be seen between the space.

The walls were matted with crimson paint, the floors, however, were coated in a shimmering black marbled tiled floor; the two contrasted with one another, giving the room a menacing yet smart appeal to it when approaching the throne bolted to the centre of the room.

Thick black rope wrapped the arms of the jagged throne, making a form of grip for the sitter to rest their arms upon; the back of the throne was cushioned with thick brown leather, padded with anything they could find, it looked hand made and cleanly sewn together to give it the oval shape.

Deep grey and slightly rusted metal ripped upon the edges, spiking up resembling like splintered wood at the top of the thrones frame; the sides were too spiked and held barbed wire within the splinters, firmly keeping it in place.

However, the four legs of the throne were even more disturbing. There were metal-made corpses, humans, and skeletons under the throne, looking as they were being crushed by the throne as they tried to keep it from touching the floor.

Seeing the appeal of the corpse to the left leg facing me, I could see its face was melting, as its hands were barely even a human shape. From men to women the statues under the throne were horrific, yet hauntingly well made for it to look realistic, as if they dipped people into molten metal.

The guards forced me to my knees, making me kneel as the woman guard stated,

"I got her, Davis, go and tell Rhovis she's ready for her, interview",

the way she said interview brought a chill down my spine, as if it was just a cover-up name for something much worse.

My knees dug into the cold marble tiled floor, the floor was so dark it could barely reflect the fire torches to the right and left side of the room, the torches were intricately made, it was shrouded by a metal grate, thick enough for the torch to hold, and wide enough to slip in oil or wood chunks to be placed within it.

When seeing nothing but the throne ahead of me, the only place in the room I could look at, I noticed there were stairs behind the throne, leading to the floors above, they were a spiralling set of metal steps, fitted with rough leather as the rails were nothing but spiked with nails, presumably just a front…I hope so.

With a huff I questioned,

"going to tell me what this is about then?",

she remarked,

"you'll know soon enough",

she wasn't informative at all, leaving me with no choice but to kneel in silence upon waiting for Rhovis.

Not long after a few minutes of deadly silence, the doors creaked open, Rhovis said,

"well look at this, the Commander kneels for another, at first it looked as though you wanted me dead",

---

16

as he walked past I mocked,

"what makes you think I still don't want you dead?",

he sat on the throne, firmly putting his hands on the ends of the arm rest, he smiled coldly as he joked,

"looks like she's even has some attitude on her too",

he leaned forward slightly as he questioned,

"so, Commander, what's your name? because you're now the new Alexandria, they told me of your status",

upon glaring at him I snapped,

"just tell me what this interview is, then you can let me go",

he laughed as he remarked,

"you think that this isn't the interview? You are thick, so let's try this again, shall we?",

his voice boomed,

"tell me, your name?",

hearing his menacingly deep voice I stated,

"Merider Black",

his frown turned into amusement, he laid back into the throne looking comfortable as he informed,

"we shot down your ship, took your people, and as 'monster' you claim I am, I recall their names well. Alis, Kamic, Mortis, Xharlot, Rhax, Qorin, Chrome, Marcella and Gina",

he sighed only to laugh as he joked,

"that's a lot of names isn't it, surprised you can even count how many there are",

he had his legs spread out as he was growing more relaxed as he expanded,

"you're probably wondering what I've done to them? Well, no need to worry, they will be eaten in time, by us, obviously",

with a look of disgust I remarked,

"is that what you plan on doing to the woman you killed? The boy you killed?",

my words clearly must have touched a nerve, his amused face was starting to frown to my words.

He was tapping his fingers upon the thrones arms as he

wondered,

"Merider, can I call you that?",

he got up from the throne as he continued,

"you think this is unfair, believe it's all my fault, but you brought your friends here in the first place, taking them somewhere where they don't belong, and for what? What do you want, Merider?",

he crouched firmly in-front of me, looking at my eyes that refused to look away as I stated,

"I came here to stop people like you, Free Liberty have stolen, and the only good people within it are waiting on death row,"

he smiled slightly as he continued,

"what about the bad people? You claim I am one of them, what could you possibly do to me that everyone hasn't tried already?",

my teeth clenched as I threatened,

"killing you successfully",

he grasped my lower jaw, firmly gripping his fingers on my cheeks as he stated,

"you will have to get through my people first to get to me, if you even try to lay a finger on me, you will have the same fate as my daughter, you saw what happened to her",

he let go of my face, letting my disgust show as I expressed,

"she was your daughter? Why do this? The bloodshed festival, the killing for a boy talking to her?",

he persisted,

"the boy was disrupting her work, she was doing just fine, that was until she met your friend, Narla. Yeah we know where you were hiding",

he captured all of my friends, but Neon was out there still, he might be able to help us from the outside. Even if he turned me in, I don't think I could have gotten in any other way.

Rhovis sat back on his throne again, building a fire of thoughts as his wife climbed down from the steps behind the throne. She wore a deep red bra that was armoured with brown leather, there were murky rags that flowed at the bottom of her shirt, if you would even call it that. Her rough brown hair was tied back in a scruffy ponytail, her fringe spiked over a thinner version of Rhovis's crown, it tucked behind her ponytail.

When seeing her move to his left the rest of her outfit could be seen; she wore a rugged red-dyed skirt that slanted backwards behind her to her left, the front of the skirt on her right thigh exposed her upper leg and the dagger holster tied around it.

She wore rugged thick black boots, wrapped with barbed wire on the outside, upon her left arm was a thick metal band but gold instead of copper. Her right arm had a modernised tribal tattoo going down to her wrist, from thick lines, clean and symmetrical triangles, to a drawing of a viper within her inner arm, it was a strange mixture, yet it worked nicely as a sleeve.

Her lips were stained a crimson red as her eyes were smudged with black paint, her brown eyebrows were thickly shaped and sharp at the ends, making her look rugged and broad as her slim face showed an almost goddess side to her, she was looking innocent yet her piercing green eyes, and evil smirk gave it away that she wasn't that godly figure she portrayed.

She had a stride to her walk as her soft voice questioned,

"Rhovis, you're going to leave me waiting again?",

when she looked to me she remarked,

"oh right, didn't know you had company",

he laughed with amusement, only to pull her right arm, closing her in on him as he stated,

"don't worry, Azella, I'm not bored of you yet",

with a frown to my face I exposed,

"how can you love someone like him? He killed your daughter",

she moved away from him only to laugh as she reassured,

"oh, he always does things like this, and Zetori was a pain too",

the guard behind me remarked,
"she was a fool to fight",
Rhovis looked impressed as Azella added,
"see, even she agrees with us",
Azella crouched as she showed me her tattooed arm as she instructed,
"look at my arm and tell me what you see",
reluctantly I examined her inner arm, seeing the viper as I said forcefully,
"a viper",
I was growing tired of their games, but my hands were cuffed behind my back, with the fine work of Neon off course, well either way I would have been bounded either way.
She smiled as she informed,
"the viper stands for death, poison of humanity and destroyer of the world. And that's what's going to happen to you, you're going to be poisoned and killed",
she smiled with her stained lips as she sighed,
"as much as it's fun to scare a prisoner, I guess I have a bloodshed festival to prepare for, sounds like this year it's going to be bigger",
she moved to Rhovis, putting her hands on the arm rests, only to kiss him passionately as she said coldly,
"better start the festival soon, we have a night to create another warrior, hopefully, one that won't fail us",
her words brought a chill down my spine as she moved away from him, glancing back to me as she remarked,
"see you dead, Merider, if not, I will do it myself",
as she walked back up stairs Rhovis sighed as he admired,
"she's ruthless I give her that",
with a frown I warned,
"just let us go, or you're going to regret it",
he sighed only to state,
"you're tied up, your friends are too, so you can say what you like and it won't change a damn thing",
a plot was coming into his head as he negotiated,

"or you tell me why you are here, I can help you",
with a puzzled look I questioned,
"why would you help me?",
he smirked as he remarked,
"well you're going to reward me, tell me something, what's the largest reward you can give me?",
seeing he was just trying to black mail me, trying to get me to give in to his little games it didn't stop me from insulting him. I threatened,
"largest reward is your death",
he looked amused as he questioned,
"do you want your friends alive or not?",
my silence answered the question as he went on,
"then I suggest you stop being smart and tell me your mission, then I can make my reward",
not wanting to tell him about the bones of Medusa, I instead told him about the Chinooks, if he's persistent to 'help' us, as he calls it, then I have no choice, my whole team didn't get over the wall just to be killed by a couple of mad people. This is on me, and as frustrating as this is, we are going to have to go by his books.
I nodded slightly, which he taunted,
"I couldn't hear you?",
reluctantly I agreed,
"fine, we're here for the Chinooks, and the downfall of Free Liberty, that's if they don't comply to my needs",
he rubbed his beard only to push,
"what needs?",
persisting to not expose the bones I stated,
"you need to get me my Chinooks first, then we can talk about that",
he was pushing more as he pressured,
"it's that, or your friends die",
I blurted,
"it's either that or you kill me, I'm not telling you the full plan when I haven't even reached my objective yet, if you

help me, then that shows me you have what it takes for the next stage",

trying to get him on my side, or at least convince him not to kill us he seemed to be swayed by my words, considering his options.

He wondered,

"hmm, okay, sounds like something I can do. But like I said, I choose my rewards",

not liking where this was going I pleaded,

"don't ask for my friends' death",

he laughed as he ensured,

"oh no, off course I will, but I'm not going to kill them",

he leaned forward as he pointed,

"you are",

with refusal I stated,

"you can't expect me to kill my friends? My team, it's not happening",

he tilted his head, seeing me virtually beg him not to do this, he sighed only to stray in thought, he said,

"you know people say we're monsters, humans, no matter who you are, where you from, what body you behold, we're all monsters",

he expanded,

"you can get me to do whatever you want just like I can do the same with you, I could even give you my wife to kill if you wanted it to be easy? But that's not happening, not because she's my wife but it's TOO easy, you believe she's evil, and you kill it",

he smiled as he wondered,

"so, it's simple, Merider, you have to pick someone to kill, they are lined up outside just as we speak, I covered their heads, muffled their hearing by earplugs, and most of all gagged them with a rag, so it's easy for you to kill them, your friends won't know it was you, but the one you kill will know, I'll make you look in their eyes and see them beg for mercy", his face had a grin of greed, evil and plain frenzy, this was madness.

I refused again,

"this isn't right, you can't make me do this",

he got off the throne, marching over to me as he exclaimed,

"you already agreed to it, you don't get a choice anymore",

he picked me up by the front of my shirt, lifting me from the ground as he explained,

"you have to do this now, it's what you are, you are like me, but weaker, I can show you how to be stronger",

he let me go as he motioned the guard to undo my handcuffs, he ordered,

"take the cuffs off, if she tries anything she won't win, I always win",

as the guard let me out she forced me to turn my back to Rhovis, allowing him to stray behind me as she kept to my side, letting me rub my hands as the cuffs were starting to chafe my wrists.

My heart was racing by the dozen when stepping outside, seeing the crowds were facing to my right, my team was lined up from my right.

When stood in-front of them I could tell who was who, by their clothes they were wearing, their body shape…it was growing harder to look at. From my left to right it was Qorin, Kamic, Chrome, Rhax, Marcella, Mortis, Gina, Alis, and lastly Xharlot.

They knelt on the floor with their hands tied behind their backs, as their head was looking around, even though they couldn't see, they were trying to figure out where they were.

The crowd stood firmly behind me as the guards made a line in front of them, stopping them from getting too close as Rhovis approached the radius.

My breaths were short as sweat started to drip from my head, my words choked,

"there's got to be a different reward, I can give you anything else", he hushed as he lurked behind me, he stated,

"you agreed, you see this bloodshed festival happens when we capture a team, normally we would be tearing at them by now, but since you're a good sport you have the honours of drawing first blood",

with a frown I looked to him as I snapped,

"what?! You said I had to kill one, you never said about drawing first blood",

he smiled as he remarked,

"you never told me the full plan, and this is already arranged",

he smirked as he wondered,

"wait, you expected us to stop the festival for you? Oh Commander, you are weak",

his words were frustrating me as he was urging me to use my rage to get the task done, but my body physically couldn't do it.

He took my katana from my left holster as he stated,

"go on, pick one. Otherwise I'll choose for you, and that won't be good, will it?",

tears rolled down my eye, seeing no way out, no one was coming, it never works like that.

He put the katana in my hand as he continued,

"you got ten seconds to decide",

as he counted down the world was slow, my tears rolled harder as it

was do or die, one must die. With force my throat lumped as I pointed,

"Gina…just bring her here",

a heavyweight pressured upon me as he put his hands on my shoulders, he said coldly,

"now that's better. See, we are a team, and once we get your Chinooks back, I can take Free Liberty, restore it to a better future",

he moved past, going behind Gina only to grasp her hands that were firmly behind her, forcing her to stumble forward, putting her back to her knees as she was placed in front of me.

24

The tears trailed down my face seeing her franticly look around; soon I could see her face as Rhovis took the mask off her head, she looked to Rhovis only to look at me, her eyes filled with red and water as she muffled pleads.

As Rhovis took off her earplugs and gag off, he walked behind me as he said sinisterly,

"here you go Merider, the first blood is yours",

Gina was in bits as she cried,

"please you don't have to do this Merider, don't let him kill us",

my eyes were filling with sorrow and guilt, I didn't know how else we were going to escape this, the people here are so evil, they are hateful and worst of all they don't care who is dead, they just want to cause bloodshed.

Rhovis was growing impatient as he questioned,

"Merider? you picked your human, go and kill it",

when glancing back at him I persisted,

"what if I told you about the second part of the plan? Will you spare the others?",

he went closer to me as he wondered,

"if that's going to be the case then it's agreed, your friends with be spared, she won't be",

I nodded, which I negotiated,

"put my friends in the throne room then, let me have that as a piece of mind",

he tried to be smart as he forced,

"tell me the plan first",

with a deep sigh I looked to Gina, seeing she was urging me not to tell him, but I have no choice, if it means my friends can be spared then it's something that has to be done.

My shaken voice explained,

"it's the bones of Medusa, we need the scientists to identify how to destroy them, for good",

he looked impressed with himself as he ordered,

"guards, get her minions inside, then let's get this bloodshed over with, seems like we only have ourselves to kill", the guards took the team into the throne room, forcing them inside as I puzzled,

"you're still going to continue the festival?",

he laughed with amusement as he remarked,

"what did you think we were going to do? If there are no people, or we get a successful negotiation from our prisoners, then we spare them and kill one, or kill them all in the festival if they didn't give us enough",

he rubbed my shoulders as he looked to Gina, he whispered,

"we are the monsters, we take and we give, but today we're taking",

he put moved his hand below my chin, forcing me to look over to my left to see his face as he continued,

"you can be so much more than this, you just need to let the monster take over, you tamed it so long you have forgotten the joys of killing, being powerful",

he slowly moved my head to look at Gina as he pointed,

"you will turn out like her, pathetic, crying over death, when we monsters face it",

he let go of me, allowing me to have my space as I stated,

"if crying over death is a weakness, showing emotions is a weakness, then I am the monster",

Gina looked afraid as I looked to my sword, seeing my eyes were straying to hers.

She begged,

"Merider, don't do this, I was wrong about you okay, I was wrong and it wasn't fair on you, you're trying to help, and Uri and I were trying to ruin it, he got us here, Uri did this, please don't let me die like this",

Rhovis was amused by her cries, he even laughed as he encouraged,

"how pathetic, Merider, she even is a tattle-tale too, well not only is she able to do that but she could betray you, isn't that the fire you need",

my breaths were focused as my tears were stopping, it was do or die.

We can't let people drag us down, take us, break us.

This is the only way to do it, with firmness, my grasp tightened upon the hilt as I requested,

"Rhovis, I need you with me, it's not just my option but it's your punishment, make sure it's done to your liking",

he looked amused, seeing I had given him the respect he wanted, giving him the authority over me as he agreed,

"see, now you're learning",

Gina's eyes were burning with red as her lips quivered,

"we were helping you, Merider, I know you were watching me in the beginning, you have to understand that we didn't know this would happen",

Rhovis cut in,

"kill her slowly. If you want me to be on your side it has to be slow, a deep penetration to the heart, then tear off her limbs, one by one",

he was growing more and more agitated as my body was building up, urging myself to do it, just get it over with before my sanity takes over.

His words reaped over again,

"kill her, just kill her already",

the crowd started to cheer in a frenzy as I raised my swords to my right side, ensuring I had the angle right before making a swing, causing the crowds cheers to muffle into silence as Gina shrieked for mercy…

It's do or die, take the strike, before the chance don't come back.

Chapter Three

Do or Die

With force I changed the sword's direction, moving past Gina's head and hitting Rhovis's instead, my swing caused me to face him, seeing the katana spray neon sparks where he stood, the edge of the blade glowed a sinister neon green. The sword cleanly cut through the top half of his skull, burning the skin, bone, and flesh it was faced with; the crowd fell silent when seeing his body slant to his right, only to collapse as the skull slid off from his body, splatting to the floor below as his exposed brain spat blood upon the floor, soon draining within the dirt.

When moving the sword back the people looked tamed, as if I just took the lead from Rhovis's hands as I ordered,

"get Azella, now",

the guard who was making remarks all the time and stuck with me through the whole thing instantly left my sight, doing my biddings as I sheathed my sword back within the holster, feeling the weight lift off me as my body didn't need to do his sickening demands.

The crowd looked to Rhovis's limp and lifeless body, silenced by my actions as I turned to Gina.

She looked to me only to stand up as she thanked,

"thank you, thank you",

when approaching her I turned her around, untying her as I stated,

"don't thank me, don't you ever think I was going to do that",
she faced me as the knotted rope was finally taken from her
wrists.

Her eyes were still reddened from upset, but she couldn't
contain her emotions, and I couldn't blame her, she probably
thought she was going to die today.

With firmness I questioned,

"Uri and you set this up? explain it to me, trust me I won't be
mad at you, I think you got your scare",

she laughed slightly as she wiped her eyes, she remarked,

"yeah I think that was unintentional for you to scare me like
that, but yeah I learned my lesson",

she said seriously,

"Uri on the other hand, he didn't have the bones, Sheriff War
will have them by now, he wanted someone to stay behind to
lower our chances of surviving out there, he didn't like me
anyway and persisted I was dead to every fail I made",

she looked to the crowd behind me, feeling slightly
uncomfortable but she knew they wouldn't try anything, it
was bizarre, it was like the Vipers way, that whoever killed
their Commander was the next ruler.

Gina expanded,

"he persuaded Free Liberty to side with him to kill you,
because that's what they wanted, kill the next Commander"

with a frown I questioned,

"to kill the next Commander?",

she nodded as she explained further,

"it's something Free Liberty has been trying to do for years,
they want betrayers and traitors on the other side of the wall
to help them take their goal. Uri and I were the fools they
trusted to do the job",

I ensured,

"trust me you may have wanted this to happen but until it's in
motion you don't know how deep this can go, just lucky this
even happened",

uncontrollably she hugged me, not knowing how else to

thank me without crying, even more, she must have felt bad for everything, she would have felt guilty, upset, and not only that but I did scare her, big time, and that didn't feel great either.

I returned the hug as I urged,

"come on, we need to get a clear head on this",

she moved back as she joked,

"you try being in my position, I thought my death was going to be ironic",

she laughed slightly, only to listen to me as I instructed,

"why don't you walk it off. There's a man that I need you to find, his name is Neon",

the guard came back as she cut in,

"I can help you guys out with that in a second, but you need to get in the throne room, right now",

with worry we followed after her, going into the throne room to see what was going on this time.

As I walked through the doors first, I saw my team to the right side of the throne room along with Rhax and his team, they were out of their binds, their hoods and earplugs, along with the gags were on the floor also, as the guard must have helped them out.

Qorin looked to me as he persisted,

"Merider, you got to talk some sense into that bitch",

when looking left I saw Azella, she was holding a revolver to them, but it didn't faze the team, they didn't even look scared, they were more worried about making a wrong move causing a death of our own.

When approaching Azella I stated,

"drop the gun Azella, Rhovis is dead, and your people are under my ruling",

she aimed the gun at me as she warned,

"you can back away from me, if you're under ruling you'll want me dead",

Kamic negotiated,

"unless you give her a reason to kill you, I highly doubt she's going to kill you now",

Azella glanced down to Kamic, only to quickly make a shot at him, with haste I tackled her, causing the shot to go blind as I forced myself on top of her.

With swiftness I took out my dagger from my belt holster, putting the edge of the blade upon her neck, forcing her to let go of the gun as I pressed,

"you make another move and I will kill you, don't give me a reason to do that",

Alis approached us, taking the gun from the floor before I got us off the ground.

Firmly I stood with my dagger back in the sheath as Azella wiped herself down, she looked at Kamic as she wondered,

"you okay?",

he laughed as he remarked,

"am I okay? You just shot my arm you idiot",

Gina reassured,

"don't worry I'll patch you up, but we do need to take the bullet out before I can do anything",

Azella pointed,

"go up stairs in my room, I have tools in the top dresser draw",

she glanced to me as she poorly covered,

"for, uh emergences",

Alis remarked,

"are they sterile?",

Azella sarcastically smiled as she stated,

"yes, they are sterile I'll have you know. I'm not crazy",

Xharlot insisted,

"Marcella and I will help you out, you'll be needing more than just one person for this job",

as Xharlot, Marcella, Gina, and Kamic proceeded behind the throne, ascending upon the steps to the second floor, we were left to figure where to go from here.

Rhax and Qorin approached me as Azella questioned,

"so is Rhovis really dead? Or are you just saying that to get me to follow you willingly",

Rhax remarked,

"you make it sound like it wasn't a choice to be his lover",

she admitted,

"well at first it wasn't, but he kind of grew on me, he was more of a man than you, that's for sure",

before this turned into a heated argument, I cut in,

"look, we need to know if you want to kill us still, because if not, we are here for a reason, and we need the extra pair of hands",

Qorin agreed,

"as much as I hate this idea, Merider is right, we need all the help we can get",

Azella wondered,

"so if I help you then what?",

with a puzzled look I firmly stated,

"then nothing, you're just helping us and saving the land you live on, if you seriously want a reward then a place in the council of Zion City will be enough",

Rhax halted,

"woah wait she can't just be handed the city",

with firmness I explained,

"I'm not handing her the city, she will just be my helping hand, if she wants to redeem herself then she can show me what she's good at",

Azella challenged,

"and what's that? You seem to know me from the back of your hand",

I looked to Alis as I reassured,

"you can lower the gun, she won't try anything",

she looked wary, but trusted my judgement.

As she lowered the gun I expanded,

"people like you I've met many times, one person, in particular, was called Deoaka, she was greedy, wanted blood, and did anything to get what she wanted, that's what you are. You went with him because he wanted you, and you didn't

like him, not at first but you went with it because it got you everything from power to money, to bloodshed, your place of power was what you wanted",
she crossed her arms as she encouraged,
"so what happens if I'm in this council position of yours?",
seeing her attitude was changing she was sounding less evil, less cynical, it was as though this completely different person was hiding within her and she let her true self show.
With firmness, I explained,
"you get the same amount of power you have here, but you get a voice, and input in situations and from what you said earlier, about those tools it sounds as if you might be a good interrogator",
she smiled slightly as she approached me teasing,
"how come it's been this long before meeting you? Sounds like you're quite fun to be around",
Mortis remarked,
"yeah she really isn't so far",
Alis laughed only to join him as she reassured,
"don't worry, you think this isn't fun, just wait",
she joined Mortis and Chrome upon the other side of the room as she was joking around with them, seeing the opportunity to just relax herself for a moment, as we finally weren't in a life and death situation, for now, that is.
Qorin questioned,
"you're an interrogator?",
Azella looked at him as she remarked,
"ah so you do civilised talk as well",
I gave her a look, making her put more effort into insulting my team less, and instead, get along with them.
She nodded before she recalled,
"I believe it was before the storm, the profession of an interrogator in the army has its perks now, I just make it my way",
he was curious as he glanced at me, seeing he was trying to be interested.

33

However, I think he was more than interested on the topic considering his past. To let them have their own conversation I motioned Qorin to continue, letting the conversation with Azella go on as Rhax and I moved away from them, moving to the entrance, meeting with the guard as she wondered,
"Is everything okay?",
Rhax looked amused as he wondered,
"you know, I like how Merider has to kill the Commander of the city here, and automatically you change your ways",
she smirked as she stated,
"well, that's the Vipers way. I mean we dress up as our own, we call ourselves the Pythons instead, as an alternate version because we may be from the Vipers clan, but it's long since been dead, we're the last of its kind",
with a perked up face I encouraged,
"wait so you're Vipers? That tattoo that Azella has is based on that culture then",
she nodded only to go into more depths about how the clan works.
She expanded,
"Azella was the last of the Vipers and so are we but she was the Commander's daughter, since coming here though people changed, we changed to stylise like the Eviliance, I think you can tell with the white and black, but we added blood upon it, show it's not the same. Anyway, I'm going off track. We came here and Rhovis lived here, we thought it was abandoned but clearly wasn't as we got closer, he let us in if Azella could marry him, so she did it, not for herself if anything but for us",
she did have a heart, after all, bet over time she grew this bitter shell to hide the fact she once cared for humanity and her people.
With knowing that I knew at least half of the people have passed on the tradition, if it weren't for the fact over half the city population were Vipers we wouldn't be able to overrule the city so easily, if you would say that was easy, it was

---

34

emotionally and physically draining.

With firmness I stated,

"well, now your guys won't die so harshly under my hands, not unless you betray me, I don't take that so likely",

she laughed as she reassured,

"seeing how you killed Rhovis, I don't think anyone will mess with you. That sword of yours, where did you get it?",

Rhax remarked,

"why? So you can kill people with it, ours especially",

I nudged him, causing him to stop his words as the guard joked,

"well I do plan on killing people with weapons, but not my own",

seeing what Rhax's deal was I curiously asked,

"what's your name? you never told me",

she warmly introduced,

"Rarla Stormer, sorry Commander, I should have remembered you didn't even know my name",

she smiled only to glance at Rhax as I asked,

"Rarla, do you mind if I can talk to Rhax for a moment? Check on Kamic for me, see how they are doing",

she walked past me instantly heading off to do the job as Rhax faced me, seeing he was going to be asked many questions until we cleared the air.

With firmness I persisted,

"tell me what your deal is, you've been off with me and my team even before this",

Rhax stated,

"we can't just accept this, let Azella and the city join our grounds",

I continued sharply, "what do we do then? Let them stay here on their own and slowly die out, we need more people on our side, and you out of all people should have understood that",

Rhax looked as though my words offended him as he challenged,

"what's that then? Why, out of everyone, am I supposed to

be the most understanding for some movement like this?",
without hesitation, I stated,

"you're a leader, you're supposed to accept change and let it happen for the better, I used to hate doing things like this as well",

he didn't seem convinced until I made an example of my statement I was making.

Hearing me out I expanded,

"okay you know what Qorin used to be a raider all right, he attacked my city under the name of his leaders, but he and his rebellion helped us, seeing that I was persistent on taking the city back, they helped me. And ever since, Qorin has earned my trust, and kept his faith with me. Do you think I should have killed him then? Kill him along with the rebellion, when an Undying hoard was marching to our doorstep",

he considered my words as he wondered,

"surely you could have survived on your own",

with doubt I stated,

"no if I could then I wouldn't have anyone with me, just myself and that's not what I'm wanting, I don't want survival just for myself I need others to survive too, we've been fighting for so long that we forget others are just wanting to live, we need to do this Rhax, not for us, for our team",

my words made him open his mind, see the picture for what it was, it wasn't sparing them, it wasn't mercy, it was a second chance to redeem themselves.

He nodded agreeing with my words, only to gather his as he ensured,

"I will get along with her and the others then, its survival, I see it now",

with a smile I reassured,

"you were never wrong, Rhax, you knew it since the start, it was just that change hasn't happened yet, but it's happening now, we can finally break free of the old ways",

I looked behind me to see Azella approach me as she questioned,

"Merider, can I talk to you in private, it's about the arrangements, of the situation the very least",

when looking back to Rhax, I let him stay with me, letting him have some role in this as I turned back to her, I wondered,

"what is it?",

she stated,

"Neon, the one that's outside the walls, he has a huge part in the plan",

without knowing where this was going, I encouraged,

"okay, go on",

she expanded,

"you know he has powers, not the lethal kind but he might be able to gain the attention of Free Liberty. We can get to the third camp and see if they are breathing, we never really check up on them, so before we go we have to find him, he doesn't know you and I are pals yet",

Rhax stated,

"you will stay with Merider and Qorin then. Narla is out searching as we speak, he thought to wait up but she didn't see the point in waiting around",

she should be fine on her own but it's a risk searching out there, the dead do get attracted easily.

With persistence I stated,

"Azella will have to announce the march then, I'm not leaving people here, they are mostly all fighters and if Free Liberty have a migration at their door step they will be vigilant, we need all we can get to over throw them",

Azella looked back as Marcella raced down the steps, she called,

"Merider, we have company!",

with a frown I worried,

"what do you mean?",

I hurried past Azella as she and Rhax followed me.

Qorin, Mortis, Chrome and Alis joined us as Marcella explained hastily,

"we were finishing with Kamic. Then we heard something odd, we looked outside and there's a fighter helicopter on its way, two maybe more",
Azella stated,
"okay, we get the march to the third campsite, build up our team there. I'll get the evacuation on point",
Rhax insisted,
"I'll help out also. Merider, you get the team on the ready we won't be stopping",
Azella refused,
"woah wait we can't just leave without her",
seeing her worries but knowing Rhax was right I stated,
"no he's right, if we delay things by waiting, then we all don't stand a chance against the helicopter",
Rhax instantly left the room, seeing the green light was go.
Azella saw there was no other way to talk me out of it, she informed,
"Narla's suit is in the lower floor, just be careful, the pillar will give way under attack, so be quick",
she left the room as Marcella questioned,
"Merider what the hell do we do? We haven't got the gear to take down the helicopter",
when looking at the elevator I persisted,
"if they confiscated Narla's gear, there then there's the start, we can know what else they have there",
when facing Mortis, Qorin and Alis I persisted,
"help Azella and Rhax with the evacuation, the team will meet you, Marcella and I will grab what we can",
Qorin tried to convince me to change my mind but I said firmly,
"now, the attack helicopter is not far from us",
they hurried out the room as Chrome approached me as he wondered,
"what should I do, Commander?",
with thought I hastily questioned,
"what are your functions? Can you take down one of the

helicopters",

his hands grew large curved claws as his legs were curved backwards, acting as springs as he stated,

"I can run at fifty miles per hour with these legs, and I can jump over sixty feet. My hands are also gripped and built to tear. So I can go on the roof when they get close",

when nodding to the plan I persisted,

"you go to the roof, wait till they get close and see if you can take one of them down, I'll join you",

as Chrome headed past us to the throne, going towards the spiralling set of stairs, Marcella And I hurried to the elevator, entering the closest one before pressing the button labelled '-1' the only button that went below ground.

As we descended within the shimmering silver elevator, Marcella worried,

"you said you're going to meet him on the roof? What are you going to do?",

with firmness, I informed,

"I'm going to take down the ships, fleeing won't stop them from following us, so whatever Rhovis has we are going to use that against the aircraft's, as you're going to attack from the ground, Chrome and I will take them in the air",

the door slowly opened, allowing us to see the large room ahead of us, it was squared with cabinets and crates upon the white walls, the bright light showed us half of them were over full with pistols, rifles, and anything else that was taken from stranded people, or those unfortunate to cross their paths.

When entering the room we searched around the room as Marcella persisted,

"We better look for launchers, there's got to be some psycho they captured who had possession of one",

instantly I could see where the suit was, it was stood within the centre of the room, cover in dust and scratch marks.

With a fast pace to my steps, I hurried to the suit pressing the centre of the chest, allowing the suit to fold open at the front.

I quickly took off the katanas clipped holsters, putting them to my right side before stepping back into the suit, allowing it to shield over my body, firmly keeping me in a protected shell as the suit lit with life again.

Firmly I took the katanas from the floor, attaching them to my suit as I questioned,

"Marcella, did you find anything?",

she motioned me to the left side of the room where she was, she showed me the opened locker as she stated,

"two RPG's, meaning we're going to have to be lucky in where we shoot. We got some frag bombs too, so you can take them with you, if you can get a hand bomb in there it could take them down",

when taking a satchel of dusty frag bombs, firmly gripping them within my right hand, Marcella took the RPG as she remarked,

"better hope you don't get in my way, that will be a story to tell",

she put the RPG strap over her shoulder, allowing herself to take a small duffel bag of rounds with her as she persisted,

"we can only take one launcher, we can't outweigh ourselves",

keeping grip of the satchel we hurried out of the room, heading to the elevator before the attack could outrun us.

As we raised I could hear a mass panic, the people were leaving but the sounds of the helicopters were loudening; Kamic stood with Gina, Xharlot, and Rarla as they were waiting on us.

When approaching them I stated,

"you guys need to leave with Marcella, right now",

as Marcella joined them Xharlot questioned,

"what the fuck is going on, one minute we saw the helicopter but now half the team's gone",

with a shortage of time I explained,

"Rhax and Azella are leading the evacuation, Narla is searching for Neon who are still out there, we can search for them later, we need to be in one piece before even thinking about going back for others",

Xharlot persisted,

"what about us? What are we going to do?",

Marcella remarked,

"be alive, we need to go now",

she turned to me as she forced,

"go to the roof, now. Chrome will be needing your help out there",

seeing as the team didn't have any choice, they left me in the throne room as they were going to the direction of the evacuation, they were heading east to where the helicopters were coming from most likely, they should be splitting up upon the bridges to ensure at least a bunch of the people could survive the attacks.

Without time to waste, I hurried up the spiralled staircase, going past floor by floor until reaching the last section where the walls curved around the staircases, leading to a door that shut me out from the rooftops.

It's all or nothing…

Chapter Four

Havocs Kiss

When opening the door to the roof I could see the large squared floor around me, no railings were squaring around the edges, just a blank concrete square to walk upon.
Chrome was within the centre of the grounds glancing behind himself when hearing me call,
"Chrome, how bad is the upcoming attack?",
when firmly standing upon his right he pointed,
"there are three attack helicopters, they weren't there before the wall happened",
with piecing together his words I theorised,
"you're saying they might have had some help with that? or do you think they built it from scratch?",
he stated,
"they either did make it themselves or we got another person to worry about, either way, they aren't slowing down, what's the plan?",
he looked to my satchel I was keeping a firm grip upon as I persisted,
"we have four chances to take them down, four hand grenades, three helicopters",
when giving him a grenade he slipped the ring on his thumb, ensuring a quick pull to the hand bomb and enabling him to use his four clawed fingers to grasp the helicopter.
When giving him the other bomb his hands were both

equipped for battle.

As for me, I took the last two upon my hands, slipping the rings upon my thumbs like Chrome did, keeping a hold of it, and ensuring it didn't fall out of my grip too soon. The three attack helicopters were skinny, painted with black matt paint causing it to appear even dirtier as the ash and whatever else it was carrying stuck to the paintwork, giving it the old appeal too.

They were gaining ground and were going to target the civilians, not unless we gave them a different target to focus on; with haste we ran upon the rooftops, charging ourselves to the edge before making a jump, activating my suit as Chrome launched himself to the closest helicopter that crept to the centre of the city.

My suits jet-pack soared me close to the second helicopter, seeing the missiles were launching at the bridges, causing them to collapse one by one.

The people were being torn by the shrapnel coming from the metal made bridges, the wooden planks of the bridges however were exploding into balls of splintering wood, penetrating the civilians on the nearby bridges. They were running faster than their legs could go, tripping over, trampling upon people it was starting to turn into havoc as the third helicopter was setting in motion, taking over the second helicopter's job as it was under attack. The helicopter was slow to face me as I curved to the left side of it, seeing the open doors as foes were using their machine guns to take down the people upon the bridges and the city.

With haste I flipped the pin from the grenade when rising to the door of the helicopter, seeing the people panic as I gently threw the grenade within the aircraft, ensuring it didn't vacuum to the other side.

The people were jumping overboard, with and without parachutes as the grenade went off, destroying the second helicopter with a ball of fire and smoke, damaging it internally before it spread to the outside, causing the aircraft to go up in smokes.

My suit took some damage as I dove downwards, trying to avoid the explosion as it rained past me, falling to where the bridges once were standing, seeing the crater below me.

The darkness of the night was flashing orbs of red and orange as the missiles penetrated the bridges and city buildings, causing fires to spread and the noises to echo upon the Dead Zone, surely will be attracting attention any time soon. the third helicopter was scouting for me as the first helicopter was finally crashing, Chrome must have used the grenades, but he wasn't there, I couldn't see him it was too dark to find a glimmer of his metal shimmering skin, but he's not dead I know that, I believe in him and that's all that counts, I just need to take down the last helicopter before worrying about the evacuation plan.

The shots were echoing louder as Marcella fired a missile upon the helicopter, causing it to go into smoke, when flying past it stopped as a second missile was shot, causing me to move backwards when hovering upon the air, seeing the missile pass my body before annihilating the last helicopter. The bright orange glow that puffed from the aircraft gradually faded; the people that parachuted weren't to be worried about, even if they ended in the city or within the crater there was going to be the Undying no matter what route they have chosen.

Hearing the deadly silence I hurried to where the people were building up, they had made it through the southeast side of the city to my left, luckily, they looked all in one piece, some had cuts, and others were bruised from trampling, but I think we're fine.

My suit gently landed to the left of the group, they watched me land as I worried,

"Is everyone okay?",

when the suit lowered my helmet, revealing my face to them, one of the women stated,

"not everyone made it out, but yeah we're fine at least",

they looked to my right, overlooking the crater and city that was gradually burning into flames, the HQ was destroyed, the homes were engulfed in flames, it was an Undying welcoming bonfire if we stay here any longer, it looks as though the smell of the crater burning was attracting the dead along with the fire that urged them to wonder there.

Marcella moved past the crowd with Rhax and Azella as she informed,

"Alis said she found Neon and Narla, but we have to go to them, we know where they are",

with persistence I stated,

"we need to get the crowd moving, I will go with Rhax and look at the situation",

Azella nodded before she questioned,

"where are we taking them?",

with not knowing I wondered,

"do you know any places in the city? Perhaps a warehouse we can stay in, we can't trust the clans around here, especially with that performance put on us",

Azella was in thought, she ensured,

"I got a place we can go, it's a store but we locked it down, there still might be dead in there but I think we can cope with it",

Rhax ordered,

"go to the store and marked down each mile you make, we'll come back with the full team",

Azella nodded, only to motion Marcella to follow her as she ordered,

"Alright everyone on me, we need to be quiet about this so keep the volume on the minimum",

as the crowd was moving Kamic and Mortis approached us as they expressed,

"we need to go with you",

Rhax stated,

"one of you can come, but it can't be you Kamic, you're injured and we can't afford to be slowed down",

45

the choice was too quick to make, but I understood the urgency, as the dead were gaining ground on us from the North, some had strayed away from the wall, going to where the commotion was erupting.

Kamic sighed as he remarked,

"well, don't expect me to not go after you in case you're late",

as Kamic strayed away with the back of the crowd, guarding the people who didn't carry guns with them, which were very few people.

They were walking blind but used the street lamps that flickered ahead to where the city was standing by the edge of the dried-out fields.

Mortis kept to my left as we walked ahead, Rhax stated,

"they are ahead, Alis said something about a situation, she didn't tell us what situation but from the sounds of things it was an avalanche of a sort from the tower over there",

he pointed to an old radio station ahead of us, it was accompanied by a crowd of holds, broken homes and apartment buildings, this place was barely even standing, the mid-central of large buildings to the left to it shortening to our right gave the impression that each place was just a little bit different, some were cluttered with building and some parts were nothing but a wasted field, makes me wonder how bad the first storm was like over here.

With curiosity I questioned,

"did Alis say anything else?",

Mortis remarked,

"to be honest with you, Commander, I don't think we even know why we're bothering, but here we are",

Rhax kept his attention ahead as he silenced,

"shh, we're closing in",

I looked to my left hand, seeing I still had the non-active frag. Mortis noticed as he took the bomb only to whisper,

"see you don't have pockets, well this can come in handy anyways, I'll keep that safe", as he took the bomb, placing it within his left pocket I looked ahead as I wondered,

"is that, Alis?",

I saw a faint silhouette that flickered to show Alis as she stood on a tipped over bus, firing upon the dead that was crowding her and clawing at the bus, some were close to climbing on top of it.

My glowing suit attracted some of them but Alis looked more tempting for over half of them, the dark street behind her looked haunting when closing in, Rhax started firing only to stop as I seized,

"no we need to use our daggers or in my case swords, we can't attract more",

Rhax remarked,

"your glowing suit doesn't help, either way, we can kill them all",

seeing he and Mortis were persistent to open fire on the dead, shooting their heads one by one as two more dead would show up, some of them were crowding us, leaving me to defend them from close, as they went long-range to the ones by the bus.

With haste I unsheathed my katanas, slashing the dead causing sparks of green to burn some of the surrounding Undying.

The ones killed had a green glow to each slash and stab to the head, oozing their thick blue blood upon the floor when falling to the damages, leaving me to finish them off with a stab through the skull.

Most of them fell, either with one strike, or stab through the head, inches away from Mortis and Rhax as we pushed forward to the bus, seeing Alis empty all of her clips on every gun she had, her last resort was to stab them through the head, causing her to be in the heat of the danger.

My pace picked up as I called,

"Alis, stand back, we'll get you",

she persisted,

"no way, I'm not going to be outnumbered",
Mortis had the body of his rifle on the Undying that was gnawing at him, forcing him to shove the creature back as a chunk of his neck was spurting from his throat, causing his curses to muffle words as he choked upon his own blood.

I raced towards him, seeing the dozens of Undying were crowding, hearing his unbearable screams and cries for help. Rhax stayed close to me as he covered my back as I pulled off each of the dead, slashing their heads and throwing them aside.

Mortis's screams were turning into whimpers as the dead were starting to target me, seeing I was the next threat, the smell of Mortis's blood was attracting the dead to move away from the bus, allowing Alis to go to the ground, and take on the dozens of Undying from the back, taking risk after risk as black and blue blood was spewing upon us, it was as though the blood still roamed around the vessels of their veins, the Undying was alive but not alive enough to know when to stop killing, when to stop eating, they just kept attacking and forcing us to give up, tire us out as they had more numbers to them over on this side of the wall.

Rhax was to my back as we forced each of the dead to the ground, as Rhax shot them I gave him my Katana before we were restricted of all movements, tearing each of the Undying's head, cleanly cutting through their heads to impaling through their eyes, dripping blood upon us as sweat dripped upon our faces, Mortis's cries could still be heard, he was alive but how alive? How bad was the damage? I couldn't know, all I could see was my suit's green glow reflecting off the dozens of Undying that were around us, seeing their skin droop from their faces, exposing the rotting flesh and bones beneath it.

The cloudy pale eyes were staring at us, watching us as we slashed at each one of them, they were ruthless enough to have their hands in the way of our attack as they tried to test their boundary's, seeing if the swords could also be eaten.

48

As our strikes were growing weaker, the crowd was starting to thin out, Alis was wiping them out from the back, as we were in the centre of the feast, determined not to be torn apart, well Rhax has more of the chance of that happening to him as I have protection, but even so, the suit can only stand so much before giving up.

The blood that was drizzling from the sword was starting to give effect to the handle, making it oily and slippery to grip on; Rhax persisted,

"Merider we need to push through your side, the grip is starting to get a little on the slippery side",

the growls were loudening as they closed in on us, forcing me to push forward, holding the blade horizontally as I grasped the end of the blade with my right hand, using it as a manual mower as I was pushing the Undying back, cutting into their heads with force as Rhax took out the ones behind us, it was working, the creatures were thinning out just by a small percentage as we had enough space to move around.

Alis pushed her way through as she persisted,

"Merider we got to go",

she approached us shortly as the gap was closing behind her, nearing her being bitten and permanently marked as an Undying, luckily she shoved the Undead back into the crowd, going to our location as we went back to back, repeating our last steps, now that we had made a bigger gap.

Alis's hair and body was drenched in blue and black blood, making it look as though she dipped it in oil as it glimmered from my green glowing suit.

Upon slashing one Undying to stabbing the next, Alis said hastily,

"can you use your shield? They are getting a bit close",

with force I fended with my left hand, pressing the shield button, seeing nothing happened as the suit announced,

"forty percent of your suit is charged, shield activation function is not available under fifty percent",

upon listening to the suits warning I stated,

"we're just going to have to be careful on how close they get, just keep doing what we're doing, there's a few dozen left, we should be fine",

the crowd that was just under four dozen had finally reached to a dozen, our energy and fortunately my suit also, had helped me take down more of them, ensuring the protection for my team, all apart from one who I don't know is alive anymore, there were so many bodies scattered around us that when killing the last Undying it felt as though there was no solid ground under us.

Alis caught her breath as she thanked,

"thanks for the extra pair of hands, I should have just went to you myself, instead of getting us in this mess",

I scouted around, using the suits perks of the targeting sight to see if there were any more crowds to come, so far none but the sound travels far, meaning we better go and get Neon and Narla before we get outnumbered again, I don't think I could do that a second time in one day.

With firmness I stepped over the bodies cluttered by our feet, hurrying over to Mortis as I tapped the side of my helmet with my free hand, opening my helmet, exposing my head, Breathing in the rancid rotted air created by the dead bodies around us. When stood to his left I could see his half-eaten body; the suit caused the radius to glow a few feet around me, giving us light.

A lump formed in my throat, seeing the dead that had fallen upon his legs, tangling them as his stomach was torn open, showing his intestines and fast beating heart.

The blood was dripping and oozing from his stomach, causing me to look into his eyes as his mouth had drips of blood trickling from it as he muttered weakly,

"kill",

he turned his head right as he reaped those words over and over, only to stop as Rhax dug the katana into his head, making his words silent upon impact.

As he took the katana out of Mortis's head, his eyes watered

50

as he stated,

"we need to get going, Narla and Neon are ahead of us",

he kept hold of the katana, seeing as his other weapons have run out of ammunition.

Blood had stained his grey hair, turning it a deep black and blue colour from the remains of the Undying.

Alis was walking to the right of me as Rhax was to hers, leading the way past the bus stop and into the darkened city streets. The glow of my suit reflected off the puddles formed in the streets, some were rain, some were oil from the broken cars, and merely the rest were formed from blood…human blood, those who were turned into the Undying, when the blood was fresh and once gave life to the person it was stored within. To the left were rows of apartments and stores, the radio we had passed was firmly locked down and windows were bordered up, however, I can say the same to the other buildings, people's homes were too on lockdown, it was a literal graveyard in this place.

Alis pointed to the left as she stated,

"they are over there, the tower fell over and Neon says Narla was trapped in there",

with the curiosity of how the situation came by, I wondered, "how did they end up here? I thought Neon was finding a way into the Rhovis city",

Rhax stated,

"Neon said he thought to see if he could slip away, he knows now that it was a wrong choice to make",

Alis added,

"he may be a coward, but he said he thought he would have been with you when giving you in as part of the plan, yet I don't see how that's helped us out",

she was right, no matter what he's done it's not helped anyone, we better get Narla out of this mess before Neon makes things worse than it already is, all I simply was asking for is to reach Free liberty, I guess asking isn't going to be enough in this world.

We took a left turn to the cross junction, seeing the Undying stray towards us, some were fast enough to run with a limp, yet others had broken and torn legs, causing them to be a lot slower.

When looking ahead, Neon could be seen trying to lift a bit of concrete off Narla's leg, she managed to be skimmed by the tower fall but even so, it caught her on the way out, this place wasn't safe we need to be quick about this before we get cornered.

Rhax stated,

"you go and get the concrete off her, I'll defend with Alis", as he and Alis took position by the cross junction where the tower fall was, our point of location, I hurried ahead to Neon, seeing he was trying to use his powers to lift the block, but it was ineffective, the slab must have been four meters tall, and two meters wide or more, either way, Narla wasn't going to be able to hold on much longer when the small bit of scrap metal gives into the weight, it stopped the block from putting its full force on her but even with that small bit of assistance it was still slowly clamping her right leg into the floor.

When taking Neon's place I persisted,

"go and help Rhax, and when we get back we need to talk", he let me stand where he was as he commented,

"I'm not going to help you because you said, I'm going for Narla",

brushing off his remark I sheathed my sword, only to put my hands below the concrete block as I stated,

"Narla, when I lift, you got to pull yourself out",

she mocked,

"if Neon can't lift it with his stupid powers then you can't", with persistence I said sharply,

"he can't even lift a ton with his powers. It's only a healing based power. Now, can you just work with me, and move when I lift",

I know she was stressed, angry and frustrated but we need to get this done, she needs to crawl when the block is off her lower leg.

With all my strength I pulled upwards on the concrete block, lifting it up with my suits assistance as it was designed and built for battle and emergencies, all suits were designed to be that way even I knew that.

I grunted,

"Narla move now",

sweat dripped from my face as I kept hold of the block, lifting it a few inches from her leg, giving her enough room to shuffle forward.

She quickly crawled out, clawing against the floor, only to be helped by Alis as she informed,

"Merider, we got another dead problem",

when letting go of the block it slammed against the floor, echoing within the city as I stated,

"then we go before it grows into an issue",

I faced Alis, only to see the crowd of dead were emerging from the left, there were five times as many as there were before, where are they coming from?

Chapter Five

The Overload

The hoard was closing in on our street, but we could escape from the right side, well the others can anyways.

With firmness I persisted,

"go, now! I'll find another way out with Narla",

Rhax and Neon left with Alis, seeing there was no other way out of this unless they did what I said.

They hurried past the small gap, as the dead were focused on me as I taunted,

"over here shit bags!",

it worked perhaps a little too well, as even though some split ways to follow the team, the rest of the dozens were coming towards us, some were running clumsily, using the floor as a guide, along with the walls as their half-blind eyes were targeting us.

I took Narla's left arm and put it over my shoulder as I urged,

"we need to get inside",

I kept my hand by her waist as I forced her to turn left, facing the closest building.

With a fast pace to us, we hurried to the door, only for me to throw my body against it, breaking the door open.

As I let Narla go, my eyes darted around trying to look for things to barricade the door with, we were in some sort of lobby, a hotel or what once used to be an up and running hotel.

The darkroom shimmered green by my suit as the darkness closed in on us when shutting the door, I used a metal bronze lamp stand to hook between the double doors, temporarily sealing the door yet it won't last that long, there's that many out there that if we don't get out of their line of sight or far enough so they couldn't hear us, we're going to be screwed.

I moved ahead as Narla had found a fire exit to the back of the hotel, we might be able to cut around.

With a pause, my suit was flickering as it announced,

"ten percent of power left",

Narla worried,

"we need to go, now",

I pressed the chest of my armour, deactivating the suit as I ordered,

"Self-destruct mode",

the Undying were growing more uneasy as they were hammering against the door, hearing the suit as it counted,

"self-destruct in ten",

Narla flung the door open as I took the katana from the hands of the suit, only to run to her, moving past the reception desk and waiting room.

The suit's red glow flickered around the room as it counted to five.

With haste, I slammed the door shut behind me when hearing the front door break open, they breached the entrance of the dusty and old hotel room as we fled the grounds.

The suit was still counting down as we hurried to the left, avoiding the junction to our right where we started. Instead, when turning to the left we were faced with a chaotic scene, cars were parked off and on the road, some of them were tipped over as others were coated in blood and dust, this place was progressively getting darker the more we discovered its grounds.

With haste I moved my right arm to Narla's waist as she hooked her left arm over my shoulder, giving herself some support with her most likely broken foot, she could barely stand on it and it looked extremely damaged, we're going to have to sort this out when we get back.

Upon passing car by car some of the dead were hiding behind it, they were gnawing at the weaker dead and some fresh corpses, it looked as though someone was feeding them; Narla was struggling to keep up as the hotels first floor exploded, causing a rumble within the ground and dust to scatter from the tower as it quaked from the impact.

Most of the dead we spotted on the way down the road were attracted to the sound of the explosion, all but one which was following us, grunting as it tried to limp its way to us.

When cutting left passing the tipped over fuel truck, Narla stumbled to the ground as she panted,

"leave me, just get back to Neon and the others",

with refusal I took her left arm, hooking it over my head as I stated,

"this isn't the way you're going to die, come on let's keep going",

her legs and hands were coated in slippery oily fuel, it was hard for her to keep her grip around my shoulder, but I kept a firm hold of her wrist, ensuring she didn't use it as an excuse to let go.

The night sky shed the smallest amount of light as the moon overlooked us, the street lights were barely working, as most of the light was coming from cars that were burning out, some were even lit-up oil drums, it was like someone was living here.

The grumbles and grunts loudened as more dead were joining the one that started following us a few blocks back.

With persistence I kept us going as I stated,

"we can do this, don't give up",

she was thinking about it but stayed with me as I approached the oil drum to the side of the road to my left, tipping it over as the junk and coal that was on fire spread across the road, creating a small fire trap as we pushed ahead, finally making a left turn to street coated with a dim orange glow.

When pushing ahead the glow was coming from a towering wall, it was a campsite from the looks of it, three people were standing on the left and right side of the wall, overlooking the long street we raced upon, the people were wearing normal clothes, well clothes that aren't to do with combat anyway, it was worn out jeans, rugged shirts, flannel shirts, they were wearing before the first storm clothing, no doubt it's the only thing they could get out here.

Narla stumbled over in pain as she stated,

"let them eat me, it will give you time",

she was persistent in giving up, she wasn't going to bother to try and help herself.

The Undying was lurking around the corner, some were set on fire from the trap, but I could see it slowly was killing them, it made them slower for sure, but they still had enough energy and life to limp after us.

As sweat dripped down my face I lifted her again, this time it was a lot harder as she wasn't going to try and help me; I gave her my katana, forcing it into her right hand persisting, "use this to help yourself out, come on Narla you're not a quitter",

as she took the katana I had a firm hold of her left arm, soon putting my right hand around her waist as we kept going, making her use the katana as a form of cane to keep her on her feet as she let the weight off her foot, almost hopping as the foot dragged upon the concrete floor.

She sweated as the pain of her foot and leg was getting to her; she kept going as the grunts of the dead were gaining on us, the people fending the gates were starting to shoot at the dead as we strayed closer to them, they were using silenced snipers, causing nothing but a small and quiet echo within the city.

The dead that were gaining on us from the right and left were accurately shot within the head, only to be passed down to line behind us, and the line before that until all the bodies were dropped.

We slowly stopped running when hearing the growls had finally silenced, the scattered field of bodies behind us masked our sent and some of the dead that did arrive were eating away of the corpses, taking whatever flesh that was left upon the ragged, and deformed bodies.

My breaths could finally grow larger as we stopped running; we were met by the wall a few feet away from us, seeing the rugged metal double gates ahead of us, rusted and yet it looked sturdy, whoever these people were they didn't plan to kill us, but they weren't looking to save us either.

The gates opened, exposing the tents and oil fires upon the others side; soon a man showed up wearing a rugged white shirt, dark black jeans, deep brown boots along with a rusty machete within his hands as he stood there, looking at us as we were struggling to see who he was, what his face looked like, the lights from behind him were surely bright, but I guess we were in the dark for some time without any lights apart from my suits dim glow.

When frowning my eyes to see his face I thanked,

"thank you for protecting us, who are you?",

he stepped out of the light, enough for us to see his face from the torches outside the wall.

He had a ruff and short greying beard, ruffled long brown hair, it was tamed and yet it looked unkempt and greasy, his blue eyes pierced at us as he stated,

"we're the Saviours, that's all you need to know",

he approached us a bit more as he wondered,

"now I can ask the same of you, what are you two doing out on your own?",

with firmness I informed,

"I was with a team, they're going to base, we had to find another way out as an army of the dead were following us, and not those you saw early, there was over fifty of them",

he didn't look convinced as he remarked,

"well your friends are most likely dead, why don't you stay here for the night, patch your friends up and we can let you go in the morning",

Narla looked to me as she stated,

"well we survived that I think the least we can do is leave the team waiting for a little bit, besides Kamic and Marcella will be waiting for them",

I considered her words, only to look to the man as I followed him inside, allowing the gates to shut behind us.

The view of the camp was mind-blowing, to the left and right were a form of a tower parking lot, there were curtains made of rags covering some of the floors presumably to give people privacy in their section of the campsite.

Some parts of the parking lot floors had washing lines hanging from one pillar to the next, it was strange to see normal clothes, made me feel alien walking through the street in my black trousers and white stained shirt.

Some of the people were up and wandering around, looking at the gates thinking about what was going on upon the other side, the street road was kept clear to walk on as the parking lots were where everything was held in, apart from the end of the street where we were approaching.

A large wall blocked the end of the street as a medical ward stood in-front of it, I say ward, it was mostly a large rectangular tent with a red cross painted on the left and right side of the tent flap.

Upon slowing down Narla gave me my katana as the man stated,

"stay here, I'll get Doctor Renlon",

as he entered the brightly lit tent the flap shut behind us, hearing the muffled talking as Narla wondered,

"this place must have been here for a while, wonder how it came by" ,

with a slight guess I theorised,

"when you have one leader persistent to make changes anything is possible, seems like the man has been around for some time",

shortly after my words finished he left the tent only to hold

---

the door open as he motioned,
"you can go in, we'll meet you here",
as Narla limped past the man he helped her inside, shutting
the tent flap behind him as he motioned,
"lets go for a slow walk, I need to know more about you
before giving you a bed to sleep on",
hesitantly I kept his left, facing the gate and the two parking
lots.
Our feet strolled as he questioned,
"Tell me yours and her name?",
with a strategy I persisted,
"you first",
he smirked slightly as he stated,
"alright fine, see how it's going to be. I'm Nathan, your turn",
I firmly informed,
"I'm Merider, her name is Narla",
he wondered,
"Merider? Are you sure that's your real name",
with a smile I remarked,
"I'm certain it is",
seeing his words were a little puzzling he expanded,
"sorry for being rude, I just thought you would have had a
prettier name",
when facing him I remarked,
"do you treat all the people you save like this? Just curious",
he looked amused as he apologised,
"Sorry, just trying to make small talk",
seeing he was trying to make talk, I have a few things to go
over with him.
With firmness I wondered,
"you can start talking by telling me who you are? What this
place is",
he joked,
"I told you who I was do you have amnesia or something?",
seeing he was starting to get on my nerves I clarified,
"you told me your name but what do your people call you?",

he caught on only to explain,

"well, they call me Saviour, and they do my biddings to stay alive, hunting for food and such, it's simple, Merider",

I approached him snapping,

"don't patronise me, this is how it's going to work with me being here for the night, you stay out of my way and I'll stay out of yours, I know how you people work, and rather not get stuck in your circle of debt",

he looked amused by my threats, he looked as though he didn't care if I figured him out by first glance, he just wanted a reaction and he got it.

He challenged,

"tell me something, Merider, if you were in my position where I created this, what would you do? You don't look like a leader to me, couldn't even be a Commander if you tried, I saw what happened out there, you were virtually cornered and we saved your ass",

he stepped on the line to where he insulted me, with a firmness I stated,

"I'm the Commander of Zion City and what you saw earlier was called being outnumbered from one to a thousand",

his face dropped to thunder as I continued,

"if I was in your position I would save every person there were and let them choose to hunt or choose what role to have, then in return, they have what they want, a house and a long life ahead of them, not do what I say or you owe me more",

he questioned,

"the hell are you doing out here then? You're meant to be behind the wall",

I cut in,

"so I can live? You and the people standing here should be behind the wall but that isn't happening unless the wall is taken down, we need Unity not 'you owe me for saving your life'",

he looked almost flustered as he didn't expect me to be the Commander of Zion City, to be honest, I didn't expect to rule the city either, it fell into my hands from what people have witnessed and they believe I am the suited role for the job. Nathen expressed,

"look, out here there's no cost, no currency, nothing but owing and debts and that's the way it is out here, but that still doesn't answer my question earlier, why are you here? I can help you if you needed extra hands",

with thought and seeing we did need the extra pair of hands I explained,

"I need to go to Free Liberty, I was on my way there but Rhovis Crater was attacked by some attack helicopters, half the people made it out and are camping in the store within the city",

he looked as though he knew where they were as he questioned,

"you mean the one on lockdown far east of here? That place right",

with a slight frown I wondered,

"yeah, sounds as though you think it's a bad location",

he looked half certain but doubted,

"no it's not that, it's a little crowded but I think they'll be fine for a few days stay",

he wondered,

"did you want me to help or not? If so we can go to my tent on the top floor of tower two",

giving it thought I didn't have much of a choice but to trust him, it's all we can do for now, see what he puts on the table, and if it's going to be enough to help, if not he can help differently.

We continued strolling to the second tower, the parking lot on our right, we walked on the drive-in point, proceeding up the spiralling roads leading from the floors, only to gradually me the fifth floor as I questioned,

"if you built this place how did you get the walls to be so sturdy? Surely the dead would have tried to pile up against it",

Nathan and I stood upon the fifth floor, overlooking the gloomy broken city surrounding us, the torch lights were in the centre of the grounds, allowing his large squared tent to stand out from the rest of the ashy and dusty parking lot.

We stood overlooking the city below us as he explained,

"I wasn't the first person here, I live with my team; my wife, kids, and four of my trusted friends, but one wasn't to be trusted, either way, we built this place before shit went down, and since then I kept building it, thickening the walls, ensuring the people were protected",

with curiosity growing on me I wondered,

"what happened to your team?",

he sighed only to continue,

"well the friend that I said couldn't be trusted, her name was Alexandria. The first Commander to Zion City, she decided that being a friend and team was nothing compared to being a leader, so she decided to leave the gates open, lure the undying in and luckily a small group, back then the groups were smaller but as you know they're getting bigger",

with knowing what happened next I theorised,

"so the dead killed your team, where were you at this point?",

he explained further,

"I was up here, living the leader's life of having the top floor",

he glanced to the tent as he persisted,

"come on, let's get things arranged, we got a few things to go over",

as he walked away first, I took one last glance down, seeing the campsite glow below us, yet outside the walls were dark and shadow looking, it seemed like the whole city was dead, and this place was the last light it had, it was almost a sad sight to see that not a lot of things survived during the First Storm.

Gradually I followed Nathan to his tent, seeing the skies above us slowly be smothered by the darkening clouds, it seems like it's going to be raining soon…not going to enjoy the smell of this rain, the bodies and rotten corpses

---

63

everywhere takes away that fresh smell of the nature being soaked by the rain.

Upon entering Nathan's tent, there was a sleeping bag to the back of the room, a small wooden dining table to the left with two chairs facing opposite one another.

There was an oil lamp within the centre of the tent to where the metal pole kept it standing, he moved to the dining chair motioning me to join him as he questioned,

"so first things first what's your deal with the Free Liberty? Why did you go here to try and take down the wall and to see them?",

as I sat on the chair facing the sleeping bag Nathan took the chair facing me, firmly sitting down after me.

He listened as I expanded,

"Free Liberty have the scientists, the advancements not only Zion City needs but every other city needs, they are dying out here and we need them to help us bring the cities together",

he wondered,

"what does taking the wall have to do with that then?",

with persistence I continued,

"without the wall there will be easier supply routes, full contact with the cities, also I'm worried that if the wall stays up the dead will continue to build up, it's a dumping ground before I took over, now it's not going to be",

he questioned further,

"so how do you plan on taking the wall down?",

not knowing the answer myself, I thought of what I know I can do first, I expressed,

"we need Free Liberty on our side before thinking about how the wall will be taken down, and I think you might know how to do that if you want to help me out",

he nodded briefly, he said,

"yeah I know how to get into Free Liberty, but the thing is, they let anyone in, just as long as you don't go snooping around, but even so there's people trying to stop you, like you said about the attack on Rhovis City, I think Free Liberty

---

64

don't want you in",

he was right about them not wanting me to have access but since when has that ever stopped me from entering before?

Seeing as this was going to be a difficult task I questioned, "okay we need to take their cities then, they destroyed two of their places so far. The gas station where Neon and Narla were in charge of, bear in mind it was a missile strike so it's a risk if you help me",

he looked a little more nervous only to persist,

"no, we're still helping you, if it means the people can finally get out of this life style then yeah, it's worth every risk",

he informed,

"the third place is close by but they are guarding The Saviours Bridge, that's far south of here so they aren't a threat to us nor to them, they simply arrange for a supply line every few months or a long space of time in this case, however the fourth and additional hands they have, joined forces, they are the ones hosting the attacks on you, they live by a military camp and market place, it's the barrier between us and Free Liberty, so we need to pass them, once that's done we don't have any attacks to worry about",

sounds straight forward, take down their attackers then we're left with the defenders, it will be a high risk for the amount of people we have, we just better make sure we don't slip up, if we do it will end up in a pile of corpses, although this place has too many of them walking around here.

Chapter Six

Night of Schemes

Nathan had more to add as he stated,

"I've been here long enough to know that outside the walls aren't safe, but you and whoever you were with seem to know how to run things, not smoothly mind you. The Forth and Fifth city aren't to be taken lightly, they are just as ruthless as the dead, but the thing is, they are on the flesh side",

with a puzzled look I wondered,

"flesh side? Are you talking about cannibalism or something completely different?",

he expanded,

"they are on the cannibal route, they survive on human meat and I know that because one of my members turned to them, he probably is living a better life on that side of things but still it's not a way I would live. It's vile and it makes me sick to think that people turned to that",

knowing about Kaylo's past, and what he was once, I knew that he changed, I don't know how far gone those people are, but they can be saved, we can result to something that involves less death, there's always people trying to change who they are for the better, trying to redeem themselves.

I leaned forward on the chair slightly when resting my hands upon the table, clasping them together as I wondered,

"what happened to your team Nathan? You tell me Alexandria went over the wall, someone else turned to cannibalism, tell me how many there were, what the hell happened?",

he sighed slightly only to explain,

"Alexandria was a woman of ambition, and frankly she was greedy, she wanted to have her own way, so she left us, seeing as there was less dead before than there were now.",

he paused only to continue hesitantly,

"I lied about the rest, I don't have a family, no one",

I leaned back as I asked,

"why make it up make me feel guilt for you",

he smirked as he stated,

"it's what I tell everyone here, it gets them to stay, and it works well",

with a frown growing I persisted,

"what makes you any better than Alexandria then, the cannibalism, which is a lie I'm presuming as well",

he looked offended as he stated,

"I never said I was better than them, I just wasn't stupid and the cannibal story is right, he was my closest friend; his name is Reece Mykel, leader of the fourth city from what I understand",

with curiosity to how he knew, I continued,

"what I find hard to believe is that you claim to be the good guy, but you lie, lie to your people, lie to strangers, so why should knowing about your friend help me?",

he was in thought which he defended,

"people prefer to hear the comfort of lies, cover up the truth because they wouldn't take it, knowing about the outside all they know about is the Undying lurking, not the cannibals in the forth city, they didn't go far enough to see that",

his way of leading, was almost corrupted, no leader should

base their role on lies and cover the truth, no matter how harsh, people deserve to know the truth.

Seeing as he was trying to be a leader I gave him a hit of truth, a harsh slap of reality, metaphorically speaking, of course.

I expressed,

"Nathan if I'm going to trust you there's one thing you need to do for me in return, you need to stop lying to your people, they deserve to know the truth, and all this covering will eventually get the truth out and people will know you're a liar, and that's not a way to go in my eyes",

he remarked,

"so you don't lie to your people? You don't try to comfort them and ensure they can breathe the night without a worry",

I cut in,

"the lies I tell are events that will affect my people if I tell them, the ones where if I tell them they will be in danger, same goes with my team",

he looked doubtful as he questioned,

"look, what are you trying to state to me? we can just argue all night if that's what you're aiming for, but I haven't got time for that",

with persistence I stated,

"all I need from you in this mission we're doing, is just be honest with me, and be honest with your people, because frankly they can't stay here during the attack on the fourth and fifth city",

he stood up as he refused,

"woah I said I would help you not get my people killed for you, what gave you that idea?",

I stood up only to approach him as I firmly expressed,

"you said you were going to help me out. Azella's people are helping, but we have half the numbers, a hundred people or less, we need extra help and you said you were going to do just that",

he negotiated,

68

"okay, if that's how it's going to be, then there's something you can do for me in return",

dreading where this was going but I didn't want to get ahead of myself, I wondered,

"what do you need me to do?",

he said firmly,

"we need to do a controlled extermination of the dead in our zone before taking the wall down",

with a puzzled look I questioned,

"is that it?",

he looked confused as he remarked,

"well don't make it sound so easy",

seeing his confusion I expanded,

"no it's not that, but we were heading in that direction anyway, we were going to take the wall down after the extermination took place. I just didn't think that far ahead, we haven't even made it past the fourth and fifth city yet",

he smiled warmly only to state,

"well, you're going to pass the third, so that's got to be something, right?",

I returned to smile at him, seeing his worries were a little less on the hostile side, all these lies and cover-ups to ask me that? well, let's just hope that talk got him thinking a little, change the way he did things around here because I'm not looking to take over his place that's for certain.

Nathan approached the sleeping bag as he said,

"We better make this official then",

he crouched down to a footlocker on the head of the sleeping bag, unlocking it as he took out a vintage whisky bottle along with two metal shot glasses.

He stood up with the cup and drink in his hand as he questioned,

"do you drink? Should have asked that before I got the stuff out",

he put the drink on the table as I reassured,

"once in awhile, yeah",

he smirked as he continued,

"sounds as though you didn't have any good experiences with a drink?",

I remarked,

"well, I know one was a mourning drink, the rest were celebratory drinks",

as he poured the caramel coloured whisky in the shot glasses he said warmly,

"well we can have a good drink for once in our lives",

he gave me a glass as he took his as he toasted,

"to the future, let our teams join and make something out of it",

he smiled as I returned one to him, holding the drink up to his toast before clanking the glasses.

We shot down the drink, feeling the taste and strong lingering smell of the whisky whirl within our mouths as the drink went down.

I put the glass on the table as I insisted,

"I better get back to Narla, she probably thinks we're having a party",

he joined me to my left as he ensured,

"I'll go with you, besides, we have a march to do, don't we, we'll evacuate to the store",

we left the tent as he went on,

"I'll get the people rounded up after we check up on Narla",

with curiosity I wondered,

"I thought you said it was going to be dangerous, surely we can join in a different place tomorrow morning? Your people need their rest",

he saw my point only to agree,

"yeah, your right, sorry I was getting ahead of myself. When you and Narla get on your way tonight, or in the morning, you'll see a park nearby, wait there and we'll come in nearing late dawn",

seeing the plan was good enough I agreed with him, giving it a solid foundation as we made our way to the street of the campsite.

With firmness I ensured,

"we'll be there in late dawn, but whether we leave tonight or tomorrow morning will be a different story, I need to see what Narla feels about it, she might want to stay here for the night before thinking about walking out there",

we entered the street, only to curve left, facing the medical ward, gradually pacing towards the glowing tent as Nathan reassured,

"well, if you stay the night, I can get a tent set up, no problems",

he was being a lot nicer to me but I think it was the fact I was going to do the controlled extermination for him, either way, whether it was him getting what he wanted, or just him helping out from the kindness of his heart, he was going to help me, all I cared about was that he was going to help me out with this complicated plan, but overall, it was simple I just have the knack of making things sound overly complicated.

When approaching the tent Nathan entered as he stated,

"you stay here, I know I can trust you, but the doctor is picky on who enters, they like a clean environment",

his words paused as he remarked,

"you know what never mind, Merider you need to see this", with the confusion I entered the room, looking around the bright glowing medical ward.

The tool table was to the left knocked over as the medical bed was tipped over and coated in blood, with a puzzled look I wondered,

"the hell happened?",

Narla was nowhere to be seen and neither was the doctor, but soon my fears were growing as I heard a growl, coming from behind the curtains separating the right side of the tent from the left, making a form of an operating room.

Nathan took out his revolver as he cautiously approached the curtain, only to drag it across exposing the Undying that found a way in, but how? I stopped Nathan as I took over, using my katana to impale through the Undying's head, causing the flesh it was eating to drop from its mouth.

As the body dropped, Nathan looked at the bloodied corpse, turning it around as he questioned,

"this has never happened before, how did the dead come in?", with a theory in mind I pointed,

"perhaps that had something to do with it",

I approached the back of the tent to my left, seeing a door that was hidden behind the wall of the ripped tent, it looked as though the doctor had an easy way in and out if he pleased to go for a stroll…in this dark place.

Nathan sighed before he remarked,

"so that's where all the noise came from",

he approached the door with me, looking out upon the other side of the wall seeing the Undead that was straying to us, some were running as most were limping.

With firmness I stepped out the door, only to grasp the handle as I pulled it back into the wall, I stepped back into the tent with Nathan when locking the door firmly, sealing it from the outside as he worried,

"what if he's out there?",

he turned back hearing a movement, only to approach the door as I stated,

"go check that out, I'll barricade the door, it can hold for a night at least",

upon dragging the operating table that was folded and broken on the floor, I heard Narla's voice in the background, she was speaking with Nathan as she said hastily,

"I was trying to find you, the doctor just left, he patched me up and said he was going out on a supply run, so he got his nurse to help out and I don't think she made it, she told me to get you, as she didn't know what to do, I tried to help but she said she could handle it",

Nathan remarked,

"well she clearly didn't",

a sigh grew as he reassured,

"don't worry it's not your fault its mine, I should have talk to the doctor about the door he made, I knew he was hiding something but never confronted him about it, just hope he can hold out for tonight",

this was what I was worried about, he wasn't keeping a close watch on his people, didn't confront anything his gut was telling him to check out, well there's only one way out of this and it's to find the doctor before he gets himself killed also.

When blocking the door with the operating table I moved past the bloodied torn corpse, only to approach Nathan and Narla as I persisted,

"we're going to stay the night",

I looked to Narla seeing her leg was bandaged and firmly tucked into her boots and covered by her trousers, she had a crutch to support her and ensure she could at least walk independently.

Although she was still drenched in the Undying's blood her broken foot was clean and well-kept at least, she looked to me wondering,

"don't we need to get back to the team?",

to ease her mind I stated,

"they will understand, besides they would expect us to stay low until the morning rises, then we can take the people here and go together, make sure it runs smoothly",

I looked to Nathan interrogating,

"about the doctor, where would he go? He said a supply run so there has to be a pharmacy around here",

he and Narla both didn't like where this was heading as he stated,

"you're not going after him, he's just one person",

with persistence I expressed,

"he's a doctor, and for what we're going to be facing, we sure as hell are going to need one",

he was persistent in joining me as he informed,

"I know where the pharmacy is, at least two of them, which

73

are close by, but we need gear",

before I could refuse his help he firmly stood ground,

"I'm going, whether you want to be the lone wolf or not",

Narla looked to me as she agreed,

"he's right Merider, you can't go out there on your own, even if you can handle yourself your body can't stand so much damage if anything happened out there",

seeing as they were both persistent I let him help me out, but Narla still needs to recover.

With firmness I instructed,

"Nathan will join me then, but get someone with Narla, set the tent up, it won't take us long to find the doctor",

Nathan turned to Narla as he informed,

"go to the first tower, find the guard on the first floor, tell him Nathan told you to set up a tent there and have assistance whilst we are gone",

she sighed slightly, seeing as she was doubting we would come back but she did what he said, leaving us from the tent as he turned to me as I questioned,

"we can't go around to the front of the city it will take us longer to get to him, is there another way out at the back?",

seeing as the door within the wall was crowded and occupied upon the other side, we had no choice but to find another way around.

On the plus side they are bunched up in one area, leaving other areas open.

Nathan and I left the tent as he informed,

"on the first floor of tower two, there's a restricted section, where we couldn't repair the damages of the tower",

we hurried from the tent, which Nathan pointed,

"just go ahead and reach the restricted zone, wait there I'll get our gear for the night search, we can't go out there without some sort of light with us, and can't rely on the fires that are out their either, the dead lurk around it",

he departed to the first tower on my left as I paced to the right, holding my sword firmly within my hands when entering the first floor, passing the spiralling road going up each floor.

The dim glowing tents passed me on my left, hearing the mumbles of the people within the tents, some were fast asleep as others were moving around, cleaning their tents and other things.

Upon passing a dark green tent, my feet stopped when hearing a girl question,

"who are you?",

I looked left seeing a girl, she wore a white shirt, blue jeans, and simple black shoes. Her black hair was tied back firmly, letting her fringe drag by the left side of her forehead.

Not wanting her to follow me I stopped in my tracks, seeing as I will only be waiting for Nathan either way, she looked to my sword as she prodded,

"are you going hunting?",

with a firmness I stated,

"yeah I am, and it's not something for kids to play around with either",

she remarked,

"well, I don't see why you have that when you have guns too",

As I crouched to her, I persisted,

"look I know this is something you're curious about but how about you go inside and stop asking questions",

she pierced her eyes at me only to look back as a man agreed,

"stop asking questions Abby, can't you see she is in the middle of doing something",

I stood up from the ground as the tanned man approached me. His dark black hair was cut short and ruffled as his stubbly beard was cleanly cut and thick, his broad face stood out as his perched lips were amid his beard.

He wore a white shirt along with a ruffed up red flannel shirt, his sleeves were rolled up showing his toned arms, he wore dark black rugged jeans along with thick broad black boots, lastly, I could see a pistol tucked within his belt, not the best place to store a gun, yet I would assume he didn't care.

His smile was smooth as his rough voice questioned,

"hope she didn't bother you ma'am, she's a curious child",

with a nod I reassured,

"yeah I can see, well I need to get going",

he grasped my wrist as he halted,

"woah hold on there, I stopped the child from bugging you, at least give me an explanation on where you're going",

he let go as I faced him, seeing it was the least he needed, but still, I couldn't risk the child overhearing, she might follow us if she knew where we were roughly going.

With firmness I explained,

"look, the doctor went out on a supply run, which he shouldn't be doing at this time. He needed it but should have waited until dawn. Nathan and I are going to find him, we know where he could be",

he then theorised,

"the pharmacy right? He told me about his secret door, didn't want Nathen to know because he wouldn't like what he would hear",

it sounded as though there was another reason why the doctor left, one which I will regret asking about, but he knows something worth taking note off.

Curiously I wondered,

"and what's that? what else has the doctor been hiding?",

the man stated,

"he's been on the drugs for a while, says that is the fix we need to end our problems. Well, his anyways. Everyone knows about it, but Nathan doesn't",

they don't seem to trust him, why is that? with a puzzled look, I challenged,

"why does no one trust him? You seem to keep a lot of things from him",

he expanded,

"look, as much as we appreciate Nathan's leadership, he's a good liar. Promised us freewill but never gave it, saying the

Undying is the only thing out there, but we know that's not true, we all know about the cannibals, the Dead Alive, they live and feed on humans, just like The Undying do and it's not right, he thinks we're thick but we're not",

he glanced to his right, looking at the exit leading to the street as he shortly continued,

"look, just whatever you do, make sure you make the choices out there",

he looked to me as he departed,

"because he will make the wrong choices if you let him have that input",

as he walked back into the tent I faced the exit, seeing Nathan approach me with two dark black rucksacks, one in his hands and one firmly planted on his back.

He exchanged the rucksack in his hand for the katana as he informed,

"we got ammo, blades, spare flare gun, and the flare ammo to",

upon putting the rucksack firmly on my back, feeling the slight heft of the items within it, I took the katana back as I wondered,

"what about the light? Did you get a torch or?",

he showed me his left hand that held a dark black hand torch as he reassured,

"don't worry I got the torch, new batteries also, well hopefully they're new I changed them earlier",

he followed me to my left as my katana was firmly within my right hand, staying by my side as we walked further to the back of the parking lot ahead of us, seeing nothing but a dead-end, that was until we got a little more closer seeing a shut fire exit door.

Nathan turned the torchlight on, shining it ahead of us as he stated,

"that's the exit, it's locked from the outside, so it opens our way, once we get the doctor we will come back here, I can lever the door open a little, not enough to be noticed by the

Undying the very least",

we reached the corner only for him to take the lead, he opened the door allowing us to see the half-demolished room of what used to be the stairwell of the parking lot, there was nothing there as we stood upon the first set of stairs, seeing the rugged and debris-covered ground below us, along with a few dead that didn't take notice of us.

I looked down as Nathan pointed,

"the pharmacy we should try first is the one behind the south wall where the medical ward is, it's under halfway to where your friends are, we can see the store from there at least anyways",

he sat upon the ledge of the steps, only to jump down as I followed him, landing upon the large concrete slabs.

The Undying closest to us turned to us from the roads, they were sensitive to the noise but not to the light, unless shone directly in their eyes.

With haste we climbed down from the mound of rubble, edging our way to the street leading to the south part of the campsite wall, we kept to the left side, using the small and slim alleyways to avoid the crowd by the wall, they looked to be building up but some were growing bored and strayed away luckily, but I can't say the wall will hold on much longer if the crowd builds up by the double.

Gradually, we edged our way to the road in view of the wall to our right, along with the crowd that was gathering there. Nathan and I made a left turn facing the east where the long stretched out road showed ahead of us, the long stretch passing broken apartment buildings and corner stores, the darkness grew as the lamps upon this side of the city were completely out, leaving us with the light of the torch to rely on and the sounds of the Undying to navigate where we should be avoiding.

Chapter Seven

Rescue Mission

As we strayed down the long roads, Nathan said quietly, "what did Darik want earlier? The man you were speaking to",
to cover up what Darik warned me off I explained,
"he wanted to apologise for his daughter, Abby. I was on my way past and she asked where I was going",
Nathan looked curious, but his question was stalled as we passed the broken vehicles upon the left and right side of the street, seeing the Undead clawing within.
He gradually continued,
"and did you tell her?",
I looked at him as I reassured,
"no I didn't, I told her specifically",
a voice cut in,
"grown-up stuff?",
I looked to Nathan confused, only to look behind us, seeing Abby as she had a pocket knife within her hand.
She had taken a small rucksack of supplies with her too.
Nathan looked around as I approached the girl, taking her wrist as I stated,

"Nathan find us a building, now",

I moved her in-front of me, letting go of her as she followed Nathan, I firmly paced behind her as we trailed to a nearby arcade, it was quiet and dark the very least.

We turned left, heading inside the arcades double doors; quietly shutting them behind us as Nathan shone the light in the centre of us, firmly he warned,

"Abby, you shouldn't be out here, you need to go back right now",

she remarked,

"well, I'm already halfway with you, so if I go back, people will only hate you more because you left a child to walk back on her own",

she smiled as she was acting mischievous, she was smart for a kid but even so she still doesn't have the strength of an adult, or grown-up to understand the consequences out here, she thinks it's all fun and games.

With a sigh I asked,

"okay first things first, did you close the door on the way out? Presuming talking by the tent told you as much as you needed to know",

she looked unamused as she remarked,

"no, I obviously didn't shut the door, I even opened the front gates too, believing the dead should walk in, have a tea party",

Nathan cut in,

"did you leave the gap open in the door?",

she stated,

"obviously I did, I'm not stupid to not know it was a one-way door, besides, an eleven-year-old like myself isn't stupid",

hm I thought she was eight? Well, she looks younger than she was, and even though it's a three-year difference to my guess she is still not capable of understanding the dangers out here.

I looked behind us seeing the door was still clear, we can get out of the arcade but I have rules to set down with a third person in the party; with a sigh I instructed,

"first rule is stay by me, Nathan is our scout so he has to go further ahead, and because you found out where we were going from fault of my own its my duty to protect you",

she smiled seeing she was getting her own way only to stop as I continued,

"the second rule is use your pocket knife when they are close to you, don't try to get any far ahead and if we pass one that is stuck or half there we kill it, it creates a pathway for us and makes less noise",

Nathan looked as though as he disagreed as he refused,

"she can't join us, she's just a kid",

without us arguing, or wasting more time than we already have, I stated,

"she's joining us, we haven't got a choice, it's either we split up and take her back, as the other goes on their own to the doctor, or we work as a team and go their together",

he couldn't argue with me as I already set the marker, we were taking her, and that's final. To know if she returns safely she is just going to have to come with us.

Nathan led the way out as he persisted,

"fine, whatever, let's just get to the pharmacy, we have two to go to but this one is closest",

I made Abby go after me as I kept behind her, ensuring none of us were weakened at the back, and I could see the whole team, ensuring I didn't let my guard down.

Nathan shone the light as he said quietly,

"the pharmacy is ahead of us, past the street, but we'll take the alleyway ahead, we will have to climb over the gate, it will be a quieter option",

we proceeded to the apartments ahead, gradually seeing the fence appear in our view, along with a dumpster bin, we can use that to climb over the fence but I'm not sure if that's going to be quiet enough.

Nathan moved to the left side of the bin as we reached the

door and apartments of the gate on the opposite sides, he went to push it, only for me to stop quietly as I said,

"wait, surely there's a better way of getting past? The second you move that bin, it's going to rattle",

he ignored me, only to push the bin, causing the wheels to squeak and creak as he moved it forward, letting the wheels roll stiffly to the rusted fence.

He stopped only to climb on the bin as he insisted,

"scouts go first",

Abby looked to me as she whispered,

"what a twat",

I glanced to her, not having it in me to scold her for the language, but to be honest she was right, he was very selfish and yes I know scouts go ahead but even so, if they know a kid is with us and we have to protect her, she should go first. I looked around the dark streets behind us, and to our left and right, the dead were closing in, I could hear the muffled growls and forceful gasps for air.

Nathan shone the torch to us as he persisted,

"hurry up Merider",

he wanted me to go next but I insist on Abby to go first, I gave her a foot boost as I stated,

"Abby when you're over the gate get Nathan to go to the pharmacy, stay there until I get there, I need to find a different way through",

as she climbed on the bin, moving to the fence to jump over it I moved the bin below her, forcing it to the wall to ensure the dead couldn't climb upon it.

The noise of the bin attracted them which I wanted but it was that noise that attracted a crowd of them.

With haste I approached the apartment door to my left, opening it seeing the door was slightly open, the lock was busted from the outside meaning someone has previously been here before, let's just hope there is no company now, otherwise that's another sticky situation on my hands.

The dead were crowding around the door, trying to push in as one stumbled ahead as I raced up the apartment steps.

The apartment lights were dimmed and flickering, it was dim enough to see but it wasn't bright enough to know what was on the floor.

I looked down the steps, seeing the dead tumble and race up the steps, most were falling down the steps as others were speeding up the stairs trying to reach me as I was closing in on the rooftops door.

When reaching the last stairs I could see a window ahead as a door to my left led to the roof, with shortness of time I approached the window, seeing the pharmacy below across the street.

The green cross was glowing faintly through the dirty window, but as I opened it I could feel the fresh air rush in as the green cross was brighter, the street ahead was half-destroyed and cluttered with broken shops, but when glancing left I could see the large superstore, it was bright and glowing with life, no doubt attracted the Undying's attention.

I looked down only to soon throw myself over the window ledge, grasping tightly upon it as the dead were ascending the steps even though I was out of sight they could smell me, I needed to climb down somehow.

I glanced down, only to put my foot within a crack in the wall, using it to shimmy left towards a drainpipe, it might not be able to hold the weight I'm carrying, but right now I can't see any way out of this without falling to my death.

I grasped upon the drainpipe, hearing the bolts creak when climbing down, it wasn't loud enough to hear from afar, but upon being this close it sounded lethally loud, it made me self-conscious to think the whole city could hear it, but that was just an exaggeration.

My body froze when glancing up, seeing the dead were crowding around the window, only to look in my direction, they were figuring out where I had gone but they couldn't see so great in the darkness.

As my heart thumped heavily, I continued to climb down slower, causing more strain on the pipe as on each bracket I stepped upon the bolts would make the smallest creek, feeling it bend after one foot to the other that forced upon it.

The tall ten-floor apartment was tiring to climb down upon but I'm glad it's not the other way around, the climb up is a lot more difficult than the way down. It felt as though minutes went past before touching the concrete ground, feeling relieved to touch the solid ground again.

When looking left and right nothing could be seen apart from darkness, the night sky was just getting darker as the clouds were starting to overcast, the rain was going to come in heavy, but we can make it back on time before it does…hopefully.

With haste I turned around, facing the bright glow that lit that part of the street, there were some Undying around it but they didn't seem to like that glow all that much, strange its as though they don't respond to certain colours.

With curiosity I approached the pharmacy, seeing myself glow in the green light, along with the dead lurking around it, they glanced at me, but thought nothing of it, it was as though I was invisible, I need to keep note of this, this could come handy with the controlled extermination.

Cautiously I walked past them, going towards the entrance; quietly I opened the door, shutting it behind me to make as little noise as I could, the dead were lurking out there, but they seem to not take notice of me entering the building, it was bizarre.

When walking in, Abby stood there taking guard of the door; she glanced back to the counter where the medicine was stored behind the counter, she explained,

"Nathan said to stay here, he's in the back",

with a frown on my face I moved her close to me, only to make her walk ahead as I persisted,

"come with me, Nathan probably might need help if he's been there for a while",

84

the pharmacy had a basic layout, to the left was the waiting room as to the right was the public accessible products like baby things, bath things, just basic stuff whereas behind the bright white counter was where the medical products were.

The door built into the counter top was already opened upon the left, I moved ahead of Abby when hearing the cluttering noises in the back as I questioned,

"how long has he been there for? Was the doctor here?",

she shrugged stating,

"he didn't let me see, all he said was to stay here and wait for you, he's been there for a while",

I had my katana firmly in my grasp as we walked past the first shelf behind the counter, passing to see the storage room behind it to our right. The noises were coming from there, perhaps Nathan is fighting a dead, yet I have a bad feeling about this.

With caution, I approached the door as I whispered,

"Abby, stay behind me, get the pocket knife open, keep my back",

she did what I said.

As she kept behind me, I pushed the dark black storage door open, letting the door creek open as it showed me the shelves full of boxes to the left and right, within the centre was Nathan, he warned,

"Abby I told you to get back",

he turned to me only to pause his words as he was covered in blood, the person he killed was the doctor, he was horribly disfigured within the face, presumably Nathan didn't want him coming back from the dead.

He got up from the floor, stepping away from the doctor as he said franticly,

"I can explain, he was going to kill me first",

he held the bloodied knife as I interrogated,

"tell me exactly what happened, every bit of detail I need to know",

he glanced to Abby as he stated,

"look, there's no other way of doing this, I needed you here, and to do so, he needed to be missing, so when we had our meeting and I told you to wait outside before Narla was seen to. I told him about the plan, go here so I can get you here, we all know who you are, the scientist told us, they spy on your land and you didn't bat an eye",

with the confusion I questioned,

"why pretend to be friends with me? make me trust you, if you wanted me to be dead you should have killed me on sight, shouldn't have opened the gates",

he changed his weapon to a gun as he remarked,

"if I wanted you dead I could shoot you here and now",

not afraid of his gun I snapped,

"then what's stopping you. He was right about you, you shouldn't have been trusted, and I believed for a moment you were good",

as I went to approach him he moved the gun into Abby's direction as he warned,

"now, don't make any hasty moves, Merider, you know what will happen",

with the frustration of not being able to do anything without the kid getting hurt, I stopped moving towards him, playing his stupid games.

He stated,

"you think I was going to help you? It was sad you believed that, I don't want you hurting my people and they aren't going to war for you, most of all your time here is almost over, the Free Liberty will be here at any moment, to collect you and your friends, I hope you're in the mood for a bit of blood",

with a snarl to my face I challenged,

"you want the only thing stopping this mess from getting worse to be killed? I'm here to help you, not kill you. The price for peace is high, but that's life, Nathan, you can't expect things to be handed for you, it's not how it goes",

he smirked as Abby went behind me, he moved the gun to

me as he mocked,

"who are you trying to be? A saint, this place was doing fine, my lies were working and the monsters that we are, the five cities that will do anything to protect Free Liberty, so if that means to kill your friends, kill the girl, kill you…then that sure as hell is going to happen",

I felt my bag was moving as Abby was searching it discreetly with her left hand, making it look as though she was cowering behind me ,but she was finding something.

Abby remarked,

"you say you let us in to help us, was that a lie too?",

he smirked as he said,

"I never was going to help you, you were going to help yourselves because whilst you and the people were doing all the work I didn't have to do shit, all because we were the third city",

he looked to me as he remarked,

"oh yeah, sorry I forgot to mention, I'm the third city, the Saviours bridge is out the circle, on the kill list of Free Liberty",

a deep rumbling sound was echoing from outside as Nathan smiled to us, he said coldly,

"hear that? that's your ride, you out of all people should know about the high technology of the scientists and builders, they virtually have everything to spy on everyone, the second you stepped over the wall they knew, and just be glad they didn't kill you, yet",

as Nathan sheathed his gun, Abby moved in his view, only to shoot a flare at his chest, causing a large bright glow to reflect around the room as his body was engulfed in red smoke and fire. He flung backwards, landing upon the back of the room in smoke, his body was slowly burning as the flames ate their way through his crisping insides, melting his skin to charcoal black as the flame covered his whole body.

The rumbles sounded louder, I looked to the left, seeing the fire exit as I persisted,

"come on we better get you back",
she remarked,
"I don't think that's an option anymore, we need to go to your friends, they will kill them",
we left the storage room, heading into the wide street seeing the store stand tall and bright, four Chinooks were landing within the radius as two were making
their way to us, but one passed overhead as we hid close by the store walls, using it as cover as we dodged the bright spotlights shining upon the concrete streets.
The Chinook that was after us had landed in-front of the pharmacy as I hid us under the store's concrete foundation, using the cool building to camouflage us as they were overhead; the second Chinook was heading in the direction of the third city, we need to choose what happens before people start dying.
Abby looked behind us as she urged,
"come on, we can get in here",
I refused,
"no we can't, the stores will be occupied, look we just need to get our way to the superstore, if we get there and stop them before they get off the ground we can save your people",
she agreed as she followed my lead, running behind me as we hurried down the street, staying close to the dark and murky walls of what once used to be store's, from clothes shops, pet shops, and food shops they were all abandoned and destroyed, a horrid sight to see when passing the pet store as the skulls of what once were cats and dogs no longer had its flesh, just covered in dust and fur.
I stopped us moving when hearing footsteps ahead, soon knowing they were human when hearing the careless gunshot noises, whoever they were they didn't plan on sticking around to make less noise.
I firmly tucked Abby to my right, we pressed our backs against a shop squared pillar with our backs to where the people were coming from. We kept quiet in the dark dusty

Street, as the people's footsteps grew heavier. They sounded as though they were wearing a full helmet as their voices were a little muffled, I glanced to Abby as I said,

"you need to make a distraction, they will know it's me if they see my face, but they won't know who you are",

she put the flare gun in my left hand as she said smugly,

"watch and learn",

she moved past me, gradually getting in the line of sight of the guards.

The torch lights were brightening as they looked upon the street, seeing Abby as she faked cried, she asked ,

"are you the good guys? I need help, I'm lost",

she moved back slightly, allowing the guards to walk to my left as the man reassured,

"we're here to help you lady, tell us where your parents are?",

the man was in my view, I could see his bright white armoured jumper along with his black shoulder and elbow pads. He also wore rugged black combat trousers along with thick heavy white boots, they copied the appeal of the Eviliance, perhaps they never left here, they just split up, it would make sense they never leave something that they want to control.

He wore a full white helmet, it rounded over his head; the wind protector where his eyes would be was a thin line, ensuring he had protection everywhere, leaving the glass strip just for his vision, same with the woman that was with him. His clan's logo was marked upon the side of his helmet, the right side that faced me, it was a simple torch to resemble the statue of liberty most likely, but it was ringed around twice to give it the clean-cut look, the logo was marked in neon-bright green to stand out from the rest of his armour, it looked to be as though they had LED's behind the logo engraved on the badge to make it glow brighter. The glow however made me visible as he was stood to my left, facing ahead to Abby as she lied,

"I don't know where they are, they left me",

she was making up a story to get their attention as I approached him, causing him to look at me as he saw me move from the corner of his eye, but before he could react I dug the katana within his neck, causing him to choke upon his blood.

As he clawed at his neck for air Abby went for the woman, digging the pocket knife into her neck before jagging it out of her. As the woman fell, I searched the man, taking his helmet off seeing his wide-open brown eyes, his ruffled up black hair looked sweaty as though he must have been in that suit pretty much the whole day.

With firmness I took my katana to his face, only to dig it into his head as I instructed,

"Abby I need you to do the same with the woman, we can't add two Undying to this place",

Abby unclipped the woman's helmet, stabbing her through the eye with her pocket knife.

As she moved away I persisted,

"we better get going, we'll go through the alleyways up ahead to our left, it will be quiet",

Abby followed me, glancing at the woman only to remark,

"my dad never let me kill them before, wished he was as fun as you",

I stated,

"it's not supposed to be fun, it's survival, so don't talk like a killer please",

she wondered,

"so, you don't get the feeling of victory after each kill?",

with a sigh I admitted,

"perhaps I do, but even so, you never express it, you hear me lady",

she smirked as she reassured,

"loud and clear Captain",

I rolled my eyes only to find her a little amusing, but right now I couldn't joke around, my friends are in serious trouble and if we don't stop the Chinooks or hitch a ride with them

90

then we're going to be at square one again, and I've been there too many times to know I don't want it to end that way.

Chapter Eight

The Cages

We crossed the street with a fast pace to our feet; I glanced back every so often to make sure Abby was keeping up, she was behind me by a few feet but close enough for me to defend her if anything was to jump on her.

Upon passing into the alleyways making a shortcut to the store, the radius was starting to get a little brighter, the street lights were gleaming upon the rugged old street, it was as though the store was keeping hold of a back-up generator keeping not only the store up and running but the buildings surrounding it.

Our trails stopped as we pressed against the left side of the alleyway wall, hiding within a doorway as I whispered, "there are dozens of these people, what are they planning on doing?",

I peered over the corner of the wall, seeing the store ahead of us, fenced off with barbed wire fences, leaving the double gates within the centre ahead of us completely wide open, however they were heavily guarded by four people, two on the sides of the doors as the other two stood within the centre of the gate.

The store raised as tall as three floors, spread across two blocks, it was huge, so I don't think that's going to stop these people from searching.

The four Chinooks were firmly parked in the parking lot in

two separate rows, the left side of the parking lot was occupied but a dozen of these people, they must have just left the Chinook after a meeting, it's usually these things go in operations and missions.

They hurried from the aircraft's, only to hurry their way to the front doors of the store that were on lockdown, whoever activated the security protocol gave us some time, or at least gave them some time to prepare for the breach.

When looking around I pointed,

"Abby we can get the Chinooks, they aren't occupied and from the looks of it the other three dozen people are clearing the area",

I took my bag off, tucking myself back in the door way facing Abby as she wondered,

"perhaps Nathan packed stuff in your bag that you can use, probably like grenades or something",

I laughed slightly before I remarked,

"well I'm not sure about that, the mission to get the doctor was meant to be quiet enough",

my words paused when taking out a hand grenade, I puzzled, "why would he pack one?",

she grinned as she stated,

"well I normally slip one in, he doesn't like them being used so when he dumps them in the dumping ground I go out the city through the fire exit, recover it and put them in the bags", upon giving her the ruck sack I persisted,

"okay we can flank them the very least, but either way I'll try to get a Chinook",

she pointed,

"no, wait",

she kept my hand on the grenade pin as we looked through the alleyway opening, she pointed,

"why not go for the gas station? It's a little closer and will definitely cause them to go to it",

she was motioning to our right, looking to the right, seeing the gas station wasn't barbed wired around, it was out in the open and it might be a far throw but I think I can do it.

Before making the throw I looked to the door as I instructed,

"Abby get the door open, once the grenade goes off breach it and we can hide",

she remarked,

"forgetting I'm a kid? I think you might have to breach it, if I try, I don't think my arm will be the same colour",

she smirked as I rolled my eyes only to face to the gas station as I warned,

"fine, look just get back I don't want you in the way",

I placed my katana against the wall behind me near to Abby, allowing myself to have the free hands as I pulled the pin from the grenade, keeping it on my finger before throwing it, upon throwing it I did a middle high throw, not too high for me to pull something and not too low for it to go higher than necessary, I threw it much like a baseball player would, perhaps the influence of the Zasalious sports helped me with the powerful throw, sadly I was on my own playing the games but even so it was a long time ago.

The frag grenade started to tick as I threw it within the distance, causing people's attention when they saw it land; with haste I approached the door, swiping my katana from the floor before approaching the door as Abby said quietly, "nice throw",

just as she said that we glanced back, seeing the gas station explode in a ball of furious flames, the echo crackled upon the lands, rumbling over to us as I turned my attention to the door, slamming my body against the door, forcing it to break inwards.

Abby was watching the flame in awe as she said to herself, "awesome",

when looking around the room to find the front door I soon saw the dark oak door at the front to my right, it was past the living room and opposite the rusted steel kitchen along with the steps leading to the floors above us.

Seeing Abby was still watching the gas station go into

smokes, I pulled her inside, closing the door quickly as the guards were running past, they were alerted by the grenade but soon were instructed to do a search of the area. With haste I approached the front door, hearing it rattle as the man on the other side stated,

"the door is locked, we'll have to breach it, no one stops the search until a body is found, dead or alive",

I looked around as I told,

"Abby get upstairs, find a way back down",

she glanced to the door only to run upstairs to my left as I hid in the kitchen, crouching behind the countertops that separated the living room from the kitchen grounds.

With a quickness I put the katana on the countertop, creating a form of distraction for them to look at when they breach the door. As I did I rummaged my holster, taking out the red dagger, firmly keeping it within my grasp as the doors were finally being breached.

From the sounds of it, someone was using their foot to kick the door down, I took a small glance from the side of the countertop, seeing a team of four enter the room.

When tucking back in one of the guards pointed,

"Is that a katana?",

the people approached it, only to be ordered by the only woman of the team,

"yeah it is. Right, two of you go upstairs, we'll check this place out",

their voices didn't sound muffled, meaning they didn't wear a helmet with their white and black armour.

The man that was with her informed,

"I've checked over the living room but there is a basement unchecked, I'll go ahead and do that",

she agreed,

"you do that, I'll look around in the kitchen",

the room was small and to think I wouldn't be thorough enough to search this place, but it was as though she knew I was here, waiting for the man to go into the basement hidden under the living room floor.

As the man's footstep quietened as he stepped down from the extendible ladders, the woman looked to the katana as she remarked,

"the damn false UFO, they are here I know they are; only they have these, and it looks used",

as she went to grasp it I stood up from behind the counter, pointing the knife outwards to her neck, she slowly let go as she calmed,

"alright no one needs to get hurt, put the knife down before we capture you dead, Merider",

with a frown I looked to her with a puzzled look, how does she know my name? the scientist knows things but they know everything, to the point of where even their own hunters know my name.

She raised her hands slightly as I questioned,

"tell me what you are doing first?",

she explained,

"our mission is simple, control, contain…and kill",

she grasped the dagger with her bare hands, not fearing the cut that formed within her grasp as she swiped the dagger from my grasp, putting her gun under my chin as I mirrored her action with my revolver, causing us to be on a stand-off as both of our guns were at each other.

The blood was dripping from her right hand where she held the pistol, she pointed it under my chin as I did the same with my revolver, soon stuck in a stand-off as she persisted,

"put the gun down or else we both drop",

slowly I moved the gun away from her, she kept the gun under my chin as she snatched my revolver from my hands, throwing it on the floor to ensure I could shoot her, or attempt another killing, I still had one more gun, but she will expect that.

She moved back aiming the gun at me as she ordered,

"move around the counter and kneel right here",

she motioned in-front of her, she was forceful in her orders but then again, her ranking was different to the others, I could tell as her logo was shimmering a red colour, it was like each rank had a different coloured logo, she must be a leading sergeant, lieutenant of a sort.

When moving to my left, gradually stepping past the counter before facing her, seeing her features as the lights were slowly flickering, the explosion caused the power to grow a little twitchy but not enough to burn the lights out.

Her tanned skin dripped with sweat as her uniform along with the heat were causing her temperature to rise a little; her deep hazel eyes watched me as I gradually stopped a few feet in-front of her, kneeling slowly as she kept the gun on me. Her dark brown hair was braided back into a spiked ponytail, neat and clean like her uniform, with no marks of blood on it apart from the streams that trailed upon her sleeve, staining the white and black armour.

She motioned,

"put your hands behind your head then, do I have to tell you everything? Surely you know how this works",

as I put my hands behind my head, I heard Abby yell,

"get your hands off me creep",

she looked to the stairs seeing the two guards bring down Abby, she was trying to break free of their grasps, but it was no use, she wasn't physically capable of breaking past one of them.

They made her kneel next to me as the woman questioned,

"presuming a friend of yours, Merider?",

I glanced at her, seeing that if I said yeah, she will be killed, but if I said no she will still lie the same fate, but without me there.

With a firmness, I stated,

"she is, yet she wasn't involved with this, she followed me",

the woman smirked as she wondered,

"you know there are three things you've done, actually four things you've done which can get you killed, executed",

the guards had their rifles aimed at Abby and I, letting the woman approach us as she listed,

"killing a Free Liberty guard, disruption of the Dead Zone, oh and attempting to kill a lieutenant, that's me",

she crouched in-front of Abby, putting the gun under her chin, forcing Abby to look at her as she teased,

"but you, well, since you don't need to be kept alive, there's the sorting lines for you, oh this is going to be fun",

she lowered the gun, only to point it at me as she questioned,

"now, do you want her alive? Or do you want to be killed?",

she looked to Abby, who was persistent not to answer.

The guards came out from the basement as the woman ordered,

"Mores, get the soldiers rounded up, we have a store to raid", he nodded only to insist,

"I'll get the raid started, the people we find will be lined up outside in the parking lot, if they come willingly",

she looked to him, keeping the gun just inches from Abby's face as she instructed,

"get the prisoners in chains, they might be a feisty as Merider, and I'd rather not go on a wild goose chase",

as the guard left, he kept the door open, allowing the bright lights from the store to shimmer within the room, letting us hear all that went on upon the outside.

As the man left, the lieutenant looked to us, seeing she was enjoying every moment of this thin ice we were standing upon, one wrong move and we both sink. She kept the gun on her only to ask again,

"so what's it going to be, little girl? Kill you or kill her", with a firmness I remarked,

"you can't even kill me, it's a trick question, you need me alive that's what your leader wants",

she moved the gun away from Abby, smirking as she knows I was right.

She glanced to the door as she instructed,

"take the girl to the line, they will be lining up our prisoners by now, I got this one",

---

98

the two guards left with Abby, leaving the lieutenant with me as she mocked,

"you see there was a rule to not kill you, but nothing is stopping me from killing that girl",

I snarled,

"you wouldn't try it",

she put the gun to my face, pressing the side of it to my face as she warned,

"tsk tsk, you don't want me to have a reason to kill you, do you?",

she pressed it harder, moving my face left as I kept my eyes on her as she continued,

"you see he said to bring you to him, never said alive, well perhaps he did but either way, I can just say I wasn't listening",

she smiled to me as she said,

"you don't have anything clever to say?",

she let go of the pressure, letting me face her as my eyes glared into hers, she was persistent to make me talk and give her a reason to out burst at me, but I didn't want to give into her pathetic games.

Upon keeping my mouth shut still she stood up, only to swing the gun to my face, causing a cut to swipe on my right cheek; my head was facing the ground, looking down only to stray my eyes to her as I straightened myself out, she looked empowered as she questioned,

"tell me Merider, our orders are to kill your friends, we can save one of them, tell us who and they will be spared?",

she didn't look convincing, I knew deep down they weren't going to be spared, they were the ones to be killed first, and from what I know she was lying, I've seen many different liars but this one, this one was obvious, I speak a word and she will fly that bullet at me, I can't do that to Abby.

My mouth was sealed as she huffed, she glanced down, seeing the katana as she pointed,

"that's yours isn't it? Why don't you take it, I surely don't want it",

she kicked the katana towards me, along with my revolver as she mocked,

"you're going to have to ask me to kick them just a little further, so they are in your reach",

I looked down to them, urging myself not to go for the katana, it was easy to grasp them, but the second I was out of position, she had a reason to kill me, this wasn't a fair situation, but she didn't care about her rules, her objectives, she just wanted to have authority over me, and feel like nothing could knock her down.

She crouched down, seeing I was persistent to not look at her as she ordered,

"look at me",

with force my eyes looked into hers, seeing her amused smile as she said coldly,

"you and that girl are going to die, either way, they said to bring you back alive and oh we will",

she approached my katana, holding the hilt with her left hand as she continued,

"but you see two hundred people are going to the prison, including the girl's people, they will be joining your team...oh we know about them too, they are a pain in the ass",

she laughed slightly as she moved the edge of the katana to me, letting the tip of the blade rest upon the centre of my throat as she stated,

"they will be saved too, don't worry but right now we have to lower the numbers, we only have six Chinooks, each with enough room for ten prisoners, we can fit more in obviously, but you know the saying....Captains orders",

without thinking my voice snapped,

"you can't just kill one hundred and forty people! They haven't' done anything to you",

she moved the katana down, she said,

"you talk now, over all things, you worry about those one

hundred and forty lives like it's your duty to look after them. They don't care about you, and neither do your team, if they did they would have come over the wall by now, they have our seventh Chinook but I think six is more than enough, besides they got the worst one",

her words twisted my stomach as I lashed out,

"do you get a kick from this?",

she put the katanas blade across my neck, causing me to faced left as she approached my face, snarling her teeth at me as she intimidated,

"it's not me, so why should it matter, so do me a favour and keep your mouth shut, even when you're talking it kind of makes me want to kill you more",

my eyes looked to the door to my left, hearing the sounds of gun shots and chaos as she smiled to me, she stated,

"it won't last long, don't worry it just means we have less to execute",

I slowly lowered my hands, seeing she was focused on my face as I remarked,

"you think my team are going to give up, they fight for the right cause",

she grasped the scruff of my neck, letting the katana balance below my chin as she raised me to my feet, seeing matters were only growing worse every time I made a remark to her, she was a time bomb walking.

She pinned me to the stair rails as she teased,

"you think your big words and rough talk will get you somewhere, well let me tell you something, you're going to enjoy the show that's going to happen",

she sheathed her pistol putting the katana flat side of the blade across my neck, holding the tip side of the blade with her already wounded right hand, the blood was streaming down her arm, causing it to drip upon the floor as she gripped tightly on it, forcing the flat side of the katana on my neck, causing me to look at the door as she stated,

"you see that? they already found some of the little friends of yours",

the dozen guards came out with a team of civilians, around twenty or more, they had their arms raised and looked as though they surrendered, they were lining them up in the street in rows of ten, making a gap between them so the guards could count how many were lined up, but I know there are more to come, they will fill this part of the street and it will be havoc, why are they doing this? They want me but why kill them for it, they don't deserve this treatment, there must be something I could do?

I tried to struggle my way out, but it only caused her to force her weight harder on me as she grunted,

"try to escape this and they all die, what will it be, Merider? All two hundred and your team left standing, or one hundred and forty, with you as their little leader",

after one person to the next, the lines were forming in the street, they stood facing on the opposite side of the street, from what I could see was forty as there were twenty in-front of the entrance to the street with their backs facing us, their was a small gap between the ten people where the door was, allowing me to see the other twenty that faced them, they all had their hands in front of them as the guards chained them, shackling their feet to each person, using either their own equipment or wires they found within the homes in the street. With force I choked,

"who even are you? If I'm going to kill someone I want to know their name",

she smirked as she said coldly,

"Karmin, the one who is going to tear you apart, break you from the inside out before the final swing, before your death", she paused the words, stopping me from struggling as she hushed,

"shh, shh, can you hear that?",

I stopped struggling, feeling the katana's weight lighten as I listened to what she was talking about, I heard feet, many of them. There were lots of people walking past the line ahead in the street, the other hundred which was Nathan's people, but soon it clicked to me as Abby could be heard yelling, "Dad, Dad!",

she moved away from me as she grasped the scruff of my shirt, she pushed me to the entrance, keeping the sword pointed to my back as she remarked,

"I think your friend just started the show, lets get going before we leave them waiting, shall we",

she made me move forward, going through the entrance and passing the gaps were the shackled civilians were stood.

I looked behind the people facing me, my team was being put in the Chinook.

Qorin, Xharlot, Kamic, Rhax, Gina, Marcella, Alis, and Chrome, who I'm glad made it out of Rhovis city okay, he must have followed them.

Qorin was the last one in as Karmin announced,

"we have Merider, the leader of your people, the one who will cause the death of many of you, once you're lined up and ready, Merider will pay the price of the crimes committed here",

Abby was in the row, I thought she was meant to be safe? She wasn't in the team, but she was with me, I thought that would be enough of a shield for her.

Chapter Nine

Sixty Left Standing

The team were escorted into the Chinook, not leaving yet until the sixty people have been chosen to stand.

Karmin made sure two guards were behind me as I stood to the left side of the street, looking down to the two rows of a hundred, they were spaced out in tens showing me just how many will be killed, why kill them? why punish me by killing their own property? The hell is wrong with these people. The two guards were heavily armoured in riot gear and both held a pistol to the back of my head, ensuring that if one was to fall the other one would shoot.

Karmin strolled down the centre of the street, only to point out random groups, forcing them to the line in front of me just by a few meters, close enough for me to see, but far enough so I couldn't intervene.

She got them walking to me, stopping gradually as the extra guards lined them up, forcing them to kneel as Karmin counted,

"ten people kneeling for the great Commander Black",

she smirked as she ordered,

"group one, three, eleven to fourteen and row ten, line them up behind these",

the ten turned into eighty people as the guards ordered them to row behind the ones closest to me, making a gap for the guards to wall past each row as Karmin approached me, she informed,

"so you might have noticed each group has a number, after this they will be reset, but in case your small dim brain couldn't pick up",

she faced me as she pointed to her right,

"one to ten",

she them pointed with her left hand,

"eleven to twenty",

she smiled as she said cockily,

"you know I could kill them all, one by one, but we're on a time schedule",

my lips snarled as I mocked,

"why kill your own property to punish me? seems elaborate",

she tutted only to correct,

"the land is our property, the people are our cattle",

the lines thinned to the last twelve people, they were grouped together as the last six dozen people were placed in the line facing me.

The Chinooks that were at the city were on their way to us, parking behind me as Karmin ordered,

"get our six groups into the two Chinooks, we'll take the last four back to base",

my eyes filled with rage as she faced me, she said swiftly,

"oh, sorry did I give you the idea I was going to waste all the six Chinooks for our cattle? You only need two, if you thought I was being cruel perhaps I should cram them into one, do you want that?",

I shook my head, holding my tongue to not make things worse for the people being put on board, I saw Abby walk past me, thank the stars she's fine, but where's her dad? The few guards that were escorting the groups stood outside the Chinook, seeing as the prisoner has no way of escaping once the ramps were shut.

As they entered, Abby yelled,

"dad! don't kill him, don't kill my dad!",

as the ramps shut upon her, the Chinooks were in motion, going east to the fifth and fourth city, or base as Karmin calls it.

My throat lumped as the silence of the Chinooks hit the street, leaving those who were going to be killed to listen to the deadly silence surrounding them, the dead were nowhere to be seen, but the bullets echoing within the background explained why, they kept them far from us but why? They might as well just let us be taken by them, they are ruthless, and frankly, I don't think this torture is going to stop here, these people are cattle…meaning food. Karmin looked to the fourteen rows in front of me, she smiled as she announced,

"now that those of you are being killed are here let's get started, shall we?",

she heard the pleads for mercy but she cut in,

"oh no don't be like that, it's simple, very simple, all you need to do is die and we can feed off your flesh, eat every last scrap from your pathetic bodies, making something from you",

the two dozen guards went from the front row to the back row, they stood behind the civilians with a rugged long dagger, it was clean and shimmering with a green glow as their symbol was embedded into the handle.

They held the daggers close to the people's necks as Karmin approached me, she ordered,

"eliminate the cattle",

the guards miss led the people to believe their throats would be slit but instead the dagger was embedded into the sides of their head, causing just a little less bleeding as Karmin questioned,

"ever had human meat before?",

she smiled with a crazed look as I glared at her in silence, she remarked, "well you can stay quiet all you like but I can tell you one thing that will make your day better",

my focus was going away from her, seeing the people be dropped one by one, only to be collected and dragged into the closest Chinook to the right side of the store, nearing the fence so they could collect their food, it made me sick to the stomach to how they just dragged them away by their tied-up feet, like they were nothing but food, and that was just it, we were nothing but food to them.

She caught my attention as she turned my head to face her, moving the katana to my neck as she persisted,

"listen to me, listen",

her voice was becoming colder as she stated,

"you and your little friends are alive, our Commander ordered us not to kill you, but he never said to not hurt you, destroy you from the inside out, he never said",

she moved the katana away as she expanded,

"you think you can just take our cattle and think we wouldn't get you for it? You couldn't be more wrong, you're in our territory, and you are going to have the best three weeks of containment of your life",

containment? If the leader wants to see me, he would want me to go there immediately.

Perhaps he wants me to break first, show me what power he and his allies have, well it's not going to get to me, I need to keep us together, but with the loss of one hundred and forty people, it's going to be hard…especially since Abby's father was in the midst of the slaughter.

I held my tongue as she ordered,

"let her go, I'd like to see how obedient she is",

the guards put their weapons down, they were still on alert but stepped back as Karmin wondered,

"do you want to be my bitch when we get to my base? Do everything I say for the three week, get full meals, get everything you want and more, because I can arrange that",

without hesitation I spat at her face, causing her to barely flinch a muscle as she wiped her face with her hand, she remarked,

"is that all you got?",

she handed the guards the katana as she wondered,

"you know that little girl had a daddy, I'll feed her his flesh, make it look appetising for her, and for you too, don't think you'll be left out from all of this",

she was making taunts, testing to see how far my patience would go before trying to swing for her, kill her before she could do any more damage, but if I did that I know that the guards will have me killed, she isn't the only leader of the city, there are two and I'm going to find the other one…and kill them both, that's a promise I can keep.

She moved in front of me as she took something from the guards as she requested,

"the tools",

I kept my attention firmly ahead, seeing the slaughter continue, only to be left with a field of corpses as they soon were being removed one by one, dragged from the streets to the Chinooks, loaded up like they were just sacks of resources, piled and toppled on one another, it was inhumane. Karmin stood in front of me, taking my hands before attaching iron bracelets on me, they were octagonal pieces of metal, chunky, and very much acted like normal handcuffs in terms of putting them on my wrists, however, the key port wasn't there, it was merely magnetically sealed as she had the controller in her hand, a small device with only two buttons, one to unlock it and the other which I do not know. They weighted them, to make sure my wrist would ache as my hands were under pressure. She looked to my feet as she said,

"we'll put the feet cuffs on when you get into some new clothes, since you're determined on being the prisoner, we will treat you like one, until the Commander is ready to see you",

with my patience running low I warned,

"you better stay away from me in those three weeks, I will kill you with these if I have to",

upon moving the chain-less cuffs upon my wrists she laughed only to mock,

"if you even try that all I have to do is press this button right here",

she hovered her finger over the shimmering yellow button as she played,

"guess what it is? The cuffs don't give it away, the scientist and engineers along with many other names are good at what they do, hiding things",

she wiggled the controls in her hands, teasing me.

I couldn't bring myself to think what more could possibly go wrong.

She sighed before he stated,

"you're not that smart to guess. They are exploding cuffs, so if I press this then guess what? Say goodbye to your hands and feet",

my eyes widened as I cursed,

"what the fuck is wrong with you? you psychopathic bitch",

she moved the case from the back of the remote, covering the buttons as she put it in her pocket stating,

"well there are many things, but to list them for you, it wouldn't be the same as killing you",

she smiled only to look back as she ordered,

"come on we haven't got all day, this one is getting a little impatient",

she faced me as she motioned,

"come with me",

she didn't get the guards to escort me to walk with her, she knew I would have to do it myself because if I don't the cuffs will explode, literally, and I can't imagine what other damages it could do.

Unwillingly I followed her to her left, staying by her side as she teased,

"aw look at that, you are already learning to be obedient. Oh,

and guess what? You're stuck with me for three weeks",
the guards kept behind us as we walked into the store parking lot, seeing the blood streaks painted on the floor along with the rancid smelling corpses stacked in the back of the Chinook we walked past.

We reached the store's doors only to turn left to the Chinook where my team was held in, they watched me and Karmin walk in as she introduced,

"Merider, meet your new inmates, seems like they are more than familiar with you, but remember one thing, if they go against us, there's no rule to say we can't kill them",

Xharlot, Chrome, Rhax, and Gina were to the left side of the room by the wall, they sat firmly within their seats as they too wore the cuffs I did.

Qorin, Alis, Kamic, and Marcella were on the opposite side facing them, their weapons were confiscated as I could see the crates with their weapons in them to my left by the ramp.

I walked on board with Karmin and her guards as she ordered, "go sit with Marcella, she's been asking all about you, well they all have but you know how that goes",

with a quiet sigh I moved ahead of Karmin, sitting by Marcella to the right side of the Chinook, firmly parked facing the other side as she ordered,

"get us up, we got some people to break",

the guards sat firmly by Gina, seeing as Karmin was beside me to my left, she was close to me, but I knew what she was trying to do, get on my nerves, show me things that she knows will get me ticked off.

As the ramp sealed, allowing the Chinook to rise from the ground, Karmin wondered,

"so, I've asked Merider all these questions, and she fails to notice my existence",

she got up from her seat as the Chinook was heading directly east, leaving the ground for her to walk around freely.

She looked to Chrome as she commented,

"well you're only a robot, hmm, that might be a problem",

Kamic demanded,

"well you're not going to kill him, he has traits, you want someone alive to keep your stupid place repaired, then leave him be",

she glanced to Kamic as she wondered,

"Chrome, you're good at repairs, yes?",

she moved to the ramp as she stated,

"tell me, if I was to shove you off the Chinook would you live the fall?",

Kamic remarked,

"are you kidding me?",

she clicked the button lowering the ramp as she held the bar beside the controls, she said snidely,

"oh I'm not kidding",

she had the controller in her free hand, flipping the cover for the control case to go to the back of it, revealing the button as she blackmailed,

"Chrome needs to go, if he don't well you guys know what happens when I click this button, bye bye hands and who knows how far the shrapnel will go, it could kill you the wrong way, turning you undead",

Chrome got up as Kamic refused,

"no you can't do it Chrome, you can't",

he didn't listen, he walked towards the ramp, looking at me one last time.

He stepped upon the edges of the ramp as he had some last words to say to Karmin, presumably not the best of words either; he threatened,

"you may kill me, you may kill the team, but you can't kill Merider, she will kill you…and I hope it's slow and painful",

he stepped on the edges of the ramp, firmly in place until he jumped down the long, long fall to the dead city below.

Chrome soon jumped, causing Kamic to attempt to get off his seat, he stopped as Rhax ordered,

"Kamic don't, he had to make the sacrifice okay",

Kamic didn't like his words as he raged,

"sacrifice? That was blackmail, he didn't even have a choice", he sat firmly in his seat as Karmin pressed the ramp button, letting it seal in place as she put the cover back over the control as she remarked,

"you better listen to your big boss Kamic, you might just thank him for it",

she put the controller in her left pocket as she clasped her hands together, she questioned,

"right, now that dramatic deal is over with, lets get moving on the questions, shall we?",

she strolled within the centre of the room, only to stop by Gina as she queried,

"let's start with you then What do you think happens with tainted meat?",

she crouched in front of her, causing more pressure on Gina as she kept silent, she glanced to me, seeing I wasn't going to add an input into her choice, she will have to speak when she wants to, I can't decide for her.

Karmin explained,

"well, first we take their heads off; usually we use the head as the stewing bowl, it makes a very nice trinket and bowl. You see the parasite is in your brain, worming around, and to get it surgically removed is possible with our technology, but why waste it on the likes of you?",

Gina was feeling more self-conscious, growing more uncomfortable knowing there was a living thing in her head as Karmin went on,

"you see, it's asleep now, your body is active but when you die it wants to take over. So we take the head off, and sew onto someone else's body who is dead obviously, then they take over we release them into the dead zone, they are the false Undying, easy to repopulate the undying especially when you get tainted meat, it's all too simple since it's a parasite based thing",

she had a sinister smile upon her face, only to pat Gina's shoulder as she got off the floor as she reassured,

---

112

"but I think that can wait, I like the fear on your face, makes you look pathetic. It's quite amusing to watch",

Gina looked to me in fear, she was afraid, but now was in an even worse state than before as her words echoed in her head.

Karmin looked at me as she informed,

"you know there is another way of getting cured, you would know it too wouldn't you Merider? The Vipers Venom, injected or stabbed in the heart and it will destroy the parasite, and heal all the damages, no thanks to the first leader of the Vipers, who was an Eviliance member bear in mind",

she sighed deeply, she teased,

"come on people I'm starting to run out of facts to give you, speak up a little, talk to me",

she faced Alis as she taunted,

"I got a question for you, you psychopathic bitch",

Karmin smiled as she commented,

"always a good start to a question. Come on then, tell me what's eating you up?",

Alis threatened,

"which way do you want to die, being put in a wood-chipper, or strangled by my bare hands?",

Karmin thought briefly as she reminded,

"now, I would say bare hands, because when I click the button of the controller, you won't have any hands left to use. So, as amusing as that little threat was, you didn't fully think it through",

she looked to Qorin as she pointed,

"however, Qorin is the person I want to speak to next, look at him, he's a built killer isn't he",

she approached him as she challenged,

"you've had human meat before? you were a raider once. Tell me, what your favourite parts of a human?",

she leaned over him, put her hands firmly upon the chair behind him as she was getting into his personal space, almost as though she was flirting with him as he stated,

"the legs, more meat",

he saw that he had to say something she would agree on, or at least be in her mindset for her not to go in another outburst. She hovered her lips over his as she wondered,

"did you ever find entertainment with the corpses? Or were you a kinder man, and just ate his victims",

his lip snarled as he forcefully answered,

"I killed them, cooked them and ate them...I wasn't sick enough to feel the need to be entertained by them",

she moved back as she said coldly,

"I know someone who found pleasure in the dead, Nayker Black, your dad funny enough",

she looked to me as she could see I didn't want to hear his name again, it already was bad enough to know I was related to him by blood and bone.

She pointed to me as she teased,

"there it is, the topic, that's the topics that gets you crying internally",

she walked to me as she wondered,

"what was it like knowing your dad didn't want your sister, but wanted you, knowing he and your mom's sister had Rosia? I know these things because my Commander does, and he knows them because he's the smartest man alive",

she stood firmly in front of me as she continued,

"don't worry though, he had what was coming to him, we have eyes everywhere and most importantly, we bugged the hell out of Nayker's city's. Seeing as he joined our forces, we gave him our scraps. Which that wasn't enough, so he built the arena, and covered up the dead bodies with those he killed in the background. You wonder, how he got away with it? Well with our help of course but we see something in you Merider, we saw you kill him and that shows that all the bad people can go away, and we can take over",

she was saying 'we' as in she believed she was doing us a favour, she is deranged and no doubt is on my hit list, these cuffs need to get off but to breach them might set them off, we need to find a way to stop this before we all get killed, one by one.

As she glanced back to her guard she ordered,

"when we get to the ground escort these in front of my home, I will like to be sure they are all accounted for",

she gradually made her way to the front of the Chinook as she informed,

"now, don't worry about me guys, I will be gone for a moment, I need to be sure we're arriving on time, the people of ours will be dying to see their new inmates",

she walked past me, heading to the door to my right at the far end of the room, passing us before entering the pilot's sector.

Upon leaving the room I looked to the guards as I interrogated,

"why the hell are you following someone like that? if you seriously want a way out of this without being killed by either of us, then join us and fight against her",

the man on the left stated,

"if we wanted her dead we would have done it, besides you don't understand how good it is, fighting with a Commander who knows what he's doing, he's curing us, saving humanity, you're just trying to destroy it along with us too",

Xharlot remarked under her breath,

"oh brother",

the guard glanced to her as he defended,

"he is strategic, the people that die will come back due to the future, humans will repopulate again but pure, not tainted or dead why else do you think he singled us out from the rest of the others? We are pure and strong, you are corrupted and belong in a grave",

the other guard interrupted,

"the Commander wishes for us to keep you alive, he knows you are pure, from the moon and wants to show you the light, show you that this path, with these people, it's wrong, they aren't from where you are from",

with firmness I stated,

"that may be but they have my heart and goal and that's more

115

than enough. I don't care where anyone is from, who they are, what they are, if they fight against the cause to wipe out our species, I swear to all the planets and moons that I will kill them, I will destroy them until there are no bad people left", they were silenced by my words, but it didn't intimidate them, more or less sceptical of me, they believed that I could be changed, so they said nothing.

These people are corrupted but for the reason being that they follow a person who thinks all are corrupted, everyone apart from them, I bet half of the people that are with him are from the outside, so what's hypocritical is that they say because I'm teamed and socialise with people outside of my lands they are corrupted, well whatever this way goes I know that Free Liberty will see the truth of this, even if it means killing them…

Chapter Ten

Base Zero

It felt as though it was hours that we were left in silence, reflecting on our plans and what can happen due course, it didn't look good in my eyes and can only lead to more death; I could feel the Chinook was stationary, meaning we might be in the landing grounds, it touched the ground shortly after descending for some time, allowing us to hear the clank and gradual stops of the propellers, leaving us in the silence of the ship once again but this time we could hear chatting and movement outside of the aircraft. From moving vehicles to other Chinook's landing I knew we were here, but it was when we can see this horrible place it was going to make me fear our end the most, I'm going to make sure no one else suffers, it's bad enough there was a slaughter of a hundred and forty, but to let my team down and half of them die too…then they will only have to blame me for that.

Our attention immediately turned right, looking at the pilot's door as Karmin stepped out into our view, she had the control in her hand as she ordered,

"alright you guys we better get this show on the run, we need to get you guys washed and dressed, don't worry we have better things for you, after all the leader told us Merider must live and you guys obviously won't, or at least if I can't help it",

she winked at me walking past, seeing as she was swimming

in glory, looking as though she had defeated us, but we were still breathing, there's still time to kill her, and this stupid base.

The ramp gradually lowered, revealing to us the dim sunlight outside, it was nearing late dawn, we must have been a few hours in the air.

Gina was to my right as Marcella paired with Qorin behind me, Alis and Xharlot were behind them, then lastly Rhax and Kamic were the last to pair up, we were in a neat paired row, allowing ourselves to stick together but also stay in Karmin's good books, just a little.

The guards were at the back of the line, keeping a firm watch on us as we stepped down from the ramp, touching the smooth concrete grounds, it was much like Base 19 but instead, there were three large warehouses, one ahead of us that was a large dome, people were mostly hanging around there meaning that's where the living quarters are, the homes and shelter for their people.

To the left was a large rectangular warehouse, walled around with barbed wire fences, tall rectangular towers within the corners of the fences, it was a prison for sure.

Guards were patrolling around and, in the fences, in pairs of two, a few dozen guards were within the inside, overlooking the prisoners who wore the shackles that we did, presuming we are going to be sent in there.

The prison warehouse was rugged and looked a little rusty, but they patched it up with fresh steel panels, it was spiked on the roof presumably so even they couldn't patrol it, because they knew that anyone that tried to climb it to escape the area or some other way, the roof wouldn't be able to be accessed by anyone.

Then lastly the third warehouse was built like a cube, it had a smooth white wall, shimmering rectangle-shaped windows that stretched down to the bottom of the building; there were ten windows spaced out upon each side, but since we were within the south side of the city we could see the large glass double door within the centre of the buildings left side. People wore the same gear as Karmin, but their symbols variated from green, yellow and only a hand full of reds, they were leading groups of yellows around the camps, telling them what their duties are as they escorted prisoners and even resources to the warehouses.

The large wide concrete grounds touched past the warehouse, covering every inch of the ground in nothing but concrete and not mud or any form of vegetation. Squaring around the edges of the grounds was a tall wall, large enough to not be able to see it but even so, the roofs of the warehouses could peak over, see the outside as we could see nothing but clean well-kept building and walls.

We all were stood firmly within the centre where the painted roads led to each place; the black painted roads led only ahead, left and right as behind us was the large gates leading out of the city, and yet even that was heavily guarded also, two towers were standing to the left and right side of the large metal door, there were two snipers placed within them, one facing the outside as the other was scouting over the city, they had a clear view meaning if you tried anything they have a clear shot, not unless we use the buildings and vehicles as cover, even then that will be a game of chance.

I heard the ramp shut behind us as Karmin ordered,

"follow me, prisoners, we have a detour to do before sending you to your cells",

we followed her cautiously, glancing left to the road leading to the prison.

They were handing coffins made of iron bars, they were elevated from the ground by an extendible metal pole, there was a control board to each one, but they all had a key which activated it, smart thinking but even so, the coffins looked inhumane, they couldn't even move in them. the cages were human-shaped and formed into their image.

Each one was wide or tall enough for the one receiving the punishment, the front was open as I could see the split, but it

119

looked as though it would need to be bolted shut, you would need a welder or perhaps it was made to look that way, if they are anything like us they would have used a strong magnetic force, it would be hard to break through them malnourished.

I looked ahead seeing Karmin noticed we were looking at the coffins filled with people in each one.She stopped by the wall as she made us look at it longer as she stated,

"they get hung up there to die, they don't come down until they are, or unless they respect and obey us, then only can they come down, we get the executioner out there to do that along with the psychologists too, they get better chances of brainwashing them, tell them what they want to know",

she continued the march as we went right, going to the large square building.

As it was ahead of us we walked past many patrol men, or presuming they were patrol men, I couldn't tell who were civilians or guards, they all wore the same gear it was starting to give me the chills.

I glanced back to Qorin briefly as he remarked quietly,

"I think she's the one that needs to see a psychologist, she's fucking crazy",

when looking ahead I saw she didn't hear that, luckily.

Gina looked at me as she said quietly,

"are we going to die?",

she was still a little skittish from Karmin earlier, and it's understandable.

I reassured,

"don't worry, let me handle it, you just do what they say, get in their good books",

our conversation ended as we faced ahead as Karmin welcomed,

"welcome to my work tower, this almost feels like bring your children to work day",

she glanced back to us as she continued,

"I'll take you to the lower floor first, that's where the

showers are. Since you're royalty Merider you get my shower, leaders orders to kiss your feet",

we entered the room seeing ten elevators as she explained, "we have ten floors, two below ground and eight floors up, don't worry we also have fire exit stairs to the back of the room there, they line up perfectly with their given elevators.", The rectangular pillars were evenly spaced from left to right, they had numbers painted in black above each shimmering metal elevator door, from the left it was '-2, -1, 1, 2, 3, 4' and so forth, ending on the elevator numbered '8'.

The tiles were bright marble white as the walls were half windows and white painted metal walls, the forty rectangle shape windows were evenly spread out from the room and I could see that it merged with the ceiling, heading to each floor above.

Karmin led us to floor number '-2' as she informed,

"these elevators are so large they can fit twenty people in it", I remarked,

"are you sure? You weren't sure that a Chinook could fit over a dozen in it",

she smirked as she teased,

"oh you, such a joker; I bet you remember every little thing I say, it's quite flattering",

she clicked the button to the right side of the door, calling the elevator. As the elevator raised she faced us as she explained, "I shall hand my guards the honour of the controller, Merider won't need it with me, I can simply just kill her. Now you guys are wondering what the fuck is going on I know, but you know just do what you're told then you shall know it all", she took me aside as she ordered,

"get in the elevator then",

the team glanced to me, seeing I looked at them, to say just do what she says.

Qorin huffed as he walked past us, Karmin gave the controls to one of the guards as she instructed,

"get them showered, dressed and out in the centre of the city,

make them stand still as a stone, if one person even makes a small amount of movement make them kneel, and so forth", the guard questioned,
"And what if I have to press the button?",
she said bluntly,
"you won't need to, and if you press it I swear to the sun you will be killed, roasted and eaten for my dinner, so, off with you",
the guards entered the elevator descending to the lower floor, I know something is going to happen to them, I just hope they don't activate the button, they need to be in one piece.
Karmin got me to walk with her as she hooked her arm within my left arm, linking us together as she stated,
"they will stand there for hours, probably even the whole day if need be, as for you, you're going to get the luxury of a hot shower, a change of clothes, sadly it's the same as theirs but don't worry we still have a special surprise, I need to arrange it so",
we approached the last pillar with '9' marked above the elevator, she pressed the button as she ordered,
"guards",
there were people all over this place, I didn't notice until three heavily armoured guards approached us as she instructed,
"take Merider to my room, I have our surprise to do, leaders orders, oh and be careful of this one, she's ambitious",
she patted the closest guards shoulder only to leave me with three heavily armoured guards, all with their faces covered, only to allow me to distinguish who was who by their voices.
They held their shotguns firmly within their grasp as the centre one ordered,
"get in the lift, we'll be watching you closely",
I nervously walked into the elevator only to stand at the back facing the entrance, the three guards stood in front of me with their backs to me, their back were, even more, armoured than the front.

They had full-back padding, leaving only but the spine expose for movability, as the doors shut in front of us I could see the wide square elevator, large for a dozen people, not two dozen like she claimed, she seems to like to make herself look good by lying.

The bright lights of the elevator shimmered upon the black marble walls, revealing the metal bars walled around the left, right, and back of the lift.

My feet were virtually glued to the floor as I wasn't wanting to make the wrong move, the guard on my left questioned, "what's your name?",

she glanced back at me as I answered,

"Commander Black, or Merider if you don't want to be civilised",

as she faced ahead she remarked,

"well, Merider, this bath is surely needed, you reek",

with a snuff I answered back,

"you try and fight over dozens of Undying and not get showered in their blood, see you barely get any dirt on yourself, so how do you fight? Verbally or prod your victims with a stick",

the guard in the centre snuffled, laughing at my joke as the woman stated,

"you watch that tongue of yours, it will get you killed", seeing as I was getting on her nerves I thought to push her a little further, because if she makes a move on me Karmin will be on her, and no doubt that isn't going to be pretty but an incredible distraction.

With firmness I mocked,

"it's not gotten me killed yet, but it sounds as though you're really taking my words to heart, how quaint",

she faced me as she persisted,

"if you're planning on getting killed, then you're going the right way about it, keep talking, give me a reason to kill you", I smirked as she pointed the shotgun to my chest, she paused her trigger finger as I remarked,

123

"but if you kill me, then not only are you disrespecting your leader, but you are disobeying Karmin's orders",

she lowered the gun as the guard in the centre calmed, "alright that's enough, if you're looking for a fight we're going to the prison soon, bet you will eat your words then", he moved the woman back from me, making her face the door as we were closing in on floor nine.

We waited for the last floor to go by before the door finally opened. The woman parked outside the door as she ordered, "you two go ahead, I'll keep watch of the door",

to tease her more I stated,

"don't forget the fire exit, the lift isn't the only way down you know",

the woman watched me walk past with the two guards, even though I couldn't see her face under the helmet, I knew she was glaring at me, I could feel it, and that's what I wanted, to make her angry.

We were in a small room that led to a bright white door ahead of us. The walls that squared around us, were shimmering and reflecting off the bars of lights going down the centre of the room, the floor was a bright white colour, it also had a marble pattern placed upon it also, giving it the feeling of class and cleanliness, this place was getting weird.

The two guards went ahead and opened the door, watching me as I entered Karmin's room, the large rectangular room stretched to the left and right side of the door, extending far and wide as I proceeded to the centre. She had a circular meeting desk within the centre of the room, made of dark oak; twelve oak chairs were circling the table, cushioned with white fabric making it look homely.

Ahead of me was the windows, and bright white rectangular pillars separating each of the eight windows.

To the left of me were four dark black doors spread out evenly between the end of the room, white wall that shimmered around the doors, along with the large wall behind me and to the far-right side of the room, but that side only had one large double door, presumably her quarters, so where do those four doors lead to?

The two guards lead the way through the left side of the room, heading to the four doors, the first guard went to the first door on my left, as the other one went to the third door, standing in front of it showing me the unblocked doors two and four, the rooms I'm supposed to be entering.

I looked around the room a little upon proceeding to door two as the guard ordered,

"enter this room first, your change of clothes are in there, then go to door four to wait for Karmin, she will want you to be quick",

the floor was made of cold black tiles, contrasting against the wall and the lounging room I walked past. There was a rectangular sofa to my right that faced the windows,

overlooking the city as a short stretched out marble white coffee table stood firmly in front of the sofa, there was a silver platter placed upon it with crimson red wine and two broad glasses, it looked as though Karmin was fully prepared for my arrival, or capture rather.

Upon walking within the second door I walked into the shimmering white bathroom, the large squared room was mainly upon the left side as the door was in the right corner of the room, it looked almost inviting and I was afraid of that, it looked clean and didn't even give off the creepy factor of Karmin, it was tidy, too neat.

When walking ahead I felt the white marble tiles painted all over the walls, it felt smooth and cold as a stone.

The toilet was ahead facing opposite the door that I made sure I locked, it was a black marble colour as the toilet paper to the left side of it was obviously going to be white, whereas the holder was black, the theme of this place brought too much familiarity, it was like I was back home yet it was upgraded, I didn't like it one bit.

My attention turned left seeing a large luxurious bath, it resembled much like a jacuzzi, it was touching the back wall

125

of the room, perfectly centred allowing the three steps to ascend from the centre of the room, allowing easy access as the left and right side of the jacuzzi bath had no steps, allowing security to it.

The water was full and bubbling slightly, the steam of the room was instantly suctioned out to the right side of the room, and upon noticing that I saw the window that let out the sight of the Base surrounding the warehouse, it was one-way glass, so I could see out, and they couldn't see in, even so, it felt strange to be in this position, why was she trying to give me luxury? Not long ago she was mocking me and showing me the worst of her, what is she playing at?

Clearly, this is some mind game she is playing, it must be.

When looking at the black coloured jacuzzi I noticed she had folded a black towel upon the floor, it was trimmed with a thick gold line on both ends of the towel.

Placed upon it was folded clothes, there were dark black combat trousers, a thick white jumper with the Free Liberty logo stamped upon the left side with a P.O.F.L labelled under it, presumably I can only guess its Prisoners of Free Liberty, the only thing that would make sense to me.

On top of that were a pair of deep grey boots; the pile was moved to the left side of the room, far away from the jacuzzi as I approached it, seeing a note was on it.

I picked up the neatly written note as I read, "don't have too much fun, you still got more to come. Love Karmin. Addition, the products are in a cabinet to your right, along with extra towels too",

I looked right seeing the cabinets tucked in between the wall and jacuzzi.

With a sigh I scrunched the note before approaching the black marble coloured cabinet, taking out the products, they were all salvaged from the stores which doesn't surprise me if there's anything left out there, they pretty much took everything.

I put the note in the cabinet exchanging it for the products

126

and an extra towel to dry my hair with.

I placed the products on the side of the jacuzzi before shutting the cabinet, I then placed the towel along the same ledge only to strip

down from head to toe from my old gear, seeing no choice but to play along with Karmin's sick fantasy world, she said I can't be harmed but she never said I couldn't instigate a fight, and that guard I was teasing earlier seems to be the perfect fit for the job, just better hope she stays angry at me, otherwise I will have to think of a plan B.

My undergarments were on the clean pile seeing as she didn't give me fresh undergarments, and I'd rather not go braless, it's just a big inconvenience half the time.

After all the preparation were finally done, I gradually got into the warm water, feeling the slightest bit of comfort.

For a moment it was like nothing bad was going to happen, but then my team was merging through my thoughts, what was going to happen to them, and why they must be punished for my goals.

If I get close enough to Karmin I can kill her, end her ways and find the other lieutenant for city five, with them both out of the picture it will leave me with the leader, and from the sounds of it he's more dangerous than her, and more intelligent.

The bruising and aches of my body were being healed from the warm water, it was hugging my body in the warmth that I haven't had in a very long time.

The natural bath of the wild was refreshing and cold, but this was different it felt rejuvenating and brought my spirits up, something about that comfort made me worry that the reason why Karmin is giving me luxury is to agitate my team, show them that I will be given good treatment as they are given the worst treatment, it all makes sense now.

Chapter Eleven

Special Treatment

Upon washing and cleaning myself within the warm and bubbling bath I soon heard feet tap towards the door, Karmin asked,

"you're not having too much fun in there are you?",

with haste I got out of the warm bath, drying my hair as I stated,

"just drying",

I don't know how patient she was and I'm not going to find out.

Firmly I dried myself, putting on my undergarments before wearing the prison clothes as Karmin stated,

"well, I'll be by the sofa, don't be too long",

as she walked away I was tying up my shoes, seeing they fit perfectly along with the rest of the clothes…Karmin, I didn't like when she said they knew everything, it was almost a little creepy.

I folded my dirty pile to the left side of the jacuzzi as Karmin added,

"oh, and put your clothes by the jacuzzi, saves more time",

as she left, I placed the clothes to where she wanted them,

only to move out of the bathroom, seeing as I couldn't stall time anymore, my damp hair flowed behind my back as I moved, it was a little bit curly and damp that it didn't move from its place so easily.

When stepping out of the bathroom the guards were still there seeing as Karmin wanted them to block those doors specifically.

I looked left seeing her sit upon the sofa, pouring out the drinks as she persisted,

"come, I said I had a surprise for you, well two surprises but one, for now, the other will be during the week",

cautiously I walked towards the left side of the sofa, only to firmly sit down a few paces from her, not knowing what was going to happen.

She had a letter in her hand, an A4 sized one with my details on it; she had placed it on the coffee table as I questioned, "what is this? Why are you being…nice",

she smirked as she stated,

"the leader told me to keep you healthy and breathing, never said about your friends so don't lose your guard too much, besides I know that there's something you've been looking for, but never got the right answer",

with a puzzled look to my face, she reached over to the table, handing me the envelope as she took a glass of wine from the table also.

When holding the letter I read,

"Merider Black",

with a frown I questioned,

"what is this?",

she leaned back on the sofa, putting her left arm on the back of the sofa as she faced me, she said ,

"you believe Nayker is your father but he's your stepfather, you wouldn't have known that it was so far ago and you were too young to remember, and in addition, I know it won't make anything better, but Nahtler's kid is her husbands, not Nayker's, the video that he showed us, which you saw, may

129

have looked very misleading, but our video team looked at it, and the camera cut for seven months, he told us himself that he didn't lay a finger on her",

she looked to me with a slight smile as I puzzled,

"why tell me this? Why clear this up when I didn't want to know any more",

she sipped her wine, gently moving it away from he rips as she admitted,

"look when I mentioned him earlier I saw the rage in your eyes, you weren't truly over it, I'm merely giving you closure, now look at the damn birth certificate already",

when looking to the envelope I put it back on the table, I didn't want to know anymore, I'm just happy knowing Rosia was Nahtler and her husbands, and not my step-dads.

Yet even when knowing that it made me feel worse knowing that because she also believed the same thing, I just wished she was here to know the truth.

With firmness she wondered,

"why don't you want to see it?",

seeing as she was planning on us being here for a while I suppose a small talk couldn't harm.

I said seriously,

"all of my family are dead and to know if there's one possibly still alive",

she cut in,

"oh gosh no, he's dead, seriously dead",

she wasn't gentle about it, in fact she looked amused as she continued,

"he was killed when you were born, accidentally of course, not sure what his cause of death was, but our leader knows that he's gone, I couldn't imagine what it's like losing your whole family",

she drunk her wine only to say coldly,

"one was killed by you...two to be accurate about it, the other was killed by a brutal raider. However, I don't think anything beats your foster parents, our failed experiments

surely do go a little bit wild",
with a frown I wondered,
"failed experiments?",
I got up from the sofa as I said sharply,
"K.I.L.O's are human, and you know what, how did you know that? how do you know any of this?",
Karmin got off from the sofa as she pointed to door four as she persisted,
"that was what I was going to fill you in on, in room four", she walked past me, leading the way to door four.
As she stood by the doorway she ordered,
"come, this is will answer your question",
she opened the door, walking into the room as she knew I would follow her in, which I unwillingly did, the team can get answers where they are but if I get something, I can use that to think of a plan of action.
When walking into the room I saw a large screen coating the opposite side of the room, facing the entrance I walked into as the lights were dimming down.
Karmin approached the left side of the room, going to the computer that was firmly on a white clean desk, the white tiled floor and the dark black shimmering walls made the screen stand out as I shut the door behind us, only to approach the centre of the room as Karmin instructed,
"stand in the centre of the room, you will know what I see and just a fraction of what the leader sees",
upon doing what she said, I stood firmly within the centre of the room, watching the screen flicker on, and exposed a hundred squares neatly in a row of ten going down the screen, they were large enough to see what was going on in each one, but not enough to see the smallest of details.
She enlarged the eightieth square, showing me a burned house, it was the Weathers home, there was nothing around it I could just see the burned house, they were using some form of a flying drone to see as she controlled it, she stated,
"this is where you first were, where we first saw you, we've

been watching you for some time, and to be honest, you've improved",

she said it like she was impressed, but all in one I was crept out that they were spying on me since the very beginning, how did they do it? How did they connect the signal from this far? it's crazy.

When watching the screen I could see the burned structure of the house, most parts were starting to grow mossy but as she flew closer I could see the burned open cage where Carey had forgotten her hamster, it was bizarre to see this place standing still, the storm was strong but perhaps it was curving east just missing it. I know it hit some of The Dead City. Karmin hovered the drone into the sky, allowing us to get a far view of the place seeing a large split separate the city as the towers and building that were once there were scattered and fallen apart brutally by the storm, I never knew how bad it was from the wait but the land looked abandoned.

She flicked to another camera as she pointed,

"see that, Saria and Aries are in the throne room, we can see what they are planning",

not having any choice she flew the drone closer, activating the sound system, as she did there was a blue glowing bar to the left side of the screen, it was the vocal movement as Saria stated,

"Merider said around a week to worry, she will come back before then, trust me on that",

Aries worried,

"something isn't right, I know it, look I can go over with Plasma, Dusty and Deago, you have Torre as your guard so you won't be left empty-handed",

her hand was able to move, meaning Plasma's sleepless nights paid off, the hand's movement was a little stiff, but it was flexible enough for her to express her words with her hand gestures.

The screen cut out shortly as the lights turned back on, the bright lights reflected off the wall and floor as Karmin shut the computer down, she looked back to me as she remarked,

"we know your moves, we know how everything will go, and when your team come here in a week, oh boy are you in for a treat",

with frustration I said sharply,

"why show me this? You're giving me all these things, and yet what is it supposed to mean to me?",

she moved towards me as she stated,

"you needed clarity and I gave you that, now you have nothing else to worry about because we know everything and you know everything, your friends know a little but even so they aren't obligated to be alive, so why would it matter if they know it all",

she moved past me, turning me around as she stated,

"right, enough of the drama we got your friends to tend to , Gina is my favourite have I told you that",

just within a snap of a finger she would change her behaviour, she wouldn't even let me have an answer for any of what she has shown me, she was fucking crazy.

Unwillingly I followed her side, entering the lounging room as she ordered,

"Guards, clean up my room, burn the certificate too, Merider didn't want to see it, so she never will have it",

the guard in front of room three moved away from the door, heading to the table as he poured my full glass of wine back in the bottle, he made it look effortless presumably meaning he does this regularly.

As he cleaned the table Karmin and I walked out of the room, heading to the elevator seeing the woman I was teasing earlier, she walked behind us as Karmin ordered,

"come with us, we have business to attend to, we're late and behind schedule",

she stood firmly behind us as we faced the exit as Karmin clicked the button to the floor zero meaning it led to the ground floor.

As the lift went down Karmin remarked,

133

"I know about you teasing my guard here, smart move. If she tries to kill you, I would kill her, and you weren't fucking wrong about that. But let me tell you something, Merider, there's no point in trying to plot and scheme, one of your friends will die from these attempts, and will have to face their punishment, now that I know of your attempt",

she was starting to grow colder, less sweet, she would change her mind and attitude in an instant just from one small little thing.

With firmness, she said sharply,

"you decide to get one of my most trusted men winded up, so I would kill them? I thought you cared about humans, Merider",

I looked to her only to snap,

"I cared about everyone, but you know something you're not what survival looks like",

I pointed to myself as I continued,

"we are the face of human survival, and people like you deserve to be put in a grave",

she awed,

"you know you can be very cute trying to act tough, it feels like it was just yesterday when I had your throat clamped between your sword and the wall",

I turned facing the door as she instructed,

"the thing you will have to do for me is play nice little girl, be the good girl and keep my room clean, wash my hair when I need it washed, and eat my meals with me when they come",

with a frown I refused,

"no way, I'm not going to be your bitch, I'd rather be hung in the coffin for a week",

she looked to me as she wondered,

"is that a challenge?",

I persisted,

"it's not a challenge I'm saying so",

she smirked as she ensured,

"what the Commander wants, she will get",

the door opened allowing us to leave into the bright ground floor as Karmin stated,

"well don't worry that's happening then, your surprise will have to wait, and frankly it fits in quite well with your surprise",

not wanting to listen to her I ignored her, keeping quiet as we walked out into the ground, seeing Qorin and the team lined up facing me, I was starting to feel guilty seeing that they didn't even get a shower, only a change of clothes as there's me, all clean…looking like I just made myself at home.

My guilt filled me up as we strayed closer to them, only to stop directly ahead of them as Karmin informed,

"so you are all changed and now showered as I ordered, but now here comes the punishment",

she patted my back as she stated,

"Merider here tried to get one of my guards to be angry enough to attempt to kill her, so I would kill them, it's clever, but not clever enough",

she ordered the guards to escort us to the prison road as she led the way with me, she expanded,

"so we better get you in the cages",

we stopped only to face the right side of the pathway closes to the centre of the grounds.

The cages were already lowered, seven of them but then that would mean someone doesn't go in the cages.

Karmin ordered,

"Qorin, Marcella, and Rhax get in the cages within the left of us",

as they walked past she questioned,

"Qorin, how would you like to be out of the cage? I can easily give you a free pass, after all, a man of your stature deserves to be, tended to",

he snuffed as he remarked,

"I'd rather die in here, but thanks for the offer",

as he stepped into the cage, Rhax went to his left as Marcella unwillingly went to his right.

With firmness I pleaded,

"don't do it, Karmin, we can work if that's what you want",

she laughed only to joke,

"work, what are we in the old times?",

she reassured,

"no we have workers for those jobs, paid and willing workers. However, our prisoners are for our pleasure, doesn't matter if they did anything or not, if they get in our way, they are our prisoners",

the doors sealed upon them, forcing their bodies in the large human-shaped cages, they gave them the biggest one to give them that feeling of space but even so they were restricted from going anywhere as they were pulled seven feet off the ground.

As they were raised from the ground the three cages were waiting for the others, however, Karmin had something in mind as she ordered,

"Guards, bring me Gina, put the others in the cages by Rhax", as they put Kamic and Xharlot in their cages, elevating them at the same height.

Gina approached us.

We faced her to the left with our backs to the prison as Gina questioned,

"what is it?",

she pointed to the last cage as she insisted,

"I won't let you go in the cage, you're infected and well I can't risk you dying, especially not properly anyway",

the guards activated the caged door, elevating the empty cage as they soon departed, seeing as they will be taken down on Karmin's orders.

She looked to me as she wondered,

"did I give you the remote?",

the guard that was with the team at the beginning soon approached her, giving her the remote as Karmin ordered,

"ah there it is",

she frowned to the guard as she went on,

"well, what are you standing around for? You can go",

the guard left us, leaving me with Gina and Karmin.

She made me sick, and I don't know what she is planning on doing with Gina, but what I do know is that she isn't going to be getting away with it in the end, we are going to kill her, perhaps not right now but we will.

We will end this insanity before it dares to progress, the spying, the death, the torment just isn't right.

She smiled as she held the remote as she wondered,

"so, Gina, you are my favourite, do you want to know why?", she was silent at first, but she reluctantly responded,

"I'm weak",

I looked at her, as to say she wasn't, but she didn't want my comfort as Karmin added,

"and you are also easy to pick on, it's because you are weak, and even you know that. There's something about you that is holding Merider back",

she tapped the controller with her finger, putting Gina under pressure as Karmin stated,

"Gina, go to the prison, you get my free pass, say it was my orders so they know what to do with you",

as Gina hesitantly walked past I could sense how helpless she was feeling, but we just got to pull through all the mind games, but what's going to happen to me? I don't care if I get harmed, but I know I won't be, and that's more frustrating because the team will see I've had it easy, they are going to have it harsher.

I glanced at Gina as she walked down the road to the prison, only to look at Karmin as she spoke to my team as she stated,

"so, Merider said that she would rather be in a coffin, so that decides your fate, as if you were her, she would want to be here, your Commander is a lovely one, but I know a man in the cage who has potential",

she looked to Qorin as she winked at him, only to look at Kamic as she continued,

137

"however, Kamic is the Alpha of all the men, he has the look to him",

she bit her lip as she blushed before she joked,

"well would you look at that I'm blushing",

she faced me as she said,

"why do you have such lovely men in your team, and yet you want them to suffer? All well, I get we all have our fetishes",

getting tired of her child play I firmly persisted,

"can we skip this madness and let me see your Commander, he wants me, not them",

she tutted as she opened the control cover, she blackmailed,

"if you want to start this game again, I can certainly play it. Or you keep your mouth shut, and everyone has their hands intact",

Marcella looked to me as she reassured,

"just do what she says, it's not being weak, or giving in, it's being smart",

she was right.

Karmin shut the controls as she stated,

"there you have it then, well whilst you guys are hanging for around three days, Merider and I have some business to attend to",

we walked to the left, proceeding to the prison ward as Karmin questioned,

"so, it's been almost halfway into the day, are you hungry?",

I remarked,

"over your dead body, I'm not eating anything you feed me",

she smiled as she said coldly,

"I knew you would say that, so I had a little, appetiser for you, get you in the swing of things",

we proceeded to the main gates, seeing the spiked fence be pulled back as the guards let us past, without needing identification confirmation, they all knew who she was.

We walked through the prison yard, seeing the guards stray around as the prisoners were watching me, seeing I was with Karmin.

There were over hundreds of prisoners, they were all stood there, they didn't have any tasks to do, all they COULD do was wander around and wait until they are butchered.

Apart from that they were all just stood there, keeping their eyes on us as Karmin introduced,

"I'm certain you know sixty of these people, but one young girl, in particular, wants to see you. Abby, isn't it?",

with persistence I cut in,

"you didn't harm her, did you?",

she laughed as she ensured,,

"oh gosh no, I wouldn't harm a little girl, I know people in here who love to have a little girl, tend to her, eat her",

she turned to me, pausing our movement by the metal double doors as she expanded,

"and with all those reasons I still kept a good grip on her, she has my protection, since you and her are best buds",

my lip snarled at her, finding her words less amusing than before.

She put the controller in her pocket as she took precaution as she stated,

"well I suppose it's not fair to keep you waiting any longer", she teased,

"but on the other hand it's my city, my land, and most of all, you are my bitch, and I would like you to say it",

with a snuff I remarked,

"to give yourself some authority around here?",

she rolled her eyes as she mocked,

"you always got something to say don't you",

she approached me closer only to hover her lips over mine as she stated,

"I want you to say it, so I know that you know where you stand",

she stayed in my space as I tried to move away, she only went closer as she said coldly,

"say it",

my eyes frowned to her.

I forcefully said,

"I'm, your, bitch",

she moved back as she smiled as she remarked,

"see was that so hard to do, trust me on this when I say you are going to love your surprise later",

she opened the metal doors, revealing the reception room within the centre.

The bright white room was shimmering as we enter the room, seeing the circular-shaped room around us. The desk ahead of us was built into the back of the room ahead of us, a man stood behind the shimmering black desk, he was wearing my uniform.

We approached him seeing the solid metal doors to our left and right; the left was labelled 'prison wards' as the right was labelled 'cafeteria', this place was too clean and organised that it was starting to scare me, just a little bit, even so I noticed the man was wearing my uniform, do the prisoners maintain this place?

How can she scare so many people to do what she says? Surely not all of them have the shackles?

Chapter Twelve

Reunited

Karmin turned to me as she stated,

"we will go to the prison first, see if Gina has taken her place",

the receptionist dared to answer,

"she has, ma'am, I just saw her walk past",

his words stopped as she looked to him, she soon remarked,

"I don't think I care what you saw, I only care what I see, and I see you wasting my time",

she firmly put her hands on the shimmering desk as she ordered,

"open the prison door when we get there, don't let me wait more than three seconds",

she winked at him before patting the table as she stated to me,

"the first rule you need to know is when I'm not talking to you, never ever try to answer the question, because it's not yours to answer",

she strolled to my right as she guided me to the prison door, the metal was shimmering grey, probably the only thing in this place that wasn't black or white.

As we stood by the door Karmin said out loud,

"one, two",

the door slid to the left, opening up for us as she admired,

"great time. Make sure to check the cameras for our return to the door, I will only be waiting one second, can you do that,

Sevis?",

she glanced to him only for him to respond,

"yes, Commander",

she smiled to him only to face ahead to the corridor as she persisted,

"come, Merider, I will show you to your room, and also Abby too, we were going to go to the cafeteria, but I think our food isn't to your taste. The prisoners, however, they love it",

she hooked her left arm within my right, forcing me to link with her as we strayed down the white shining corridor.

The smooth white floor reflected the long bar of light cutting down the centre of the hall, the wide spacious hall gave us a five feet space from between us to the black painted cell doors, the doors were made up of four thick bars, I could see the small rooms within them.

The walls were bright white like the halls and the lights were inbuilt into the ceiling, presumably so they couldn't be broken so easily. The black-framed bed and the white quilted mattresses were to the back left of the room, most of the beds were occupied.

The prisoners variated from men and woman, they were either sitting on the edge of the bed, looking at me through the bars or some were sleeping, trying to wake up to something different.

They all wore the same clothes as me, it was starting to feel repetitive.

The many, many doors to the prison cells felt endless, the only thing that was different from the rest of the doors was the one at the far end of the hall, it looked as though it were a set of stairs leading to the next floor; when glancing left I could see a cube to the left of each door with their number on it, it was a lightbox styled light, the numbers were cut in the front left, and right side of the box, so you knew where each room is and how far it ends.

When looking at the doors to each cell, I questioned,

142

"you didn't think to put locks on it?",

Karmin smiled as she jerked us to a sudden stop to cell twenty.

A large muscular man was on the other side as she ordered, "step back prisoner twenty",

he snuffed only to step back, allowing Karmin to open the gate, by simply holding the bar, pulling it open and leaving it as she explained,

"why need a lock when they do what you say? And they know the consequences if they do leave their cell. They get cooked, and it's a fine meal, it's a win for both of us",

she slammed the door shut, only to pull me to walk back with her as I remarked,

"what's the win for them? all I see is that you get what you want, and they die for nothing",

she cut in,

"no, not for nothing they get eaten, they don't just decompose. If that was the case they wouldn't be in these cells, sheltered and branded by us, you see this prison can make them of two things",

she looked to me as she listed,

"one, they can be our delicious meal and ultimately have a gourmet ending if that's even a thing",

she looked ahead as she continued,

"then secondly, if they show their worth they will be on our team, live and breathe our air, but it goes down to if they listen to my orders and most importantly participate in the Arena, it's a gun free zone, but swords and other melee are welcome in it, we want our meat to be clean",

with a frown I wondered,

"what's the difference? You put them in these conditions",

she stopped the walk, seeing as we must have been at the prison cell with Gina.

She looked right as she stated,

"we make sure their hygiene is on point. Look, Merider, I know this is all going fast, but it's very simple, you can't boss me around because I'm the leader of this place, and you're supposedly the leader of Zion City",

Gina approached the cell door as she defended,

"she IS the leader of Zion City, and she will take you down too, she's been through that much that this mind game you're playing won't last at all",

she faced Gina as she wondered,

"ah there she is, I know a few ways to get you angry, I'll keep note of that. Now, Gina, can I ask you something?",

she opened the gate as she pointed,

"this gate was open just so you know",

as the door flung open, Gina went to punch her, but stopped her fist a few inches from her face as Karmin raised the remote, she stated,

"you make contact with my face, and not only will you suffer the consequence, but Merider will too, and the others, to think of it, most prisoners here will suffer. This remote will spread the damage, think about your choices next time",

Gina moved away as I ordered,

"Gina, just do what she says",

she unwillingly went to the door, only to slam it behind her, putting herself back in the cell, I know it was unfair but if we do this right we can get out of this psychological game once and for all.

The aim I'm going for is to get me and her alone, just us and then I strike, take the control and end her before this continues; she turned us around, making us walk out of the prison as she stated,

"you know, I would have shown you Abby, but after Gina's attempt to beat me, I don't think that's happening, so instead I got something else",

we left the prison ward as I questioned,

"when will you let me deal with this with just you?",

we reached the door to the reception room as she remarked,

"well it's not me you're having this fight with, it's my leader, what he says is the law, and you know something else, I've tolerated a lot of your bullshit since you came here, I've been nothing but a fine guest. But don't worry, we still got the second surprise to make up for that",

she would say surprise like it's a good thing, but so far, every surprise I've retrieved have been nothing but a nightmare, I think if she's building up for this surprise, it must be bad, really bad.

The doors opened allowing us to enter the reception room as Karmin ordered,

"Sevis, the isolation room please",

he sighed as he clicked the button, elevating a circular room in the centre of the reception room as she ordered,

"well there you go, I'll take you out when I'm ready",

the cylinder-shaped room was large enough for one person to stand in, not even to lay down either, it looked like a coffin.

The open door way that faced me showed the inside of the dark room, perhaps Karmin can cool off.

I glanced to Sevis as she persisted,

"go on, Merider, you said it yourself, you would rather be in the cage, and this cage is more than enough for you",

with firmness I grasped her by the scruff of her shirt, only to slap the remote out of her hand. I soon kicked it over to Sevis on the other side of the room, I said firmly,

"you and your ways will be locked in here, for however long it will take, I swear to god if you're not dead I will kill you myself",

I forced her to the entrance as I barked,

"Sevis, close the room, now!",

Karmin looked to him yelled,

"you listen to me, if you shut that door you will be cooked and roasted like your wife!",

with firmness I remarked,

"not if you are locked in there",

I pushed her back into the room, seeing Sevis turn the switch on as I did, causing the room to descend, she tried to climb out, but as the room was descending her left hand got stuck,

145

it was clamped where the rooms roof met the floor I stood upon, it was cut off with a rugged tear, I could hear muffles below, but it wasn't clear in what she was saying, but I could sense she might be in a bit of well-deserved pain. Something out of character for me to say, but she deserved the suffering, she caused many to die, but now her brainwashed soldiers are left to deal with.

I don't know how I'm going to do this, but now that she is a captive, I needed to keep it that way, the only way I see it is I'm going to have to overrun the prison.

Sevis approached me as he unlocked both the doors as he stated,

"we haven't got time to stand around, the guards will know that she is missing and will search, if we need her down there, we're going to have to turn the grid off",

with a firmness I stated,

"no, she will be taken out at some point, but for now, we need to worry about arming ourselves. My team is outside in the cages, they are safe at least, but I've noticed the snipers",

I moved to the control, picking it up as I pressed the blue button, deactivating the shackles.

As I did, Sevis took the remote as he stated,

"well, if anything this can be destroyed, with the control not being used as a leverage the prisoners will have their own thoughts to use",

he put the remote on the floor, only to unsheathe a gun as he shot it with accuracy, the control blew into bits, breaking apart on the floor as it was finally over, but not quite over just yet.

Sevis went to the desk, jumping over it as I questioned,

"where did you get that from?",

he hit the alarm button as he insisted,

"I got it from the armoury, it's past the cafeteria, come on we better get going, the camp of guards will be coming for us",

he threw me a pistol, with one clip of twelve bullets, I will have to make each shot count when going to the armoury.

146

He vaulted over the desk as the prisoners were out of their cells, they were all heading the same way, it was as though they had planned this for ages, but how?

How did they communicate? With questions rising we followed within the crowds, trailing behind the prisoners, I wondered,

"Sevis, how did you know this would happen? Have you guys planned this for some time?",

he was to my left as he explained,

"we all worked together and the only words I told them was Alarm to Armoury, that way they knew that when the alarm comes on we all go there, we don't plan to fight them with our fists",

the large guy I saw before, prisoner twenty, he joined us as he said with a low voice,

"Sevis, the guards are on their way, should I get the launchers",

the man was darkly tanned and broadly built, his jumper was rolled up, exposing his tattooed arms, there were Egyptian hieroglyphics marked upon his arms, a passage of a sort, either way, it was well crafted and it looked as though the message was saying about slavery and to come on top, I'm not too skilled in that department but I knew people on the moon who were interested in that, and they focused on slavery and ruling ironically.

The buff man had his short black hair buzzed cut, it thickly domed around his head, his rugged beard was shaven at a point to his shin, giving his broad face a slick and cleanly cut appeal even though he looked unwashed for a few days.

He shortly left as Sevis ordered,

"get to the towers, the snipers are to worry about, once they are down we will fight on the field, take over before we all suffer",

we shortly entered the cafeteria seeing the bright scene, the flashing yellow lights replaced the normal lights, as if they were built in with the alarms to cause an ambient effect.

147

The room faded from darkness to a yellow glow as we raced past the white rectangular tables and seats.

We hurried past them only to reach a large double door, they were locked only to be breached by prisoner twenty. He used his body as a ram to break down the door, taking down the double door completely as the prisoners flooded the room. Sevis and I were by the centre of the room, flipping the table closest to us to our right as I stated,

"We got our weapons, we need to defend the position until the prisoners can take over",

it was starting to buzz with enthusiasm as the prisoners left with a few pistols and ammunition, some wore bulletproof vests as others decided to go un-armoured, it was calm chaos as Sevis and I hid behind the table, waiting on the guards to enter the cafeteria as we pointed the guns to the entrance.

With curiosity I questioned,

"tell me who you are? Do you know prisoner twenty?",

he expanded,

"me and Horneck weren't from here, we were from a land far east, below Kerivous, or rather known by the name The Storm's path, it touched our land too but not Egyptverus we lived, it's been years since my wife and I have separated but she found her, and killed her when I was disobeying her words, it's wrong if you ask me, but no matter, our Pharo will be pleased to have his lieutenants back",

with the confusion I wondered,

"lieutenants, this place of yours, how far is it? Will you think it's safe to be in?",

he remarked,

"safe? It's the most dangerous place alive, people kill and steal, the Pharo will try to hold it together, to be honest, we've had so many Pharo's it won't be a surprise if our one is dead, he wasn't the best ruler in the world",

the alarms were quieting as the power was being shut down, no doubt to give us a slight disadvantage, but even so the light from outside was more than enough to expose who entered the room.

Horneck approached us as he stated,

"the snipers will be taken down, you get the prisoners out the cages, they will focus on me, wait for the signal",

the prisoners were crouched behind us, taking cover behind the table and the other tables scattered around the room, some had night vision goggles on, I could see the glass shimmering upon their goggles, the green material was flashing before it went back to dark seeing as they were hiding with the darkness.

Horneck left the room with two prisoners, they were in riot gear, and no doubt ensuring his protection for outside, or to get a higher ground as I saw him cut into the prison. The two prisoners in riot gear were parked outside the prison ward, facing the entrance of the prison also.

He motioned me as he stated,

"let's get in the armoury, we can gear up with what is left",

as we left into the dim glowing armoury, the people had left torch lights around the room, allowing us to see the lockers to the right side as the armour was hung to the left, the weapons were stored on racks upon the wall, it was like a weapon haven.

We approached the armour, fastening the bullet proof vest over our jumper, when putting on the riot helmet, Sevis questioned,

"you know of, Abby? The girl who I protected in the dome?", with a frown I wondered,

"yes, I know her, why is she in the dome?",

he put his helmet on as he continued,

"she is pictured as the fresh youth, Karmin wanted Horneck to look after her, guide her to the dome for the show, they cage the children and bid on them, do what they please. These people do it with the woman and men too, they all get shown off in a cage and bought to become either a new meal, a false lover, or even worse a beating bag",

with sympathy I said,

"I'm sorry, I can't imagine what this was like for you, you've been here for years it sounds like",

he smiled softly to my words, he reassured,

"the loss of a wife is sad but we have time to stop it from happening, never grief something you couldn't help. Grief holds you back but it never harms to cry",

he was down to earth, I liked him, he was straight forward, and most of all had a level head of wisdom.

I looked to the wall of guns as he stated,

"the confiscated weapons are in Karmin's building, they are locked in the lower floor, the very bottom floor but for now we deal with what we got",

he put the pistol in his holster as he took a rifle, storing the ammo in a rucksack nearby as I wondered,

"sounds like you miss a weapon of yours? I have a Katana, perhaps not my original one, but it's pretty effective, it does burning damage with each successful hit",

he smiled as he stated,

"I have a spear, the tip is golden and curved back in a shape of an upside down heart, it crosses with another heart that points up wards, creating a sort of sand timer if you wish",

as I grasped a bright white rifle from the wall I added,

"sounds like a fine crafted tool",

he nodded only to expand,

"it's been with me since I was a child, it's hard to believe that it took only but a harsh bitch to take it from me, well she's not going to get in the way of the takeover",

we left the armoury, heading to the reception room as I persisted,

"we can't leave the prison until the towers are dealt with, but we need to keep an eye on the door, see how many people are out there and think of a plan of action",

he nodded before he questioned,

"Merider, you say about your team, why have one?",

he was curious as I explained,

"well it's not taking people down with me, they are helping

me, staying by my side because when I need them the most they are there, I have more of my team over the wall, we're gaining control of The Revla Lands",

he went to my right as we kept behind the right side of the door, seeing the reception room and the entrance ahead of us.

I kept the rifle close to me as he wondered,

"so you are much like our Pharo, they hold places to their name and do as they please",

I corrected,

"I don't do as I please. I change the systems there, make it safer for the civilians and Unite the cities, then work from there",

he looked as though he liked my way of things as he questioned,

"could we be of assistance to you? I would return to my home lands with Horneck, but the Pharo wouldn't be pleased or any of them, once you leave the lands you become a traitor",

with a frown I curiously asked,

"but why return if you know they don't welcome any returners?",

he smiled as he expressed,

"I think it was the home sickness, I want to go home and see the beautiful Pyramids, the sand, and the obelisks. It was much prettier over there than it is here",

with a slight smile I ensured,

"trust me this land may be dead but over the wall, it's a little nicer, apart from the red lands I guess that place is too dangerous to wonder in",

our conversation cut short when hearing the door being kicked, the two prisoners barricaded the door with beds from the closest cells, luckily it stopped their access but the doors were wide open, allowing us to see over it all.

When glancing to Sevis I said shortly,

"do you want to be on our team? You and Horneck, then show me what you got", he remarked,

"without the spear, I'm less impressive, but a rifle, I am a little rusty",

we hurried behind the wall seeing the beds were forced out the way, moving to the centre of the room as the dozen of armoured guards entered the reception room. They had their riot shields, they weren't messing around when they send their clearing squads, we need to get them down somehow, the darkness of the cafeteria will help us with that.

We tucked ourselves in the room, hearing the fire shots as the guards were tackling the prisoners in the riot gear, as for the rest of us we were waiting on the ambush.

I quickly shoved the guard as he entered the room, catching his attention as we brawled upon the floor, with haste I unclipped his helmet, only to struggle as he went to choke me, his arms were on my neck as he pinned me to the floor, the prisoners were charging into action, taking down the ones they could see as those wearing the night vision goggles could take them out.

With haste I grasped the helmet, only to hit the left side of his head with it, getting him off me as Sevis grasped the man's shoulder, pulling him back, making a shot to the guards face. He joked,

"see your katana is your best trait",

I got off the floor as I remarked,

"well it's a little dark in here",

the fighting instantly stopped as the sound of an explosion rumbled outside, presumably Horneck has taken down one of the towers.

Sevis ordered,

"get to the grounds, take cover and free those in the cages, they are in much danger like us, let's go",

the prisoners filtered through the door, killing the last guards before roaming the grounds, we were outnumbering them by hundreds, the prisoners on the floors above us in the prison section were coming down and passed us, meaning we have even more to our name.

Karmin had one mistake, she can't tame a beast that doesn't want to be tamed, the only time we monsters show is when something to our hearts tells us it's wrong, and we must fight to save ourselves before its too late.

Chapter Thirteen

Sevis from Egyptverus

We raced into the large city grounds, hearing the second tower erupt into a ball of cloud and fire.

Sevis kept with me as the prisoners fought back against the guards, taking the cages down and soon uniting me with my team again.

Qorin, Marcella, and Xharlot met with me as they informed,

"Rhax, Kamic and Alis left to Karmin's tower, the prisoners told us of the plan, and how they were going to the confiscated section",

it sounded like a good plan, but I was still in thought about something, where's Gina?

I turned to the prison ward as I worried,

"Gina might still be inside",

Sevis persisted,

"we need to decide what to do, we're out in the open",

with a brief time to think I persisted,

"Qorin, I need you and Sevis to join me, we captured Karmin and no doubt she will die before we kill her first",

Marcella and Rhax had a more important job as I ordered,

"I need you to get Abby and free the prisoners in the dome, I'm not sure how long we can hold out the siege, but the more people we have with us the better, can you do that?", Rhax confirmed,

"you can count on us Commander",

they left us, allowing me, Sevis and Qorin to return to the ward, not wanting to free Karmin, but if we are going to kill her it needs to be by our hands, not by a trap.

We hurried into the prison ward as the scene ran within the background, people were falling, and yet our people were pushing through, it was going to be tough but I think we all wanted to see it through, push through this mess and clear it up once and for all.

Sevis, Qorin and I approached the desk as I explained,

"Sevis and I have her locked here, underground in the trap room, her hand sort of came off so she can't bleed out down there, not until we deal with her properly",

I climbed over the desk as Sevis pointed,

"the button to close the door is in the centre of the desk, you can see it by the paperwork",

I moved to my right, going to the centre of the desk when seeing the red button on the side of the desk.

Upon clicking the button the small cylinder elevated as Qorin questioned,

"why to keep her alive for a little bit longer? It's all she'll needs to overthrow us again",

Sevis doubted,

"she's one hand down and half of her men are gone too, she won't be much of a threat to us weak and helpless",

he

looked to me as she instructed,

"you and Qorin deal with her, patch her up and take her out into the main grounds, I need to go to the confiscated section, there's something I need",

when letting him go I could tell Qorin was a little curious to what he was collecting, I had the faintest idea that perhaps he

155

wanted to get his gear, no doubt he fights better with it and I need him at his full potential.

The room finally rose, allowing Qorin to grasp Karmin out of the isolation room; he moved her to me as I vaulted over the desk, seeing she was holding on to her left wrist as she grunted,

"you left me down there for however long only to dig me up? The hell is wrong with you",

I cut in,

"you deserved to die don't get me wrong Karmin, but this isn't just us that need to see your end, it's the people you imprisoned here, they deserved to see the very person that tortured them for all these years be put down",

Qorin looked to me as he insisted,

"I'll patch her up, it won't take too long for her to be killed", he took off his jumper, tearing it apart as he forcefully took Karmin's bloodied stump, wrapping the jumper firmly around it as he stated,

"once you die this is over, you won't be able to do anything to anyone again, and I'm glad a scum like you is being put to the dirt",

he firmly knotted it before letting her go, she faced me seeing she never ran out of words to say to me, she was filled with the rage of defeat and anger that things didn't go her way.

Nothing gets past us, and no matter what, no matter how long or short it takes we sure as hell get the job done, as a team we work independently and work together, that's why we work so well.

She glared at me as she questioned,

"so are you happy now? Took my city, took my slaves and prisoners? You think all of that was worth it? just so you can kill me",

I stated, "you caused this, if you were civilised, not brutal and frankly weren't hostile it would be a different story",

she wondered,

"well what if I said I could change?",

Qorin snuffed remarking,

"don't be fooled by her lies she wouldn't change, she never changes, people like her don't change at all",

he was right and yet she looked desperate to be spared, it was convincing me to keep her alive but if she can kill many people in this way, cook them, destroy their family's then it's not a hard choice, it's mandatory that she is to be executed.

As she could see my choice was solid she begged,

"please, Merider, I can change, just give me a second chance alright? I never hurt you, I don't see how I hurt you in this at all",

with a sigh I though momentarily, I stated,

"you never hurt me, but you hurt my friends and people who I don't know, all those people you hurt and you don't feel a thing",

with shortness I firmly persisted,

"Karmin you're paying the debt to death, and you can't run from it anymore, it's too late for you to change",

I looked to Qorin, motioning him to put her hands behind her back, he guided her behind me as I ordered,

"we're ending this battle right now, before your people fall too",

publicly exposing Karmin would not only show her defeat, but it can tell the guards fighting for her to put their weapons down, end this madness before they all turn out to be like her, they are on the brink, but it can be absolved.

When walking out of the prison the fight ended abruptly, it was as though everyone in the whole place was alerted by the sight of Karmin.

The people stood watching us, both ours and the guard's side, they were virtually drawn to us as we guided Karmin to the centre of the pathway, seeing the four routes and the field full of ours and her people.

When stopping walking I faced her, making her kneel on both knees as I announced,

"Karmin of Free Liberty has been captured, we won't kill

157

each other anymore",
the people walked towards me, crowding around us in a large circle as I spoke further,
"we are people of The Revla Lands, whether we're born from another area, from over the sea we are homed here, we are the people of the lands and it's not said otherwise.",
I looked ahead to the dome's pathway, seeing Abby in our uniform, she was accompanied by Marcella, Xharlot, Rhax, Kamic and Alis, they were changed into their clean gear as when they were confiscated the guards most likely were going to use them, so they cleaned my teams gear to be reused.
Shortly after Sevis joined me, he was wearing his clean gear too, it looked very intricate. His golden shoulder pads were pointed from near his neck to over his shoulder, marked with blue, and golden vertical lines within a golden trim, the pattern resembled much like the ancient Egyptian marking on a gods mask.
His upper arm was exposed as his forearm was shielded by a long golden gauntlet, the bottom had the same trimmings as the top, below his elbow, was edged with a horizontal blue line, giving it an edge to it as it pointed just slightly in the centre.
Within the centre of each metal golden painted gauntlet, it had the face of Anubis upon it, painted with such care as it showed his long snout facing directly ahead as a silver line pronounced the nose, making the shape stand out from the dark black face behind the snout, the white eyes sharply pointed along with the ears curving upwards like a split spear, leaving a gap in the centre showing the squared head of Anubis, whoever made this had ritually designed it to give each lieutenant a purpose, or perhaps they all had the same design, to show they were the judges for the Pharo's foes.
His metal chest plate was golden painted with the details of the abs and chest of a man, but filling around the golden details was a black painted chest, resembling once more like

Anubis, with the dark black colours, I could even see deep cuts across the chest and six pact abs, Sevis must have been in that for a while, even during wars no doubt.

It fit his body snugly within the full chest plate as it curved around his waist, making it look as though it was a part of him, as the leather strapped belts kept it firmly in place.

The back of his arm was just golden from all I could see from this view, however I could see the detail of his lower armour perfectly clearly, his thighs were armoured with golden painted edges as the inside of the trim was painted black, it looked as though the maker kept with them when making it, however, with the feet of the armour it was just golden as the trims dragged down to the legs and finally down to the feet, leaving the back to be shielded with gold as the hard leather belts firmly held the gear in place.

The two very last details of his incredible armour were that he had black under armour for the legs and shirt under the chest plate, to prevent chafing and other things no doubt. Then finally he had his spear, it looked just as beautiful as he described it to be, he held it firmly within his right hand, letting the Anubis bust, on the hilt of the spear, touch the floor.

The bottom of the hilts where Anubis neck was had a golden ring around it, allowing it to connect to the bottom of the pole, black stained leather was wrapped around firmly on the spear's body, twisting clockwise like to show that time will always go on after the death, well I see it like that anyway.

The leather-wrapped around to the top of the spear reaching just above his neck height, the finish was ringed with a centimetre thick ringed of gold and blue rings twining around one another, letting the spear point at the top stand firmly upon it.

The spear top was shaped like two flat black hearts, the top heart was upside down as the point of the one below it joined with the spears pole, another two hearts in the very same manner, crossed in the centre, it looked much like an inverted sand timer, the roundness in the centre and the points at the bottom and top.

Sevis stood behind me to my right when I faced Karmin, I announced,

"this bloodshed ends here, death and the inhumanity of this place will end now; we need a leader that will show their people remorse, show their people sanity, and hope of the new world, we can't fight those we don't know anymore, It's not right and if you people want to do something about it, we need to burn the jumpers",

I took my jumper off, revealing my bra and upper body as I didn't care, I wasn't ashamed and for this reason, and only reason, these shirts were meant to be taken off, no one needs these and this is the key that will free us from these shackles.

I raised my jumper in the air, making sure I looked to everyone in the circle as I said loudly,

"you people have been here longer than us, and it only takes one action to get out of this, take off the jumpers, find your gear, your clothes, get your life back and change out of these, this will set us free officially",

I put the jumper on the floor, letting it land on the dusty concrete as I continued,

"the Free Liberty who are left on the field, the ones who want to hear what I have to say, you know that all this violence, rape and torture was because of Karmin, she told you what you had to do, not what you want to do, and it's something I can redeem in only one condition, you take your helmets off, destroy the logo of your old Free Liberty. We will create something better, not everyone here were killers and its time to show that, its time to show that you know between right or wrong",

the prisoners were taking off their jumpers, exposing their upper bodies as women either had vests or bra's on as the men wore either nothing underneath or a vest.

One person at a time put their jumpers in the piles to Karmin's left, far from

160

her as I was watching them, but far enough for everyone to see the hundreds of jumpers being thrown onto a mound. Shortly after, the guards were adding their helmets on the pile, and wrapped them around the jumpers, as some would tumble off. Soon it was a pile of white helmets and jumpers, as each person went back into the crowd as they were starting to accept change, accept what path to go down, it's never too late to change, I learned that from Kaylo, Qorin, Sihlar, Azella, Mersa, everyone from raiders, to bad guys I know what they once were, but they never dared to go as far as Karmin did, perhaps they did the worst of it, but they saw what they did was wrong, they left and risked everything on the line, they did that for them, not for anyone else, they wanted to better themselves and that's what I want with these guys, Free Liberty will have a new logo, the white circle in a ring of red, blue and black, shrouded with the colour of a golden background as it shows they have changed, are purifying their hearts to something, being someone.

The white circle within the centre resembled the jumpers, the prison, the enslavement, they will remember it but know that it can never come back, it shows that they came from all these dark places but raised from it.

As for the red, blue and black rings around the white circle, they represent foreign lands from here, everyone was different, and we came together to make something better, turn this land into unity again, it's all we need to survive, not who's the most powerful, who is the better leader, it's simply we unite and survive as one.

Karmin looked at me as she wondered,

"so what now big shot? You may kill me, but you have to get through the fifth leader",

understanding her mind games I know that she already killed the fifth leader, hence why she's calling every single shot in this 'so-called' joined city, she already defeated the fifth leader, and just tries to get her way out of things, believing I don't keep my words.

I looked to my right, seeing Sevis stand by my side as he stated,

"you killed the Commander of city five, you lie, and she may not have been here longer than any of us, but she and we knew the same since the start, we could have killed you then, but we waited, left you to grow lazy until someone with the power of Ra showed us the light, and we found them",

his Anubis bust was faced at her, letting her see the detailed metal made head, the eyes were made of gold as the neck was ringed with a necklace of red, blue and golden vertical striped trimmings on top and bottom of the arched design, meeting with the bottom of the slightly domed shape of the spear.

He aimed it at her firmly as he persisted,

"you killed my wife when I got here, my men also. You ambushed in our soil, and took us in your ark. Taking us across the sea, marking us traitors of our lands we can no longer return to without a fight, and now you just receive the judgement of Anubis",

I stepped back seeing as this was his judgement to make, how he killed her was his choice, he was kept here longer than me, and lost more than me, he had every right to give her judgement for smuggling his men and family over abroad, for what reason I don't know, but from the looks of it they needed more people and her leader knew exactly where to send her to get some.

She remarked,

"oh please, if the ancient gods were true I would be with Medusa by now, I can't believe you fools believe in that stuff",

he pressed the ears of the bust to her upper forehead, causing two perfect streams of blood to run down it, meeting her eyebrows as he released pressure as he stated,

"the beliefs I have are much different to yours, perhaps someday in the afterlife, you will change, you will see that",

#he moved the spear's hilt backwards as he pointed the

spear's tip to her head as he said ritually,

"with the power of Anubis and the funeral to be set ahead, may you have his judgement and be set to rest",

he jabbed the spear through her skull when he moved back slightly, causing a short burst to move to her, extending his back leg behind him as the spear perfectly entered the centre of her forehead. Her body went limp as he ripped the spear out seeing as the shape of the tip allowed it to leave as cleanly as it entered. He held the bloodied spear, letting the blood stain his hands as he held it upright, allowing his body form to be strong as Karmin fell to the floor, lying on her front as the blood-soaked upon the ground.

Her body was growing cold as stone as the people looked at her, seeing that it wasn't a fantasy, it was REAL, she was finally gone, and this enslavement and torture was over. Sevis looked to Qorin as he stated,

"we usually wrap those in fabric, but we're not in my lands anymore, presuming Merider wishes to burn the jumpers?", he looked to me, as did Qorin, letting me decide how this goes.

With a nodded I ordered,

"she can go on the pile, and the new beginning of this place can start; the guards can first get the prisoners their stuff back, after that, we will no longer be prisoners, just survivors.", Qorin smiled agreeing,

"couldn't have said it better myself",

he picked up Karmin's blood dripping corpse, letting the patters of blood trail behind him as he held her in her arms, only to throw her upon the centre of the pile, lying on the jumpers that stained with her blood.

When facing the pile as the guards and people were going to Karmin's tower, or once was Karmin's tower, Sevis stood with me on my right as the team rounded to my left, we stood at a safe distance from the soon to be bonfire as a few guards returned with oil, drenching the pile as we spoke to one another as we watched.

Abby was to my left as Xharlot was to hers.

Then Alis, Rhax, Kamic, Marcella along with Qorin shortly after, we were finally back as one but it was starting to feel a little chilly. I looked left as Abby had something in her hands, she handed it to me as she stated,

"we thought to get your things when in the confiscated zone. I'm glad you're okay, sorry for what happened...I shouldn't have followed you",

I took the bloodied shirt, putting it on before taking the pile from her hands, seeing my holster intact with my dagger firmly in it, the pistols were lost but I have another one so that's fine, but my katana, however, I will prefer that by my side than a rifle for certain, it doesn't feel natural without it.

My gear was stained from the blue blood of the dead and the red blood of the foes, but it was dry at least, it still made me feel murky but I can change later, I just need a moment to take in what happened, a liar and a brute finally got caught in her game, and it wasn't like the prisoners or once were prisoners didn't know what to do, they did, but they were letting her gloat and have this glory because they knew that someone would come along, and take it from her very hands.

Sevis looked back as Horneck approached to his right, he had my jumper as he joked,

"you missed one, rather not go through this effort for one jumper to be left unburned",

he approached the pile, only to throw it on, covering Karmin's face by accident, but it was fine, she was dead either way, and it was like she was given a little remorse to what happens next to her body.

He stepped back by Sevis's side as he questioned,

"so it's really over then? No more listening to that bitch",

Sevis cut in,

"she may have been our enemy, but we respect the dead, once they are gone, they are never to be mocked when they are in the afterlife, you know that too",

Horneck nodded briefly, he apologised,

164

"sorry Sevis, it's just that it's been a long three years of imprisonment, it's nice to not be bound by chains anymore", he took off his jumper, seeing as his jumper was the last to go on the pile, but he decided to use it as the igniting start to the bonfire, he took an oil can from the guard, pouring it on the jumper as he stated,

"we'll use this as the rope, the chain that will burn this mound",

he put the jumpers left arm against the pile as the right arm was pointed at me.

Horneck used the last of the oil near to the arm touching the pile, ensure it ignited properly before throwing it on the pile also. He moved back to Sevis as he pointed,

"do you want to do the honour of banishment?",

the guards stepped back, watching Sevis approached the end of the jumper, dragging the Anubis bust across the floor, letting sparks fly off it before sweeping it forward to the pile. The sparks bunched to the sleeve of the jumper as he stepped back.

He moved to my side as the jumper went alight, trailing to the pile, soon igniting the front half of the bonfire.

The fire waved its way to the back of the bonfire slowly, allowing us to see each jumper burn to grey and black as the helmets were crumbling into the concrete, marking its existence on the ground, ensuring it won't be forgotten.

The smoke was puffing into the air, it looked entrancing as the golden orange flames rose high, stretching tall enough to blend in with the smoke above it.

I hope the leader can see this, I hope he knows that he was messing with the wrong people and that we aren't their property, we are survivors.

Nothing can change that, death will wait, and when it's time to go I know I did all I can, and I'm not going to stop fighting for what's right until that day, until I see the sunrise and my friends around me

Chapter Fourteen
Fire of Survivors

The fire burned brightly, leaving us to gaze upon it as Abby questioned,

"is that over with then? no other people to come after us?",

I glanced to her as I stated,

"she wasn't even the person we needed dead, she was the obstacle. The real person behind this chaos is her leader, the same with the man before in the crater. You wouldn't know about it, but he fell the same fate, leaving us with his wife",

I looked to her as she wondered,

"did she die too?",

with a slight smile I ensured,

"she was willing to change, and speaking of which where is Azella?",

I looked to Qorin as he explained,

"well, from what we all know is that Azella left us, she parted as she said she was looking for Neon and Narla, other than that, we let her go",

with an unimpressed look to my face, I knew I couldn't be mad at him, it's something he would do, but I guess Azella is more than capable of looking after herself.

Marcella and the team rounded to me as Sevis and Horneck were to my left, far from the warm bonfire, as we were making our next plan of action.

I know there are things to do but the leader, Karmin's Commander needs to be killed also, he can warp their minds like that and using them to do his dirty little deeds, none that will help with the survival of humanity, he doesn't even sound like a sane human either.

I looked to Rhax and Kamic as I persisted,

"I need to sort not just the city out but the armoury for the guards, without their helmets it's obviously a disadvantage, can you two get a blueprint to the blacksmiths, I know Kamic is very talented in the building department",

he smiled as he remarked,

"I didn't say for you to stop giving me glory",

he laughed slightly as he reassured,

"don't worry Commander I'll get something of your style in the city. Well, something to protect the guards and people with, it will take some time for the production, but I can make something to speed that up",

he got lost in thought as he explained,

"you see, I got this machine blueprint that I always remember, it creates at least ten helmets per day, folds the melt, welds it, it's very fascinating",

Rhax cut in,

"we'll get that done for you, Commander, good to be back in charge again",

they walked around the left side of the bonfire only to head to the dome, were most likely the workshops are placed upon.

Marcella looked around as she wondered,

"not only are Azella, Neon and Narla missing, but where's Gina?",

Xharlot looked to me as she pointed,

"Merider might know",

I expanded,

"she might be in the prison ward still, I saw which room

she's in, but I thought she would have joined the siege",
Sevis insisted,

"I shall search for her Commander. Horneck will stay guard of you",

he went past us, cutting through the team as he proceeded to the prison grounds. He was protective, but I guess it's a default thing, after all, him and Horneck were protectors of the Pharo, or known as Pharaoh by the common history. I felt protected though, even though my team was protecting me it felt like I could have my back turned in any situation on the field or anywhere and they would have it watched, it sort of made me feel a little relaxed.

Qorin pointed to Horneck as he wondered,

"so are you going to introduce us to your friends, Merider?",

I smiled slightly as I reassured,

"they are fine. This is Horneck and the one that walked to the prison is Sevis, they came from Egyptverus, most of the people were from there, they are our new additions, we could use some more arms in the upcoming battle",

Xharlot wondered,

"you don't think the Commander of Free Liberty will put up a fight to us? He seems like he was only bluffing and wanting to play mind games",

she then expanded,

"besides, we go there now in our state, we have nothing to fall back on, no offence, but two towers were rocket launched to dust",

she isn't wrong, without the proximity of the radius around the city, we haven't got a chance to know of any upcoming attacks, and not even a secured shield to take cover behind, perhaps we can be stationary for a while, just a few weeks tops, I can't let the commander have a chance to build up his defences.

Seeing as Xharlot was enthusiastic, and wanting input, I questioned,

"did you have an idea on how we can build the towers in a

week? Or make a temporary defence whilst its being built",
she took a moment to think only to look at Horneck as she
wondered,
"your people, what were they?",
he smirked as he joked,
"we're not slavers and labourers if that's what you're hitting",
she rolled her eyes only to change her words as she explained,
"no, that's obviously not what I'm going for. Look, I need to
know if they are soldiers, or they were civilians, because I
can get them in their right groups, have a group of workers
paid in rations and weapons and coin when we get to that
stage in here",
I could see where she was going with this, and it made a lot
of sense, organise people into their skills, and that means not
only will the others be built but currency can be made here
and most of all the civilisation can be restored to this place, it
was virtually a death factory in here, but with our brains put
together into our interests we can get this place standing up.
Horneck thought a moment only to inform,
"Sevis, a group of ten men and women were guarding a
migration, the people are doctors, labourers, witchdoctors,
priests' and priestesses, we may not have enough people to
build the towers on our own, but we have enough to share the
knowledge and contribute to it",
that was two years ago, would they really kill the whole
migration if they wanted to? I certainly hope they were
spared for the sake of their gifts and traits.
I looked to Horneck as I interrogated,
"how many of your migration have survived?",
he thought only to accurately say, "around a
hundred people were in the migration. Ten doctors, ten
witchdoctors, forty labourers, ten civilians, ten farmers and
ten experienced builders",
Qorin looked impressed as he wondered,
"how do you remember all of that? I wouldn't have even
remembered half of that",

he was trying to give it a go, be nice to the new members, as he knew I would pick on him for not putting effort in it like last time.

I smiled to him slightly as Horneck joked,

"well I would be the worst protector if I didn't remember who I was protecting",

seeing them both talk spawned an idea, they both are strong, good in shape, and most of all, know their way around weapons, perhaps I can get them to do a training club of a sort, the guards can know how to fight our way, and most importantly get used to us. If they see we are helping them, they will want to cooperate more, become survivors and not slaughterers.

I got their attention as I interfered,

"guys I think I have a task for you both",

they looked to me as I continued,

"the guards here, the people here need to know how to use a weapon, whether it's a sword, gun or any other thing, they need to know how to defend themselves, and I know how much Qorin likes to spar, so there can be a club held every afternoon, people who are interested can show up and you both can instruct them in a sparring circle or firing range",

Horneck looked enthusiastic for it as Qorin had some questions, he wondered,

"if we do this where would we hold it? There's a lot of spaces",

I looked around behind me, to ahead of the dome, I soon drew my attention to the left side of the prison, seeing the standing tower that didn't explode into pieces, just below it was a football pitch size of concrete grounds, the six Chinooks were near the wall by the gate to my left.

But in-between the prison, and the Chinooks, there was a large bit of concrete ground, easily able to put the sparring ring in place and firing range by the wall ahead of us.

I pointed to the blank field as I stated,

"you can put the sparring ring near the Chinooks, and the

firing range can be facing the wall, so no one gets shot accidentally, simple, clear, and most of all the tower isn't broken into bits, so no repairs are needed in that sector", Qorin looked to Horneck as he said firmly,

"alright then, lets get going. Horneck, you got some things to learn from me",

as they left I glanced to Qorin, seeing his smile made me know that he was finally at ease for the moment, I've never seen him so unhappy when he couldn't do anything, but I'm glad that situation ended like it did, quick and easy, no need to stress about calling Karmin her bitch, that was going to get annoying very quickly.

I huffed slightly, seeing as there was going to be a lot of planning, but I at least have a distraction for people, and most importantly I know that the Egyptverus people can help me with building the towers back to their original state along with the medical side of things too.

Marcella looked to me as she remarked,

"yeah, there's still more to do",

she smiled briefly, she then questioned,

"was there anything you need us to do?",

seeing as she always asked me if things need doing, and she does them, I think she needs to take it easy, she's like me, always needs something to run upon before tiring herself out at the end of the day.

With a slight thought, I instructed,

"you can go with Abby and gather the Egyptverus people, they are most likely collecting their things from the lower floor of the HQ behind me",

Marcella motioned Abby to follow her as she encouraged,

"come on then trooper, I need to show you the ropes of being one of us",

Abby kept with her to her left as they walked past me, Abby looked more than fine to go with Marcella, it was forgetful of me that she also has a kid of her own, no wonder she was able to convince Abby to go with her so easily.

As they left, it was me and Xharlot left to deal with the last things.

I approached her as she questioned,

"so what now? It looks like everything is virtually covered", with a firmness I informed,

"almost everything is covered, we have the missing three to find, and sorting out the people in their desired jobs",

Xharlot wondered,

"why not team them with their skill. So, for example, a labourer in the works?",

seeing her confusion and question, I explained,

"that one labourer could also be skilled in music, performance art, this place needs the entertainment to perk them up. So if we get to know the hundred by making them stand in groups of ten, that way we can easily see how many have attended, then from there, I can sort them into groups",

Xharlot saw my point as she wondered further,

"so how will you do this? Call them one by one and group them behind you",

that will take far too long, it must be a simple thing, swift. With thought I stated,

"we will have five markers behind us. First one will be labourers, second marker will be entertainment in all different areas from music to other things, the third marker will be arms and guarding duties, the forth shall be the building designers, along with weaponry and armour then lastly the fifth marker will be the doctors and other medical professions",

Xharlot agreed as she said impressed,

"so you do have this all planned out then, so the markers, what will they be?",

with not knowing I wondered,

"perhaps the soldiers of Free Liberty can represent each line, I need five people in that profession, that way they can get the people right at home",

she looked around, seeing the guards splitting ways, helping with the patrols, and moving rubble form the large pathways, she remarked,

"well, it might take me a while since I haven't got a clue who does what, but I'll ask around",

she went past the bonfire, joining with a patrol of four people as she asked around for specific people of theirs, she won't have any issues with it, besides if we're one person short I know enough to get people in place, it will just mean getting recommendations to put their work station in.

The team was all occupied and busy with their given tasks. Now all that's left was for me to check on Sevis, I hoped he might have found something.

When proceeding to the prison ward road I took a glanced to my left, seeing Qorin and Horneck plant large bits of concrete in a neat circle, it looked as though Qorin was bossing Horneck around, but he looked as though he didn't mind, they were even joking around.

It brought a smile to my face to see Qorin was finally taking my words seriously, or listening to me at least.

When looking ahead I saw Sevis leave the prison ward, he approached me as he informed,

"Merider, your friend is not right, skin is pale blue, eyes clouded like the blind, I think you need to check it out",

with a frown, and not wanting to alert Qorin or anyone else in the camp, I turned him around, making him follow me to my left as I persisted quietly,

"where did you find her? What happened?",

he explained,

"the lights were dark. but the power turned to brightest it could go, and she was visible in the cafeteria, she must have left her prison cell and got trampled, for the worst-case scenario",

not wanting to believe it I only knew what my eyes would see when we get there, I hope she didn't die that way, it would not only be unfortunate, but an undeserved death.

We approached the door, seeing the beds were piled to the

left far out the way of the doors nearing the prison ward walls. Sevis moved closely behind me with his spear drawn firmly as we entered the cluttered cafeteria, the tabletops faced us as we tipped them to make our cover previously, but soon I saw what Sevis had explained to me.

Gina was walking with a limp on her left leg as she must have been trampled on during the siege, not only if she must have been turned, others might have too, we will need to clear this place to be safe.

I motioned him to put his spear down, letting him take my gear as I unsheathed my dagger as I stated,

"Gina is my kill, I promised to keep her safe, and I will do that",

he nodded respectfully, allowing me to approach Gina's walking corpse as she faced me. Her clouded eyes were glaring at me, as her virtually broken right leg caused her to have an extreme limp, not only that but pain, if she could feel it, I wouldn't know if she did feel it, or if it even bothers her at all, yet I knew she wouldn't want to be this creature.

With swiftness I flipped the dagger to face the floor, allowing me to raise it across my left shoulder before embedding it into the side of her head, making her heavy grunts stop suddenly.

Her body fell limp as I yanked the dagger from her head, making her crash to the floor, lifeless, motionless, not even a single breath to be exhaled as the parasite no longer had use of her body.

I looked to her dark blue bleeding wound ooze the blood upon the floor, forming a puddle under her head.

Sevis stood to my left as he stated,

"if she turned from the stampede, we should be safe and look in the prison ward for any more people in her state",

I nodded to his words, which I then agreed,

"we better get going",

I moved past him, allowing him to scout the cafeteria, as I went ahead to the prison ward.

When looking in each room, and taking care of my steps, I could see a few people who were killed in their cells, some were head-shots, but the ones who weren't executed, I ensured that they didn't return from the dead, I'd rather them be dead properly, not walking corpses. I would want someone to do the same to me if I died through a bullet in the heart, it's not the brain, it's not the core to where the parasite wants to control.

After one body to another, I dragged them to the reception room wrapped in their bed sheets, even if the blood stained through, I didn't want to stack them up as they were, it felt wrong to do it either way.

Sevis joined me shortly, he took a few bed sheets and mattress covers as he ensured,

"I will bring the ones in the cafeteria here, you can leave after you're done",

when putting the tenth body on the line, I stopped him from entering the cafeteria as I questioned,

"What do you mean I'm done after this? We have five floors of prison cells to do",

he had the five mattress and quilt covers folded under his right arm as he firmly had his spear within his left hand, he firmly stated,

"you've done enough. Besides, once I'm done I'll let you know about it",

he shortly added,

"and you need to slow down, you already cleared the first floor, as I just finished the cafeteria with four undead within it",

he was looking out for me, but I was perfectly fine, I was upset about Gina's way of death, but I couldn't do anything about it, what's done is done and we move on, it's always been that way, and its staying that way, I can't let every death affect me it will slow things down.

I firmly reassured,

"I'm fine with carrying on, I can wait for you to catch up if that's what you want, we can do it together then, do one floor at a time",

he nudged his head to the table as he pointed,

"that sounds perfect, your clothes are on the reception desk, just so you know",

he walked into the cafeteria, putting his spear on the floor as he wrapped Gina first, he took such care with her, it was strange to see someone so gentle. He wrapped her up tightly enough for her body to stiffen in place, allowing him to pick her up firmly. As he approached me, I walked into the cafeteria as I insisted,

"I'll help out with the covering of the dead, can't let you do it on your own",

he smiled slightly as he walked past, placing Gina's body on the floor as I went inside the cafeteria, seeing the four bodies laid on the floor to where Gina was, they were placed to the left of where Gina's blood puddle was.

When taking a cover I placed it above the dead's head, allowing me to pull them onto the clean sheet where I avoided the blood puddle, I didn't want it to be too bloody even if the dead was bleeding blue blood, I didn't want the cover to be soaking in it.

When wrapping the Undead guard, Sevis joined me to my right as he did the same with the next Undying. He glanced at me as he recalled,

"you have the same traits as my wife, well in the terms of being stubborn and persistent",

we both smiled to each other, seeing his point as I remarked,

"well it doesn't harm to be on guard every so often, so many times people tried to kill me, and so many times I nearly let them, it's not fun being a human target",

Sevis agreed,

"I felt the same in Egyptverus. I would be the main target for being the Pharo's guardian, the people and us would call him a Pharaoh like you should do, but he didn't deserve all the letters, he tainted the name so we gave him a different one, to ensure the bloodline stayed clean, as his would always be tainted",

with the wonder of his past, I questioned,

"what was he like? You speak of him like he is the nightmare on Earth",

he finished wrapping the body, giving me his full attention as he explained,

"his name was Tukan Ohra, he enjoyed the power of being a god of Egypt, he was related to Osiris his older brother who was named after the god, they used that as there way of getting the place of power when the storm hit, and now they brought back their history and their corruption, they wanted everyone to obey them",

he and I stood up as he picked up the wrapped body.

He persisted,

"you wrap the bodies up, I will carry them",

when going to the next body, I questioned,

"so the leader was corrupted, he sounds like I need to deal with him",

I smiled at him, making him perk up as he stated,

"he would not stand a chance with you, but if I'm by your side, and the team rise with you, then he will surely be defeated overnight",

he put the body on the pile not placing it on the singled out body, presumably it was Gina's.

He approached me as he stated,

"Tukan was much like the walking storm that passed us over twenty years ago, he took everything and destroyed everything, I was around nine at that time, they had me trained to be this guardian of the Pharaoh when learning my ancestors were a part of the protection of the very first leader, they found out as I kept documents of my great grandmother, she handed me all the relics of our bloodline, she passed it on to me because she knew one day I would have a wife, and it was true",

when finishing wrapping the third corpse, I moved to the

177

fourth one as I wondered,

"so you have a blood of a guardian? That's pretty cool when you think about it",

he smiled as he agreed,

"yes, I too think It gave me purpose",

he crouched to my left as he showed me this necklace he wore.

It was dark black and made from obsidian, eyes were curved at the ends as it had a golden painted Egyptian point to the end of it, the ears were squared at the tips as the face was too a little broad.

I moved from the body as I held the necklace in my view as he stated,

"you see, this was passed down from every guardian, every husband, father, and son, to me. It's the only thing I have left to my name, as my relics are most likely destroyed, I have hidden them, but they no longer matter to me, I can no longer return to my lands. But with this necklace, I have the protection of Bast",

I gently let go of it, letting him hold it as I wondered,

"the protection of Bast? I know my gods well, but I didn't learn that one in specific",

he smiled, seeing I was interested as he explained,

"this one was made for cats of Ancient Egypt, they cared of the people by taking down beast and creatures of the farms and homes, so insects for short",

I smiled to him as he finished,

"they are sacred animals to Egypt, killing one would be a crime, wouldn't know why you would kill a cat anyways. But my great-grandmother told me of a story that each guardian died of old age, all because of this necklace, and so far believe it",

he

returned the smile to me, only to cause me to avert my attention from him as I stated,

"We better get finishing with these bodies, I'll wrap the last

179

one",
he took the wrapped body to the reception room pile.
As he walked away, I watched him, I was inspired by him, he had such hope that I wished I could have.
He's a good man.

Chapter Fifteen
Building Hope

After one corpse to the next we piled them in the reception room, soon moving them on the pathway one by one, ensuring that they could be identified before the burial, they may have not been my people, but they belong to the Free Liberty people, they may have fought against us, but they were told to until Karmin was put down into the ground. After the three dozen bodies from the prison were laid out, Sevis took Gina's body to add to the line of burial. Fifteen bodies were lined to the left and right side of the prison ward road leading to the bonfire within the centre of the camp, their feet faced the pathway, just a few feet away from it so people didn't get put off by it, but close enough so people can approach the bodies to identify it.

Gina's body was on the row to my left as Sevis was trailing down the pathway with me with her body in his arms.

He gave me his Anubis spear to hold whilst he handled Gina with the utmost care, he put her down gently upon the left row, at the far end nearing the bonfire that was still burning proudly.

As he placed her down, Marcella approached me, only to look at the body as she questioned,

"is that, Gina?",

I nodded before I informed,

"she was trampled on by the siege, most of these people were.

Some, however, were shot or stabbed in the heart and not the brain, we had to finish them off",

Sevis approached me as he reassured,

"the body of the dead will rest during burial, no matter if it's the Egyptverus way, or not, these people will be at rest when the burial is over",

upon giving Sevis his Spear back, I looked away from Gina's wrapped body as I turned my attention to Marcella, she had a form of an envelope in her hand, something that looked too familiar.

She handed me the envelope as she informed me,

"well on the bright side of things the guards didn't burn this in the end, they said they kept it under the Commanders orders, not Karmin's orders, but the big boss that we need to deal with next",

I moved past her as I stated,

"I don't want to know who my family is anymore, seems like they are just secretive, don't tell me the truth and just want me dead half the time, Nahtler I will remember, and so will my mother, but even so, I just wished it wasn't this complicated",

she could sense my frustration as I threw the envelope in the bonfire, letting the weight of the stacks of paper inside anchor it to the centre of the bonfire, burning it from piece to piece, seeing my name melt and disintegrate to the ashy pile of flames. The jumpers were burning slowly but the paper was engulfed within the flames.

I looked to Marcella as I expanded,

"look, I know they were doing me a nice gesture but I can't know who my father is, if I know then I don't think I will ever let go of this, it's been with me all this time and now that I know I have one person to find, I'd rather not go looking",

she smiled slightly as she understood,

"if that's how you feel then we're all behind you on the choice", she soon said warmly,

"besides who needs a family when you got us, bickering half the time, fighting together as a team, couldn't ask for anything better",

I smiled slightly, feeling her warm words as she was right about us, we may have had our lows and downs, but no matter what we always work together, have each other's backs, and I feel like finally it's going to stay that way.

With thought I wondered,

"I haven't asked you about Erilk yet, they said you both were here",

she bit her lip as she explained,

"we landed, but they didn't know Saturn was on board, I asked her to return to Londelis with Erilk, I told the pilot was sending us over, made a few white lies to cover his and my back",

I couldn't imagine what it was like to let your kid go like that, but I know Sevis knew the feeling too well as he reassured,

"you made the right choice. My son too is left in my home city, perhaps not willingly, but I would rather him be in there than here. Perhaps when coming home some day he will be a warrior, labourer, I won't know, but I do know is that it's the right place for him, he wouldn't have liked it here",

Marcella smiled to him, taking in his words before changing topic as she stated,

"well, besides that, we have something for you to look at. Xharlot, Rhax and Abby are looking at the south east tower over there",

she pointed past the bonfire, allowing us to see the builders moving the rubble.

I looked to Sevis as he persisted,

"you will be safe over there, I will tend to the dead, mark their names before creating the burial site",

I nodded to him, seeing him walk away before moving with Marcella, curving left of the bonfire as we walked over the east pathway to the dome, cutting through it to the large rectangular field of concrete.

She glanced behind her only to look to me as she questioned, "Is Sevis okay? I think he might be missing his home", with agreement I explained,

"he's been here for a few years, and from what he described to me of his city, it's a lot more appealing than this place", she wondered,

"perhaps we could go there some day, bring him home, even if he says he couldn't, we can try",

seeing her persistence I ensured,

"someday he can return, but for now we all have a job to do, sometimes I wished I could go home but there's nothing up there anymore for me, the same goes for Sevis in the terms of when he returns he won't return as a hero or survivor of a slave camp, just a traitor",

she could see my point, and could also see I was passionate about the subject as she questioned,

"I think it should be me asking if you're okay?",

she laughed slightly as I smiled to her words, I reassured, "I'm fine, just been a long day of torment and it only took a simple trap and the city is ours, it felt too easy and when that feeling happens I know it was planned, I know that the Commander wanted us to take this place",

she thought on that too, and I think it was making sense for both of us that this was happening for a reason, perhaps so the Commander could take it back, he would do that because nothing is happening over here, just the dead walking.

We strolled to the grounds surrounding the tower, Rhax and Xharlot were talking to some builders as they wore their rugged leather armour, their shoulder pads were spiked on the edges, their chest plates were ruffed and fit rightly around their torso.

The under armour was nothing but a rugged white shirt, along with a deep brown pair of trousers and black boots.

Most people were wearing that gear over here, presumably the builders from the Egyptverus migration, they got ahead of me and rounded them up along with a few guards in the same skill, they had their white armour but no helmet until Kamic made some which I'm assuming that's going just as good if Rhax isn't with him.

Marcella and I approached Rhax and Xharlot as the two builders left to do their jobs, they both turned around as I questioned,

"see that things are progressing, where's Kamic? I thought you were meant to be with him?",

Rhax reassured,

"he's with a guard, the man is an inventor, mind you, I felt uncomfortable around that guard",

Xharlot joked,

"Rhax said that the guard was crazier than Plasma",

she looked amused as he explained,

"well he's very eccentric then, I don't mind Plasma but you know how she can be",

seeing as he was trying to make his words less insulting to the guard I reassured,

"I'm not going to be mad at you, if you think I'll be mad at what you think about him. As long as you don't say it to him, it's fine",

he smiled slightly as he wondered,

"so, not like I don't mind you being here, but",

he wasn't trying to be rude and I understood that it was a little out of the blue for me to go over there, but I needed to see the progress, how things will be going through out the weeks to come.

With understanding, I informed,

"I was taking a closer look at the progress of the tower, Marcella told me about it, and I thought to get a better look at the plan of action",

upon recalling what she said earlier, I wondered,

"speaking of that, where's Abby?",

Rhax looked to Xharlot as he wondered,

"I thought she was with you?",

she looked behind her as she soon faced me as she reassured, "I'm sure she just wondered around, she couldn't have gone far",

trying not to flip out at them I said calmly,

"can you just look for her? please, she doesn't know about her father yet, and I don't want her to explore the wrong places of this camp, we still need to find out where the bodies of the execution of a hundred and forty people are",

Rhax said firmly,

"I'll look for the bodies, and check to see if she isn't there, what did you want us to do with the bodies?",

burying them would be impractical but what other choices do we have?

We can't burn them it would only attract the dead and if we do burn them then it's not respecting the innocent that died.

I approached them closer so people around us couldn't hear the conversation as I stated,

"we are going to have to dispose of them, to bury them will take a while, and to burn them will attract the dead, we haven't got a big enough land for a hundred and forty people to be buried singularly in this place, and we can't bury them together, it's not right. Find a furnace or do something to dispose them, if they are underground, perhaps seal the room",

Rhax nodded before he questioned,

"what if we need help with it?",

with his point I expanded,

"then get the guard to help you, they know about the bodies location, but only a hand full of guards no more than that, we can't draw attention and it stays between us three, and the guards you chose, understand?",

he nodded firmly as he left us, strolling to the dome as he talked to a few guards on the way there, as for Xharlot we need her to do something else, find Abby.

I looked around as I questioned,

"where do you think Abby would have gone to, did she say

anything to you at all?",

she thought as she recalled,

"she said she wanted to hang out with this Egyptverus child, but I said we needed to watch her, then she wondered off with him, so perhaps she might be in the",

she paused only to look at the dome as she cursed,

"shit, I think she's in the dome",

I rubbed my forehead only to sigh as I calmed,

"alright no need to panic yet. Look, us three are going to have to search in the dome, if we see Rhax, briefly explain the situation, he might even see her",

we hurried left, curving our way ahead to the dome stood firmly on the edge of the pathway, as the walls covered behind it. The dome was shimmering from the bonfires light, as the white cloudy skies turned yellow and orange.

The dome had many triangular windows and walls that stretched vertically to the top of the building, curving inwards when reaching the circular top of the building; the white walls of the building streaked evenly apart from one another, letting the windows and parts of the triangle pieces of wall filled between each one, revealing to us that we have six floors to explore as the floors could be seen in the windows when closing in on the main doors.

The glass double doors ahead of us revealed the large grounds inside, it looked like a garden in there.

A large tree grew within the centre as a curved line of water fell behind it, a man-made waterfall and most likely the purest water system I've seen, whatever this water is they recycled it no doubt.

The lights inside shone around the tree as the natural light circled on the tree, it was perfection and surprisingly out of character for a once brutal and murderous place.

We finally entered the garden, seeing the clean white floor circle the edges of the room leading to stairs to our left and right, the other side did the same, but with two elevators in circular tubes of glass behind the tree to the centre-left, and right side of the garden, touching the concrete ground as a small pathway led to each one.

A large pathway met the centre where the tree was as it ringed around it too, as a large ring of water was inside of it, touching the trees grassy circled path and flowing under the concrete path touching it, this design was a complicatedly made green garden.

We strayed up the pathway as Xharlot questioned,

"where do we search first? This place is huge",

we stopped in our tracks when I heard rustling in the tree, I frowned, only to focus my attention on the tree as I stated,

"go to the third floor where the tree stops going, use the stairs",

Xharlot sighed as she moved past me, moving to the stairs behind us to our left.

She gradually made her way floor by floor as the stairs crossed one another above the door, going from floor to floor. I approached the pathway touching the tree, seeing marks and scuffs upon the tree where Abby could have climbed up, she could be up there, but I won't know until I go up there myself, I have Xharlot on the side, so she can navigate within the sidelines, as for Marcella as she's going to watch me possibly fail this.

I took off my waist holster, handing it to Marcella as she questioned,

"you can't seriously be considering climbing up there?",

with a firmness I took a few steps back as I stated,

"well, it's either be certain they aren't messing around up there, or we lose them for a day. Besides, its no harm in having a little fun whilst we're searching",

with a quickness I raced to the tree, putting my right foot on the trunk as a leg up before grasping the branch above my head.

With a firm grip upon it, my feet walked on the trunk, allowing me to mount on the branch as Marcella remarked,

"you're going to fall, kids can do this, but you're an adult,

heavier than a fucking child",
when stood on the branch I joked,
"language, Marcella, swearing when kids are around is a no go",
I heard giggling above me, knowing that they would find it funny, they soon stopped laughing as I called,
"I knew you were up here, stay there, I'm coming",
Abby responded,
"you got to catch us first!",
with a smirk I knew this was now a challenge, only this one time accepting I will act like a kid, but that's if nothing else is going to distract me.

With persistence I jumped and leapt from one branch to the next, making my way up as leaves were falling onto Marcella as she watched, who was fearing the worst, but I'm not rusty, perhaps on the rough side, yet if I'm quick and kept my movements light. then there's no need to worry about falling branches, this tree has a lot of thick branches anyway, so it's not likely.

My feet stood upon one large branch that lead to many leaves and branches around me, shrouding me in leaves in all directions as the trunk was behind me, when looking right I could see Xharlot above me, she was leaning over the side of the glass fence, I was nearing the top.

With a frown, I called,
"Abby? Can you give me a hint",
I could hear chuckling from below, only to soon move near the trunk, seeing the gaps leading to the far bottom of the tree trunk.

With an unimpressed look, I stated,
"Abby that's cheating, you can't just go back down the tree!",
She and her friend stood with Marcella, who also had a smirk on her face as she remarked,
"I said to you it wasn't necessary to go up",
with a slight sigh I remarked to myself,
"Abby thinks she's won, but I think there's a more

impressive way down",

I looked to where Xharlot was, the glass fence was close, it had a metal bar above it, I can reach it if I jumped.

I hurried to the branch on my right, making a stretch, only to step upon it, using my balance and raised branches to reach the edge, seeing Xharlot far ahead of me, a long leap away. The leaves were dead on this side where the branch reached out for the third floor, it was a good meter or two away from the fence, but if I run I can make it, I have good balance, so nothing to worry about.

Marcella, Abby, and her friend watched as Marcella called, "Merider, don't be an idiot and show off",

the kids, on the other hand, were cheering as they chanted, "show off, show off!",

over and over, causing me to run on the branch, feeling the branch wiggle under my feet as Xharlot moved out the way, seeing me jump off the tip as I reached for the metal bar.

My hands grasped the bar, allowing me to hang off the edges of the fence, hanging three floors from the garden below.

I pulled myself up, using my arms to hook myself to safety.

My legs walked on the side of the elevated floor, giving me access to climb over the gate as Abby and her friend cheered, Marcella could be heard in the background, she cut their cheers as she snapped,

"alright, enough of that Abby. She showed off for you, you better stay here now she did that",

I stood firmly on the ground, feeling relieved to touch the ground from landing that jump.

My right arm was hurting, perhaps my muscle was strained a little from holding myself up, it's been a very long time since I've done any extreme activities like that, well, reckless activities anyway.

Xharlot approached me as she said impressed,

"that was quite a jump, for a child, that was easy work",

I rolled my eyes when as I joked,

"you think that was easy? Why don't you try it",

189

she laughed as she stated,

"I jumped off a tower and landed on the one below in the dead city before, it was fun, broke a leg from the landing, but it was worth it",

she smirked to me as she walked behind me, going around the large curved open grounds, heading to the steps to the second and first floor.

When walking with her, Xharlot remarked,

"so, oldie, see you hurt your arm",

she laughed as I stated,

"well, I pulled a muscle. I should consider caring for my body a little bit more",

she smiled as she informed,

"you need a personal trainer, or you know just a daily routine of fighting for a few hours, I work with guns. So perhaps not me, neither Marcella, she works with guns",

she thought only to point out,

"well, what about Sevis? He works with a spear and he might even work with a katana",

I never really gave it thought, but perhaps he could train me, besides he seems to know his way around a spear he might know his way around a katana or sword.

It's training in a sort of way, probably will be learning a little bit more but it's mainly to keep myself active, and let my limbs work a little better, I do move rugged when fighting and stopping for a few days, no wonder I feel achy most of the time.

After walking down the flights of steps, we finally met up with Marcella, Abby, and her friend, I could finally get a closer look at him. He wore a rugged brown shirt, dark black trousers along with a deep brown pair of shoes made of leather. He had shoulder padding made of leather and tied to his chest plate, too made of leather, that was laced on the left and right side as his back was shield by leather also.

He had dark tanned skin, deep brown eyes, shaven black hair matted over his head, he had a slightly broad nose and a

---

chiselled squared chin, he was a nice-looking boy as he smiled at me, he looked nervous. To ease his nerves, I thought to ask him questions, nothing too intense, but if I show interest, he might not be so afraid of me. He looked to me as I questioned,

"so, after all of this trouble from Abby, I might as well know the second trouble maker, what's your name?",

he smirked as he looked to Abby, as she was too in a giggle about being a pain in the arse, but she's now my pain in the arse.

He turned his attention to me as his slightly low voice informed,

"Byzer. My father is a soldier in Egyptverus and my mother is the witchdoctor of the migration, she took me with her, obviously",

I smiled slightly as Abby stated,

"he's really cool, can I hang out with him a bit more longer?",

without a single doubt I reassured,

"you can still hang out with him, I'm not stopping you, but I need you for a moment",

she looked to Byzer as she asked,

"what about Byzer? Can he stay?",

with firmness, Marcella stated,

"Byzer will come with me, we'll be outside don't worry",

Byzer left with Marcella and Xharlot as they left me to it, allowing me to just talk to her on my own, I could feel the pressure rise again, I didn't want to tell her, but she will know, and I have to find a compromise if she requests to see him.

I approached her looking down at her as she said puzzled,

"what is it? You look sad",

I crouched down to her, I know she was smaller by me by just a few inches, but I wanted her to be comfortable, relaxed and not intense.

She knelt down with me as I said carefully,

"Abby, there's no other way to say this, and I wished I didn't

need to tell you this",
she looked concerned as she wondered,
"Is this about Gina?",
I shook my head before I finally said,
"It's your dad Abby, he was killed in the execution when you were loaded on the Chinook",
she looked heartbroken, her eyes were watering as her face went from concerned to stone cold, she didn't know what to do first, cry or hug me, but she did both as she said with a trembled voice,
"can I see him? I want to see him",
I knew she was going to ask that, but I couldn't let her see her father, she wouldn't want to see it, it will just give her nightmares, and that I couldn't have, she can't end up like me, and see those she loved to die around her, there has to be a way to convince her.
I will find another way she can deal with her grief.

Chapter Sixteen
Grief Lurks

I moved Abby off me gently, so she could look me in the face as I stated,

"you don't want to see him, you may think you do but trust me on this.",

I had my hands on her shoulders as she still wept,

"trust me Abby, you don't want to see him",

she wiped her eyes as she sniffled,

"what happened to him? Maybe if I know how he died, I might not want to see him",

seeing as she was demanding to know I stood her up off the floor with me as I persisted,

"Abby",

I really didn't want to tell her how Karmin's men killed her father, but it's the only thing that might get her to not want to see his corpse, I can't let her do it, not for my sake, but for hers, I've seen so many bodies of my friends and family that it will hurt me to see her look at her father's corpse...because I know exactly what she will feel, and it was that pain that might not make her the same again.

With a deep breath I explained,

"he was stabbed with a dagger in the side of the head, if there's any consolation to all of this, he won't come back",

she nodded as she smiled slightly, she expressed,

"it's funny how I can't even be angry about it, because what you said is true, I wished there's was some other way",

she sniffled as she wiped her tears, drying them as the marks of the sadness streamed down her face, the hurt and pain, I could imagine how she was feeling, but the horrible part is I'm the adult and I couldn't dwell on it, feed on my pain.

I had to lock it away and hide it as she's the kid, she will need my help to get through this, but how can I when I don't know how to do it myself?

She looked up to me slightly as I expressed,

"it's no point of me saying I know how you feel, it's not a competition and frankly it won't resolve anything",

I paused only to say lightly,

"why don't you hang out with Byzer, he and you seem to get on quite well and will certainly do a better job at cheering you up",

she perked up a little, but her eyes were red and irritated as she agreed,

"yeah",

she moved to my left as we slowly walked down the pathway to the entrance, she looked to me as she added,

"you know you're not as bad as you think you are. You can be a little intense, serious and very scary in battle situations but you're fun",

with a slight smirk I thanked,

"thanks, say, you're not bad yourself, just maybe be a little less rebellious",

she broke a small smile as she recalled, "my Dad said the same all the time, but it was worded as 'don't be a pain in the ass'",

she looked a little happy, but the pain wasn't going to go overnight I knew that, she might feel better the next day, but I knew deep down it will still weigh in on her.

I just hoped this was enough for her not to want to see her father's corpse, I don't want her to be hurt even more.

Upon leaving the dome Byzer looked to Abby as he approached her as I questioned,

194

"are you okay? What's happened?",

I looked to him as I persisted,

"she might need a friend to hang out with. You and Abby can go off and do your own thing, she needs a little cheering up",

Abby left with Byzer as she said shortly,

"come on, we can watch the tower get built, I can explain on the way",

Marcella watched her pass with Byzer, she then to faced me as she asked,

"how did it go?",

Xharlot was nowhere to be seen, presuming she had something to do, other than wait around for me, I didn't blame her though, it looked like the sun was going down. The people were wandering around the camp still, but they were fixing the lampposts so they all glowed up tonight, just over half of them were fixed.

Marcella approached me as I informed,

"she took it well, doesn't want to see her father but I still can't count on it, she might sneak in, so we are going to have to fine Rhax and the four guards he took with him",

as I went to go into the building I was stopped by Marcella as she persisted,

"about that, Rhax has returned to the HQ Commanders quarters",

I faced her, seeing she was telling the truth.

With wonder I questioned,

"did they find the bodies?",

she scratched the back of her neck as she pieced,

"from what he said, someone, meaning Karmin, was one step ahead. Something about there was a furnace station underground of the dome",

a dark idea came to my head as I puzzled,

"wait, you don't think they used the bodies as a power supply?",

she nodded, agreeing with my theory as she explained,

"she said she ate people, I think she covered that up so that she could transport the bodies in the dome, then underground for burning them to fuel",

I rubbed my face, seeing it all made sense, Karmin lied about how she fed people human meat, claimed she could do all of these things, solely so she could have privacy and do things in the shadow, she was too clever for her own good.

With the confusion of the dome I questioned,

"so hold on, with all of that being a cover-up, what about the cages? Sevis told me that Karmin kept people in cages in the dome, and that was the goriest place on the planet?",

Marcella explained,

"people hung around there, but never went inside it, they knew all these things that, NOTE, Karmin said was in there. It was her way of getting people to leave her stuff alone, and it sure as hell did work",

the cannibalism, the cages it was a way for Karmin to have the dome by herself and a way to get people out of her property, she made this place to imprison people not to make a city, they were stupid enough to let her lead them, she must have been killing her own guards too, for one thing, I know the truth, it felt a little relieving to know she wasn't this cannibalistic psychopath, but she was still a murderous psychopath.

I looked at the dome as I wondered,

"did they seal the place off?",

she moved to my left as we faced the domes bright entrance, she informed further,

"no he said he was going to leave that choice to you",

firmly I approached the door, heading inside the garden as my words trailed,

"we need to see how many bodies there are left, we can burn the rest of them, I don't know what this contraption looks like but if it's a power generating device the bodies would be tossed in like a coal furnace or something",

we walked around upon the grass field, heading to the elevators pathways that lead directly to it, it curved from the main pathway in-front of the tree but I couldn't waste time by following the path.

We entered the elevator as Marcella clicked the floor going to minus two, going two floors underground. We could see the Earth and dirt surrounding the glass cylinder passing as the floor lowered deep within it, the lights were rimmed on the outside and placed inside the metal support bars ringed around it every few meters.

Upon descending I questioned,

"I haven't seen the guards that Karmin had with her in a while, I feel like they might be up to something",

Marcella ensured,

"we'll worry about that when we get to it, we have to check this place out, and know what your next plan of action is. They won't be going anywhere anytime soon",

she was right, but the thought that they might be up to something was strong, definitely will investigate after this. The lift made a gradual stop to a bright room ahead of us, large like a hall virtually.

The ceiling was made of rugged and spiked brown rocks as the ground was smoothed over with concrete, giving the cave-looking room a flatter and even floor. The door slid open to our right, allowing the door to curve in the back of the lift as we entered the room; it must have had a setting to stay stationary until the people took the lift back to the ground, a good security measure to know who is using the elevator.

We walked upon the concrete grounds, seeing the second lift to our far right, ahead of us was a large square-looking furnace, it had a large door with four gaps to see the fire and feed the flames inside the contraption.

Marcella and I approached the machine as I questioned,

"the shape of it, it just looks like a regular furnace, but outside of the wall it's supposed to be embedded in",

the machine was thickly cased with metal, rusted mind you and it looked to be encased in lumpy black residue, it was like its been down here for years.

The warmth it emitted was intense by the door but not by its left and right walls.

I touched it as I wondered,

"whatever is covering the metal wall of the furnace, it's keeping the heat in,",

Marcella touched it, only to wipe her hands off from the black charred powder that came off it.

She stated,

"I think whatever it is it's a man-made material, it's designed to keep the heat in, and absorb it",

I looked around the left and right side of the furnace, seeing large wires stream off it. They lead to the two pillars on the left and right corners of the back of the room we stood within. The pillars were made up of kinetic cogs, steam wires that transported the air through the system, turning the cogs as it was being ejected through a pump, pushing the steam to go faster, allowing it to move the pillars of cogs as they powered up a generator on each one, sparking power as the electrical cords entered the ceiling, flowing through the city.

The cogs were made of wood, polished and varnished to make sure they could last a very long time without rotting away, or breaking apart so easily, I also understand that using wood is much lighter than metal, it can do more spins and harness the city more power, how did Karmin receive such a complicated idea?

The only answer I can think of is her leader, and he will be met by the face of death soon, very soon.

I looked to Marcella as she theorised,

"with this much heat and steam the city must have been going on for centuries, but where's the steam coming from?", with a slight idea I stated,

"human urine, sweat, blood. The bodies burn, the liquids of the humans rise, and it channels into the inner pipes she probably has installed inside of the furnace, then flows into the generators system, simple science",

Marcella smirked remarking,

"well for you it's simple, for me that's just mind-blowing", she looked to the furnace asked further,

"well, what are you doing to do with it? If this thing is powering the whole city, won't the lights go out, especially for this kind of power, it won't last after it's turned off",

she was right, but what can we do? The bodies stacked in there are burning, and I'm not burning humans in there, perhaps the Undead,? after all, we are trying to do a controlled extermination. We need a better way to access this place if we're thinking of doing that, we can get a lot, but we can't move up and down to stock this place, and we can't stick them in piles on the floor that's not right.

With plans coming into my head I informed,

"we need to keep it, the bodies in there are still burning and it will last a few weeks, but we will replace the human bodies with The Undying, they might have fewer liquids in them but they still have their dead blood, there's got to be something left in them to power this thing",

Marcella thought as she negotiated,

"perhaps we can test it out, don't make it certain unless we know for sure that The Undying can keep this thing going, and if they can, we might be able to keep this way of power",

that was one thing covered but the transport, how can we kill so much and return it here? It might take a lot more thought than I realised, I questioned,

"what about transportation? Not only are we going to have to kill a dozen dead a day to keep this going for a year or so, but then there's the problem of having too many corpses to travel down within the lift",

we thought briefly.

She schemed,

"perhaps Kamic can do a transport lift, park it outside the dome walls, lower the car and we have a tunnel leading to here, it might take a few weeks to even dig something of a size but that's the only thing I can think of at the moment", she glanced to the elevator as she stated,

"We better get back to Rhax, inform him of the situation, and that we will test the theory before making it solid",

we both agreed on that idea as we headed towards the lift we came from.

The yellow flood lights on the left and right side of the large room gave off a sinister glow when walking past it, it felt like this place was haunted, it just gave me the chills to think that people were stowed down here like coal, and thrown in when no bodies were burning in the generator. Our feet firmly stood within the lift as we ascended up to the ground floor, as we did I questioned,

"do you think we're doing the right thing?",

she wondered,

"what do you mean?",

with hesitance I expressed,

"I don't know what it is, but I feel like burning the dead after killing them is overkill, and most of all, it feels like we're just throwing people in the fire",

she thought on it as she stated,

"well okay perhaps we can think of an alternative route, make solar power for the place or wind farms, either way there's no rush in the decision, you have till tomorrow afternoon, Rhax will want to know by then",

she gave me a little less pressure to think through all of this, I will just be as bad as Karmin if I kept that generator, even though its well-crafted I can't stow people in there, I could perhaps alter the furnace to boil water but even then we haven't got enough water to share, it's so scarce over here that we can't afford to waste it like that.

This might be a hard choice, but I know what has to be done, no one is going to like it, but we're going to have to shut it down.

The city may lose its power when the fuel runs out, but it's happening.

I knew that's what is going to have to happen.

When reaching the ground floor, we strolled past the tree as she wondered,

"you think a tree like that shouldn't be hidden away, but in this place, I think having it expose might be ten times as worse",

we both stopped walking, gazing to the large tree as I said in admiration,

"I've never seen a tree that large before in life, it looks to be an oak tree I believe",

she recalled,

"before the storm hit I was around ten perhaps even nine it's been that long ago. There was a tree I used to play on after school was over, playing out in the garden, making a swing set and my mother told me don't play out there for too long or the night monster will get you",

she smirked as I joked,

"did you believe in that? the night monster",

she nodded as she remarked,

"when I was a kid I even believed Santa was real, but turns out to be the parents work",

she laughed slightly as she sighed,

"see how simpler things were back then, worried about school, bullies, being popular and just had your place",

she looked to me as I stated,

"but now those bullies would be dead because all this time of being this big figure, they were nothing but small mice. I know it's not a plus side but I don't think I would take back the world of before",

I pointed to the tree as I continued,

"you get to see things like this, go places where you shouldn't, all just so you can make the world a better place, back then you couldn't even get help in school all because the bullies were crying and you weren't",

she and I related on the level that we both have our past, our mistakes, but in the end, we came through it and now are starting the best thing we've seen in a long time, a beautiful rising tree.

We took a breather as she questioned,

"I've never asked you about what it was like on the moon, the schools said it was a Utopia for the good students, and hell for the bad students, they used it as a way to get us to be good",

a bizarre way of training kids, but what do I know, most of the kids I've spoken to have died from the fault of my own.

I wished memories could be wiped without being triggered by certain things, it was killing me in the inside as my face was blank as a stone wall on the outside.

Not knowing what to recall first, I might as well bring up the times of when I first became a biologist.

With firmness, I informed,

"my childhood was mainly okay, I didn't talk to anyone all that much, and frankly they just didn't want to talk to the kids on the moon anyway, they thought they were idiots. So that caused us to be our best, they saw something in us and I became a biologist and an expert in plants and herbs, that was when people started to try and talk to me, I didn't allow it though. It led to many years of being called the Larva",

she looked puzzled as she wondered,

"why would that be an insult?",

I smirked as I explained,

"it was because my foster mother Beliss White would shield me all the time, keep me away from social activity and it kind of made me want it more, at first I ignored the people but when I wanted to talk to them Beliss would cut me out and ensure I never spoke to them again, so I was called Larva, the maggot belonging to Beliss and will be shielded until I bloomed into something else",

Marcella looked as though she understood my situation as she uncovered,

"my father was the same in terms of shielding me from boys in school, and body in general after the storm. We found a campsite and it became our home, it was Base 19, back then it was nothing but one warehouse but I'm impressed in how it grew in over the years. Anyway, that's not where I was going with the story. I met a man named Adrian Rayline, we were inseparable, he liked what I liked, and I liked what he liked, it was a match made from heaven",

she looked almost saddened as she must have missed him, clearly, something not only happened to her father but her husband too.

I encouraged,

"what happened to them?",

she glanced at me as she expanded,

"my father left me in the end, said he couldn't handle the way the Eviliance have turned out to be, haven't seen him since and could be alive for all I know, just a very old man by now. Then my husband died shortly after I had Erilk, he was out on the field, and the Scorpions ambushed him and his team, not leaving any of them alive, back then the Scorpions were a strong presence before the Vipers left hiding and started the Scale war, after that, things died down",

we faced each other as I wanted to not be rude to end the topic so short, but I wanted her to not relapse into a grieving mood, it won't be any good for her, it was a long time ago and she still can't do anything about it now.

With a warmness to my voice I said,

"sorry about your husband, if any consolation your, father could still be out there living like you are, no doubt you got your strength from him",

she smiled as she said,

"my father was strong yes, but not after his wife passed, but even so, can't say you didn't try",

she smirked as she joked,

"you still are a little rusty on comforting people aren't you",

with a smile growing on both of our faces I stated,

"I'm a leader, I haven't got a soft heart",

she remarked,

"yeah that's what they all say",

203

we gradually walked away from the tree, strolling down the pathway as I mentioned,

"you know that now we have virtually the whole island on its feet, we could be called saviours of the world",

she corrected,

"rulers of the world if you think in a villains mind, they believe they can conquer the lands like its their own, but it belonged to us since the start, and 'US' meaning survivors of the first storm",

we were around halfway upon the pathway as Sevis walked through the doors with his staff firmly in his grasp, he looked as though he had some serious news yet he always had a serious face so it was hard to tell.

He approached us, stopping us in our path as I questioned,

"is everything okay?",

he nodded shortly before he explained,

"my people wish to greet you, I rounded up those who are not at work, they want to hold a meal, for you and your friends who want to join in the occasion",

Marcella wondered,

"the occasion for what exactly?",

he saw that he only half explained as he continued,

"oh right, I might need to tell you more on our ways in Egyptverus. In our lands, we welcome high ranked guests, or new leaders with a feast and a gift made from one of us, which in this case a gift from me as you gave me the honour of being within your team as you call it. Your friends can come if they want to, if not we won't take it too offence, merely that they have too many things to do and for us, that's more than reasonable",

I looked to Marcella as I wondered,

"did you want to come?",

she saw no reason why she shouldn't as she stated,

"I will see if Rhax, Xharlot, Kamic, Qorin, and Alis will come. Where is the meal taking place?",

Sevis looked pleased that we were all going to make an effort as he informed,

"we completely cleared the cafeteria, made it look appealing and to our tradition, you will know what to do when you get there, a seat will be waiting for you all",

Marcella left the room as she said warmly,

"we'll be looking forward to it",

as she left the room Sevis still had a few more things to say, and to be honest, I always have time for him, he's an interesting man, and I find him quite favourable.

He wondered,

"didn't you want Abby and Byzer to come? They were talking to his mother in the preparation of the cafeteria, she looked quite sad, she could use something to perk her up", with his kind gesture I informed,

"her father was killed in the execution of a hundred and forty of our people. I'm not certain in how she can be cheered up", he thought for a moment as he said,

"I will show you your gift, perhaps I can do the same for Abby, make her feel safe",

he rummaged in the satchel tied to his belt, taking out a gift-wrapped with white fabric and tied with rugged string.

Upon holding the gift it felt as though it was weighted, I couldn't be sure of what it was until I opened it, but from Sevis's slightly loosened face he seems to be certain that I will like it.

Chapter Seventeen
The Closure

Upon opening it he watched my every move, from untying the knots to peeling back the four corners of the fabric until finally seeing the gift within the palm of my hand; the necklace was beautiful, the centre piece was the one-inch oblate spheroid disc, much like a sphere shape but is flattened into a curved and nicely rounded disc.

The texture of it was smooth as it looked bumpy underneath it, perhaps a type of resin was used to seal the white rugged centrepiece, if so that's very clever of him; the top part of the centrepiece pointing at Sevis had a form of double joined golden horn, it stuck very well to the centre piece as the points were dragged far from the rock, just by a little bit so

you could see the points curve away, much like an Egyptian headpiece which is probably why it brought some familiarity. The chain of the necklace was recycled, it was a bronze colour, stained to look bronze, or maybe it really was made of it, until it rusts to green I won't know for certain.

Upon holding the fabric in my left hand I held the amulet as I thanked,

"thank you, it looks very well made",

I was going to ask him how he made it but he explained,

"I didn't make it before you think I did, my craftsmanship skills are not great. This was a gift from Byzer's mother, she opted for this to be your gift, and for a good reason too as she told us the story behind it",

as I put the necklace on, feeling the slight weight of the centrepiece, Sevis went on to tell me more of his interesting stories.

He went on,

"the full moon is the representation of Khonsu, the god of the moon and healing. He is said to be the reason the moon shines and most of all the reason why we keep going, the moon to us is like the sun, a sacred thing that shouldn't be taken advantage of. It resembles life and resembles harmony, but with that necklace on you she said that you will be able to be healed by it, loved and cared by it, she saw darkness in you",

with a frown I wondered,

"Darkness? Do you mean to say she sees evil in me", he shook his head slightly before he reassured,

"no she knew your aura was pure by speaking of you, she only had to give you a glance to know the grief in you, the very dark space inside you that you never had the chance to show the light",

I wasn't certain about his word, grief? I'm definitely not grieving, if anything I'm stowing it away, not hiding it, saving it for a time where there's no point in keeping it there anymore, let it filter through myself, and see there's no point. Even though I accepted his gift I expressed kindly,

"I appreciate the sentiment of the gift, but I don't need myself analysed, okay?",

he smiled slightly only to motion,

"in that case, come, the meal will be starting soon, the sun is down",

I followed him to his left, leaving the dome as I put the fabric in my pocket, seeing as the city was already a dump, I couldn't add more waste to it until the wreckage of the siege was cleared up, which that was my fault for letting Horneck use the rocket launchers on the towers.

When walking outside I looked up to the sky, seeing the stars were shimmering through the fading clouds, it was nice to breathe out here, but the drafts of rotten flesh put me off the scene, it was rancid.

So much dead walking around it, almost made me feel bad for them, seeing them change from people to half-eaten corpses, dragging their feet's, flesh hanging off of their faces, they were to be feared but the smallest parts of us knew that they never intended on becoming these horrid creatures.

As my thought was straying away, Sevis and I slowly strolled down the pathway as he questioned,

"I thought the dome held cages, destruction, but it's, so",

knowing what he was going to say, I finished his sentence,

"peaceful? Yeah, I was thinking the same when I went in there, just wished we saw this everywhere",

he said with reassurance,

"someday you might, perhaps not the green field going for miles, but cold mountains perhaps, deserts stretching far, allowing you to see the inner beauty of the canyons, this may just be what we see for now, but someday it will all be worth it",

to his words I couldn't help but smile inside, he was positive, peaceful even when his wife was no longer here and his children were separated from him.

Which that in mind, I wondered,

"Sevis, you're not like any other person I met before. You've been through all these things, witnessed things, and yet you stay positive all the time",

he laughed only to joke,

"sounds as though you don't like the positivity",

we made our way left, seeing the burning bonfire go with its last flames.

I explained,

"it's not that I don't like positivity, but it's just strange to see someone who almost forgives the world for what it has taken",

I tried to find a way to say that even though he's been

208

through a lot he acts as though it never happens, he never seemed angry, dwelling upon everything.

He pieced together his words as he stated,

"life isn't about holding what you've lost, it's about taking something back from it, whether it's the one that killed someone you loved or taking a city back to its peaceful state Always take back from a loss",

I never thought about it that way, I've been taking and taking but not for myself, but for those that the world has taken from me, and that's too many to count, perhaps I will never stop taking, but if anything it's for the right cause, if humanity needs to stabilise and ensure that the right people are walking the lands then I will continue to fight until no one is left to turn on us, it never ends with one person against us, there's always more and a puppet

master behind the strings I've known that with Deoaka, she played people and got them killed for the sake of riches and power.

Sevis was a lot more spiritual than the rest of my team, he may have the words to give me answers, but my friends, those stuck in the Storms path knew that no matter what was said to me, I could figure a way out of my loop, they knew how I would let people have their say, and they'd let me decipher my ways on my own, but the difference from them and my team with me now, is that they refuse to leave my side.

It sounds as though it's a bad thing but perhaps it's not so bad after all, if they aren't with me they are with someone else in a team, and even then I know where they were the same in reverse order; the team with me now, all of them are virtually foreign from me apart from Marcella and Qorin, it's strange how much that even though that we were from different soil we treat each other like a family, just the way everyone should treat each other, like no one is different at all.

Upon having that thought, I stopped us in our tracks as I questioned,

"Sevis you've been here longer than I have, do you know if the city has a radio station? I need to contact Aries and my team in Motahvada",
he faced me as he asked,
"Can't that wait?",
even though I was looking forward to the meal I might just have to have mine leftover for me, I need to be sure Aries doesn't come our way, the missiles clearly didn't come for us, otherwise I would be seeing heavy missile artillery around, we have rocket launchers here, but not the ones that could take out a whole gas station.
With persistence I stated,
"the meal will have to wait for me, you guys can go ahead with my team, they should all be there by now, perhaps if this place doesn't have a radio station I can go out in the field to find one",
he nodded firmly seeing he had no other choice but to accept my actions, he stated,
"I will have to stay behind then, you will be safer on your own, but wait here, I will need to get you some gear for the journey, if you walk in you won't be able to slip away so easily",
I grasped his arm, stopping him as I stated,
"don't worry about that I can handle myself, just tell me where the radio station should be",
he moved back in-front of me wanting to refuse as he worried,
"you can't go out there with no gear",
I cut in,
"I've been in that sort of environment without gear before, perhaps not with as many Undying but if I'm careful it will be fine",
he sighed, only to see I was determined to go there with or without his permission, he informed firmly,
"there is a beacon west of here, just where the brighter section of the city is, you can't miss it, its by a large store",

I have a rough idea where it is, but how far away it is might be another story, if I'm out there till the morning then the team will go searching, Sevis will need strict orders for this.
With firmness I expressed,
"I'll be going now if I want to reach there, the ride here took over night so it will take longer to get there by foot",
he wondered,
"perhaps you don't need to go by foot",
he glanced back to the prison, only to motion me to follow by his left side as we walked to the pathway going to the main gates to our right, he stated,
"there's two wheeled vehicles you can use, they are parked outside the walls to stop the gates from making to much noise, they are to your left and keys are in it already, just do one thing for me when you get out there",
I glanced to him as he added,
"don't get killed",
we were halfway down the field, meeting the pathway ahead of us to our left, soon walking upon it as I informed briefly,
"when I'm out there, tell the team not to worry, and if they do, simply tell Kamic to make a radio, by the time I get there they would have figured it out and contact me to tell me how stupid I was",
he smirked slightly as he wondered,
"do all of your friends tell you that?",
I glanced to him as I puzzled,
"you don't think that?",
he looked as though he agreed as he stated,
"perhaps stupidly courageous would be a suited word for me, but if you know what you're doing, there's no need to worry",
he seemed to have faith in me, or at least trusted my word, was that a good thing or a bad thing though? Usually, I go in a pair if people doubted my survival skills, but he didn't bother to join, perhaps he was trying to teach me a lesson.
But either way, I'm persistent in getting there and back in one piece, the wall of the city is made from metal and

concrete bricks, strong enough to hold back a hoard of them if that happens.

When meeting the gates, the guards opened the heavy metal doors, it was large enough to let a truck through at least, perhaps they once did before things got hairier; the doors opened enough for one person to move through as Sevis persisted,

"are you sure you want to go?",

with a firmness I reassured,

"I'll be back before they know it",

I walked towards the gate, moving past the guards before behind shut out from the city, seeing the darkness fill ahead of me along with the dead lurking towards the noise made by the gate as it slammed to a stiffened lock.

The silence filled around me as I walked to the motorbikes stowed to the left, the four bikes were lined diagonally against the wall, facing away from it, looking to the roads ahead of me.

The north side of the city looks as though the south side of the city led to a direct road to the third campsite, claimed to be south but from what I know they aren't to be prodded with, they don't seem to be even the slightest bit interested in me so hopefully, that means they are harmless and not scheming.

My feet were tapping away on the concrete grounds as I approached the closest motorbike, feeling the handles before finding the helmet on the left handle, the lights out here were non-existent, the city kept its lights on the inside as they never shed any form of light outside.

Even though the glow gave me away, the dead didn't seem to be interested as they could see the light from where they walked.

With pace to my movement, I put the helmet on only to soon turn the key, allowing a beam of light to show a gleaming pair of eyes stare back at me, the make of the bike was a BMW, old-style and has a problem with the exhaust as it rattled when moving away from the city, turning myself right to the road that led to the west.

Upon mounting the bike the rumble echoed as I drove on the roads, passing the Undying that limped its way towards me from the buildings to my left, it was trying to chase after me but I soon sped off, leaving it behind in the darkness.

The bike kept jittering every so often from the debris on the road, I tried to avoid it, but there was only more debris in my way, the roads weren't safe to drive in, but I didn't care, I was going to get to that radio station, it's not far from the city on this bike, but I hope it will be able to last the drive back. As the journey began, the sun lowered into a darker red, ending to a complete pitch black as the night came. The moon shone brightly with the stars, as the clouds were clearing up, the volcanic clouds seemed to clear up from this place, and drifted where the wind took it. I was glad the very least as the moons glow could allow me to see puddles ahead that glimmered from the reflection.

The dead were straying to my location as they were starting to wonder on the roads, they were attracted to the sound of my broken engine, the clatters coming from it caused them to follow me, and kept following the direction even when I'm out of their sight, they followed what they last saw, meaning they might come to me on the way back from the radio station.

My dagger was firm to my left side, staying put in my holster as my gun rattled from the bike's vibration. The exhaust wasn't the only problem of this thing, but if it's working, and burning fuel, it doesn't matter, it seems to want to keep pushing until it finally breaks down.

My eyes wandered ahead as the glow of the superstore could be seen peeking over the buildings, there should be a road that squared around it, so hopefully, I can patrol it, scout out any radio towers nearby, it should even have a light blinker on the top of it.

The sound of the bike was making me nervous as the dead were lurking further onto the roads, seeing as they could hear the bike first before being able to get close enough to see the blinding lights, they were half-blind creatures, but it was strange to see that even with that defect, they were able to see, perhaps not from afar, but the smells and sounds would have advanced by a lot.

My speed was reaching up to ninety miles an hour, turning to a hundred when seeing the dead were closing in onto my left and right, they were getting in my way ahead of me, seeing my light and knowing I was going in their direction.

I couldn't do much to stop them getting to me apart from shoving them and swerving out of their way, they just seemed to grow thicker and thicker as the crowd of the dead were marching towards me, a form of migration was taking place and for whatever reason, they were heading to the direction of the Base Zero far behind, perhaps sneaking out like this wasn't all in bad terms, we didn't know the threat that approached us.

With firmness I took my pistol out, seeing perhaps I can't take down the dozens in-front of me, but if I make bait, they might not want me if their own is dead, free food for them, and not a risk of me being killed too brutally.

I aimed at the dead to my right and left, seeing ones that were a little slower as I shot at them, taking down six with my last twelve bullets.

At first, they were attracted to the gunshots but then started to split ways when smelling the flesh and rotting corpse that was put down into the dirty.

I threw the gun away before taking the chance to grasp the handles of the bike, twisting them to speed me back up to a hundred when the gap formed, the large and narrow pathway was slowly starting to close on me, seeing as the flesh wasn't enough to distract them but they were followed into wanting the food more, their hunger begged them to.

The sound of the dead zoomed past me, hearing barks, growls, and grunts briefly commotion before finally reaching the end of the street, going a sharp right turn before suddenly

214

stopping the bike, even with getting past that hoard they would only continue to the Base, I can at least draw them away and delay the attack for a little while longer.

I rumbled the bike as my lights glimpse to the crowd of blinking eyes, they grunted as their feet's dragged behind them as I revved the bike, making the engine roar as I yelled, "come get some",

they were more up for that idea than I was, most of them were running ahead as the rest limped with fastness to their feet, as the ones that ran were less damaged, their flesh was mostly intact as their faces were deformed and mutilated along with their arms and chest, they might have been the ones that survived a bite, but hid themselves away before it was too late for them.

The bike has smoke trailing off it as I darted ahead to the turn leading to the right side of the superstore/shopping centre; the bike turned left, meeting with the long road that stretched far to the pharmacy I was in previously with Abby and Nathan. The lights glowed as the dead were lurking around it, they were looking to me as I sped over twenty miles an hour, just fast enough to be out of reach of the running Undying but close enough for them to see me in the bright lights of the street, I glanced back seeing the fifty dead run for me, the twenty that could run lurked behind them as the very few who were unable to run were limping with a slow pace, like a gradient effect almost.

Muffles of their feet and the loud growls of their voice, pressure was starting to build as I needed to figure out how I can shake them off; when reaching the corner curving left past the pharmacy I could see the green and red blink of the radio tower to the west side of the super store's burning garage, the one that is still burning even though it was destroyed only two days ago, whatever was left still burned until it will finally give up and die down, knowing it can't revive itself into a bigger fire again.

When passing the stores entrance I heard a person yell, they called,

"Hey, hey over here!",

when stopping the bike, I looked left to the entrance, allowing the ruffed up woman to approach me.

At first she didn't see the dead running towards us, but soon took the chance to jump on as I snapped,

"get on, now!",

the second she grasped on I sped ahead, moving towards the alleyway as I persisted,

"look, don't talk, don't say a thing when we get off this, just trust me when I say you need to jump right now",

she was going to argue, but I soon gave her no choice.

I quickly jerked the bike left, causing her to fling ahead as I soon let go of the bike's handle. The bike was going in a loop still as we tumbled upon the floor, soon meeting the side-walk of the outskirts of the superstore.

When getting up I noticed scuffs and blood on my hands and arms, but it didn't bother me.

The smoke of the motorbike cycled in a loop as we had our only cover from behind seen by the hoard, the smoke covered our scent, but the woman was just almost in their view as he got up.

She wiped down her ragged white shirt and dark black combat trousers, she looked at her boots only to face me. She looked firmly at me with her deep brown eyes, she went to march in rage but her left foot was twisted, causing her to stumble forwards, luckily behind the smoke trailing to our right, out of view of the dead as they were slowing down, seeing the bike but I know they were wanting to go around it to find the bodies on it.

I forced her to her feet, pulling her to the alleyway on our left, she pulled away as we reached the edges of the alleyway, she argued,

"what the fuck is wrong with you?! You should have driven away, not throw us overboard!",

I cut in,

"listen here, I know who you are, you're one of the guards belonging to Karmin. She's dead, so now you listen to me", she pushed me as she remarked,

"who the hell even are you? Some self-righteous bitch who thinks I'm going to believe that bullshit",

I unclipped the helmet, showing my face to her as I said firmly,

"this self-righteous bitch IS Merider Black, and I swear to the sun that if you stop me from saving your ass, then I'm leaving you here",

she paused her words, seeing she knew my face all too well, whoever she was she was surely ruffed up and tired of being a punching bag, she had bruises everywhere...not just from the crash I caused. Her dark black hair was let down in a scruffy style, not too wild but just scruffy enough for it to be flat just by a little bit. She looked back at the smoking bike, seeing the silhouette of the dead that were prowling past the smoke, seeing where we have gone, she darted after me as I proceeded ahead of the alleyway, keeping a hold of the helmet in case I needed it for close combat, I can just use my dagger, but it won't stay sharp forever.

Chapter Eighteen
Self-Righteous Bitch

We raced through the alleyway as the dead were catching our scent; the rugged wall was skimming past our shoulders upon running in the tight space. The walls were brittle and dusted upon our arms when taking turns and corners, as we headed west of the city. This side was a lot darker than the rest, the night masked most of the streets but the alleyways were the darkest parts of the city, the only way I could navigate was looking up every so often to see the moon shining down on us with the glittering stars with it.

Using that, I could tell when the next turn was, the woman kept close to me as her voice echoed,

"where the hell are we going? The stores the other way, we need to get the rest of my team out",

with persistence I hushed,

"can we keep your voice down, and just not talk, we have to get to the radio station, no arguments",

she kept pulling my arm back until I finally gave in to her annoying ways of getting my attention.

I took her wrist as I dragged her to the left side of the alleyway, taking the left turn, going to an apartment room with the door that was opened slightly, perhaps occupied, but right now she is going to get us killed if I don't answer her questions, it won't shut her up if I keep her silent on the trip. I moved her inside as I shut the door, I stated,

"look around, see if anyone is in here and I can answer your questions without being interrupted",

she looked around, the dark tipped over room, she questioned, "how can I search a thing when it's fucking dark?",

with a sigh I turned around as I thought of a solution, I moved my hands ahead of me as I persisted, "

navigate with your hands, not your eyes, and listen closely for foes if they are nearby, hopefully, there's a kitchen on this side",

when moving forward I felt the tipped over sofa, carefully moving around it to my left as I felt the wall close in on it, I was passing the living room and headed into the kitchen when feeling the counter pressed against the wall ahead of me.

When feeling the counter I soon crouched, searching the drawers from left to right, the first draw was utensils as the cabinet below it were the plates and bowls, nothing of use for me.

The woman heard my movements from each drawer and cabinet as she wondered,

"have you found anything?",

when searching the next drawer I took out a small iron cooking pot as I instructed,

"I need you to help me here, can you get some of the sofa fabric, it's only to last five minutes so I can answer your worries",

she snuffed as she remarked,

"and how am I supposed to take the fabric without a knife? I don't know if you've noticed but I'm unarmed",

I put the pot on the counter firmly, making a heavy thump as I continued searching the draw, taking matches that I could find as I remarked, "just come over here",

when reaching my way back to the iron pot I took the fabric from Sevis's gift he gave me previously, placing it in the pot as I took any form of paper, from newspapers to an old phone book, leaving it in whole to ensure it would light for a longer time.

I lit a match, lighting up the musky and grey gloomy kitchen I stood in, seeing the woman's face as she approached my location; when putting the matches in I lit another one just to make sure the fire burned a little faster as the pot finally lit up in flames.

When putting the matches in my pocket I said firmly,

"first of all you tell me what your name is, and then you have three questions to ask me",

she was going to argue,

"but that's not fair",

with a sharpness I cut in,

"I have an important mission to do and I can't waste my time explaining to someone I just saved, so ask me what you really want to know or we can get over this and we can leave without wasting time",

the flames heated my right side as the glow from the orange furious flames illuminated our body's just barely.

The woman shortly introduced,

"I'm Iren",

she went on to question,

"Look, all I need to know is why the hell are we going to a radio station, and why won't you let me tell you about my problems? With my team in the store",

perhaps I gave off the wrong impression on not wanting to help her out, I did but my mission needs to go first.

With firmness, I ensured,

"I will be able to help you and your friends but first the radio station. I'm fearing that my friends over the wall are making their way here believing we are in peril, I can't allow them to come over when we're fine", she wondered,

"that's it? If you let me explain the situation I could have told you about the truck radio we have",

feeling like I just wasted a trip I persisted,

"well it's too late to go back now, besides we will need a permanent source for my team anyway, if I can hook a radio there and connect it to my team's frequency. I can easily station some of my people there, guard it and build it into another city",

she looked doubtful but she remarked,

"well it seems like you're stuck with me, so does that mean you will go to my team after this?",

the fire was burning dimmer as I reassured,

"yes, I will help you out, are we done? Can we get on with this mission",

she was silent as she and I both were wanting our missions done, it was just the case of getting to our points.

As she and I approached the door I led the way, opening the door slowly ensuring nothing followed us as she was yelling for an answer earlier, but when looking left at the long stretch to the corner on my right going behind us, it looks as though we are clear, for now. Iren kept close behind me as we went left, heading to the long stretch as the radio station blinker hid behind the

building towering on our right, I could finally see the blink of the red and green

lights, but it would always creep behind the buildings as we gained closer to its location.

The corner ahead of us went right, finally going to the exit of the alleyway, and the small opening leading directly to the

radio station tower; when finally going through the corner and seeing the radio station ahead, I noticed the lights were working around here, the streets were glowing with pure artificial lights of the lampposts, even some of the

apartment's lights shone too, who is keeping these places up and running?

Something tells me I don't want to know, but seeing the layout of this place, we needed to tread carefully, and be ready to take down some Undying.

The barbed wire fences squared around this large radio station in front of us, it was three floors tall, perfectly rectangular long ways but it wasn't tall, not as tall as the antenna placed upon the centre of its flattened roof.

The antenna stood on very strong support beams that stretched into a large point when raising around seven floors more if measuring in apartment floors, it overlooked the tall apartments at the back of the opening.

The street around the radio station squared around it perfectly also, this place was a little more well kept than the rest in terms of less debris, but even with that it still looked gloomy like the rest of the Dead Zone.

The dead were limping around, most were on the verge of starvation as they were crawling around the place, yet one was already being targeted by a group of five dead, tearing its limb like it was a buffet, they had a limb each as the fifth dead was devouring the body of the dead.

We could see them on our left far from the alleyway entrance, and fortunately far enough for us to take it as an advantage. The gateway was to the right side of the radio station fence, it was a risky move but we both can make it if we run, however, I recall that Iren can't run...she hurt her ankle earlier.

I looked around as I persisted,

"Iren I can't believe this is happening but get on my back",

when putting the helmet on the floor seeing as I couldn't carry both her and the helmet she refused,

"no way, I can run",

Iren went to move but she couldn't even stand on her ankle, she was already in a lot of pain, but I don't know how else she can follow me at my pace, the door isn't far it will just mean that I have to push ahead.

I lowered myself slightly as I snapped,

"just do it before I ditch you here",

222

with a deep sigh she approached me, only to hop onto my back as I held her legs firmly, she put her hands awkwardly around my neck as she joked,

"wow from first base to ten in five minutes",

with persistence I moved out of the alleyway, moving across the right side of the street.

Iren looked warily behind us as she whispered,

"Uh Merider?",

I shushed,

"shut it",

she repeated,

"Merider, can you just",

with yet again another hush to not get us caught early I snapped,

"can you wait?!",

she soon blurted,

"can you tell that to the dead then? They are following us you dumbass",

I looked left, only to see the Undying were running at us, they had dropped their limbs and ignored the dead body, seeing two fresh bodies creeping away from them.

I quickly let her down as I persisted,

"go to the gate, lock the door, and get inside",

she refused,

"I'm not letting you-",

before she could try and argue and refuse I approached the dead, unsheathing my dagger, leaving her with no choice but to get inside the radio station.

The first dead was running to me, wanting to tackle me but as it got in view I step to its left, impaling the side of its head as it fell past me, taking the vigorous blow to the head.

As it fell I pulled the dagger from it, giving me the access to another hit as I pushed the next target backwards, causing the four dead to stumble before proceeding to limp towards me, instead of running.

It allowed me to stab each one through the eyes, centre of its forehead, and firmly through the right side of its head.

With each attack, my teeth clenched as grunts came from me, using every part of my aching body to ensure the Undying were eliminated.

The deep blue and black blood dripped from my hands when seeing the bodies scattered on the floor, they were cluttered in front of me as the last dead was picking itself off the floor slowly, using its fragile body to push it from the rugged ground.

When turning the dagger to face behind me I stormed towards the last dead, only to quickly jab it in the eye.

Its growls froze as its mouth was locked open, allowing me to see the rotting yellow and black teeth as its tongue was barely even human, from this close it was hideous but worst of all it was alive, it was virtually a gift to kill this poor man…or what once used to be a man.

When letting his body fall, as the dagger exited his skull, the growls continued, but not from him, from the hoard that was filtering through the alleyway.

I looked left only to back away as the dozens and virtually hundreds of dead were coming towards my location, with haste I turned to the radio station, running to the gate as the siren of growls and grunts were chasing towards me, they must have figured out where I was, or heard Iren from earlier.

I ran to the gate, seeing Iren at the doors as she franticly tried to barricade the gates, she persisted,

"you think you can come in? No fucking way I'm getting the hell out of here, thanks for telling me about your friends, they might come to rescue me",

she raced inside, passing the cars in the parking lot, only to turn left where the pathway led to the dusty white radio station.

When looking at my options running around the fence was no use I will only be outrun, I looked up, seeing the barbed wire on top of it, it was razor wire, shaped like a V as it was wrapped on a metal support, in that very same shape, perhaps it's a risk I'm going to take.

With haste I started to climb the fence, using my upper strength, what I have left of it, to insert my fingers within each grate. Climbing higher until cautiously looking at the razor wire, the nervous thought reached me, but seeing the dead below me, and the hundreds of more dead that were shaking the fence, it causing my movements to be quick as I climbed over the fence, using my feet to step on the razor wire as my hands carefully held on the metal frame underneath it, causing it to scratch at my hands, creating a few more cuts to my previous injuries before I finally jumped down clumsily, seeing my balance was knocked off course from jumping off the gates, it definitely wasn't going to stand for much longer I could feel it.

I fell on my front, causing myself to roll before getting my balance back, I was on my hands and feet when forcing myself to stay stationary.

My right foot was feeling incredibly sore as I got up, as were both of my wrists, the landing sprained my wrists for certain as the feeling was memorable.

When looking back I searched my pockets with caution, trying not to hurt my wrist when trying to find my dagger, it wasn't with me, I think I must have dropped it on the other side.

Without a thought I hurried away from the door, seeing the gate started to cave in as the Undying were piling on each other, they didn't care about themselves, they only cared about their dinner, which was going to be me if I don't get inside, right now.

When running my right ankle was thumping with pain, swollen immensely as I tried to run on it, my right leg would dip regularly as I put pressure on my foot, it didn't want me to run on it, but my body doesn't have a choice, it's either we make it to the radio station, or get torn apart…then die after bleeding out, not a way I want to go if you're asking me.

The gate was creaking and croaking as the dead were tipping

it inwards from all the pressure, my heart raced as some of them tumbled over the fence, shredding their skin, and tearing their clothes from the razor wire, it was a horrific sight when glancing back at them, seeing their skin hang off with the blood dripping off it, some of them had their eyes torn out, it was stuck on the razor wire that was virtually touching the ground.

My breaths was heavy as I turned a sharp left when running, using the floor as guidance as I stumbled, not wanting to tumble over as I raced as fast as I could to the door ahead of me, which yet again, Iren had blocked, what an asshole.

She used the furniture in the reception to block the door, from red sofas to dark oak tables, I couldn't see a damn thing inside. Luckily with the bright outside street-lights, I could hastily look at the brick walls of the radio tower, only to spot a fire escape ladder to the corner of the building, nearing the left side and past the cluttered cars. They were blocking something upon the other side but with the height, I can use it, the dead can climb the vehicles blocking the back way but they can't climb ladders, I swear to the sun if they do that, they are evolving.

My face was sweating drips to the floor as I pushed myself to the vehicles, climbing it, only to see what it blocked. There were half torn apart corpses crawling around in that sector, it looks as they were from the accident over the parking lot on their side.

There were iron beams and billboards embedded in the ground, some of the dead were still in one piece but only five or less, they were feasting on the half-torn corpses but soon were attracted to me as they could hear the sirens of growls following the radio station.

When looking right I soon approached the ladders, seeing the dead were making the car shake, trying to reach me as I franticly climbed from their grasps.

My wrists hurt so bad, it spread around me like wildfire, causing me to quickly grasp each step as I just needed to get to the roof now, the dead are down there but there's nothing stopping them from getting in, after all, they follow what they last saw and will take any route to get to me.

Each step I climbed, the rust stuck upon my hand, flaking off to the ground as my feet stomped upon the steps passing; my foot was under so much pressure, but it wasn't long till I was on the roof, there's a way in from up there, unless Iren blocked that too, that would be the final straw for me.

Upon finally reaching the roof, I crawled upon the floor, feeling relieved to finally not need to put pressure on my hands. When stumbling back on my feet, I could see the whole street surrounding me, along with the apartment buildings. They towered taller than the radio station, but I could see the superstore within the background ahead of me, it was peering tall, and was brightly lit, making it stand out from the rest of the gloomy dark city.

The dead growled with a sort of low rumbling ambient, it sounded inhuman to the amount of dead that there were. With all their rotting lungs groaning at once, it sounded as though I was going to be met by death any moment.

I glanced down from the ladders seeing the dead clawing away at the wall, they were urging themselves to climb the walls, but it was no use, their fingers were just grating and tearing on the brickwork, looks as though I might be safe, that's until I find a way to get the hell out of here.

My first thoughts were to find Iren, not only will she need to be dealt with either with a hard lesson or perhaps a light warning, fortunately for her I'm in the worst shape, and not only has she hurt herself I've hurt myself also…no thanks to her. I turned to face the single room that encased the staircase leading to the radio stations ground floor, blocking most of my view was the large beacon.

I approached it as I snuffed,

"who needs a radio tower to contact people, just use a truckers radio",

when looking around, the wires of the beacon wrapped the

core of the beacon, flowing down to the stations within it.

When hunting the core of the beacon, I walked towards the beam, seeing a large metal splinter I can use as a dagger, but to get there surely damaged my hands.

I took off my holsters, taking off the holsters clipped to the belt as I wrapped it around my hand, firmly clipping the belt together as my right hand was tightly sealed with the belt, virtually like a fingerless glove but without wrapping it around the fingers, the holster was too big to do that with, it might not be the best protection but it's rusting a little, it will be enough for it to be torn out the support beam.

Firmly I grasped the large shard of metal sticking out the beam, using my left hand to pull on my right as I started to jag it out of the beam, my swollen wrists soon forced me to yank the large shard, causing me to move back slightly.

With the shard facing downwards, I approached the wire as I remarked,

"you may have locked me out, but you have no clue on using this without the beacon",

the largest wire was where it all bunched into, the obvious place the very least, if this was the Eviliance work, it would have been more complicated to find the route.

To ensure I don't get electrocuted, as I remembered what happened last time, I took my holster off, wrapping the end of the shard with the holster, it was mixed of rubber and fabric, it shouldn't pass through it, I hope.

My worries of it being dangerous faded as I started hacking at the wires, seeing the sparks flicker and tap against the tip of the metal shard. The wire was growing weaker as the lights of the beacon started to flicker uncontrollably, only to cut to darkness.

I got up from the floor seeing the cable was cut jagged and ruggedly in half, the sparks were twitching from it from the left side where the power was coming from, well I better not go near it.

I kept the metal shard in my hand, I might need it when I

reach Iren.

Chapter Nineteen
A Self-Made Trap

I limped around the broken beacon, avoiding the twitching and sparking cable.

When hurrying to the fire escape door I noticed it can't be opened from outside, I slammed my hands on the door as I cursed,

"motherfucker; when I get my hands on her she's going to know what to fear in a minute",

with a huff I collected my mind, seeing being angry now won't do anything, perhaps I can find a window below, my wrists were sprained and achy but it can't last forever.

When going past the room I looked over the side, trying to see if I could spot a pipeline, window ledges, anything at all to climb down. When almost feeling like all hope was lost, I spotted a door that was half opened, it was still blocked on the outside, but the seven Undying that could walk around were crowding around it, seeing that they saw a person inside, no doubt it was Iren's doing, but she got clumsy and didn't block the back door, how the hell do I get down there though? When quickly looking to the left and right side of the back of the radio station walls I found a pipeline finally, but it was in bad shape, the plastic and rubber pipe was warped slightly from the heat and cracked from the immense and sudden change of weather.

The brackets were in too bad shape also, the bolts was rusted, it looked as though if I climb down it's going to break on me, but what other choice did I have?

I kept the rugged dagger, if I should even call it one, in my hands as I approached the far right side of the building, letting my body hang down. The blood that previously stained my hands were printing on the rusted metal bars when climbing down, my cuts were triggered as I pushed my self to drop and catch the pipe swiftly. I kept doing that to make this quick, as the dead were attracted to the clanking of the dagger, and the smell of my bloodied hands, I was just lucky that the fence touched the left side of the building, otherwise the hoard would have circled around by now.

When I finally touched the ground, my right foot caused me to lose a little grip, it didn't want to lay flat at all, it made me to have a slant to my stature as I stood there, seeing the dead head towards me.

The door was behind them to their right, as a car was far on my right, perhaps I can draw their attention and run for the door. They limped and walked towards me as I yelled,

"come and get me you freak's!",

I hit on the car with my dagger, causing an echo so loud that no doubt the hoard will find me again, but if I get in the damn building site I don't care. They were trying to attack me as they went around the car, they were finally on the right side of it as I faced the hood of the car, seeing the entrance ahead of me, I could see the glow of hope, it was so close but so far away for me to run to it, my limp didn't help but no matter what, I was going to persist to get the hell inside before this really gets messy.

The crawling Undying could see me, they were slowly making their way to me as I darted for the door.

The seven Undying that was running after me were closing

by the hood, they all tried to attack me before I ran off, fortunately for me they barely just skimmed my arm when I ran.

With force I threw myself at the door, making the furniture go back.

I kept pushing when hearing the growling grow louder, they were breathing on me as I shimmied past the door.

The small room I was in joined to the fire exit ahead of me, and the open stairwell to my far right. Within the centre of both was the reception room no doubt, and to hell to that, I'm not letting the hoard see me, they will break through those doors like it's nothing.

I hurried behind the door as the dead closed in, trying to squeeze their way past the gap of the door to get to me.

With haste, I pushed the sofa that was blocking it, no wonder they could push through but if the doors close and it takes them a while to open the door again it gives me time to find Iren. The large sofa was finally pushed back to shutting the door, causing the dead's arm to be stuck as I let go of it, there should be something else around here to block the door with, give me some more time before this becomes infested with Undying.

I looked around the small rectangular hall, I couldn't see anything but the sofa, the furniture here must have just been that, that's bizarre, perhaps Iren didn't want to go in the reception room, after blocking the doors and windows.

With hesitance I approached the door leading to the reception room, only to open the door, pushing it just slightly so I could see what was inside.

The bright room was virtually empty, the furniture, desks, and computers were walled at the back of the room, it looked previously done, but she moved any furniture that was left in place by the door, the sofa, and reception desk.

There was nothing else to use for the barricade in the back, it should hold out the very least, I went to go and hunt down Iren, sure she was missing me.

I carefully closed the door, hurrying to the staircase to my right, if she's anywhere she would be in the studios trying to find a radio like me, but not for us, just for her.

When climbing up the white and grey steps I observed my surroundings, ensuring there were no traps set, she would have if she had time but it's just for precaution. From the walls on my left and right were broken picture frames of the people that worked here before the first storm, they might have lived but I have my doubts that all of them could live. The frames burned and some were shot, I don't know what happened here but the people who moved in didn't want to see their faces, all I could see in each photo was a man and woman dressed in modern clothing, neat and styled for the pictures, there were a few with a whole team of twelve people, their faces were burned, scratched off or shot, but there was always one person that was shot, a woman, the only clear picture I could see of her was her shot in the face, light blonde hair that was tied back firmly, it looked as though she might have been the first one to die or the last one standing, it's always those who people hate that end up standing on top or falling in a cold grave they dug for themselves.

When passing the last steps I could see another set go to my left ascending to the second floor to then the third floor, the door ahead of me was where I needed to go, it was a large double door painted red, it even had an 'ON AIR' sign on the top left corner of the door.

When going to the door I feared it would be locked but it opened, showing me nothing but darkness as I entered.

The dark office was brightened as I opened the door widely, seeing the curved desks scattered around the room.

The room was a theme of red desks, dark black chairs, and thin grey computers. The walls were half red on the upper half of the wall as the bottom half of the wall was dark black, the lights were turned off, not cut out, which from observation I knew that.

The wall to the left had a radio room, the lights were gleaming under the door, she could be there, or she could be hiding here to distract me.

When walking in I closed the door firmly, going to the right to find the light switch, only to soon find the four switches that lit the four light bars hanging on the ceiling, stretching from the front to the back of the room.

The room lit up brightly, allowing the light to gleam through the closed windows, the shutters were all down meaning she already had the lights on previously.

When carefully walking down the room I called,

"Iren? You think you can just lock me out and not think I would return",

I tried to scare her, make her believe that I was this invincible being, she has no idea what I went through to get here but she is going to be told.

I heard shuffling behind me, along with a click of a handgun as she stated,

"you can stop trying to sabotage the radio station, I already sent the broadcast, I know parasites like you would find a way through, just needed time to send the message",

with a shake of my head I faced her, smirking as I remarked,

"you seriously believe that they are going to trust your story over me? they will come here, see me and when I say that you tried to kill me not only once, but TWICE, they surely won't let you breathe after that",

I had the dagger firmly in my grasp as she persisted,

"you can drop the dagger, I have a gun, you know who is going to win",

she was confident that she could beat me, but I wasn't planning on killing her, I only wanted to teach her a lesson for being a selfish prick, and frankly I feel like that's not an option anymore.

Carefully walking towards her I remarked,

"you're going to shoot me with that? I highly doubt that old rusted pistol can even project anything", she tried to be smart and shoot the laptop behind me, showing off that it works, but she wasted a bullet, I don't know how many more there are, but I can easily get her to waste more.

She firmly approached me, putting the pistol on my head as she stated,

"this will be able to kill you, and kill your friends when they get here, because when I show up on that roof, you're not going to be there, they will land to see where you are, and that mistake will get them killed",

my eyes glared at her, seeing her hand shake as she couldn't bring herself to click the trigger, not because she cared about me, not because it was wrong…it was all because there were no bullets left in it, whoever owned it left a bullet behind, for those who wanted to end their misery of the first storm, and the creatures that lurked behind it.

To throw me off guard she hit my head, causing me to stumble towards the desk, feeling the pounding pain on the left side of my head, feeling the warm blood drip down my face as I looked at her, she ran out of the room, using the chance to get a head start as I ran after her.

I slammed myself against the door as I pushed it open, only to look right when seeing the fire exit door was closing slowly, she was going to the rooftops. My hand stained the walls as I used it to guide me up the stairs, feeling a little woozy from the blow to the head. The blood was trickling past my ear, curving around my chin before pattering against the grey shimmering floor; I could hear her footsteps clutter up the steps, she was in the same state as me in terms of she couldn't run that fast with her damaged ankle, the downfall to that was neither could I.

However, my rage and determination I forced myself to step on my injured foot, feeling the sprain shoot a long heat of pain up my leg, causing me to grunt as I raced up the steps, reaching the top floor as the door slammed behind her, causing me to pull the handle seeing her on the roof.

She looked around the beacon only to face me with fear as she pleaded,

"please, Merider, you don't understand I'm just trying to survive",

with fury I tackled her, putting the dagger to her neck as I barked,

"Survive? You were surviving when I told you what to do, you were supposed to let me in not barricade me out",

I firmly put the knife up, making her quiver and cry as she wallowed,

"I'm sorry okay, I didn't want to die. I DON'T want to die, please, I can let you take charge, I can let you help me",

the sparking cable was closing in by her head to her left, it was waving around like a snake, taking tumbles and rolls, giving me the opportunity to grasp the hand sized cable, moving it not too close to her face, but close enough for her eyes to widened with fear as I warned,

"if you're lying to me, you will get this shoved down your throat, and I won't help you out this time, you will be electrocuted until nothing is left of you but a chard burned human corpse, do you understand?",

her breaths were quick with panic as she Begged,

"please, I won't try anything, I'm just trying to survive, please, please!",

I got off her, throwing the cable aside as I stated,

"surviving isn't about throwing people in the deep end you hear me? you left me outside the fucking gates and you darn nearly killed me, TWICE",

she cowardly sat up, she looked as though she was going to keep on crying until I said things will get better, that she will live forever, and that one day she will stand to the burning earth.

With anger still turning through my eyes she stood up as she apologized,

"I'm sorry",

I cut in,

"don't you dare say you're sorry, that isn't going to work, and frankly enough, sorry never does anything",

I approached her as I said firmly,

"you want to show you're sorry? tell me where you're people are in the store, and then you wait here and tell my friends to land in Base Zero",

she puzzled as she sniffled,

"but you don't want me with your friends, that was what you were stopping me from doing",

I expressed,

"I was stopping you from killing my friends like you were saying. So, here's what you're going to do, when they get here, and they land on this stupid roof, you're going to tell them I'm heading to the superstore to help your friend and to meet us in Base Zero, since it's already too late to warn them off from this place",

she dried her eyes as she questioned,

"why trust me with something like that?",

I approached her as I snapped,

"because if you don't, I know where your loyalties lie and I can never trust you again, you hear that Iren",

she nodded as she bit her lip,

she stated,

"loud and clear, Commander",

when moving back from her, seeing she has had all the warnings I could possibly give her, now it's her time to stop being a coward and face up to her job.

I moved past her as she questioned with a shaky voice,

"how are you going to get down? They are surrounding us",

with thought I looked over the side, seeing the hundred Undying crowding below me at the front of the radio station, they looked as though they were close to breaching the station, perhaps that's not a bad thing, I can get down the fire escape ladders.

Carefully I moved back as I questioned,

"tell me about your people, what's their status in the superstore?",
when going to look back at her, she said swiftly,
"sorry, it's for survival",
she pushed me off the side of the radio tower, making me plummet from three floors and heading in the direction of the undying crowd below me. I grasped the side of the building, trying to find something to grasp before making an impact on the crowd of the dead.

I could feel the pressure of my head bruise, followed by my chest and stomach, winding myself as the dead were lurking around me, I closed my eyes when seeing their heads crowd, only to catch a glance of green impaling Iren.

She was stuck on the radio station rails, it was as if the green glow was made of a shard of metal, glowing from the roof, and hanging her like a decoration, exposing her for what she did.

The glow was familiar, but soon was confirmed when the dead were mowed down, piling on me as my body was cushioned by the ones I crushed, their heads made an impact with the ground when falling on them, luckily for me, I wasn't bitten, but it wouldn't have mattered anyway, we're all infected with the contact of the ash-fall and bites of the dead.

I heard Narla as her voice called,
"Merider?! Where are you?!",
Azella stated, "
I saw her over there, just glad Qorin told us about this idiocy",
the footsteps approached me.

As I tried to move, my back was broken, no doubt, it felt as though I was paralysed.

The bodies were taken off me, allowing me the freedom to breathe as they piled the body's on the left.

Neon was fighting off the rest of the dead as Narla approached me, she still had an injured foot, but she could walk on it at least, whatever Neon did, he made it just a little bit more bearable for her to walk on.

Azella crouched down as she questioned,

"can you move? That was a hell of a fall, Neon tried to get there faster, but he could only kill the woman who did that",

Narla looked around as Neon stated,

"the dead are dealt with, for now, but with the gunshots and stuff, I don't think we will be alone for long",

I felt a warm sensation at the back of my head, I think I hit it to a deep wound, it made me feel dizzy as Neon was glowing with a green aura, his hands were engulfed in green serum, very much like the blue serum's effect. He walked to my feet as he questioned,

"what's wrong? Has she broken something?",

Azella examined me as she urged,

"Neon, you need to heal her, now! I don't care what it takes, you need to get her in one piece",

his voice was muffling as he explained,

"Azella, if I do that I'll-",

she cut in,

"I don't care what happens to you. If Merider dies, the Commander will come for us, and we will be reverted back to the old way, I can't let that happen again, I risked enough trying to find you, the least you can do is revive her before the world is doomed",

he walked around her, going to my head as Narla refused,

"you can't, he will die if he does this. Maybe we can partially heal her?",

Neon expressed,

"Narla, I don't want to do this either, but I know I have to. This was never me, the power I harnessed was a project, this is part of my end, what I have in me, it will be in Merider, that's the only ways she can survive if she has my powers",

my words were trying to tell him no, but it was too late, he already had his hands on the sides of my head, making my eyes grow tired as he hushed,

"I know, Commander, I know",

he knew what I wanted, this wasn't it, to be infected again, I didn't want this.

Not being given a choice to die, he made my body go into a sleeping state, letting me see nothing but darkness.

The things I could feel, the bones that snapped in place, it was painful, yet the serum made it seem painless.

The glow shone through my veins, I could feel the serum filter its way from head to toe. The skin was healing, the flesh was sewing back together, as the blood was reproducing within me, I could feel everything, unlike the blue serum that put me into a hallucinogenic state, this serum was leaving me in the dark, and shrouded unconscious state, allowing me to feel every part of the healing process, yet like I said before, it didn't hurt, but it sounded as though it was painful and I knew it would have been.

Even though I couldn't move, I could feel myself being carried by two people, they had my arms around their necks, pulling me to a vehicle from the sounds of it, and they weren't alone. I could hear a rumbling sound of an engine, an aircraft, perhaps it was Aries with Diego, Dusty, and Elria...whoever she's with, she ensured to pick the right people, I know that for certain, I hope Azella and Narla stick around, I don't want to have to go hunting for them again.

They placed me in a car, letting me lay upon the floor as Narla stated,

"I'll stay here with Merider, you go and see what that Chinook is about, they don't seem to be wanting to hunt us, so perhaps Merider was trying to contact them",

Azella left as she stated,

"just keep watch of her, and if the people attack, get the group to fight back",

I heard Qorin's voice as he got on the vehicle, from the feel of the air, I think I was in an open truck I couldn't be sure, but I heard him sit next to me on my left as he questioned,

"is she going to be okay?",

Narla explained,

"Neon put her in the unconscious state, and gave her his powers. Oh, and he's dead by the way, if you even cared about him",

he argued,

"you and him went under the radar, he had it coming, but you're right, I don't care",

she remarked once again,

"yeah, I see that, Qorin, I don't think Merider knows who she should be friends with. You out of all people in the world should have been killed by her, yet I see she never got the chance to",

Xharlot cut in,

"alright, pack it in, if she's unconscious like you said, she will be hearing all of this, can we just stop blaming people and accept the fact Neon did this voluntarily, don't let his death be put to waste, he wouldn't want that, you know that Narla",

she was speaking to Qorin as she persisted,

"we didn't come out here just for the sake of Merider either, we came to be sure she did the job, and we saved people on the way, so can you BOTH just pack it in",

she got on the truck, moving herself to the opposite side of Qorin.

He was worried I understood, but what he said about Neon, that wasn't right.

Narla is right about the fact he would be the type I would kill, but he changed, and I need to make him see that he is my friend, not my enemy.

Chapter Twenty
The Sacrifice

My unconscious state was wearing off as I could feel myself be laid within a bed, my eyes opened when seeing that for certain, the power was still going strong, the cell room was lit brightly as I was tucked in bed.

When sitting upright I could feel my whole body, it was refreshed and even with my blood-stained clothes my face was cleaned, I brushed my hand down the left side of my face, feeling the blood wasn't painted on my face anymore, it was cleaned by someone.

I took off the quilt sheet when feeling like I didn't need to rest anymore, I don't know how long I've been out for, but I don't want to rest anymore, we're already behind and worst of all people blame me for Neon's death, better make up for it.

As I stood firmly on the floor, Xharlot walked in, she had a damp cloth inside of a wooden crafted bowl, she paused as we were face to face, almost colliding with each other as I was eager to leave this place.

I backed away letting her in the room as she questioned,

"you look better than you did yesterday, do you feel any different?",

with a puzzled look I questioned,

"what the hell happened last night, all I remember was me being shoved off a building by Iren", she wondered,

"that woman was Iren? Oh right, well Neon killed her; we saw you get thrown off it and we took down the hoard with the gear that Karmin had, she has armoured vehicles, a lot of guns, we wiped out all the dead in the area",

she put the bowl down on the bedside as she continued,

"Neon healed you and he died from giving you his powers, used everything he had, you were in bad shape",

I sat on the bedside as I sighed,

"so what do the team think about the situation then?",

Xharlot looked hesitant only to sit by me as I pressured,

"just tell me, Xharlot, what have they been saying?",

she explained firmly,

"Qorin and Narla have had a fall out, which I'm certain you know what he said. But to be honest, she's not wrong about him being the type of person you would kill though",

I didn't want people to fall out over this.

With stress, I said infuriated,

"I didn't ask for him to save me, in fact, it felt as though I was ready to die anyway. I mean why is it that in any situation I have to be the priority",

Xharlot said softly,

"Merider",

she looked sorrowful for me which was odd of her to do as I cut in,

"don't even try to comfort me, you know it's true. Qorin wants me alive no matter what, I know he likes me and I think I feel the same to him, but it won't work, we have our jobs to do, the world is relying on me, and worst of all with every death of a friend people
blame me, since the very beginning",

Xharlot didn't know what to say, she instead questioned,

"the beginning? That's an exaggeration much",

seeing as she didn't know I told in-depth,

"it's true. When I landed here two, to probably three years ago now, I met the one I was talking to in space, her name was Karli. I went to the ground because I was speaking with a lander, the earth people as we called them. Next thing I knew I met this woman called Macey, turns out it was her sister and things were looking good. I hung around with them, went on searching and soon met with the Eviliance, then that was when things went downhill",

Xharlot looked intrigued as she encouraged,
"what happened next?",
with a sigh, my words continued,
"The Eviliance wanted me, as they saw me as some gold mine and a superior figure to them. In the end, we moved out the shack as they burned it. We all got out, and I told them about a petrol station not far from us, we camped out there, and an attack of the Undying happened. I got bitten but cured after the whole ordeal when we all split up. The Eviliance wanted me in return for Mrs.Weathers, their mother. Macey came up with the idea to trade me in, and I went with it to make things right for ruining their shack, and next thing I knew Karli had to kill her own mother because we tried to ambush them first, I dragged her out, and honestly, I can't even finish that story…",

I looked to her as I skipped,,
"after that event Macey turned on me, took their little sister and left Karli and I. Then even after all of that, Karli turned on me",

Xharlot looked sorry for me, she even was stuck on what to say, but she could always find the words in the end.
She expressed,
"that wasn't your fault, if anything Macey should have blamed her sister for killing their mom. Look, Merider, I know this isn't what you wanted, but it was what Neon wanted, he wouldn't have sacrificed himself if he didn't want you to live on. Besides the point, you shouldn't be thinking that it's all going to be your fault and everyone will hate you

for it, they aren't like Macey, and frankly I feel like she just needed someone to hate, and you were the perfect fit",

she stood up as she persisted,

"look, with you and Qorin, the way he is around you, it's not fair for him to take it out on people, perhaps you can talk to him about it, he's with Rhax and Marcella in the HQ",

I got up as I wondered,

"Xharlot, wait", before she was going to leave the room, something about her was strange, she was nice to me, she was wanting to talk to me, unlike before.

As she turned to me I questioned,

"why now? Why care for me then ask about how I'm doing, what my worries are?",

she smirked as she remarked,

"sounds like you never had anyone care about you",

she explained shortly,

"There's something about everyone you know. Qorin, Marcella, Rhax and Kamic, they won't ask how you are because they know you don't want to be asked, but people like me, like Sevis, they will want to worry. Abby was worried, even Aries was worried and we all knew you were fine, we just didn't see you open your eyes",

she soon remembered something whilst on the topic of my team as

she added,

"oh and I forgot to mention, the powers are temporary, we've examined you and it looks as though the power rejects your body, it won't flush out, it will just go out with every breath you take. So from what Kamic and Rhax have been saying it lasts around a week perhaps a little more if it flushes out through your lungs",

she smiled to me slightly as she wondered,

"did you want to join me? I can take you to Qorin at least, I have jobs to do in the HQ anyways, but I think it's good for both you and him if you talk, he hides his feelings well, and

so do you, probably why you were made for each other",
I rolled my eyes as I approached her as I stated,
"we weren't made for each other, it's just, I don't know how
to explain it, when I'm around him I feel",
she answered,
"safe?",
she took the words from my mouth, perhaps it's a phase and
it will blow over, but either way, I do need to have to talk
with him about yesterday night, he was acting off, it didn't
look fair for Narla.
We walked out of the prison ward, she walked to my left as
we proceeded to the reception room as I expressed,
"it's not like I'm falling for him but he just makes me feel
safe",
I glanced at her as I expanded,
"but that's what a guard does, makes you feel safe",
she shrugged as she stated,
"Mortis made me feel the same, but when he died, it felt like
my world crumbled, especially how he died. I was told by
Rhax, I didn't want him to give me the half details",
I looked to her as I realised,
"I'm sorry for your loss I can't believe I haven't even taken
note of my team members",
I rubbed my forehead as I said angrily at myself,
"I've been so hooked on trying to be this good guy, this
warrior, this saviour and I've not taken note of the people
around me, the ones that care about me",
we left the reception room, walking out into the bright sunny
campsite, the sun was blazing down upon us at the bright
blue sky was flooding over the skies, not a single cloud to be
seen.
We stood for a moment as Xharlot pointed,
"you do what a leader does, find things to occupy yourself
that will not only benefit you and the team, but all these
people. You made this happen, Merider, and I don't think
people remind you enough that no matter who hates you,

246

what happens, whatever it is that you face",
she glanced to me as she continued,
"you're not alone, you won't be alone, and if I have to remind you every day, so be it",
she smirked as she walked with me, we were at a strolling pace so I could collect my thoughts, figure out what I was going to say to Qorin, and most of all what our next plan of action is, I can't let my thoughts down, but I can build things up as I did earlier, I know it's frustrating, but I can get through this, I can build myself up, I can't keep knocking myself down with every situation that's out of my control, Neon was a good man and I'm thankful he saved me, revived me if that's the right term.
As we walked I joked,
"so when were you such a counsellor?",
she laughed before she stated,
"well I may show myself as this arrogant asshat but I know when someone needs advice and when to give it to them, you just needed reminding that you're not to blame for this, for any of this, you are the cause of the campsite being freed from Free Liberty, the old one anyway",
upon recalling about Aries and the Chinook, I changed topic,
"I know this is out of context but who showed up with Aries? What happened to them?",
she explained,
"they landed in the field, they saw that following us in the Chinook would attract the dead with their lights and sound, so they hitched a ride with us on the heavy artillery truck",
she looked to me as she went on,
"Elria, Deago, and Plasma. They said they went for the sake of Saria, but I think you know that Elria was here for you",
she smirked as she questioned,
"you get a lot of crushes no doubt?",
I raised an eyebrow as she wondered,
"no doubt? Sounds as though you think it's not a surprise that people have an interest in me, I think it's plain weird, I

always attract the dead",
she remarked,
"well they don't look dead to me, not yet anyway",
she analysed,
"you know I think I know what your problem is",
problem? Oh boy, which I thought would be fun to hear
someone else needing to analyse me and tell me what is
wrong with me, I'm fine.
With a slight sigh, I encouraged,
"okay fine tell me then, tell something I don't know about
myself",
she smiled as she explained shortly,
"you don't want to fall in love, do you?",
I looked to her as we stopped as she went on,
"you say you don't know how to feel with Qorin, I think you
already know and whatever is going on between you and
Elria, that's because you push her away, like you do with
Qorin",
with wonder I stated,
"so, you think because I don't want people to like me in that
way, that I don't want to be in that way",
she nodded only to continue walking with me as she
remarked,
"you're like me in some way, don't care if they like me back
I just pushed them away, and you know with Mortis, I liked
him, well right term I loved him but it's too late to say that
now, but yeah, I regret not telling him about what I felt",
not wanting to talk on the matter I persisted,
"fine, so I don't want to be in that way then, but it's not
forever don't get me wrong on that, but it's after this mess is
over",
we stopped outside the HQ doors as she wondered,
"and when will that be?",
she looked smug with herself, seeing she had a point, when
will this mess be over? It goes on, and on, and on it doesn't
seem to end and every time I hit a bump I avoid it again, not

wanting to lie the same fate again.

She walked in as she departed,

"tell him when you're ready, better not say 'until this mess is over' though, it never is",

she walked inside, heading to the elevator to the far right, going to the penthouse of Karmin's, or just the luxury room in general.

When watching her walk away, I thought to myself, if she could read me so easily I must be like a book to other people; they can see through me, perhaps if they aren't observant they won't think anything of me, but if she could tell me all of this just by a few words and how I act, I must be like a museum, everyone knows what I'm doing…what I act like, it's strange to think that all this time of be doing what I was doing, people knew how to approach me, unless they had important things for me or wanted to warp my mind like Iren, they needed to ask for my help and all my attention was on them.

Before heading into the HQ I saw Abby, she was calling my name as Byzer was behind her, they were running over to me as I turned to face them, seeing them run past the burned-out bonfire.

Without even thinking I hugged Abby as she was going to hug me, I didn't want to hug her, my head was telling me all these things, not to want to fall into the trap of having another child under my wing, but I couldn't help it, I hugged her seeing she was nearly in tears of joy as she worried,

"where were you? Sevis told us how you snuck off, most likely because Qorin was on the verge of beating it out of him",

Byzer stood behind her as I could see him, he confirmed,

"it was true, nearly got knocked out by Sevis",

Abby let go first as I stepped back as I questioned,

"tell me what happened when I left? What's this about Qorin and Sevis",

Byzer stood to her left as he explained,

"we were sleeping, and all of a sudden we heard yelling", Abby added,

"we went out of our prison cells and saw Sevis was being moved outside by Qorin, he was saying something about why didn't he tell him before, and that it was his fault if you die", Byzer went on,

"yeah and it got really nasty as Sevis was beating up Qorin, Qorin was returning the hits twice as hard, but Marcella, My mother, and Rhax broke up the fight",

I'm glad they told me the truth, gives me more to bring up with Qorin, I can't believe he was going alpha with Sevis, why the hell is he being like this?

I know he might like me but why get protective over me, let's face it if Qorin didn't tell the team to get me I would have died last night, if it wasn't for me being a pushover and thinking I could save a stranger, but then again, they saved people last night also, who were Iren's people?

With that in mind, I questioned,

"Abby, they were talking about people yesterday, did the team return with anyone?",

Abby shook her head before she explained,

"well they had a few people, around five, but I haven't seen them since they arrived here the last place I saw them go was in the HQ behind you, apart from that I don't know",

without thinking yet again I ruffled her hair as I reassured,

"don't sweat about it, off with you, I need to talk to Qorin about his behaviour last night",

Abby smiled as I ruffled her hair a little,something wasn't quite right, was I , accepting myself? Was this how it felt to change? To evolve myself into a better person.

Before leaving Abby, she had one last thing to add, she stopped,

"wait, Merider, I thought to tell you before you wondered why I'm gone so long, and in case you didn't know where I'm going to be all day",

I heard her out as I encouraged,

"go on",

she expanded,

"I was going to make that tree a memorial tree, not just for my dad, but for the people that died in the siege, and those who died in this camp. Byzer and I were going to go around the campsite, get some names",

with a smile I stated,

"well, be certain to ask respectfully, if they are anything like me I won't want people to pry, but you're a kid, you get away with it",

I nudged her arm as she smiled stupidly, she looked a lot better since yesterday, I think this memorial tree is going to do her some good.

As I watched them walk away I wonder to myself if this was natural, me…smiling for knowing that Abby was okay. I shook off the thought as I kept myself serious, only to turn around and walk into the HQ, seeing that Qorin had beaten me to it as he descended from the luxury room.

Within the empty and echoing room Qorin asked,

"Merider, Xharlot said you wanted to see me?",

he was pulling the 'like nothing ever happened' card, I know he was raging, and angry but he was mostly worried about me and I could see that, I couldn't have it I don't want him to end up like the rest of my failed relationships, they all died, ended up being dead and most of all it was all my fault, every time, it was going to be and always will be my fault and I know Xharlot was right at parts but I know now that I'm not ready to be with someone, I don't want to settle and I think that was what I've been hiding the whole time, no wonder people get mixed signals from me, I don't make it easy for them to figure out what I want.

With firmness I stated,

"don't play that game with me Qorin I know what you did to Sevis yesterday",

he defended,

"he told us you left an hour ago, he let you go out there and you darn near got killed out there, if it wasn't for me you wouldn't be here",

I agreed,

"and I know that but you didn't need to ruff him up, you got me help and that's all you needed to do, not ruff him up, get mad at him, blame him for my death if I did die out there, but you know something I was lucky Neon sacrificed himself for me",

he didn't look satisfied as I defended,

"no, don't you even dare get mad about that, it's true and you know that its true, he saved me you told the team to get me and they did, I went there solely because the team over the wall, OUR team were going to come for us and they were going to be stuck here, which they are, if they go over the wall again they will attract more of the dead to the wall, rising our risks",

he didn't look satisfied as he challenged,

"and what's that supposed to mean? Where are you going with this?",

I cut in,

"I'm saying you need to stop protecting me, when I want to take a risk you need to let me go, I don't care if I die if I want people to help me I will let them, but not the way you helped me yesterday, I don't mind you trying to help me and send me a team, but when you beat up your own member, and the team has to split it up then it's not good is it",

he looked guilty, he looked as though he knew what he did was wrong but then again didn't seem to regret it which was the worst part.

He questioned,

"okay so what do you want me to do then?",

I listed,

"don't start fights, if you protect me don't try and kill our own members",

he looked angrier and angrier until I said softly,

"the last thing I need is for you not to get killed, you acting

252

as you did will get you killed, it will disrupt our team work, and most of all split us apart, and if that happens I can't forgive myself for it, and I know you won't be able to do the same for yourself",

the debate was heated but I tried to make sure at the end of it all he didn't feel like the bad guy, I cant tell someone off for caring for me, but I can tell them how to do it right if they plan on staying by my side, these people know how I work but I think Qorin was in it for himself, he wanted to prove himself, he has nothing to prove he is part of the team and he shouldn't fell the need to compete with anyone, especially not over me.

He said warmly,

"Merider, I just",

he paused as I finished,

"love me? yeah I know you do",

he looked surprised as I stated,

"I can't...Qorin, I can't be with anyone and I know it hurts but",

he cut in,

"all you needed to know was that I love you, that's it, I don't expect you to want me there and then",

we were both shocked that all this tension for him to just get something off his chest, to create this smooth slate, all this time we've both just been on the wrong roads and decide not to talk personally, but it only takes a few minutes.

To really get things off your chest it only takes a few minutes and ends in harmony or unfinished, either way, I'm glad he and I are on the same page now, I just hope this means he won't go alpha on me again...it gets annoying when everything is because of me, and happens for me. I never asked for it, it happens and I suck it up, and I will this time when it happens.

Qorin changed the topic as he glanced back, he questioned,

"did you want to go up? Aries is up there too, she's worried sick", we approached the elevator to the far right side of the room, going to the luxury room as I stated,

"well I'm fine now, that's all that matters, and for respect of Neon, we won't speak of what happened that night, not the negatives, not the fights, let's just remember the sacrifice that he made to keep me here, because for a raider and for a gang leader he cared for humanity, he just followed the wrong path",

I glanced to Qorin, reminding him that he wasn't what he was before, and that he should be proud of how far he's come, how he stuck by me and that I just wanted him to know his past is gone.

The future starts now.

Chapter Twenty-one
Liberty in Pieces

When meeting with the main floor the door was firmly shut, I could hear Aries as she argued,
"Xharlot, we need to do something",
she explained,
"Aries, I can't just make up solutions for this, we all need to be here, Merider should be up here soon, we just need to wait",
upon opening the door to the luxury room I could see who was here.

Aries was sat on the left side of the table, facing opposite the table to Xharlot, Rhax and Marcella, they were looking at a map that was previously drawn by someone. To Aries's left, Elria and Deago were sat upon the seats, they were talking with one another only to soon spot Fuel, she was stood by the table where the blueprints were that Rhax was looking at.

They looked up seeing me enter as I remarked,
"so I'm alive for another problem to solve, what is it?",
Aries smiled at me as she got off the chair, she looked as though she was going to hug me but she stopped, she took note of the others watching us as she changed her hug to a

pat on the side of my arm as she said warmly,

"Glad you're alright",

I smirked as I stated,

"well the sacrifice was great for it, and I'd rather not be reminded",

I tried to say it nicely, so Aries didn't feel offended, or felt as though I didn't miss her, I did, but it was just getting repetitive.

I approached the table as I questioned,

"Is this about the Commander of the Dead Zone",

Elria explained,

"well, from what Xharlot says I don't know if they're even his ones",

with a frown I puzzled,

"what do you mean?",

I leaned upon the table as Fuel projected an image on the centre of the table, allowing us to see this large domed building.

The blue hologram shimmered the image, allowing us to see the buildings structure and the surrounding around it; the head of the statue of liberty was by the entrance of the building facing me, it was a curved large arched doorway, it looked to be a picture image of it, but 3D printed, how did she get this?

And how could she project such an image? When looking at it, Fuel explained,

"Plasma had a camera installed in me to be able to project images from a drone, we did a full rotary image of the place, but from what I've seen it's abandoned, watch",

she played the image, allowing the drone to hover around the building, giving me a full view of the place, the trees surrounding it were barely even breathing, they were falling apart, and worst of all the drone kept glitching, causing the images to spike in places as I questioned,

"why does it glitch at that point?",

the image was clear when going near the door, but at the

back, there was something there that caused it to glitch, perhaps the place is occupied, how else is the power spreading so far.

Elria pointed,

"say didn't Alis tell us about the statue being built there?",

I looked around as Alis came out of the second room, the one I couldn't enter a few days ago, she came out with her bulletproof vest on, white rolled-up jumper along with dark grey combat trousers, her dark black combat boots thumped against the floor as she moved her holster a little, arranging it as she approached, she said,

"they might have not built it, after all, we were told they were given the statue of liberty to be our truce, seems like it worked but because of the wall, not the truce gift",

she stood to my right as she looked to the map Fuel projected, she wondered,

"Is this legit the big city? It looks isolated",

upon looking at it I had a theory in mind as I wondered,

"the statue is made of copper isn't it?",

Alis looked to me as I expanded,

"perhaps the place isn't isolated, what if the person using this place had melted the statue, piece by piece",

Aries was catching on as she wondered,

"wait but why would they take it down? Wasn't it a part of the American history? Something that marked its land, why would they destroy a relic like that",

my eyes wondered over the table, seeing Sevis with this woman, she was bizarre looking but perhaps could be one of the witch doctors, after all, he seems to know her quite well. Horneck was by his left, they were quiet, probably why I didn't notice them the first time, but the witch doctor had an input, she might know the answer, but I wanted people to think the same as me, so they are on the same page as I was.

The woman turned around along with Sevis and Horneck, they were starting with her as they approached the table opposite me, she had her dark black hair braided back, attached with feathers on the edges as she had golden and bronze beads at the end also, the braids were tied back with a firm rugged light brown thick hairband.

Her skin was smooth and dark as the night, entrancing light blue eyes and deep red lips as she painted them. She wore a light brown thin shirt, it hung over her right shoulder as it missed her left, the shirt acted much like a dress as it stretched over her left side of her left thigh as her right was almost virtually exposed. She wore a rugged red shirt made of feathers, long feathers that reach just above her knees, it was half dyed so the top half was red as the bottom half was golden yellow, it was vibrant and intricately made. She had a silver band bracelet tightly on her left arm, a golden one under it then finally another silver one below that, it was spaced out and looked very modern for a tribal look.

Her hands were wrapped with thorn looking gloves, they had gaps in between most of the vines, they also ended before the fingers like fingerless gloves if I'm correct.

The vines wrapped up to her lower arm, just below her elbow, giving her that final touch of the earthy feeling as she pointed to the map with her golden painted nails, they were matt and not too shiny, making it look like they were her natural nail colour.

She was pointing to the statue of liberty as she stated in her smooth voice,

"they wish not to respect their relic, they want it to be gone and they will use it for power",

I agreed,

"precisely, with the power of the statue they have all the copper they need to build something with it",

Alis wondered,

"if that's true, how can one person melt something so large?",

Marcella pieced,

"he had twenty years to do it, think about it whoever this Commander is they wanted to destroy the earth since the start, they wanted to take it piece by piece, and if they had planned to harvest the copper like that, then no doubt they are dedicated for the next plan of action no doubt",

with that in mind Fuel turned the projection off as she explained,

"the person who wants that much conductors will be wanting it to do something, a project no doubt, whatever they are building they need power, lots of it why else would they allow other cities to be here, they want power and they want people in their name, and since we have taken then them they will get their project in motion",

the question was, what is the project? All this for one thing, what have they been using the copper for? Guess we're going to have to find out when we take them down.

Sevis expressed,

"we must go to the Commander of the Dead Zone before the project gets a chance to run. We won't need cars, just our feet, we will attract less attention",

with a problem in that I added,

"but we can't leave the city without a leader, we need at least tow people over watching the city",

the witch doctor stated,

"Horneck and I shall take the job, after all a witchdoctor like myself knows how to calm and ease peoples minds, and with his strength we can tame the city when you leave for your journey, today",

Xharlot cut in,

"woah wait, we never said anything about leaving today",

Sevis expressed,

"listen to Fortrela, she knows what she's talking about",

Fortrela, the witchdoctor, continued,

"the sun rises high and the dead will see you, but you can see them and it will make things much easier for you to get there, by foot it will take days, by vehicle it will take mere hours, whatever you decide it must be a quiet route, as the dead don't wait and you know that",

she was right about us needing to go in the sun rise but why now? I didn't understand the urgency, but she believed we should go when we can, and I don't see why we shouldn't, this Commander has a large plan in mind and we haven't got a clue on what the person is playing.

With firmness Rhax stated,

"if we are going we have to be prepared, we can't return without knowing for certain that the dome is empty",

he stood up as he continued,

"Marcella, Deago, and I will meet with Kamic in the armoury, the gear will be piled up outside waiting for you guys, we need to have everyone geared up",

when watching Deago, Rhax and Marcella leave, my attention turned to Alis as I questioned,

"who else is coming?",

she looked to team as she stated,

"Xharlot, Aries and Fuel are coming without a question, Qorin too",

we looked to Sevis as he added,

"I shall come also, whatever you go through, I go through too, Commander. Like I said before, I am your guard and so is Horneck, whenever you're ready I will be too",

I nodded firmly and briefly, seeing the team was settled, even if Fortrela and Horneck are leading on their own, the camp seems to trust them both, and I don't think anyone would go against them, anyone apart from those saved by the team last night.

Qorin joined me to my right as Aries stated,

"I will get Fuel and I downstairs. Xharlot, are you coming?",

she got up from the set as she agreed,

"yeah, I need to make a few preparations before the mission, let's hope we all make it back",

Aries persisted,

"no we are going to make it back",

Fuel agreed,

"yes we have faith in ourselves",

they left the room, leaving me with Horneck, Fortrela, Alis

and Qorin.

With thought about the survivors last night, I questioned, "who were the people saved yesterday?",

Qorin informed,

"it was a few guards from this place, to be honest, they were glad to see a stabilised city, they said Iren was plotting to take the city and had this genius plan on being a victim, well you already know what she did",

I don't know if I trust these people, from what I know now is that they will say anything to be alive.

With persistence I stated,

"keep an eye on them, if they were with Iren no doubt they would have plans of their own",

Horneck reassured,

"if they plan anything they will be killed, no mercy unless proven innocent",

I nodded as I joked,

"yeah perhaps try not to kill them, be sure to prove them guilty before killing them, at least",

he smirked as I reassured,

"sure thing Commander, whatever you say goes",

Fortrela moved around the table with Horneck, moving to my left as she questioned,

"Merider you still have the necklace I have gifted you?",

I looked to my chest, pulling the intricate necklace from under my shirt as I reassured,

"it's still with me",

she smiled as she wondered,

"were you told about the meaning of it?",

recalling what Sevis said I ensured,

"Sevis told me about it being the god of the moon, the god of healing; Khonsu",

she nodded briefly, she expanded,

"that necklace is given to all of the good witches, the amulet of Ra is given to the most evillest witches",

she untucked Ra's necklace from her shirt, it was very much

like mine but instead of it being white coloured within the inside it was a fiery orange.

She rubbed it as she stated,

"this one belonged to my mother, the one you have belonged to my father, they claimed she was evil but he knew she was far from it. She had the heart of Khonsu but this showed up on her doorstep when passing the witchdoctors trials, everyone went through it",

she went on,

"they put you in a test to heal a corpse, my mother resurrected one, claiming her evil when they gave her a dead man, those who couldn't resurrect a dead man were good, the ones that healed a living injured man lived, those who healed them with side effects were evil, but even so, my mother was persistent on getting better, she made potions to heal and sold them to the village, people claimed she show them the light like the god of Ra, but no matter what, she was good",

she smiled to me as she finished,

"all I'm saying that even with these it doesn't change you, it just adds to your story, be sure to keep the necklace with you at all times, it heals you, shows you who you are and be certain of the choices you will make in the dome, you will be challenged I can see",

Alis smiled as she wondered,

"you must have had a past on you",

Fortrela stated,

"I do and if you want to know you will have to return, use that as a motive if you must, after all we never like questions unanswered",

she winked at me, seeing she knows how I didn't like questions not answered.

She moved with Horneck to the back of the room as she stated,

"you better get off on your journey strong ones, I see the ending and it won't be sweet with a late arrival, I can assure you",

Qorin looked at me as he whispered,

"better get going, she creeps me out",

he smirked to me as we turned to the door, leaving the room letting Horneck and Fortrela go over and plan things for when we leave the city.

We entered the elevator, heading to the lower floor as we faced to the door behind us, seeing the walls pass us as we went over a few things, Alis stated,

"when we get out there we use only melee, that's until we meet the Commander that is, we don't bother with negotiation we just knock his lights out and end it",

with the thought of the commander, I questioned,

"what if the Commander is like Neon? No doubt Narla and Azella would want to join",

Qorin informed,

"Narla and Azella are staying here under my rules, I stated that they are needed here not out there, besides they keep wondering off",

Alis theorised,

"perhaps they are searching for something, where are they now?",

he sighed seeing where this was leading as he stated,

"by the cafeteria, they said they were on break since the morning, no doubt they are having a blast",

the elevator opened, allowing us to walk out the HQ as I stated,

"you guys go and get prepared, I will go and talk to Azella and Narla, it's not going to be a long debate it's just to see what they know",

they kept with me as we went to the prison ward, seeing Rhax, Marcella, Fuel, Aries, Xharlot and Kamic gearing up outside, they had a pile of armour, a pile of weapons and a few rucksacks of supplies, they weren't joking about gearing up, and to be honest the way I've dealt with things I no doubt need to gear up myself when I get the chance.

Alis stated,

"well don't be too long, the only thing I can ask you to ask them is about Neon and his powers, if you know that then you might know the Commander a bit more, and if they know about the Commander they can tell us more about the person, we're on a thin line here",

they went left, join the team as they geared up, they watched me walk past as Kamic asked Qorin,

"where's she going?",

he explained in the background,

"gaining some more information on the Commander that we're going to face off with, we might not get anything at all but it's worth a shot",

when entering the prison ward Narla could be heard laughing with Azella as they were with the guards they saved yesterday, they seemed to be having a blast...like Qorin said earlier; when approaching the room Azella glanced to me as she said shortly,

"hold on, I'll finish about the one about the bronze crown in a second",

she got up the table, approaching me as she questioned,

"how are you? Don't know if you remember much about yesterday",

I said briefly,

"I know what happened",

with firmness I questioned,

"I need to ask you about the Commander of the dead zone", she didn't want to tell me about it but she saw the determination in my eyes, I wasn't going to leave without some sort of answer to this question, I needed to know something about the Commander, anything that can help me, and if she can't tell me that she can tell me about Neon, or Narla can if she knows little about it.

She stated,

"look I can only tell you what I know, he deals things in the shadows, sends letters, scrolls, or even projects himself if need be", with a puzzled look I wondered,

"projects himself? Like a hologram",

she shook her head shortly, seeing she was going to need to explain it in a way where it made sense, you can't project yourself with a hologram without light, so how can he show himself? She went on,

"he has this power where he can show himself without needing to leave the dome. I see him as a man with short brown hair, a bit toned up, dressed much like an Eviliance member with a white jumper, black bullet proof vest, that style. Narla said he saw the Commander as a woman with skin like sand, hair like a goddess, calls herself Medusa",

my eyes widened as I recalled,

"hold on a second, Medusa? I saw Medusa when I was near to death in Zion City",

she looked even more worried as she questioned,

"well what did she say to you?",

with thought I recalled further,

"something about the bones of Medusa and that they were going to be destroyed by the priestess, it was hazy but she was very convincing at what she said",

Azella looked concerned, she seemed to be in thought about the situation too, why does the person project himself as man and woman? Why project himself differently to other eyes but project themselves the same to my eyes, why to show me Medusa, like with Narla, perhaps she can answer that for herself.

Narla walked over as she questioned,

"you both seem to be glancing at me, what is it?",

Azella answered,

"Merider, said she saw Medusa, as you did",

she looked confused as she questioned,

"Is that true, Merider? But how, how did you see her?",

I explained shortly,

"look, I saw her when I was in Zion City after I got stabbed, she warned me about the priestess saying the bones are going to be destroyed in the fire, it's hazy",

I soon added,

"I can't put my finger on it though but I feel like I was seeing a different person, the real Medusa or something because Wyet changed, she was there and went into Wyet or the priestess changed her",

Azella reassured,

"look whatever happened there it sounds like you saw the Commander, made the priestess see her and changed Wyet, he might have been playing all of us, he or she I don't know, the Commander is clearly trying to cover up who he or she really is, because in the end they knows that people will turn on them, and that's what's going to happen, isn't it?",

seeing as they didn't know the plan and I had a little bit more time to explain I informed,

"we are, virtually the whole team is going. Sevis, Qorin, Kamic, Alis, Rhax, Marcella, my team over the wall, it's going to be a fight we will remember that's for sure",

Azella smirked as she stated,

"well for one thing be sure you guys return, not only do we have him to deal with but I've been worried about the dormant bomb this whole time, understandably people like to fight, I know I surely love it, but when I went missing, looking for Narla and Neon, I was searching for the bomb too, and I found it, but I can't disarm it alone",

she looked worried about it, she feared it and I understood, she lived on this side of the world long enough to know what the bombs did to the world, I never knew, my younger self was on the moon at the point of the bombs dropping, the world was surely selfish back then.

With shortness of time I ensured,

"once this mess is over we can deal with the bomb, we have the dead to exterminate also but I think it can wait, besides I'm sure we can figure this out",

Narla agreed,

"it's worth a try, but I don't see it ending without it being activated",

Azella was hopeful as she said with confidence,

"we won't need to activate it, Merider will have a solution to it, she always has for something",

as she walked away she said shortly,

"good luck out there, come back in one piece you can't be revived twice",

yeah, thanks of reminding me about that Azella, it felt horrible what I did, I didn't want Neon to sacrifice himself, but what's done is done and no matter how guilty I feel it won't help, I'm just going to have to get myself out of the loop, as I've always done.

Narla glanced to her only to face me as she stated,

"I know how she feels, wanting something to not happen but it does",

she was most likely talking about Neon as she persisted,

"but please if you have a solution that doesn't involve disarming it then tell her first, don't lie, don't try to get her hopes up",

she patted my arm only to soon hug me as she said softly, "don't get killed",

she smirked when moving back as she joked,

"Neon would be super pissed if you did get killed",

she walked away, joining the table as Azella continued her joke,

"so about the bronze crown. I was walking in the throne room and my husband was saying about how I should take what I want more often, so I took his crown, as I stated 'if you say so, by the way, you're going to need a new crown, this one's mine'",

she laughed as the people wondered,

"what happened after that?",

seeing as they were in the zone as Narla and Azella were up to date, I guess it was time to finally be on the journey to meeting the man or woman behind the manipulation.

Chapter Twenty-two
Journey to Death

When leaving the prison ward I approached the pile of armour and weapons to my right, gearing up with a white jumper as I placed it over my murky shirt.

Upon clipping the black bullet proof vest on Qorin questioned,

"are we ready to go? What's your plan when we get there?",

with firmness I tightened the vest as I stated,

"we focus on getting there first, no doubt the Commander has a few things in store for us on the way, they would have struck us by now if we didn't have any back-up",

Kamic wondered,

"what makes you say that? they could easily be wanting us to go there, I can feel it's a form of trap",

seeing his point I explained,

"it's not about a trap or about what he will do, he already knows we're going, he won't know about what we'll do when we get there, I know something about these kinds of people and they would know we're talking about it right now",

Alis and Marcella looked agreeing on my words, perhaps it

was the truth, or I was just being superstitious, even so, the thing I do best is think about every solution before it happens, sometimes it's over the top for something so small but if the problem is solved then what's the harm in it? Besides this Commander seems to know everything because certainly, Karmin wouldn't have known about it on her own, no offence but she was a cocky liar, not smart.

We were geared up with white jumpers, black and grey bulletproof vests, deep dark combat boots along with a white and black padded jacket.

They had the free liberty logo on it, but the batteries and power charges were taken out, causing the logo to not glow as they kept it for different uses. Rhax had his jacket firmly zipped up as he carried the large rucksack, like he was carrying air even though you could clearly tell it was full of ammo and weapons along with other useful tools.

He had the dark black skinny rifle firmly in his grasp as he informed, "we can get halfway by sun down, we have to walk down the main road going east, but then we will be faced with an alleyway, we avoid it",

Xharlot questioned,

"Avoid it? It will take longer, can't we cut through it",

she joined the circle as we rounded up to the left of the armour pile as Aries remarked,

"Xharlot, I don't think you want to be in those alleyways, they are unpredictable and we could easily walk straight into a hoard, if we go on the main road we will be able to see what's around us, even a genius doesn't have to see that",

Alis smirked as she joked,

"Aries don't call her stupid, she might not understand the word",

Xharlot looked to Alis with a sarcastic smile as she added,

"well, I better hope I'm not dumb enough to shoot my team member",

Rhax cut in,

"Alright that's enough of the jokes, we need to have some input in this. Xharlot, are you okay with the route?",

Xharlot glanced at Alis only to face him as she agreed,

"yes sir, I think it's a GREAT idea",

she was being sarcastic, but he didn't care, he took the agreement as he remarked,

"well good, you can suck it up and we can get on our way",

Kamic walked with others. Rhax, Marcella, Sevis, Xharlot and Deago.

Alis, Aries, Fuel, and Qorin walked with me as we strayed behind them, letting them take the lead as we kept watch of them, being the back-line and watcher of the group.

When leaving the city it felt as though someone was following us, shaking off the feeling, I stated,

"Alis, can you and Fuel scout the roads",

she wondered,

"why Fuel?",

Fuel was straying behind my feet as she remarked,

"I'll try not to take that to offence",

with a smirk I picked Fuel up by her body, seeing she didn't mind as I stated,

"you will need Fuel to use the little radar she has",

Fuel corrected,

"the radar goes approximately two hundred feet around our radius, so I wouldn't say it's little",

I passed Fuel over to Alis as she joked,

"well, you are little, Fuel, now be a good parrot and sit on my shoulder",

she put Fuel on her left shoulder as she sighed,

"I'm never going to hear the end of this, I seriously need an upgrade",

Aries stated,

"Plasma is working on it",

Alis pointed to Aries as she persisted,

"you better not, Fuel's cute sized",

she walked ahead of us as she looked upon the left side of the

270

road, we were heading west passing the east side of the road, going far from the dead city to where the country side is, but the rest of the city was far ahead, we could see the stretch going to the left and right side of the horizon.

The gloomy atmosphere brought familiarity when glancing at the muddy grounds, and dried grassy fields, the place had no moister to it, like the rain water didn't even land at all on this place.

Aries glanced left as she wondered,

"I still find it impressive that a seventy-foot wall could be built upon the lands like it was nothing, well it took under twenty years to build but still, it's crazy",

Qorin questioned,

"why build it? I know it was meant to keep people out but why make it for that reason? People always find a way to get over the wall, no matter if they are bad guys or the good guys they still find a way",

Aries stated,

"well it was the Alexandria's blood line idea, the first Alexandria birthed the idea and the blood line created it, they said it was to stop free liberty from returning, they said that they were a great threat to them, they never said it though",

Qorin snuffed as he wondered,

"then how do you know they were the biggest threat to them?",

Aries smirked as she explained,

"well they wouldn't need to say it, we all know the wall was built to keep them out, and not because of who they were or what they did, it was because the Alexandria blood line were afraid of being over ruled, the Commander of here is said to be pretty strong",

Qorin didn't help as he stated,

"well, Merider is no doubt the strongest leader",

I cut in,

"no, definitely not. There are people that can kill me, but people decide to bring me back to life, cover my ass, and you

271

know it gets a little on my nerves when people claim I'm indestructible",

Aries look to Qorin, only to back me as she felt a little awkward as she stated,

"well, clearly you two need to talk, I'm gonna go skull hunting",

I looked to her as I questioned,

"skull hunting?",

she smirked as she reassured,

"you'll know what I mean, don't worry I'll come back by the time you're done",

she was venturing the far left of us, keeping in our sight but far enough so I can just get my words out to Qorin, it was killing me, I really wanted to tell him what I felt but he got the idea that I love him, I do but not the way he thinks, I don't help with the situation either, it's just I never had to explain my feelings to someone before, tell them the opposite to what they want to hear.

With firmness, Qorin questioned,

"is it about earlier?",

without trying to hurt him but I couldn't soften my words, I expressed,

"Qorin, I wasn't trying to give you the wrong message earlier, I really tried to tell you, but you know how I'm like I don't help myself when trying to explain something",

he said firmly,

"Merider, just tell me",

I finally said,

"Qorin, I love you as a brother, I think everything of you, but it's not the way you want it to be",

he frowned only to snuff as he remarked,

"that's it?",

I looked surprised when facing right, going to him as I questioned,

"wait, hold on, you're not going to be mad at me for it?",

he laughed slightly as he reassured,

"I'm not mad, I find it amusing you thought about it too much",

I rolled my eyes only to pointed simply,

"well it's me",

he nudged me said,

"well don't worry about it. I know what you been through",

I added,

"well what I've been through in the past shouldn't affect me in the future",

he said firmly,

"well you learn from the past, build yourself in the future, see me for example, I used to be a raider, a guy you would kill, but now I changed and you didn't kill me",

he smirked as he glanced to me only to pause as he blurted,

"what in the hell of fire is that?!",

I looked left only to move back as Aries stated,

"see? this is what you call skull hunting",

she held a good large skull, it was like a human skull but wider and flatter at the top. It had four eyes, the top two were nearing the sides of the head as the other two were below them; it didn't have a lower jaw, probably fallen from decomposition. Its top set of teeth were spiked and shimmering a red colour; it was three times larger than her head, she had it in both of her hands, she looked chuffed, but Qorin and I were quite the opposite…we were a little horrified I couldn't lie.

We kept walking, keeping up with the group as Aries explained,

"this skull belonged to a K.I.L.O. Don't know what it's doing out here though, they did stop the experiments sixteen years ago, wonder if this is as old as it is back then",

I put my left hand out as I sighed,

"alright, give it here",

she was trying to get me in the game she was playing, guessing what it was and how old this K.I.L.O was, what power it beheld.

She placed it in my hand, letting me feel the weight of it as I held it. Looking at the skull as I questioned,
"where did you find it?",
she pointed by the field to her right as she stated,
"around a few yards back in the centre of the field",
I scratched the mud stating,
"well, if you found it on the surface and it barely sunk in the mud it's around five to one years",
she looked surprised as Qorin wondered,
"so it could be recent?",
I couldn't be sure, I'm not specialised in corpses or bones either, but in biology, I know about the plant life and nothing touched this, not even covering the head, I couldn't even see sights of vegetation that she could have pulled of, I think this was placed here quite recently, perhaps not even years.
With wonder I looked to the city ahead as I questioned,
"I think this K.I.L.O was dumped over on the fields",
I passed it back to Aries as I explained,
"the skull wasn't touched by any form of vegetation. Moss and mould would be all over that. You told me you found it on the field? Did you find anything else over there, the body perhaps",
she threw the skull on the floor.
She patted her hands as she stated,
"well it was on its own, presuming whoever dumped the body wanted to be sure it never came back, it's surprisingly clean so maybe it was clear and dumped as a warning",
it's a thought, perhaps the Commander did this, showing he can give power and take it, like with Neon he said he was a test subject, I need answers.
I looked to Qorin as he theorised,
"well from what I can understand of this bullshit is that he can take what he likes, and if he did kill that K.I.L.O he probably is experimenting on people too, turning them into creatures",
when looking past him, I could see the horizon of the city to

the right, this place was abandoned where we were walking, this countryside or what it feels like a countryside, it looked as though something used to be here, what happened to the buildings in this place?

When looking around I wondered,

"Aries, what happened to this place?",

we were closing into the team ahead, seeing nothing was coming for us from the left or right, the dead were occupied by the wall, but near the centre of the walls structure, they seemed to only want Zion city, perhaps it was a tactic that the commander sent, if he can tame K.I.L.O's or experiments rather, he would be able to give orders to the dead.

Upon giving that thought Aries explained,

"well, I've been living in Motahvada for the years being here, I've never understood the wall, but when asking around for a year, I found out that the Commander of the Dead Zone singled themselves out, people would say it was Medusa but others would call him Death, the reaper or something like that",

she faced me as she continued,

"so yeah that were the names they called this Commander, but other than that, all we know is they created Medusa Cursed or were the birthplace of the mutated humans, the K.I.L.O's for short",

that brought more questions to this situation, this Commander has more secrets to them, more than I needed and I think it gives me a theory in mind.

Xharlot was straying to us as she was hearing the conversation as I theorised,

"perhaps the Commander is both, perhaps not the Reaper or Medusa. But the Commander behind the K.I.L.O's was also the maker of the Medusa Curse, or trigger them at least as the parasite is made in the volcanic ash of the mountain.",

Xharlot was to my left, cutting past Aries as she wanted to walk next to me as she added,

"well if that was true then you would blame the Commander

for the dead zone, or the first storm whilst you're at it",

seeing as she had a thought of her own Aries questioned, "alright then smarty pants, what do you think then?",

Xharlot had her rifle firmly pointed to the floor as she explained,

"well the Commander is the creator of the K.I.L.O's for certain, it's no doubt because you can harvest the red serum from the volcano, and yes before you mention I know there's a huge fucking wall stopping the Commander from getting to the other side",

Aries was going to make that remark but was instantly quietened as Xharlot continued,

"as I was saying, he could have made his own copy, when the wall was built some people went on the other side, those people being the Free Liberty and they were everywhere before the wall was built, so they would have brought a few samples over, take Neon for example he created the Green serum, but I don't know how he made it to not affect a person, change their form, the one he made didn't do that",

Aries pointed,

"so how would you explain the skull I found then? it as mutated, four eyes, looked pretty much like a K.I.L.O to me",

she expanded,

"well it could be a failed experiment, the first try never succeeds we all know that",

Alis strayed towards us as she stated,

"we're around a few more yards till the city, say a dozen perhaps more so we're not far, better catch up slow pokes",

she had a smirk on her face as she went ahead to the team, we were straying behind the team, only to soon join in the centre as we lined up, heading to the large city ahead of us, the building was half torn, a little crooked and met the face of fire a few times, they were burned out, this place was slaughtered compared to the rest of the cities.

I glanced back as I wondered,

"Say I know it's a bit late to mention this now but where is

Elria?",

Xharlot wondered,

"I was thinking the same, I thought she was coming?",

Rhax stated,

"she's on her way, she said she's just gearing up, in her words she's going to be fucking loaded and armoured to the teeth",

well that sounded like her, I just hope she doesn't go over the top. Rhax, Kamic and Marcella were to the right of Qorin as Alis, along with Fuel and Sevis were to Aries's left, the team was rowed and marching with pride, it made me remember the feeling of when going towards the Eviliance city, the city of Eden but now it's the city of the dead, perhaps it's habitable now I didn't see the storm take it down when leaving the place.

The feeling was strong. I felt as though nothing could take us down,but I've learned to think that way is never good, something bad always happens and everyone not just myself should be prepared for the worst, although it's easy to say that until it happens when you least expect it, you could say we are never prepared for the worst, we focus on now and I think that's all we can do, we can never prepare for what the future

holds, we just face it.With firmness we entered the large stretch of road ahead, the alleyways were far ahead of us, a few miles out before reaching it, it felt as though it didn't take us long to reach this point, but the sun was already reaching halfway, where does the time go? It felt as though it was like sand, running through my fingers, as if time could slip past you in a blink of an eye, the worst part of this journey was thinking that perhaps it might take longer than the rise of the moon for us to finally settle briefly, this

mission will be long and time isn't on my side, I feel as though we shouldn't stop but everyone needs rest, it's not forever it's just to have some kip and get a better drive for the journey to The Reaper, I will name them that instead of

Commander, the person doesn't deserve the name, anyone who puts themselves first and their people last don't deserve that name.

The buildings stood over us, shadowing half the road with their dark sheets as their roofs were soaking in the warm afternoon sun. Most of us were growing hungry and were feasting on protein bars along with any other snacks people had packed before leaving, I was eating a bag of seeds and peanuts, the least popular treat they had but for that reason, I had it so they didn't have to eat it, the other reason was that I secretly liked it, it was bland but the peanuts were the best parts of it, added the salt and roasted flavours to a bland bag of trail mix that's for sure.

The people on guard had their pistols firmly in one hand, as their other hand held their bar of food , ensuring they could protect us as we ate our food at a fast-enough pace to slightly enjoy the food we ate but just for the sake of survival and needing to breathe without a cramping starving stomach.

Minutes passing, and we threw most of the trash on the floor, the paper trash from the trail mix I scrunched in my pocket for starting fires with, normally I'm against littering but let's face it no one is changing the bins around here.

I had my holster firmly tighten as I ensured the pistol I loaded was working fine, checking the clip, and ensuring the safety was on, I'm still making that mistake but I hate guns, never like them but I use them for the sake of needing to, at least I'm a kind of a good shot up close, but if you ask me to use a sniper I think you will be dead, that's for certain.

I looked to Xharlot as she questioned,

"where did your katana go?",

Qorin smirked as he joked,

"the number of times I say that to her you wouldn't believe it",

I smiled only to state,

"I've probably lost it in the armoury, I didn't check to get my stuff so I took the things for the pile for now",

I looked ahead to the alleyways closing in as I said firmly, "we better stay quiet, the dead might be around here, looks abandoned though",

the team was quiet, we were starting to split into two half's again as Rhax persisted,

"Xharlot, Kamic, Aries, Alis. You guys come with me, need to be sure the way's clear, the rest of you can have our backs and scout for anything useful",

as they walked ahead Sevis, Deago and Marcella joined us, teaming to my right and left as Qorin stuck by me to my right, even after the talk he's still protective of me, I wished he wasn't but I can't control what people do, they make their own choices.

Upon thinking that I glanced back, feeling like something was following us as we turned the right corner, heading to the long road squaring around the alleyways cluttering to our left. I paused for a moment when hearing something as I questioned,

"can you, hear someone yelling?",

Qorin agreed,

"yeah, where the hell is that coming from?",

the team with me looked to the right, only to see Abby.

She wore a bright white jumper that was rolled up, she wore a dark black bullet-proof vest along with black combat boots and baggy dark grey combat trousers, she even had my katana attached to a back holster. Not only was she carrying that, but she had a belt holster with two pistols. She followed us all the way here, I moved towards her as she ran towards me, she was yelling my name earlier, I thought I was going crazy again.

Abby approached me as the team was behind me, watching as she said,

"Merider, I was trying to call you from across the field, you probably didn't hear me",

I firmly snapped,

"Abby, why the hell did you follow us? We can't look after

279

you",
she snuffed as she stated,

"I have two guns and this katana, your katana rather",

she took the katana off as she handed it to me as she persuaded,

"If I give it to you will you let me join the team? Join this mission that you guys are having",

I snatched the katana off her, unclipping from the holster as I stated,

"you're not joining us because we have to",

I attached the katana to the holster behind my left gun as I continued,

"you're joining us because we have no choice, and you have three rules to follow, alright?",

she looked eager, but was a little annoyed that I was angry at her for following us like this, I wrapped the holster in a neat wheel before stowing it in my ruck sack as I listed,

"rule one is don't leave my sight, ever, you are going to have to stick with me no excuses",

she was looking less and less pleased to have found us when I continued,

"rule two is don't use the gun unless it's absolutely necessary, and the last rule is don't get in the way",

I moved her arm, moving her ahead of me as I stated,

"you're walking with me, the team will be behind us",

she wondered,

"but why can't I just join you guys as a group?",

Abby and I were in the centre of the teams perimeter as they walked far behind and far in front of us, I wanted to be sure Abby didn't get in trouble and that she was in our sight, she was foolish to follow us but she did it and now we can't take it back, I could let her walk back on her own but she will no doubt get killed, she was lucky to even reach us on her own, I didn't see any blood on her or any of the undying blood on her, so she made it to us clean, she might have just run through, she has the energy for it.

Stuck with the babysitting job, just great.

Chapter Twenty-three
The Campsite

Abby stuck to my left as I told her to do, but even so, it just felt as though she didn't know what she was doing, she might have not known but just being a kid, being so young I don't know; judging by that it made me look bad, I can't always assume that every kid I meet with, turn out...well you know what I mean, I just can't face losing someone else and if its another kid on my hands they seem to die, all the time, same with anyone else that I cared about, it feels unfair to take it out on her but I can't be soft on her, I need to bring the better out of her so tough love is the way to go, perhaps not too tough, she only just lost her father, but even so I don't want her to be morning forever it's not good for her.

It will take a few months for her to get the loss of her father from her heart, but I know it gets better, she pulls the brave face, but I know she's breaking in the inside.

People always saw through me every time they could see I was hurting inside, I made it obvious but singling them out, snapping at them and pushing them away made it too obvious that something was wrong.

I glanced down at Abby seeing even though I gave her the strict rules she was still happy to be with me, she didn't smile she was keeping it serious, but every so often I could see her glance up, smirking a little before looking at the surroundings trying to pass my looks, but I would catch her out when I kept checking on her, making sure she didn't stray from my side.

Xharlot went ahead as she informed Rhax about Abby, telling them about keeping their guards up, it was a risk Abby being here but she might not be so useless, she was good at searching and scouting, she found us and we were far from the city, perhaps we didn't leave so discreetly but even so she must have been following our trail for some time, perhaps I should ask her, might lighten the atmosphere a little, the city was quiet and us being silenced by it was even worse to deal with.

The city was watching us walk past the ruined roads, seeing the cars scattered around us as the skeletons of those dead during the storm were left where they were, stuck in the windows, wedged between car wheels as the drivers were flung to the wind shield, it wasn't a pretty sight and I could imagine the situation for that to happen, it was survive or die trying, and they did try, but never made it.

Abby was hesitant of the skeletons as she was curiously looking around with her eyes, finding things to occupy herself with only to face me as I questioned,

"Alright, Abby since you're stuck with us you might as well tell me how you followed us, when did you leave the city?",

she stated,

"well you didn't make it a quiet exit, so the second I heard you left I geared up, Byzer helped me, he got the guards attention, I slipped by and left, I knew where you were going it's pretty obvious",

I smirked as I wondered,

"oh really, it's that obvious?",

she went on,

"the only place that's standing is the Commander of the dead zone, and you are a Commander too so you want him dead so you can take his place",

I corrected,

"I want him dead to have no one in his place, I don't want it",

283

she curiously asked,

"well why? You get more power",

I said with firmness,

"power isn't everything, it's what you do with yourself that gets you to somewhere, so, for example, you like to climb trees and that's a form of power, because you know how to get up and down the tree without falling, most people would climb up and be stuck, does that make sense?",

I wanted to make an example that would catch her attention, something she likes to do, and I hoped it worked, it felt as though it worked, but I couldn't be a hundred percent sure about it.

She said with an agreement,

"yeah I get what you're saying, but what if that's not enough to climb a tree? What if I want to climb to the sky?",

I smirked seeing she was using my example, with thought I said shortly,

"then you take a spaceship and go to space, no matter what you do as long as you go to the highest point of your life at the end, it's all worth it, you get knocked down but you always find a way back up",

she said with a smirk,

"so you do think power is something then",

I sighed seeing she got me in a trap, I did technically just say that power was great, building higher and higher to your peek, but then again there are two ways to go about power, the right way and the wrong way which will catch her out for trying to be clever with me.

With firmness I stated,

"well you see if there is a tree with steps to go up to the top would you take them?",

she joked,

"trees don't have steps",

I looked at her as I said,

"just pretend one does, alright?",

gradually I continued,

"so there are two trees, the one with the steps can get you to the top, without the effort put into it, and it's faster, but the other tree doesn't, so you climb it",
she encouraged,
"yeah, and?",
my words expanded,
"you take the tree with the steps you take the bad route because it's easy and faster, but take the one without it and its more effort, more rewarding and you reach the top at a slower pace, but you get to your point and reach it",
Abby looked as though she had yet another clever thing to say, she's a kid so it's expected she will always find something to pick out from my words.
Abby said slyly,
"If taking the stairs is faster, and it gets me to the same point as the other tree, then why is it bad? What's bad about it?",
I kept glancing around, ensuring we weren't talking too loud in this isolated place, it enhanced our whispers to a talking volume as I went on,
"I didn't tell you that the one with the steps on it are rotting from the centre, meaning every step you take will risk you falling, not being able to stop yourself from crashing to your death. Look what I'm trying to say is the easy route gets you killed, it turns people bad for wanting the power then and there, you have to earn it and this Commander didn't earn his like I did, I don't want his place but I do want his people to be looked after, which will happen gradually",
she smirked as she chuckled,
"well why didn't you say that at the beginning?",
with a puzzled look to my face I stated,
"well you wouldn't have gotten it otherwise",
she caught on as she teased,
"oh right, because I'm an eleven year old, so because I'm a kid I don't get the adult things, well you're not wrong but I thought it was amusing",
I rolled my eyes as I stated,

"well I was trying to make you bored but clearly it didn't work, well this isn't supposed to be amusing, why don't I give you a task to do",

I pointed to the car tire on the road as I persisted,

"drag that tire over there, and when we get to a campsite and hold down, you can make it into a seat, or something",

she rolled her eyes as she remarked,

"or this is just another way of saying this is your punishment", without denying I said swiftly,

"yep, now get going, I will be with you all the way, because you have no choice",

I approached the left side of the road, seeing the crashed taxi car, the wheel from the front part of the car was popped out, lying upon the concrete floor.

I took out the holster as I remarked,

"well isn't this just a coincidence, it can be wrapped around and you can drag it with this",

being quick I tied the holster firmly around the wheel, making a loop at the end to make it easier for Abby to drag the tire as I stated,

"all right there you go, we've wasted enough time talking, we are meant to be on a mission",

Marcella and Sevis watched with amusement as Abby dragged the tire, moving the holster over her shoulder allowing the tire to balance on the floor vertically, she was cheating but I didn't want her to slow us down so I let it pass as she remarked,

"see it's easy, just a little heavy though",

Sevis joined us along with Marcella and Deago, they stuck to my right as Qorin was behind us, he wanted to keep watch as Sevis stated,

"we should be far I hope, may I ask about the tire?",

he had a smirk to his face as I explained,

"Abby carries that to the campsite, her reward for following us",

Abby remarked,

"punishment more like",

Marcella stated,

"well it serves her right for following us",

she looked ahead as she pointed,

"good luck Abby, we have a turn going left, you may find it fun to drag it but turn and drag? That I would like to see".

Rhax, Alis, Aries, Fuel, Xharlot, and Kamic were just ahead of us, they were turning left but soon retreated to cover as we heard gunshots.

Seeing what was shooting us I moved the tire off Abby before dragging her with me as I stated,

"we got raiders, Sevis come with us, Marcella cover us", Sevis joined Abby and I as we hid behind a tipped over fire truck, not seeing an oil spillage I think it was safe to keep us covered.

When standing behind the truck I looked to Sevis explaining,

"stay here and defend Abby, I'm going to join Marcella and Qorin, see what's happening",

Abby went to argue but I wasn't wanting it, I said firmly,

"no arguments Abby it's not safe for you and I'd rather not have another dead body in my hands", I looked to Sevis saying firmly, "don't let her out of your sight",

he kept my words playing in his mind as I left, he never let me down and I know he won't mess this up, it's just keeping an eye on her whilst I go out on the field, hopefully, nothing serious is happening and we can just take out the raiders and be on our way.

I hurried to Marcella as Qorin dragged the tire with him as he stated,

"they look like some buggers who want to be killed", Marcella observed,

"around twenty of them, they look like a clan of a sort",

Th team lined up to my right, seeing the twenty people approach us, they were heavily armoured and looked to be wanting a fight for certain.

I glanced right seeing Qorin as he questioned,

"the hell do we do?",

when observing the clan I might be able to find a way to kill them, some of them have guns whereas most hold swords or gauntlets morphed into blades, it covered their hands making it look as though their hands were the blades.

They wore rugged brown jackets that had holes torn within them, they wore grey, white and dark red shirts that blended in with their rugged appeal they were going for. They had ruffed up baggy black trousers, along with brown leather boots, they even weaved chains in their trousers that trailed over their boots, giving them a sound to their walk, the creaking of iron and the dragging of chains gave them a rusted appeal, a haunted effect to them, as if they were the ghosts of the raiders if that's even a thing.

Their arms were coated in a ripped brown fabric that was tied together with bike chains, fishing nets to give them a robe-ish look to them when moving their arms slightly, as the breeze of the wind would make them drift a little.

They had car number plates on their shoulders, welded and hammered to their form, as it was tied to them with chains swirling down their arms.

Some wore incredible looking helmets looking like rusted skulls, they had two small holes on the left and right side of the helmets head, as their eyes showed in the eye space below them, resembling much like the K.I.L.O that we saw previously.

They had short horns on the left and right sides of the forehead, however.

The leader in the centre had a Spartan looking décor going down the centre of her head, it was made entirely from car number plates, it stretched from the front with a spiked flick going up as it ended to the back of her head in a short curve spike going downwards, she looked as though she took pride in whatever this clan was, they obviously reused things in the surrounding to create this gear, it's magnificent, yet I couldn't admire it too much, they could, and probably will want to kill us, yet we are the same to them.

Upon approaching us the woman stopped her people, seeing they were hungry for bloodshed as she stated,

"hold your positions brothers, let me handle this",

she had a smooth yet rugged accent to her voice, she had her rugged swords in her holster, when approaching us I could see the hilt of her swords with better detail, they were cased with biked tires and glued with heat, I could see the burn marks of where they wrapped it around the swords frame and cased the hilt with the rubber, very clever. She stopped walking towards us, letting her luminous green eyes scour at us, she was infected with the green serum two, perhaps The Reaper didn't just experiment on him but someone else too.

The woman pointed to me as she stated,

"you are the, Commander, are you not?",

Qorin was prepared to throw the tire, I had a feeling he was going to use it as a weapon. But I motioned my team to stand down, Rhax refused,

"we can't hold our weapons, not until we know they won't kill us",

the woman snuffed as he remarked,

"you all hold your weapons, but ours are down, I'm pretty sure we should be the ones to worry",

Rhax saw her point as he reluctantly disarmed his weapon, lowering it as I approached her, she questioned,

"his words are true then, you have come to the Dead Zone", with hesitance I interrogated,

"if he says I am here then he wants me dead, and most likely sent you to kill me, didn't he? Why did you shoot my team", she looked to Xharlot as she explained,

"well she shot first, but I forgive and forget, no doubt it's because of the appeal",

she was bizarre, she acted highly and thought much of herself, that's what it felt like anyway.

She went on,

"anyhow. Yes, he sent me to come here, I'm assuming you

didn't know him, who he really is",
with a puzzled look I asked,

"tell me about him, we only know what people say over the walls, not inside of it. It's almost as if no one inside the wall knows anything about their Commander",
she agreed,

"and it's true, only those who were his subjects or requested to see him knows who he truly is, he is also Medusa, the hallucination of the Red Zone and past the wall, the one people worship",
Aries questioned,

"so he's Medusa?",
the woman sighed as she explained further,

"yes, he is. He made her, a way to scare people over the wall and also to keep them from touching his projects, the Medusa Cursed are made from the ash from the volcano but he has long since kept it going, he has a machine in his dome that connects to the one underground, it creates quakes and so forth",
she got carried away as she informed,

"anyway I'm not here to give you the history of the Commander or the behind the scenes of the Medusa Cursed, I'm merely here to help",
I was confused, why would she want to help us? She would want to kill the person that made the green serum, the K.I.L.O's, the one that made her powerful, why would she want to do that?
Qorin dropped the tire as the woman remarked,

"you can drop the tire, Qorin, I'd rather not get hit by one",
she looked to the fire truck stating,

"Qorin, get your friends from the truck, Merider and I still have more work to do, well some clearer things to talk about",
Qorin snuffed,

"hey, you may know my name and have these shitty powers but you can't order me around",
I looked to him as she stated,

"Qorin just do it, I don't think it's helping anyone by refusing",

he was quiet for a moment, seeing that if she can't order him around it was going to have to be me, funny enough he did what he was told and got Sevis and Abby from the cover I told them not to move from, I hope they stayed there otherwise its another wild goose chase and I'm getting sick of those.

He went past me as the woman ordered her guards around, she instructed,

"guard our perimeters, don't move until I say so",

the ten guards lined behind her as the other ten filtered past us, going to the other side where the fire truck was, keeping a firm ground on our location as the woman clearly didn't want us to go, it felt strange to trust her, but so far she hasn't given us a choice to not trust her, it was mandatory that we did or we all end this with bloodshed which she didn't want.

She looked to my team as she observed,

"well, once your friends join us we can talk, I'd rather them all be here than wait and explain myself twice",

she looked to us one by one as she said intrigued,

"hmm, this is peculiar, some of you are from over the wall; Marcella, Merider and Qorin are from Londelis, different soil, why trust them?",

she looked to Rhax as she asked again,

"why would you trust someone from a different soil?",

not wanting to answer he said shortly,

"we are the same to them, end off; it's not about the soil it's about how much we all want to survive",

I could see a smirk through the helmet, her lower half of her face was exposed, the spiked teeth of the helmet met her upper lip leaving her lower half of her jaw exposed, you could see her smirk as she said amused,

"good answer, see your team are loyal to you Merider. Something the Commander of the dead zone does not have",

Deago said firmly,

291

"why can't you just tell us his name, you call him the Commander of the dead zone, we barely even know who you are so what you say could be lies",

he was right about it, she kept herself a secret, she knew us but we didn't know her or who her disciples were.

She introduced,

"Marella Quarry. I was a subject of the Commander of the dead zone and in return, I watch the city barrier to his little dome, but obviously, it's running a little thin out here, we dress ourselves in the ruins of the city and in return we get our food, our fun and most of all we survive much like you",

Marella went off-topic as she questioned,

"what is this robot? She looks nothing like an android",

she noticed Fuel was perched on Alis's shoulder.

Aries remarked,

"I thought you would know that?",

Marella explained,

"I would but she's a robot, so I can't read her mind, much like the Commander he too is one like her, not an android",

Marcella questioned,

"wait the Commander is a robot? Can you make sense please",

Abby and Sevis joined us to the left with Qorin as he said shortly,

"there you go",

I could sense he was being narky.

Marella said briefly,

"now that you're all here I shall introduce myself again, like what I feared to explain myself twice but shit happens; I'm Marella Quarry, I came here to help you kill my Commander, well he isn't mine I would say Merider is my Commander when it comes to morals, but that won't happen until he's gone",

she took off her helmet, exposing her head as she stated,

"I recall the campsite was ahead of you, you were heading my way actually, but this time we will be taking it, they

292

won't want us back there so I hope you all are prepared to kill some people",

she smirked slightly with her red painted lips, she had smooth tanned skin, deep brown hair braided back into a spiked ponytail that flowed behind her as it released itself from the pressure of the metal helmet, it looked ruff and spiked, would say her hair was sweaty as she must have worn it all day.

Growing more puzzled by the situation Alis thought what I was thinking as she questioned,

"wait you're talking about your own campsite? Why the hell would you kill your people for us to camp in the area, and why help us?",

Marella didn't seem in a rush as she expanded,

"look the campsite is a corruption that I created, I built it so the Commander could see me as his own, and since I can't read his mind he can't read mine because he's programmed to harness Intel not read minds, he harnessed the Intel from me. I tell him everything I know but now that you're here you could say I planned it from the beginning of your arrival",

she winked to me as she put her helmet back on, she stated, "enough chitter-chatter, guards lead the march",

the guards by the fire truck moved past us, leading the way with the other ten as they were going left, moving around the alleyways and going right, to where the city grows shorter and shorter, most likely to a forest or another empty field, either way we have no choice but to go with her, she probably knows everything about us and what our plans are, and if we separated from her or refuse her help she will surely turn on us, want us dead for not having trust in her, and I still don't, yet it's one of those 'you just have to trust them' situations, one that will impact me if we get betrayed by her.

We followed her as she walked with me to my right, the team kept their distance and trailed behind, making sure she didn't make any sudden movements, but from the looks of things she was doing what she said.

Chapter Twenty-four
Marella Quarry

When walking with her she was making herself comfortable as she answered peoples questions.

Abby questioned,

"so what are you?",

she corrected,

"who are you is the correct way to ask about me, young lady",

she expanded,

"so you must have heard about K.I.L.O's, yes? Well, I am one of them. Neon is my brother, he passed away though",

how did she know that? I couldn't be certain that she read our minds but I'm going to be the one to look stupid to ask her this.

With curiosity, I questioned,

"how did you know he passed?",

she was by my right as she stated,

"well, I would say I read your mind like you're thinking, but that would be lying; Neon, the one you saw was dead, but he lived because of the Green serum hence why you are alive",

the team trailed from left and right side of us, however, Qorin and Rhax were trailing behind, keeping watch of us as

Abby was getting too comfortable with Marella, I don't know if that was a good thing or a bad thing, but I know one thing is for certain, I don't trust what she says.

She was leading us to the outskirts of the city, we could see the fields going to the right where we were heading.

There was a large campsite ahead, the torch lights were attached to poles circling the site, the torches were pinned to the ground allowing it to be replaced easily.

The tents were made from rugged grey material, they were shaped from squared to a rectangular shape, this camp was entirely built by hand, I could tell by seeing the patches of different grey to black patches of fabric, some even had brown patches to, they used what they could find to make the camp stand tall.

We stood on the outskirts of the city as Marella's guards were lined in front of us, they were waiting on the call to start the battle, they were acting as a shield for us, blending us in with the scenery as we firmly crowded behind them.

I pulled Marella aside as I ordered,

"Sevis, hold the team with Qorin and Rhax, I need to talk with Marella",

I made sure we were far from the group before going face to face with her as I warned,

"you better not be playing any games with me",

she questioned,

"what do you mean?",

I don't know whether she was pretending to be dumb or didn't know at all, so I expanded,

"you say you want this Commander gone but to do that you will risk killing your own people? Tell me why you want them dead? What makes them corrupted?",

she expressed,

"they are like my guards, I tell them to do something and they will do it, if I tell them to kill themselves, they will do it",

she went on in a softer tone,

"you believe that they wouldn't do the same for you?",
she was talking about my team, but she was wrong, they didn't do anything I told them to do, not unless it was important.
With firmness I stated,
"they wouldn't die for me even if I told them to",
she said smugly,
"ah but they would die for you like my men would; however in your case it's because they weren't ordered to do so",
she changed topic as she wondered,
"why are you doubtful to my knowledge? My words are true and that no matter what you think of me, we both want the same person dead",
with a sly smile to my face I challenged,
"for yourself or for the good of the people?",
she simply answered,
"both, now if you're done interrogating me I think we have a campsite to visit",
she walked away taking the lead as she ordered,
"march to the campsite, leave no one alive",
the guards headed towards the campsite, stomping their feet firmly upon the floor as they marched, her people were dressed from head to toe, thinking about it they didn't even show their faces, or any part of their bodies, I don't know if I trust them or her, but she's thinking she can run the place, and no doubt the green serum affects that as she was ordering my team around.
She marched to the city with her guards, going to the people that were straying around the place; they were armed with guns and rifles, but they didn't even make a move as she ordered,
"Kill yourselves",
the guards with her didn't move as my team was thrown off, the people in the campsite were slaughtering themselves, taking a bullet to their heads with their pistols. Their blood was staining the fields as the gunshots echoed within the

surroundings.

They just, shot themselves no doubt the green serum isn't as sweet as it makes itself to be, whatever she was, she wasn't human, she wouldn't make people just kill themselves to take over like that…yet she did and that's what made me not trust her.

When straying towards the bloodied campsite Marcella questioned,

"you made them kill themselves? Why bother having us help you at all if you can do that",

Marella stood outside the campsite with the team, facing them as the guards were lined behind her as she stated,

"it's very simple. If I have those who can help me bypass the dome, it will be easier to take him down. Now, this, on the other hand, I wanted you to see what I could do, prove myself, and most of all didn't want you to miss the clear up", she faced the guards, raising her hands as they glowed a green flame on each, she streamed green glowing vines from each of her hands, wrapping her guards in twists as their armour disintegrated, exposing their red rocky bodies, they were Medusa Cursed men, they were shimmering green and irradiating with a bright glow before falling into heavy green powder.

The smell was sickening as it was smoky and burned; the ash gradually rolled over the city as Marella moved her hands out, whipping the vines towards the campsite, it was streaming upon the floor, discarding the bodies to ash just like the others. The glow was oddly entrancing as the team watched it return to Marella, seeing it return to the flames before it finally left.

She looked to her left as Abby said in awe,

"cool, how did you do that?",

she smirked as she stated,

"perks of being an experiment is you can make it what you want it to be, even death can look beautiful",

I hurried past the team, pulling Abby behind me as I argued, "you stay the hell away from her",

Sevis took Abby as I stated,

"you believe you are good and might be, but I can see through you, if you are capable of killing you're people you are fully able to kill us",

she looked as though my words didn't have any affect on her, she explained,

"if you think that was killing my own people then you're no better than I. You killed your people remember?",

she went on,

"The Scorpion, Vipers, your own kind, and yet I am no better as I've killed my own also, have you wondered why it's only a hand full of people out here, I control them, I ensure they don't step out of line and if they follow me they know they follow me till their death",

my eyes glared at her as I remarked,

"you believe that if you compare myself to you that it will be one happy family",

Marcella cut in,

"Merider, we need her",

Marella stated,

"well, whilst you convince Merider I will be in the tent in the centre of the campsite, until you're ready to hear my plans then I'll be waiting",

she smugly walked away, she still was wearing her helmet, I don't know about you but wearing it when not in battle means she has something to hide or believe it gives her a symbol, well I don't need to know what else she thinks about herself, but to hell that she thinks I will follow her.

Marcella stood in front of me as she stated,

"guys get in the campsite",

Qorin expressed,

"to hell to that",

I looked to him, not even having to say anything as he said reluctantly,

"Aries, Alis come with me, the rest stay here, that's the only compromise",

Fuel was going along with Aries as she reassured,

"don't worry Merider, I will scan the city",

as they walked past Xharlot and Kamic were to my left as Rhax and Deago were with Marcella.

Sevis was behind me with Abby as we were still discussing the situation.

Marcella expressed,

"we have no choice",

I cut in,

"we always have a choice, and I can tell this isn't going to end well, did you see what she could do?",

she argued,

"she is infected with the serum, we can find a way to get her cured, or get rid of her for certain, but we haven't got a choice now. At this point, we need to have her on our side",

Rhax agreed,

"I'm with Marcella on this one Commander, it's not like we don't trust her judgement, but as you said, you've seen what she can do",

he walked into the campsite, going to Marella, the way he worked, the way he did things it was from fear.

Whatever he planned to do he was going the wrong way about it, to run by someone with fear and not loyalty is wrong, you get killed in the end.

Xharlot defended,

"she ain't wrong on that Marcella, we can't trust that bitch. It should be her needing us not the other way around, I don't know why you're wanting us to be in a trap",

Kamic compromised,

"Clearly being at each other's necks isn't going to work out. Marcella why don't you go with Rhax, see what Marella's plans are, and I will talk to Merider",

she glanced to me as she said shortly,

"just trust my judgement on this, otherwise you'll ruin things", she walked into the campsite, entering the main tent within the centre that had a flag sailing within the centre of it, the flag had a unique sigil, most likely to resemble her name or whatever she believes she is.

The sigil was three-rings circling a skull, a four-eyed skull like her helmet she was wearing, the background was a bright green, yet again resembling her power, what was she trying to prove?

She has power, so she can do what she likes? I've never felt so infuriated by someone before, the way she was feeding Abby's curiosity, and was making the deaths look like it didn't show pain, like she was performing.

I looked down to Kamic as he stated,

"Merider, walk with me, okay, let's just clear your mind for just a second",

I glanced back as I quietly sighed, observing the team as I stated,

"you guys get in the campsite, don't relax. Sevis, I need you and Xharlot with Abby at all times",

Abby argued,

"but Merider she won't kill us, you can trust her",

I said with firmness,

"when she gives me a reason to trust her then I will but for now you stay with those two, I don't want you wandering off, you got it",

she frowned seeing her little journey with us wasn't going to be pleasant, I didn't want it to be, if she joins us on the mission she needs to do what I say and not relax and let her guard down.

As they walked into the city Kamic and I walked to the right, straying down slowly on the road seeing the outskirts of the city on our right as the fields were far on our left.

The lowering sun gave the sky an orange and red glow within the horizon as Kamic questioned,

"what is it about her Merider? I know she's a little threatening, wants to kill people, and let's face it she has

every trait to be your worst enemy",
he looked up to me as he went on,
"but she had healing abilities, shows her good side, even hospitality in her own strange way",
I stated,
"that's the point, she is friendly and yet she killed her guards, they were like strands of grass in a wildfire, it was too easy and that being said we shouldn't be going down this route",
I paused as I looked down to him as he wondered,
"what's bad about an easy route? We've gone down many of those routes and we turned out fine",
I gave him a look only for him to change his words as he said,
"well we turned out okay",
he smiled as he saw his words were amusing as he stated,
"look, Marcella wants us to get along with her, not for her sake or ours but for the future, just like what you want, you do want to make the world better don't you?",
I could see what he was doing, making examples, relating me to my team, but he wasn't wrong and that's why I couldn't be mad at him for wanting us to follow Marella's ideas, but one thing is for certain she isn't in charge of the situation, she may have us but she doesn't own us…we're not her bitch.
With a sigh I looked back to the campsite as I stated,
"yeah I know; and you're right but doing this for the better of the future still has the right path, and if we are going to do her plan we are doing it my way, the better way, the one that will get us all alive",
Kamic look doubtful but I didn't not want to make promises I couldn't keep, he stated,
"perhaps not all of us live in the end, like you know people always side, and like you've experience there always has to be a sacrifice even when you didn't want them to make",
he smiled softly as he motioned,
"come on Commander better get yourself in the campsite, we have an imposter trying to out beat you, and I certainly can't let it get you down, so you better show her who's the boss",

I smiled to him only to walk with him back to the campsite as I admitted,

"I just think she might not be the person we need on our team, she kills easily, she worries me but what worries me more is that I think Abby is starting to like Marella",

he wondered,

"and that's a bad thing?",

with a puzzled look I questioned,

"wouldn't that be a bad thing? She has powers to kill, she can manipulate easily, what if she gets Abby to turn on us",

Kamic reassured,

"I don't think you will let that happen, so she is fine as long as you keep your head clear and go with it, being a part of the plan and get the Commander down. If you get to be on the top of the throne, metaphorically speaking of course, then you shall not fail",

he had the wisdom to his rugged voice, Kamic was silent throughout the journey, but when I needed help with unscrambling my thoughts, let go of my worries I knew who to go to.

When entering the city Aries approached us as she stated,

"Merider. Rhax and Marcella are in the tent with Marella, I didn't know if you knew but I thought to tell you, to be on the safe side",

Fuel was sat on her left shoulder as she informed,

"there appears to be no sign of stress levels in there, you, on the other hand, is boiling with it",

trying not to look uncomfortable from her observation, I questioned,

"did you notice anything else scanning the campsite? Energy levels of Marella, if she gives off an aura that calms people, or something",

Fuel's screen flickered as she was checking over something quickly, as she showed a picture, it was an inverted image of the main squared tent in the centre, I could see a table in the centre of the tent along with Marcella and Rhax on the other side, I could tell as their gear was more padded than Marella's.

With that in mind I noticed that Marella was glowing with green as the others were yellow, I questioned,

"what does this represent? What are you showing me?",

Fuel stated,

"the yellow aura of the non-infected, aka Rhax and Marcella shows they are under her influence, they are meant to be orange like Kamic's aura. We all have a form of aura in our moods, orange is neutral, red is stressed, angry, and so on",

Kamic wondered,

"so is green a positive aura? So that could be why Merider isn't fully",

Fuel finished his words,

"under her influence, and neither am I. I am a robot so we can't be easily infected, and the reason being is that if a human is seriously stressed the positive energy can be cancelled out, but the same with two positives make a negative, so if you are very happy, or like Merider, very stressed, it's much harder for her to take control, that's if she doesn't verbally manipulate you",

that's interesting to know, Fuel has some advances and I know for certain they will be thinned out when she gets upgraded, with that In mind perhaps she and Aries can take out a task with Alis and Deago, I need them to be on their feet and not sink into the aura.

With firmness I persisted,

"Aries you take Fuel, Alis and Deago. Go around the campsite and take note of what's in the tents, if they are spotless, something is definitely wrong here, if one has something of interest take it, it could help us or might give us a back story on the guards that worked with her, I'm certain they didn't come willingly",

they walked ahead into the campsite as we gradually strolled behind them, taking time to have a thorough look at the campsite.

It looked normal, it didn't have any unique traits about it.

I look to Kamic as I questioned,

"Abby better not be venturing this place, it just, looks normal...what do you think?",

he remarked,

"there's many campsites that looks the same, to be honest",

we were nearing the Commander's tent as I stated,

"Vipers tents are green and they have banners with their sigil on it, the people here only used what they saw and don't go with a colour, just black and grey. The Scorpions have a brown and red theme to their tents, torture pikes and they have banners with their sigil on it",

Kamic pointed,

"the Commander has their banner, so it's the same as the rest",

he reassured,

"look, perhaps you go in there and talk to Marcella, Marella, and Rhax. I will round up Sevis and meet you here with the others",

he walked away as I met the door of the tent, the silenced doorway was giving me the chills only to approach it further to hear mutters and muffled talking behind the tent wall.

With a sigh I approached the tent room, seeing the table and the backs of Marcella and Rhax, they moved back from the table as I joined them in the centre as Marella wondered,

"ah, Merider, glad you've came around, what would the world be without, Friends by your side",

she had a sinister touch to her words, but her soft voice made it a little less chilling, her helmet, however, gave off the creepy effect, she didn't take it off even inside the tent, she showed us her face earlier as she was expecting not to show her face again afterwards, something about that gave me the feeling that perhaps she wanted us to forget her face, or she wanted to show her power, who knows, but I do know she is planning on taking my team from my hands, and that isn't happening.

I looked firmly at her as I questioned,

"What's your plans Marella?",

she looked pleased as she said shortly,

"hmm guess you're not the one for messing around, I shall get to the point then",

she pointed to a blue print as she stated,

"the dome is a complicated building, the walls are made of concrete, the inside is filled with connectors, vents and mainly every other things buildings have, including the pipelines and flushing systems",

she went on,

"the last layer is a sheet of metal, the walls stretch wide and high allowing the Commander to walk around in",

with a firmness I questioned,

"right? So what about him in general? How many floors are there? If we're taking him down we need to know the inside-out of this place, not how many layers are in the wall",

she has a sly smirk on her, she was trying to figure me out and I could feel it, but she couldn't break through my negative emotions of doubt, and frustration to having her in our team, let's hope once when this whole ordeal is over. She will either leave us for good or I end up killing her myself, even someone proclaimed invincible can be killed, it's just the case of killing them right the first time, much like those infected by the Undying's Parasite.

Marella stated,

"very well. Commander Artell is a robot, like I told you before, so he specially made the dome to keep him safe, charged and no matter what, he never runs out of power as long as he is in the dome, he can roam outside but it takes twenty-four hours for the charge to run out",

Rhax frowned,

"Plasma doesn't need charge and she's an android, even Fuel has a longer power charge than that guy",

I looked to him, seeing he just exposed Fuel's power charge as Marella said wondrously, "ah so that little robot is Fuel, who is Plasma?",

Rhax informed shortly,

"Plasma is an android of Motahvada, she's a trained repair woman from what I know, she knows a few things about robots. She's creating an upgrade for Fuel",

he was just willingly giving her information as she encouraged,

"so what about Fuel, you said she had a longer power charge?",

before he said anything else I cut in,

"she isn't involved with your games all right, she's my team member and if I want her story told it will be from me",

Rhax glanced at me either with annoyance or hatred, either way, he wasn't impressed and I know why he isn't, she already influenced him, something about this aura is stronger than it sounds, she's powerful.

Too powerful.

Chapter Twenty-five
The Aura

When looking upon the map of the dome there were three interesting features to it. The shape itself, which was obviously a dome shape, I don't think there are rooms in that place at all, and if she said about the connectors and copper stuff being on the outside, I think it's used as a source of a lightning rod, gives the station some extra power, as he is using what other sources to make his own. With the lack of resources here I can only think of the kinetic power like the furnace or wind power, perhaps even nuclear.

Thinking about that Narla and Azella were talking about the bomb they were trying to find, hopefully, they are searching for it as we speak, but if they can't find it I have a pretty good idea where it could be, this dome is suspicious and worst of all I can't even talk to my teammates about it, they will tell her or if I even dare to think it she will read my mind, but if I stay negative in emotions it will be hard for her to break through, that's all I can hope for that my negative and stressed state will keep me shielded.

The second curious feature was that she circled the areas of interest, or perhaps they were markers for something else; it made a triangle shape if joined together by lines, one on the left, right and at the top of the map behind the dome, perhaps they could be generators to disarm the full power, leaving it on the back-up power until fixed.

The last curious feature was the ring at the far front of the map, it didn't fit in but there was an arrow pointing to me as it read 'The Red Valley' with curiosity and no other way of thinking my thoughts without them being read, I questioned, "what's The Red Valley?",

Rhax looked at the map as he didn't see it before, he looked to where my finger was pointed as Marella explained,

"The Red Valley is much like The Green Valley, the one over the wall, you think the red serum would be within the red lands but obviously its found its way over here",

she went on,

"the valley is the one route we can cross but anything around it then the Commander will certainly see us, no matter about my concerns, it's your choice after all",

with a slight frown I cautioned,

"what do you mean by that?",

she smirked as she stated,

"well you seem to hate me so what I say won't make anything better; so why don't you come up with the plan then, genius?",

with a deep huff I questioned,

"tell me about the Commander then, what's the purpose of this tower, you said he charges in there but nothing else",

she seemed to find it amusing that I didn't trust her, and my team did, they didn't trust her for the sake of it I know that, but they were putting a little too much faith in her.

She informed,

"well, Commander Artell uses that place for his charging station as I said, but he also hunts people down with it and like with me he has experimentation rooms underground, he has his scientist in there too, he, on the other hand, wonders the dome and checks in every so often",

Marcella wondered,

"so the scientists are in there? Why does Karmin have the Chinooks I thought he would have wanted them close so no one leaves",

309

Marella said firmly,

"he likes to see people run, so he doesn't bother to keep the transport close, however, the other reason was he didn't want the scientist to be freed, he wants them for himself, so he kept them hostage",

with doubt I challenged,

"if that was true then why have the low security? Anyone who doesn't want someone to leave would put everything to the line to make sure that didn't happen",

Rhax agreed,

"She's right about that, if they are so precious to him he would have made sure to put up security",

Marella pointed to the three circles as she stated,

"these are his security methods. The three clans, go ahead to The Red Valley and you will see The Morkarik Clan, much like the Scorpion's appeal, but the wrath of the moon cursed, the serum has infected them over time but they are easily killed by their own substance, of course, Merider, I know you already know this",

she was patronising me, she really knows how to get on people's nerves.

Trying to keep my cool she continued,

"the left side of the city is Clan Quarry, they live obviously in a Quarry, a mining post for coal I think, or quartz? I'm not certain what mine they nest in, but I do know that they are different from any clan you've seen",

with doubt I wondered,

"in what way?",

she went on to explain in depth,

"so for example you get the Medusa Cursed, they are much like them but don't go insane and try to kill not only humans but themselves too. Clan Quarry is made up of people with rocky and tough skin, they resemble much like rock in other words, to kill them would mean you're in for a tough fight",

I cut in,

"not unless you know how to kill them",

seeing for once I knew something she didn't I explained,

"Alis gave me a dagger made of red rock and red serum, it able to kill the Medusa Curse with one hit, perhaps it could kill them",

she cut in,

"perhaps it can get us all killed whilst we're at it; so let's go over the last option before you get any ideas, no doubt ones that will kill us",

I bit my lip holding back my words as she continued,

"the last options is the Village of The Cursed",

sounds as though this village in particular was related to magic and curses, lets hope it is and not some more freakish experiments carried out by Artell.

With curiosity I questioned,

"the village sounds as though it shouldn't be touched",

she agreed,

"it shouldn't",

she said firmly,

"that village is off boundaries. The people there are different, they hold powers like me but not the serum, something else, a fire or something that they call it, no doubt the idea was from The Red Valley they have a ceremonial bowl of red flames, much like The Green Valley, but to think about it, the Quarry is a small trail from it also",

Marcella added,

"so, perhaps that's the Commander way of contacting them, is with the fire of the ceremonial bowls",

Marella wondered,

"but he's a robot he can't just telepathically go to flame by flame",

with a sly smile I wondered,

"yet you can?",

something was growing on me, she knew about the flames and didn't tell us about the Quarry, she knows everything she's just playing dumb even I could see that, and that's not me saying I'm dumb to clarify, I just always trust people to easily, I can't make the same mistake again.

Rhax questioned,

"Merider what are you getting at?",

I looked to Marella as I stated,

"she can telepathically go where she likes, the flame makes her presence stronger, maybe you were the one that turned the priestess against us, took Wyet from us, and most of all you are Medusa",

she snuffed as she questioned,

"and where's the evidence to prove this?",

not wanting to make a fool of myself I firmly stood my grounds as I went on,

"One person I've known in my life who could teleport, it was more of a connection of when I was infected with the same batch of serum as her. But even with that aside you hold her power in the non-harmful Green serum, that's what you claim or what we thought it was",

she puzzled,

"it's not harmful",

Rhax persisted,

"Merider, we just need to get through this alright, can we save the interrogation for later?",

ignoring his words I continued,

"you think I wouldn't notice your people, they were Medusa Cursed in armour, their hands were cased with weapons",

she laughed slightly with amusement as she remarked,

"wow you really have lost it haven't you; how on Earth would I control them?",

without doubt I stated,

"Artell made you his tool, so he knows how to tame the Medusa Cursed, you can destroy bodies and I know full well you can resurrect them, because the serum heals and damages, it doesn't work both ways and you know when you said Neon was already dead and was a walking corpse, so are you, it heals and damages, you're already dead and you never even knew it",

312

she looked to me in silence, seeing something in me, hearing my words for once, it's as if I found a soft spot to her.

She bit her lip before she challenged,

"if I'm already dead, then you can't kill me. You will just have to live with me being here. You know something, what is it like being incomplete?",

with a pause Marcella glanced to me as Marella continued, "well your family didn't want you let's put it that way, everyone you met tried to kill you, apart from one. You know nothing about what your family was like before the storm or even if what you know is true at all",

Rhax and Marcella were feeling the intense tension between us as we were in a heated conversation, she was trying to get me angry and prod at me as I stated,

"you're saying this for your own glory, what are you trying to prove?",

she said smugly,

"that you are no better than I, that even with the regular teasing that you give away you're story through the windows of your eyes, they tell me what I need to, you listen to Fuel and she told you about the aura, I'm merely testing her theory",

with wonder I halted,

"hold on, Theory?",

she was playing with me, she was telling me what I needed to know but she was finding little things to get me angry, to see if anger restricted her from reading my mind.

She informed,

"look I told you what you needed to know and when you were out having a strop, on a very simple choice mind you. I was talking with Fuel and Aries, told them what they liked to know and how I was going to test out my power, trial and error and you certainly weren't letting me read your mind, until I mentioned your family that is",

with firmness I slammed my hands on the table, only to clench my teeth as I stated, "you leave me out of your pathetic games, I'm only here to kill your stupid Commander, and if you don't watch your mouth I will have to do the same to you",

she looked into my firm glaring eyes as she remarked,

"you can't kill something that's already dead",

as smirk grew on my face as I said shortly,

"clearly you've not fought the Undead before",

when facing away from her I looked to Rhax as I said,

"once you and Marcella are done here meet me on the east side of the camp, we're going to take The Red Valley and work our way around",

when leaving the tent, Marella took the chance to remark,

"that won't work, you can take but you can't keep taking",

I left the tent not satisfying her games as I hunted for Aries and Fuel, get the answer straight from themselves and see what they had to say, better hope they have a good excuse this whole messy situation is bad enough as it is without some manipulating K.I.L.O on our hands, I've killed them , and seen some killed before to know when its over for good…unfortunately I don't have enough things to kill her with, and as much as I hate to agree with the team on this but we need her.

When searching the campsite I paused my tracks, seeing Abby on the south side of the campsite, when approaching the outskirts of it I could see her playing with Aries, she was searching for something, no doubt the bizarre bone game that Aries made up, but they looked happy…very happy, sometimes I forget that Aries is just a little older than Abby by a few three years.

I watched for a while seeing Abby was smiling as she was talking to Aries.

Fuel was with Alis and Sevis who were wandering far from them, they were searching the fields, keeping an eye out on the perimeter until it was time to move camp.

Sevis was speaking with Alis, they were also happy, perhaps this intense atmosphere I was creating got them to do other things, occupy themselves as I was determined not to befriend Marella, but I'm still not going to.

I walked away only to be met face to face with Deago, almost bumping into him as he questioned,

"woah watch yourself Merider; you okay, you've been a bit intense around here?",

well that confirmed my worries, I can't believe I let this take over me, but I couldn't help it, trusting people over and over again only to be betrayed by a handful of them, it's just getting harder to trust when people are determined to stab me in the back, I have too many scars of those, it's starting to mark me .

I noticed Deago changed his gear to black and white like me, he had his helmet attached to his back, it was there for when he needed it, he didn't have a rucksack either to store ammo, in-fact he just had two clean white hilted and black bladed swords by his sides, he had a new look to him it was refreshing to see him in something else for once.

He and I walked into the campsite, straying to the east side of the campsite, facing to where the next city was.

As we walked I stated,

"it's just I can't trust her, she's telepathic she knows more than us",

he wondered,

"perhaps you're worried that she would see something in you that others can't, because we all have our secrets, but what you're hiding shouldn't be let out by a simple read of the mind, is that what you're worried about?",

in a way I guess I was feeling insecure about it, it was like with Macey, she was able to control my mind and turn me against my friends, or turn my friends against me, it feels as though I've met her again, but as someone much worse, and more obnoxious than before.

With a slight sigh, trying to collect my first thoughts I said simply,

"she brought up my family, she was trying to get me angry

and I was worried, she was saying about speaking to Fuel and Aries about the theory, but even so, I feel like as though she's trying to get me to be angry at her, I don't know why",

we stood on the east side of the camp, seeing the city stretching ahead of us, probably nowhere near the dome but if we keep going east we can find The Red Valley, but something tells me we should go southeast to The Cursed Village.

It's like something isn't being told over there, they are rumoured to be cursed, but I'm not so sure about it, something about the place seems off for certain, but if all brings death, then that place wouldn't bring the worst of him. Deago and I stood firmly, taking the view in as he wondered, "Aries and Fuel were talked into the plan? Or were they involved with it?",

not seeing it as a big deal anymore, I reassured,

"probably both but either way, I know that if Marella is going to try and get on my nerves she's going to be in a grave by the end of it",

he laughed shortly only to agree,

"well, she sure as hell will be, maybe from you more than me, Xharlot is even getting annoyed about it",

I looked to him as I wondered,

 "where is Xharlot? Is she with Kamic and Qorin?",

he confirmed,

"yeah, she was the last time I saw her. They were talking about creating some gear, seeing as there's a graveyard of a city they might get lucky and find something",

whatever keeps her busy then I don't mind, to be honest, it seems like we're sitting ducks here, nothing is happening and it's starting to get my feet cold, to wait around killed me, but I usually prepare during it so we have some form of action going on, but this is the silence I feared, not moving a single step.

With that in mind I informed,

"well, since they are doing that I can go over our options on the leave",

he listened firmly as I went on,

"Commander Artell, the one Marella works for; he has three clans keeping his ass safe, The Red Valley is east of here in front of the dome. Southeast is The Cursed Village, presumably, it's the name that makes people not want to go there. Then lastly, we have Clan Quarry, the people nest within The Quarry northeast of here to the left of the dome",

he took note as he wondered,

"Which route will you be going for? After all, this is your shot more than hers",

with slight thought I recapped on Marella's ideas and mine, I stated,

"Marella wants us to go to The Red Valley, because you can kill the infected clan with their own serum they have within the valley. But I also wanted us to take all clans, starting from the weakest one which most likely is The Cursed Village, to the strongest one which could be Clan Quarry",

he agreed,

"well, from what you explained they sound tight in those orders, besides she thinks taking one of the cities will do us fine but that gives the other clans a chance to take over",

he was on the same page as me, I'm glad he didn't give in to much to Marella but then again I saw he was avoiding her completely, along with Xharlot, Kamic, and Qorin, they most likely took my warning and stayed far from her, or it was just coincidental.

Deago glanced back as he stated,

"heads up",

I looked back, only to sigh inside, she was persistent to talk to me.

I don't know what games she was playing but it was starting to get on my nerves with the patronising voice, the good to the bad side of her, it was like she barely even knew herself.

I looked to Deago as I stated,

"go over to Rhax and Marcella in the tent, tell them about the plan",

Marella watched him walk past, frowning slightly as she faced me, he wondered,

"what plan? Presumably, you are still going with the whole 'liberating everywhere' plan",

with firmness I stated,

"if we don't do this they will attack us from the back and ambush us when we least expect it",

she cut in,

"look, Merider, I wasn't trying to make you feel like I was being hostile",

with a slight snuff, I wondered,

"and what are you trying to do?",

she said firmly,

"I was trying to impress you, and I've heard all about you; yes I know I have telepathic traits but it really just depends on if the person lets me in, or is too weak and lets me in",

she was trying to butter herself to me, but it wasn't going to work as I persisted,

"it doesn't matter what you want from me, or what you're trying to do. All we both have in common is wanting your Commander dead",

she added,

"exactly, so can we start on a clear slate",

she put her hand out expecting me to firmly grasp her arm, but I didn't.

With firmness, I stated,

"the only time we start on the clean slate is when we never meet again after this or you are dead",

she slowly lowered her hand as she wondered,

"why are you persistent to hate me? is it because of what I said earlier, being incomplete?",

I stated,

"no it's not that and you know what, since you're on that topic you were more than wrong about me",

my words turn colder when I expanded,

318

"my family may have not wanted me, apart from one, but even then, it wasn't for the right intentions, but even after all that, I discovered something about my family that everyone doesn't want to be faced with",

I approached her, looking her firmly in the eyes as I stated, "we don't like people in our way, and those who want us dead",

her eyes were flaring into mine as she wasn't giving into my threats.

She said with a stern voice,

"there are things you don't know about yourself, Merider, and the same goes to me when you decide to make me an enemy, I will be the worst person you've ever met",

she soon said with a lighter and softer tone,

"or if you stop with these accusations of me plotting to kill you, I can be the best ally you've ever had",

she moved back as she stated,

"we will move on you Commander but if you want my advice, wait for Kamic, Qorin and Xharlot to return to camp, they might just have something in mind for us",

she winked, I could just barely see her eyes through the helmet but the neon glow made it much clearer, I think she wore the rusty helmet to prove she was infected, and to show those she first met that she isn't to be messed with, but even a person with a thin amount of armour can be feared, it's what they are capable of that will scare them, not their appeal.

Seeing her walk away made me wonder more about her, why she played games, experiments with herself and her powers on other people, was she learning still? I thought having a decade, or a few years would have told her what she knows, perhaps she never listened and felt as though she never needed the lessons.

With that thought in mind, I strayed my attention to the city far ahead, seeing the towers, the sunrise was lowering between the buildings. Seeing the orange glow warmed my body, the atmosphere cleared my head as I thought simply on the mission at hand, not her, not what she can do or what I fear she can do, we just need to cross the city, and finally meet the three clans with our guns and swords, if they are his protectors they certainly won't welcome us with open arms and we won't do the same to them.

Those who ask for mercy we will give them it, but those who won't and will want to keep fighting until they die a horrible death, then that's going to have to be the case, I'm not messing around anymore, people keep on taking me and my team for granted, and its time to stand our ground and fight for what is right, even when we must be paired with someone you don't trust.

Even a leader must do things they hate for the sake of their people…in my case, it's trusting strangers.

Chapter Twenty-six
The First Marker

It took nearly dusk for Xharlot, Kamic, and Qorin to return, they had a few parts rolled over to the camp with a rusted trolley, apart from that they didn't carry anything else; the parts were mainly computers, components, metal sheets from cars and wall panels, just things like that for whatever reason they need it for.

They dumped the items in a pile by the north side of the camp, directly in the light and visible enough to see it within the darkening atmosphere.

Kamic shuffled the parts as I questioned,

"what is this stuff for?",

he picked up a pipe as he was midway into sorting the pile out from components to plain metal objects as he stated,

"well, you will need people to stay behind here, so I opted to stay. Qorin wanted to help collect the resources faster",

Qorin moved past Kamic as he reassured,

"trust me they will be fine, besides Elria is still needing to catch up, she was delayed on preparing for the journey; she said she had some things to gather up, she probably is coming with the whole artillery you know what she's like",

he laughed shortly as I gave him the smallest smile as I stated,
"well we better get going then, we waited long enough",
Kamic apologised,
"I do apologise about that Commander, Xharlot is a talker",
she nudged him only to state,
"I think it was you picking up too many things, glad Qorin
came, I don't think I could have pushed that trolley on my
own",
she smirked, only to have the face of thunder when facing me,
no doubt Marella is behind me...she has that sort of effect on
people.
When turning around I was faced to face with Marella as she
was joined with Deago, Rhax, and Marcella.
She questioned,
"as the team is back, are you ready to go, Merider?",
I glanced back to the team as I informed,
"Kamic is staying behind to wait for Elria, she possibly
might have something handy, or can be our back up",
she looked to me with a smirk as she wondered,
"that sounds promising, don't think you're quite convinced
though",
she was finding things to annoy me with, but even so I
looked past it as I stated,
"my team, my choices, if they think it's wise to stay behind
then I will let them, we have plenty of people, and I swear to
the sun if you speak ill of me or to me again, you will be
killed and that's a promise",
Qorin stood firmly to my left as Marella was put in her place,
I couldn't deal with her annoying threats and remarks
through the trip, so if she knows where she stands then we're
going to be able to work this out.
I moved past them as I ordered,
"you guys go ahead, I will collect Sevis and the rest of the
team",
Qorin stuck by me as Marcella, Deago and Rhax left with
Marella, going east within the fields large stretch as we

headed to Aries, Alis, Fuel, Xharlot, and Sevis they were by the outskirts of the camp within the torch light glow, they saw me as I approached them, seeing I had business to deal with.

Sevis approach me as he questioned,

"what's wrong Merider? Is it Marella?",

the others rounded to his right as they faced me, I explained shortly,

"we're going to the three clans, they all have traits of their own and I will explain as we go along, but one thing is for certain I need Abby to be guarded at all times",

when walking with the team Qorin was to my left as Sevis, Abby, Aries, Fuel, and Alis were on my right, we headed through the fields seeing the other half of the team far ahead of us, they were doing what I said and were drifting to the southeast side of the city, to at least pre-route ourselves for the mission ahead.

Upon explaining each clan in depth to the team, I soon dragged it onto about Abby.

I know she is younger than Aries by a few years but still, she's just a kid and not an experienced fighter like Aries.

I expanded,

"Abby will need to be kept watched by all of us",

Abby cut in,

"I know I'm a kid but I can fight",

Sevis wondered,

"out of one to ten would you say how you are skilled at firing a gun or using a blade?",

Abby said with thought,

"uh, six with a gun, that's up close, but far, I would say one", she felt awkward as she knew that wasn't very good for anyone, she went on,

"well I'm good with a sword that I can carry, definitely say an eight",

Aries reassured,

"perhaps you can just work on that but if you are going to

survive out here you have to get better at fighting",

Abby remarked,

"that's easy for you to say, you were in an arena for some time, you know everything about fighting, and yet you don't get treated like a child",

Aries explained,

"you get treated like a child but not by certain people, for example Alis treats me like a brat but that's because she's my sister",

she motioned to Fuel as she went on,

"Fuel treats me like an equal like everyone, for the sake of my skill, and it's generally all it is, if I didn't know how to fight, people would be protective over me just like Merider is of you, she's just trying to be responsible",

Aries knew how to get Abby on the same page, she was understanding that to be treated like a kid wasn't all that bad, perhaps it gets annoying but she needs to prove that when she no longer has to rely on our protection then and only then will she not be a child anymore, or helpless.

The sun shimmered across the thick dry grass, giving us that smallest bit of light to allow us to rummage around in our rucksacks, taking out hand torches.

We shone them ahead as we caught up to the other half of the team, Qorin was firmly with Deago as we lined up on the field, we kept the formation to see who was with us as the field grew darker.

Our feet crunched against the dry grass as the thick smell of rotting flesh and smoke weakened, it was as if we were finally getting out of the Dead Zone, yet we were still behind the walls, perhaps this sector of the Dead Zone is untouched by the Undying, perhaps the Commander doesn't like them or rather not be in contact with them, that will mean he definitely wouldn't want contact with us.

To think that a person like him would not only trap his companions but he wouldn't let them breathe without his say so, this place runs on corruption and half of it's breathing with free will, this sector might be the last to finally breakthrough this wretched system and bring back the lands that once breathed the fine air, perhaps not that fine but enough for it to relieve weight off peoples shoulders.

Our feet were pacing across the fields, meeting the outskirts of the city as I ordered,

"we go through, the clearest way to see where we're going is through the large roads",

Marella didn't have an input in the choice, she must have learned where her place is, I don't mind her having some form of an idea, but not when it comes to knowing a safe route, I need to be certain about the choice.

I'm no expert but when it comes to the past, my trials and errors, I've learned that alleyways aren't the best way to go, besides the clear roads ahead show us what we need, the cars and the abandonments of the buildings where shrouding over us as we walked through the centre of the roads.

When taking a glance to the buildings on the left and right of us they had their windows smashed in each one, some had no windows at all as they were glittered and scattered across the dark grey roads of the streets we roamed past, our feet were quiet, but it was those fragments of glass that made us noisy, the crunching and scraping of the glass against the floor didn't help us with the discretion.

The areas we walked past were complete silence, our feet were the only things making noise out here as the buildings creeks were whispering warnings in the background, alerting people of our arrival as we were drifting to the southeast side of the city, things were getting darker as the buildings were getting more and more burned, if the dome is as big as the map shows it to be, we should be able to see it from miles away, but with a building that big it can't just be one large charging station, that would just be impractical, there's more to this, and I knew full-well Marella knows, perhaps getting her involved with the team won't affect me, but it will warm her up to being open with us, even if I hated it, she's still helping us at the end of the dead, she didn't kill us yet if that's a motive.

I looked to Qorin as I stated,

"get Fuel and Alis to scout ahead with Rhax and Marcella, they can collect things on the way if they are handy",

he wondered,

"what about Marella, she's going to be isolated virtually",

he was concerned for her but not enough to care, just wondering why I would want her singled out, with firmness, I explained,

"that's because I'm going over there and talk it out with her, we have along stretch of road ahead and if I'm neck and neck with her it won't do us any good",

he smirked to me as he remarked,

"and that you want her close, you keep your friends close, but your enemies closer",

I rolled my eyes as he left, seeing he made a cliché quote, well, either way, he wasn't wrong in my plan, yes it's bad to be her friend for the sake of keeping her close to me but she will just be a bigger explosion if we leave her to wonder in her own mind, pondering of ways to kill us one by one and that won't be good for either of us.

Qorin went to the right as he got Fuel and Alis as he went ahead to Marella and the others, they were walking a few paces to the left of us, she wanted to keep a distance as the others were sticking by her, not for her sake I hope, but mine, if not then they generally do trust her words, I'm still figuring out whether or not she is to be trusted at all, but that's a fight with myself I haven't won yet, perhaps she was right or perhaps she was wrong, I don't know what she wants or what she is after.

Yet from all of this, I know that we must stick together and even when you don't trust the person or dislike them you don't have a choice, they are there, and they are on your hands also, that's until they betray your trust and you know what to do.

As he left with the team, Sevis questioned,

"what is happening, Commander?",

to get him on my speed I explained,

"I need to talk with Marella on her own, I'm getting Qorin and the others by her to be on guard and patrol ahead of the roads, ensure we don't get surprised by anyone else on the way",

he then wondered,

"so why did Alis have to go?",

I reassured,

"It's just to look more convincing, the more people on patrol the more likely she will believe I didn't plan her being on her own, besides even if she knows we can do with the extra precautions, I don't know about you but this place is too quiet if you ask me",

Sevis agreed,

"you're not wrong there, a quiet ruin always holds haunting ghost, in this case, brutal foes and Undying",

he looked to Abby as she questioned,

"did you just say haunting ghost?",

he smirked as she stated,

"well ghost of Egyptverus are hauntingly terrifying. They curse families, Pharaohs and even the deadly Pharo",

Abby then wondered,

"what's the difference between the Pharaoh and a Pharo",

as they were going over his history Aries joined in with the conversation, she was keeping guard along with Sevis, but either way they were both interested to find out more about Sevis, my curiosity was growing but I saw Marcella, and Rhax leading the walk with Qorin, Alis and Fuel, their lights were shining cross the buildings, floors and small fenced off alleyways to ensure we didn't face any trouble on the way to our first marker, that's where we want our problems to be we really don't need any more before barely even reaching the midway point to the fields surrounding the dome, the reed valley I will be cautious of but you can see it easily so it's very easy to avoid fore certain, but the Clan Quarry sound just as unpredictable, they may nest in the Quarry but even that isn't enough for people.

With firmness my feet wondered to the left, straying to Marella as she sighed,

"Merider, I'm not saying anything, you made it very clear", when keeping to her right I expressed,

"no, I came to apologise",

she looked surprised only to look at me as he wondered, "you're planning something aren't you, you wouldn't apologise unless you want something",

I added,

"or when I realised I've stepped out of line",

she heard me out as I expanded,

"look I shouldn't have singled you out and not even give you a chance. I still don't trust you but it doesn't mean my team members can't make the choice themselves, and they proved to me that you aren't as bad as I make it out to be",

she laughed slightly as she joked,

"you're very great at apologising has anyone told you that?", with a smirk I stated,

"well, I never usually have to apologise, but when I do, it's when I know my actions were wrong and they could seriously affect the way my team and I work",

she looked to me as she wondered,

"why don't you trust me?",

she wasn't being cynical or cold, she generally wanted to know why I didn't trust her.

My words trailed on,

"well, you don't make it easy for people to like you. You killed your own men and discarded them like paper in a burning flame, the list goes on",

she smirked as she expanded,

"well I wanted to impress you, as I said at the beginning about being incomplete; it makes you want to be someone you wished to be, or at least a figure you want to follow", it sounded as though she was trying to be an admirer to me, she was taking inspiration from me somehow, but I haven't shown her anything, she hasn't seen me do anything to want her to become like me, or behave like me.

With that in mind, I wondered,

"you say you admire me, and see something in me, but then you insult me for one, then you claim these things, and you just go back to normal as nothing happens",

she went into thought as she explained,

"the serum makes me naturally aggressive, if I feel threatened and angry it's the first emotion to show through. You would know with the serum as you have had your experience with it, but even so you got rid of it, I can't do that with mine because then I would really be dead",

how did she know about the serum? Oh, right she just read my mind because I relaxed for a moment, the stress levels were down low, and I felt like nothing was going to harm me when I was around her, but that feeling was dangerous, no wonder Rhax and Marcella are around her so often they feel this sensation of safety and protection from the outside world.

With thoughts straying I wondered,

"why do you need to use your telepathic powers all the time? It feels as though you need to know what peoples thoughts are",

she smirked as she revealed,

"well the thing is I can't help it. My powers tell me to read their minds and I do it, they tell me my body is weak and with human contact or using it regularly it makes me stronger",

knowing about the serum I used I stated,

"sometimes being too strong gets you killed and if what you say is true and that without the powers you will officially be dead, then the power's aren't worth living for, you will be harming yourself and people around you",

she snuffed,

"you say that like it's a good thing, to let my power go and cure myself to only die, that's not happening and you won't understand what it's like to be under his project, he made the serum so if we decided to betray him we would be dead anyways when we cure ourselves, from all the wounds we sustained from battle with the serum, they will reappear and kill us for good",

that was strange, it's as though the serum remembers where and when the person was killed or stabbed and injured, and it will give it back to the body, like some form of schematic when they are dead, I wouldn't want to die like that.

With wonder I questioned,

"okay perhaps that wouldn't be a good idea, but the serum isn't good for you, even with the one I had, I still was connected to people made in the same batch of the blue serum. It turned me against my friends, it hurt me and made me do things I didn't want to do, the serum was gone but it came back to me again, perhaps I'm still infected now but so far from what I've went through nothing has activated it",

she wondered,

"perhaps killing the serum won't work but you tamed yours, how did you do it?",

without any other choice but to tell her I explained,

"well I killed those who had Macey's genes in the serum, mine was related to her and we killed her, but I had to kill a companion infected by her, she took over and tried to kill Londelis but I stopped it by using the broaches of Macey's that she gave to her companions, each one half a fragment of her pure serum, and I got rid of it",

she admitted,

"to be honest that sounds complicated, how will I find my batch?",

with a shrug I didn't know that answer myself, and the green serum was far different than the blue, I wouldn't know about what she can do, but I can give her ideas, maybe if I help her, she will be more likely to be closer to me, gaining her trust a bit more.

Giving her a slight idea I stated,

"well if Artell knows all about the serum then he will be the best person to answer the question, and he is a robot, like you said, so we can take his memory core back to camp, and hook it up to a computer",

she looked doubtful as she stated,

"his memory core is as tall as a forty-foot tree, the scientist have it underground so if anything we can take over the lab, perhaps then it will be safer to hack into",

she wasn't wrong, but the strangest thing about all of this with me and her, was that she had the calming aura of her, she didn't seem hostile to me anymore, but how can she do it? Perhaps it was a seriously bad sign, but so far, nothing horrible has happened yet, and I say yet as if it's going to get worse when walking deeper and deeper into the calming energy she emits from herself.

I glanced back to the team seeing Sevis was doing fine, they had stopped talking for a moment, so Aries could show Abby the ropes of the gun, showing her how and how not to hold a gun, they were laughing as Aries pointed the gun to Sevis like a gangster, tilting the gun sideways.

A small smile peaked upon my face before I turned back as Marella questioned,

"you really care about them, don't you?",

seeing as she was trying to start a different conversation I stated,

"well I care about all of them equally",

she cut in,

"I highly doubt that, you seem to have something for Elria",

with a puzzled look I wondered,

"I don't know what you're talking about, can you clarify on that?",

she smirked as she reassured,

"well, I won't tell anyone what you were thinking earlier about Elria",

I blushed only to state,

"can we not. Okay, I need you to promise me you won't read my mind, unless it's absolutely necessary",
she said with a smirk,
"no problems Merider, I think I can limit myself",
she seems more relaxed around me now, hopefully this bridge I built will stop the team from feeling uncomfortable, I know they know it's me being protective and it is, but something about Marella didn't sit right with me, she would be willing to betray her leader, kill her people and walk with us to get rid of each of his people, maybe this was for her and not for me, she is planning something but I won't know until we get to the dome, only then will her true colours show.

Our feet trampled upon the empty roads, passing time with small talk as we joined with Sevis and the others, they were uneasy about Marella but because I was there they saw it was okay, for now at least; they always trust my judgement without a doubt, but even so, they still have their own thoughts deep down inside and if something is clearly bothering them, then they would mention it to me for certain, I don't like to cancel people out when it comes to the free will of speech, it only depends on if they have a reasoning behind it.

So for example they can have input with a plan, but they must expand on it for it to make sense to us, to at least make them stick to the ground a bit more.

Perhaps I'm too full on when it comes to having control of things, but in the end, the team understands that and they explain their points so I can be convinced on what is the right choice, and with Marella's perks of being the puppet to Artell we can easily get this mission done, but if it's too easy then I know we barely even made the first step, I'm worried that if we get Marella to do everything or even participate in the battle she will get her wish of power, she said she gained it from using it so we limit the use.

Even a puppet can kill its own controller, it only takes one small hiccup for them to cut the string and be their own person, let's hope I'm enough to stop that from happening.

Chapter Twenty-seven
The Daunting Gallows

When creeping further and further out of the city we were met with two roads, one going ahead to the valley in the form of a high way, it looked as though the roads were untouched and undamaged from the first storm, the only things that were damaged were the cars dotting through it, the traffic lights were torn and bent to face the floor, the signs were even torn from the roots from the fields surrounding it. However just like with the green valley, there were sticks of glowing red lights going from the centre of the road, they were built in, emitting a sinister red glow all over the cracked concrete.

The glow was vibrant but it shimmered red making it all the worse to walk through to see what we were getting into, I looked right to the second road, seeing the scruffy made pathways of pebbles, flint, and large scraps of tiles from homes previously destroyed from the storm no doubt, why was that pathway different from the others, perhaps is a lot darker but if it leads to where you want it to or at least where you presume it does, then there's no harm going for either. Marella questioned,

"Merider, you can't still be wanting to go to The Cursed Village, is there a way we can compromise this?",
the team rounded on me, having their backs to the glowing road as I explained,
"we can't go the easy route, the light is what helps him see us, we make our way in the darkness, we use our torches and listen with silence, talk is on whisper level when we get to the off road",
I looked to Marcella, Alis, Fuel and Aries as I stated,
"since you all are careful, quietest and excellent scouts you guys are going to be team one, walking ahead of our team as we follow behind, we keep our voices down and if you have any problems Marcella knows the signals to stop the group, we round up to you and we go on from there",
Marcella nodded firmly as she ordered,
"alright, team one, on me",
they paced ahead, going around ten feet from us as we trailed behind them, having their backs as my orders were to continue, we may have their backs but we don't have our own, the sides of the pathways are even more unpredictable, the fields of darkness didn't give the welcoming feeling as we went further and further from Red Valleys pathway.
The quietness was growing deafening as we didn't even make a whisper, we were all afraid of making noise as our feet tapped on the ground, Marcella and her team were ahead keeping the lights on the pathways but occasionally drift to the left and right as the grass was rustling and crunching.
A smell of rotting and decay was closing in on us, but not the Undying it was as if someone just died recently, I made sure Abby stuck to my right as Aries was to my left, Marella was next to her as Deago and Qorin were trailing behind us, being the barricade and last line of defence against any ambush, it made me feel a lot safer knowing they had our backs, but I still glanced back to them, only to hear Deago put his helmet on, it made him feel safer no doubt or to scare anyone we met on the road, if Marella wasn't enough with her skull helmet

there's Deago with his Spartan looking helmet, just a little on the sharper side.

Sevis was keeping a firm place to the right of Abby, making sure she didn't touch the end of the wide stony pathway, this road could bring carriages down it, vans even, it was wide meaning they had built this road for a reason, perhaps it's still in use but I don't know if that's entirely true.

I mean the roads were isolated; the rocks were dusty, ashy, and not even a print to be seen, maybe the curse was that it was inhabitable, nothing we need to worry about as we aren't planning to stay, but even if that's correct we need to be certain that no one lives here.

With caution Abby questioned,

"Merider, why did we go down this road again?",

she was scared but she couldn't be, she needs to not be afraid. I said firmly,

"it's the route that won't get us killed, we aren't going to risk being seen by the dome",

I glanced left seeing the spec on the horizon, it was the Dome, but even a spec can be large when examining it up close, it was far away and so were the cities, but that's to be expected, if he wanted to be found he would have made it easy to be seen, but it's the travel that people fear, I may be ageing but my legs are working like they once did, perhaps a little achier. My word went on,

"we take this by the hilt, the sooner we get through this then the more markers we kill, besides, you're too deep to turn back now",

she looked to Sevis as he said to her quietly,

"perhaps you would want to hear a story? A one about The Lone Girl",

she looked uneasy as she wondered,

"is it bad? Is it going to be like a scary story because I'd rather not hear it if it is",

he smirked slightly as he reassured,

"no it's a life lesson story",

she remarked,

"oh. One of those, if it's good then I don't mind",

Sevis looked around, keeping sure his side of the pathway didn't have any lurking foes as he said cautiously,

"The Lone girl was poor, she lived on the streets, she never even had friends they all single her out all because she was a kid, she must belong to someone, right? Well, she didn't, her mother died giving birth to her and soon was raised by her godparents, however her father would travel the sea's with her, only to be killed by the captain, and she was thrown overboard, luckily found by a sailor",

Abby remarked,

"how is this supposed to make me feel better?",

Sevis cut in,

"not all stories start off in the right side, it always shows their struggle to how they heal, now where was I",

he collected himself only to continue his intriguing story, I wondered where it was going.

He went on,

"so she was found by a sailor, she ended up being traded to a slave trade and one day she had enough of being given away, for her birth, for spite, for greed, she decided it was time to make something for herself.",

Even though the story was getting intriguing I couldn't let my guard down, every time I looked at Sevis my mind was being distracted, it didn't help that Marella had the aura to calm either, she made me feel safe and if she stood next to Aries she was making her feel a little lazy, but Aries was persistent, she had her pistol on the go, she had it aimed to the floor until it was needed.

Sevis continued,

"she went on to be a warrior of the land, taking peoples lives who would take from others, giving people the wealth of protection and teaching those to not take anymore than they needed, if the person takes and takes they will only get greed, but it's only what they give afterwards that will make them

look less greedy",
Abby wondered,
"so you're saying that all of that happen and she became this warrior? One that was giving and taking",
Sevis added,
"and she was also your age, you don't need age to be a warrior, if you're one and taking down small bugs you are warrior, if you are ten and taking down hyenas you are a warrior, if you are twenty and taking down the ferocious villains in your path then you ARE the warrior, the protector", she smiled slightly, seeing as Sevis overall was just saying to her that it takes time to be what you want to be, to take is to give, as long as what you're giving will make the person you're helping live a happier life.

The story brought some comfort to me only for me to shake it off as I stated,
"we better keep the volume on mute for a moment, we're passing through a forest",
with my luck I needed this silence to be sudden, we were entering the forest and Abby was still curious about what other stories Sevis knew about, but we can't go the journey with the talking, not at least without a few quiet breaks, we really need to hear our surroundings it won't help any of us if we are heard by anyone.

There was a slight ambience to the area, it was strange it sounded like a low hum; the trees were shrouded with red leaves, they were oozing red thick goo, but it never dropped from the leaves, it just coated the top of the leaves, showing us the reflection of our torches when looking at the surroundings.

Sevis looked to the bushes and shrubs by the edges of the wide pathway as he stated,
"the bushes are the same colour, I wonder if this was a bad idea",
he glanced at me as he stated,
"the liquid doesn't move either, I think it's a type of thick

338

poison, we shouldn't touch them",

with the agreement we kept away from the edges of the pathway, keeping a safe distance from it as we listened out for anything odd, but this place was already giving off that vibe, not even Marella's aura could stop us from feeling unnerved of the surroundings.

The trees were chattering as a form of fog was starting to grow, it was coming from warm water springs, whatever was in them clearly didn't mix well with it, it turned a deep purple colour, the water was smelling almost like gas, like methane.

We kept our pace as we didn't want to tire ourselves out and move faster for the sake of the atmosphere growing darker as we headed deeper into the pathway. The noises within the background were sounding like whispers, I know it was the wind, but it was like an enchanted orchestra within his place it was starting to chill my spine. Not only were the leaves of the trees were swaying and chattering, but the hot springs were bubbling, spitting, sizzling like they had their own mind pattern. Shrubs and bushes were too contributing to the chilling orchestra as their leaves shuttered, their bodies were shivering, it was as if they were watching us walk past, each of us felt as though we were being watched either from afar or something was breathing down our necks.

The fog was heavy and trailing by our feet, making it harder and harder to see what we were walking on, the only thing that helped us know we were still on the pathway was the large split from the left and right side of the deathly forest.

My breaths were growing more shallow as I questioned,

"Marella, you didn't mention that this would be on the route?",

she remarked,

"you never asked me",

I rolled my eyes as I said firmly,

"okay, next time I ask you something tell me what I should know",

---

Aries stated,

"Merider I don't think you should be talking",

she was warry of something as I said with an even quieter whisper,

"what is it?",

she glanced left as she shone the torch, she questioned,

"can you hear that?",

she kept it there as the team stopped walking as Sevis got Marcella and her team to stop, they looked left as I questioned,

"the hell is that?",

Aries remarked,

"I don't know that's behind that tree but I think we should just keep going, feels like we should be looking at it",

the thing behind the tree looked like a person, something was below it, but I couldn't tell it was so dark and gloomy, the thing below the person was a platform of a sort, they didn't touch it though, perhaps my mind is playing a trick on me but it was curiosity that was urging me to check it out, see what it was.

I looked to the team as I questioned,

"does anyone want to go with me to check it out?",

Qorin remarked,

"well I don't think I have a choice do I, look let's make this quick",

Marella stated,

"you really shouldn't check it out",

with curiosity I wondered,

"do you know what it is?",

she didn't know herself I could see it on her face, there are some things that need to be found to ease our minds or scare us into working a little bit faster.

She admitted,

"no I don't know what it is, but I think it should stay that way",

I moved past her as I said firmly,

"it will be quick",

Qorin walked with me as we went off the road, moving past the shrubs that stained our black trousers to a shade of red, just enough to see that the plants marked us.

We soon were walking on the flat grassy grounds, the heavy fog made it hard to see where we were stepping, but we trod carefully, going further and further towards the person behind the tree, they had their backs to us as their left side of their body was visible from where we stood.

With slight hesitation we walked around the large wonky tree; our lights were shone on the person stripped of all clothing, marked with an equilateral triangle in the centre of her chest, there were two small circles to the left and right side to the points of the triangle.

When moving further behind the tree I could see the platform or rather known as gallows, where the platform door lowers, and the person is hung for a crime. When looking at the scene I could see a line that was marked where the point of the triangle looked to the floor; a circle was above the vertical line as a circle was marked below it just past her belly button.

The markings were made of deep cuts, it wasn't enough to spill her insides out, but it was enough to see the flesh behind her pale grey skin. Her dark black hair was put behind her head as the rope around her neck was made of barbed wire, it was to make sure she died from the fall or the barbed wire digging into her throat, it was sad to see something so barbaric, what was I even looking at. The blood drizzled from her stomach, twisting around her legs as a puddle was below her feet, from human bowels excretions to blood, dark red. The woman must have been around twenty, she was so young, but for what reason was this needed? The extremity of this punishment was inhumane and wrong, with the markings she was prepared for this before being hung that's for certain, the only place I know where we can get the answers is The Cursed Village.

When hurrying back to the pathway Aries questioned,
"what did you find?",
Qorin answered,
"some sort of punishment ritual, she was marked chest to stomach in markings created by deep cuts",
Marcella said firmly,
"gives us more of a reason to go to this place, if that's there and the corpse is still bleeding that means someone is there and we need to stop them, before they kill anyone else", Marcella left with her team as we trailed behind them, the smell of the corpse and faeces stained my nostrils, it was slowly wearing away, but the sight didn't leave my head I couldn't believe something that was still going around, being hung is the worst way possible to die but she had barbed wire around her neck, certainly whoever wanted her to die wanted it to be the most uncomfortable way for her to end.

The trip was growing more silent upon our discovery, The Cursed Village must be into some sort of punishment system for delusions and hallucinations; thinking about the forest and what plants are here, no doubt there has to be a side effect to being here for far too long, they might even see Artell as some sort of sign and will do what he says because of what they see, perhaps that's why the woman we saw was killed in such a brutal way, because people thought she was something that she wasn't, it makes a lot of sense but I can't prove it without seeing the place for myself, see the way they act. It could be like with Bharkry Island with the purpose drugging, but instead, this one was a natural drug dosage coming from nature's vegetation, perhaps it was the hot springs and their unnatural arrival in the lands, they might hold a chemical that had a short-lasting effect when here temporarily.

Then maybe when they've been here for decades they made a form of clan, a symbol for themselves then Artell took the chance to take advantage of them.

Maybe the effects are permanent after a decade or so, it

makes sense, but it scares me to know that none of them can be saved, not unless they have an antidote to this and move somewhere less toxic, they might call it The Cursed Village but all I see it as is a damsel in distress, they don't know how to leave and the longer they stay there the worse they will get, I just hope that the leader knows something, or if not, then we will have no choice but to kill them before they can do more harm than good.

With that in mind, I looked to Aries as I stated,

"the people of The Cursed Village might be drugged by the springs, I might know a way to taint them to normal but I don't know how many springs there are",

Marella answered,

"over fifty-five springs so if you do plan on trying to clean the springs then you are in for a challenge, the best case is to kill them",

Aries defended,

"well they might not even know what they are doing, properly anyway. They know they are killing these people but they might not know it, not what they think, they are innocent in some ways and if we can try to help them first then we take that risk, don't you take risks?",

Aries was laying the heat on Marella seeing as she likes to take the easy route all the time, and it's understandable with her powers and traits but I can see why I never wanted to end out like her, the power made things easy and that's never a good thing, to succeed in what you want it has to be difficult to reach, because when you grasp it you can feel what you earned, not what you bought with power.

So that we weren't be loud we kept our voices low as Marella stated,

"well, if you read their minds you would know that they don't want to be cured, all they think is death, and how to kill the next impure wonderer",

seeing as she was telling us half the story of these people I encouraged, "can you tell us exactly what these people are? Perhaps with a better understanding of this situation I might be able to come up with something else",

she said with a slight sigh,

"well they are The Cursed Ones, the ones that live and breathe the hot springs air, we don't get infected by the fog, not unless we go directly to the source, so I highly recommend we don't go there, something we really should do is go by the springs",

she carried on,

"but that might be hard as if you want to see the leader, his fortress, as he calls it, has a hot spring in the back, so perhaps we can linger around the village instead",

with firmness I agreed,

"well until we know how to bypass the springs that's going to have to be the case",

 seeing as she knew much about the person and the clan I wondered,

"what about the springs here? How did you know how many of them there were?",

she explained shortly,

"when leaving I was told to visit each city, read what they had to say about their status and what to have in return for them for giving me that information, so in this case they wanted more hot springs which Artell did himself, he was able to create them with his charge of powers, and he returned a day later to change back to normal",

Artell sounded as though he had a secret to him, for a robot to have powers perhaps he runs on the serum, or his charging station is a mixture of serum for his blood and electricity for the kinetic movements of his limbs, it would make sense.

The idea of him was overwhelming, he has more power than I have sought to believe at the beginning of the whole mission, he can create springs, a made anomaly that was created by nature not him, but he was able to make it himself, perhaps when we meet him he might be able to be turned off but a switch, he is a robot, not a human, and the one perk of that is they always have an off switch, or a way of killing them by overloading their power circuits, either way, I have a rough idea on how to kill him but the dome I don't know what beholds inside of it, and it doesn't sound good to me. Our voices were quietened by the sounds of the forests rugged movements, and the sounds of chanting, the real voices of people and not natures made whispers, it was starting to make me feel very unwelcome seeing the trees ahead turn into huts, a large circular ground where the homes circled facing a huge squared platform within the centre of the village.

The platform was a gallows station, there were one hanging ropes for each direction, the gaps in-between were dipped into the floor, creating ramps leading to the platforms and the villages stony pebbled grounds.

The ropes were made of barbed wire to ensure the person stayed in place when the floor dropped, and it was raised by a wheel to the left side of the regular metal frame holding the rope upon it, it was like a rotary frame, it would lower the wire to the person, hook them on and when they dropped and choked to death they were lifted, hanging like a decoration for them.

The homes were made of old stone and wood, the floors around it were large and spacious, but the sides of the huts were making it look bigger, they were two floors tall, but they were skinny, they could possibly hold four rooms in each one but in this place they don't eat in the huts. We walked in the village, feeling the dark eerily sound of silence, the people weren't here or were inside the homes.

The platforms frames of the ropes showed the large hut at the back, two floors wide and three floors tall, it was larger than the rest of the huts but the thing that crept us out the most was that all the window lights were turning on, lighting orange to our presence.

Perhaps this was seriously a bad choice of judgement.

Chapter Twenty-eight
The Dreaded

After one light to the next people were waking up or at least that was what it looked like. No one came out of their homes, it was starting to give me the chills as I ordered,
"Sevis, keep watch of Abby, stay here with the team",
seeing as it was a risk for all of us to enter the centre of the village to get a better look of the place I took the risk of going further by myself, that way only I get injured if something happens, if not then this place is safe, even when it looks like it's going to kill us.

Being Marcella, she followed me as she stated,
"I don't trust this place for you to wonder just a little further, besides whatever is here looks as though they have abandoned the place",
the village was overlooking us, watching us as we moved closer to the gallows centred in the ground, why would they even have these in the first place? what kind of drug causes them to kill and do deranged things?

We lurked around the gallows, seeing the large hut behind it, the Commander's hut, and frankly, the one we should be staying clear of, the hot spring behind it was smothering the hut's floor, making the dense fog scatter on the floor.

With caution I turned back to the team, shaking my head as I motioned them to come towards us, even though it was safe for them to move I kept watch of them as I said to Marcella, "when learning about the plants back in Base 19, didn't we read up on it? well, you did the background checks on the books when you joined anyways. Wasn't there something about hot springs because we were figuring out the Bharkry drugging system",

she recalled,

"perhaps, to be honest, I kind of wanted to forget I did that much reading, it was a VERY long time of reading",

I smirked slightly seeing even the most loyal and smartest people get bored easily, well, fortunately, I was the nerd and read all night, well tried to at least. The team rounded up on me as I explained,

"I will split us into two groups again, but this one it's not about who can do what, we need equal balance so we both survive",

with a firmness I informed,

"Qorin, Abby, Fuel, Marella, and Alis you are team one",

Qorin made sure Abby stuck by him as I went on,

"Aries, Deago, Marcella, Xharlot and I will be team two, but obviously that leaves us with an extra person so Sevis can go with who he pleases",

He joined Qorin's team, seeing as Abby was his priority of protection, which I needed someone to be by her side, he was a perfect guard, and couldn't have asked for any more of him. My team and Qorin's team were set to go, now it's the case of not getting us caught in a trap.

 with firmness, I ordered,

"Qorin, you take your team and search the perimeter, if you hear any commotion what so ever, you return here or you leave, because you don't get any other options, is that clear?",

he nodded as he got the team to follow him to the left side of the village, cautiously walking to the homes with their light on, wondering whether it was faulty electrical connections or generally was a haunted mess, either way, I don't believe in superstitions of ghost, but even so I've learned in this new world that anything is possible, you just have to see it with your own eyes.

With firmness, I went over my team's instructions as I expressed,

"we haven't got a choice to avoid the hut back there, we are just going to have to risk it and go to it",

Marella stated,

"we can't. Trust me when I say this, but the house is a time bomb, it's unpredictable, the last time I was here the people darn near killed me",

Marcella wondered,

"what are these people? You gave me the impression that people were here?",

she said firmly,

"people, but not what you think. You know that red stuff on the shrubs? That's them",

with a frown I questioned,

"hold on what? I don't think I heard you correctly can you expand on what you just said",

the goo we saw can't be people, it's physically not even possible, why would they hide in the forest, and not the village within the forest? This is getting weirder and weirder.

Marella explained,

"look I know it's strange but it's true, the people are fucking curses or something. They just turn into that goo and form into their original state",

with a frown I puzzled,

"but how can they do that?",

she pointed as she said calmly,

"like that",

when turning back I soon saw a red cloud stream on the floor, I ordered,

"Qorin, get over here, now",

Qorin and his team could be heard approaching behind us as we stared in horror at this thick blood-red smog cut through the white dense fog.

The red cloud's trail ended as it paused in-front of me,

forming a human with its vine-like movements.

It ravelled the body to look like muscle, only to soon form its skin and clothes, the man that stood in-front of me had short dark black hair, pale white skin, deep red eyes along with blood-stained lips.

The man was wearing a robe of black and red shimmering colours, the trimmings were made of a metallic red colour, looking much like thorns and vines as it ringed around the end of his sleeves, bottom of his robes, and the parts going parallel on the front of his robes.

The hood on his robe was down, it was flattened against his back as it pointed to the smoggy floor, underneath the robe I could see his cut chest, deep scars of wounds he had, presumably the ritual they were doing, it looked much like a triangle edge below his collar bone, but his robes covered the rest of him, so I couldn't tell if that was true or not. He had a rugged dark black pair of trousers on that touched in with his leather brown boots, they looked as though they were bounded together by thorns and other things to keep it in place. He had a rugged short beard that coated his jaw and upper lip, it was boxed on his cheeks as the thick facial hair connected cleanly. His eyes were watching me as he said with a soft voice,

"you are not Marella",

he was darting his eyes around as I looked back to the team, seeing that Marella changed her eye colour to her original brown shade, she was hiding from him, why? Well perhaps she doesn't want to be killed by them but then again neither do we, they look like they mean business, that's for certain.

He drew his attention to me as he questioned,

"what is your business here wonderer?",

my intentions were to kill them yet I don't think that's going to happen so easily, to cover up our tracks I stated,

"Artell claimed this place will help seek us answers",

he looked pleased as he said firmly,

"I see, well he says the same about you; he sees you have

answers he needs but he claims you are what we need",

my heart started thumping as his words chilled down my spine, his smile, his appeal, it isn't going to lead into a bright path that's for certain.

My lies continued as I said with a fake convincing smile, "well whatever you need answers for I'm sure we can help you",

he had his hand out as he said warmly, "welcome sisters and brothers; to continue our journey you must shake the hand of I; Commander Thorn", I could feel the heat of the team telling me to say no within their head, I could feel that they were looking at me, persisting me not to do it, but if I didn't this lie would be exposed and we will all die if the whole forest is the clan.

With nervousness I grasped Thorn's hand firmly, only to flinch it away as I breathed in sharply, seeing my hand was burning a mark upon it.

I looked to the palm of my hand, seeing the marking that the woman had on her, the triangle, the two circles on the left and right point, the vertical line going down the palm of my hand and end with a circle, as the last circle met at the top of the line nearing the bottom tip of the triangle.

When looking to him he showed his hand, seeing the razor like thorns creating the shape of the mark, he had marked me, branded me.

Deago looked to my hand as he questioned,

"the hell is that?",

he looked to Thorn as he explained,

"the leader of the wonderer's pack must be branded, as for her team they will be killed",

with a puzzled look I tried to move, only to question,

"the hell did you do? Why can't we move?",

he had a smug look on his face as he stated,

"the fog is mine and the power is mine, the people here cannot handle the wrath of the springs behind my home, that is the heart of the queen of the springs we drink from within

the forest, however, I am strong enough to drink from the direct source",
the outside of the village was turning red, every corner and turn there was red smog entering the village as his words continued,
"you see every wanderer is a liar, they pretend to be something they are not. So we simply cure them, by death or by our rituals",
the people that appeared were young women and men, this power gave them youth and their rituals were the cause of being a psychopath, they didn't do anything it was a false belief that they follow, to give them power over life itself as they live for as long as the springs are around.
The people were wearing slim red and black side cloaks going on their left or right side, they wore a rugged black, red, or grey long shirt underneath, padded with a leather wrist band, clamping the shirts to their wrists.
The bands went halfway up their arms, trimmed with metal and held together by chains and rugged leather belts, they wore rugged black, red, or dark brown combat trousers as they were tucked in firmly with their trimmed black boots, the appeal was very dark and sinister, the colour coordination reminded me of the devil themselves, no doubt that was their inspiration for such a dark clan.
Over their shirts, I noticed bloodstains of the markings showing through.
It was painted on with blood and it looked like their own, it was strange to see it, what did it mean? Why did they religiously follow the symbol and live upon these hot springs? Eternal youth isn't a gift, it's a curse, and the day the sun crashes you will still be breathing afterwards and have nowhere left to turn. The people were a grey colour, as if they were walking corpses yet they were breathing and acting just as alive as before, but a lot younger than they must have been.
The people of Thorn were just as clean as he was, the

woman had either their flowing red, black, brown, or blonde hair behind them in different styles.

Some had shorter hair shaved on the sides, the men were too the same, they were all different and some were the same as the other; they all looked after themselves, but it was what they had to show for it was their creepy crimson red eyes. They circled us, rounding up behind us as he ordered,

"the girl please",

a woman approached her as she said softly,

"to be ours, to be in bars, you are going to become like us, or you will pay with your heart",

she was guiding Abby past us, I couldn't move from my spot, my feet felt like they were cemented into the ground as I warned,

"don't you lay a finger on her",

the woman with her had silky dark brown hair, she had an innocent look to her as she reassured,

"oh no I won't be touching her at all, that isn't my honour", she made Abby face us as she couldn't move either, she was controlled to stay in one place like us, she tried to move but the floor wouldn't let her as she cursed,

"let me go you piece of shit",

the man tutted,

"see that was what I was worried about, the foul language of humanity, what have you become to show such dishonour", he approached her as he informed,

"Ariala why don't you go and get the gallows prepared, we have to convert this one first, she's not going to change as of yet, but if she continues to be like this Commander, then she won't be able to be saved",

Ariala walked past me going to the gallows as I raged,

"you don't get the right to kill people like this, the fuck are you to kill people without them fighting back",

the people were even more disgusted, I wanted them to be angry at me, I needed them to be wanting me dead not Abby, I don't know how I will worm my way out but I hope

Marella does something before we all suffer an excruciating fate.

He approached me as he stated,

"we hold nothing for you wonderer, the marker is on you, you are pure, these are not",

without hesitation I spat on his face before I snarled,

"you hold something of mine, if you want her you're going to have to kill me for her",

he wiped his face as he wondered,

"let me get this straight you're saying you want to challenge us?",

Marcella said shortly,

"Merider don't do it are you crazy?",

Thorn looked to her as he remarked,

"see your friends are wise Merider, you say that you can take us to combat and yet they don't have faith in you",

Deago blurted,

"we do have faith in her you asshat",

the last tick to Thorns anger as another person insulted him, he approached Deago as he stated,

"you clearly need a lesson or two as well",

Thorn snapped his fingers, making the fog clear a pathway as he remarked,

"come with me the man who hides his face, you want to challenge me then make the first move",

I warned,

"Deago don't do it, don't",

he went ahead and stormed towards Thorn, shooting his face over again and again but soon he ran out of bullets when meeting him ahead of us in-front of Abby.

The fog quickly covered the pathways, trapping Deago as Thorn remarked,

"you shot me many times and that's admirable",

he grasped Deago's pistol, melting the metal as he stated,

"but you have a few things to learn",

the gun was wrapping itself on Deago's right wrist, wrapping tightly as he tried to take it off, the metal was solidifying, looking like a thorn vine as he was starting to grow into incredible pain as the band was finally completed, the thorns were tight around his wrist, creating a bloodstream to drizzle down his hand.

He looked to Thorn as he threatened,

"you think you're invincible? Wait until we find your weakness, let's see how it turns out then",

the fog was thickening as our lower legs were soon being hidden by the smog as Thorn stated,

"you think we have a weakness, it's not like that I'm afraid, we don't have anything to hide",

he approached me as he questioned,

"now that you know empty threats don't do anything here, where is Marella, and I might just let your friend go",

I stated, "you don't get to blackmail me", even though I didn't want to protect her clearly these people were wanting her for a reason, and I can't throw someone in the deep end, it's just not right.

Even though my attempt to hide Marella was good enough cover for her she soon blurted,

"I'm Marella okay, just don't hurt them",

I turned back as I stated,

"Marella, don't do this they will kill you",

she could walk past us as the smoke made a small gap as she walked to Thorn.

As she moved past me she said under her breath,

"I can't be killed, remember",

she approached Thorn as she questioned,

"why the hell do you want me badly?",

he kept her stationary in place by the fog, using it to his advantage as he took off her helmet, he

examined it as he wondered,

"you wore this? Hmm that's not very leader-like is it? A leader must always show their face", he looked to me as he stated,

"because if they don't the foe won't know who they are after",

a smile grew on his face as he threw the helmet on the floor behind him, letting the smog engulf it as it melted into the pebbled ground, how is he doing that? clearly, the main hot spring is a different form of serum, that can only explain why he can do all these things, the people can do the same also, perhaps they got the weakened versions in the other springs, it might be filtering out the strongest part of the power, giving him more than the rest.

He wondered,

"Marella, no need to hide your powers, we know what you have",

her eyes started to glow back to neon green as she threatened,

"when Artell hears about this",

he cut in,

"he already knows dear sister, it's a shame you can't read my mind to know that, because in here you have no power",

he teased,

"go on, try it, see if you can choke me like last time, trying to burn me into ash like you did with a hundred of my people",

she tried to use her powers but it didn't work here, it was like her powers were no match to his as he remarked,

"the only thing you can do here is not die, that's what your powers can do, we're going to have a lot of fun with you",

he said in a chilling voice,

"you will be ritualised, you will be prepared, perhaps I might spare you of your dignity for the sake of you being Artell's legionary, but even so, he told me to punish you for your betrayal, he said you might learn if he taints the springs to repel the green serum, which as you can tell it's working very well",

he was trying to kill her, but in a way where she doesn't die, but her head will be in a bad place, I need to figure out how

355

to cure the springs, when that is done the power source will no longer be there and their powers wear out, they have lived with their power from the smog but also drinking directly from the source, maybe the powers are temporary.

He formed chains on her as he snapped his fingers, creating red metallic thorn wrist bands, they connected in the centre as they were entwined with one another.

His minions grasped her along with Deago as they were both tied with the thorny cuffs as Thorn instructed,

"take them to the preparation chamber, I'm certain that Merider won't mind attending the ceremony, after all it's an honour given from the Commander",

as they led them to the hut behind him he said with a sigh,

"ah, well that deals with two of them, we still have a child here, but not to worry we have plenty of plans of you",

he looked to Sevis as he continued,

" a man of Egyptverus shouldn't be here, however",

he got Sevis to the front, with the help of his minions Thorn wondered,

"what are you doing here boy?",

Sevis glared at him stating proudly,

"my purpose is to eliminate threats against humanity, I'm looking at one of them who will face Anubis's wrath",

Thorn approached him warning,

"your gods are no use here, they stay in their homes",

Sevis cut in,

"they are with us wherever we are, no matter what gods you follow. If you believe or not your beliefs are always with you, and they are never wrong for your judgement",

Thorn corrected,

"they are never right either; you see we hold the devil's drinks, well that's what Artell names it, it's really the fountain of youth, it holds all we need and all the power we need, our beliefs are survival of the pure race, not the survival of the idiocy and derange obsession with being the hero", he said coldly,

"there are no heroes in a world of darkness, only the saviours",

he is out of his mind, these people can't be saved Marella was right, I should have listened to her, but I had to see if for myself to believe her words were true.

Sevis said firmly,

"the faith you follow isn't real, it's all lies; you believe a simple experiment held upon you will bring you life, you never see it but you are Artell's experiments",

Thorn yet again corrected,

"we are his children and he gives us what we need to survive",

Sevis was trying to make them see the truth, not this made up fantasy over a stupid experiment, but no matter how many times he changes his words and tried to explain to Thorn about the situation he wouldn't listen, he would deny and deny until finally, he broke into an outburst of rage, he was growing sick of people telling him he was wrong even though it was true...he was wrong about the springs being a gift from Artell the godly figure they follow, they were there just for them to be turned into these things, they were experimented by him not birthed by him, they were once people of the earth but now they belong to insanity and delusions, this can't get worse.

With my fears growing wilder over the minute, Thorn explained,

"look you children wish not to see what we see, but until you do you won't understand what it's like, being in a haven of Artell",

he blabbed on,

"Artell isn't a figure, he doesn't exist in the world but he shows in the smog when he wants to show himself, he is the forest and the world needs more of them, he will create the lands again, raise them, take us from the ashes where we burned", the people were growing inspired by his crazed words as he carried on,

"the world before was taken because it was wrong, it wasn't his way. So we take this opportunity and make sure the real god Artell has the chance to show us rejuvenation, we will become pure, we may kill our own kind but they are in the wrong, we change there ways to what he wants",

his words grew a fire in me as I was growing more angry at him as his persuasive words echoed,

"we are the face of human survival, and nothing will get in our way",

the people were cheering, clapping, taking his words to their hearts as we were on the death rows.

How the hell do we get out of this alive?

Chapter Twenty-nine

Artell's Influence

Trying to make sure no one else got in trouble I stated,
"Thorn you know you want me not them, just tell me what you want and I can try and do something, anything just please don't hurt anyone else",
he snuffed as she approached me as he expressed,
"what part of we don't want you dead do you not understand",
with a puzzled look I questioned,
"we saw what you did with that woman, she looked dead to me, what are you trying to prove?",
he said firmly,
"it's proving what we can make of you and your poor followers, the sheep behind the wolf",
with firmness my teeth snarled,
"if you're going to speak in references, then they are wolves in sheep clothing's, one way or another we will get to you first",
he looked amused as he stated, "come with me Merider, take a walk with me",
the pathway cleared as I refused,

"you think I'm going to walk with you? I'd rather drown in a lake",

he smirked as he remarked,

"I can arrange that",

he walked away from me, allowing the team to watch me follow him, not wanting to but Deago said firmly,

"just go with it Merider, seems like playing on it does more good than bad, for now, that is",

I glanced back to my team seeing Rhax and Aries nodding shortly, Fuel was looking at me also, doing the same as the team agreed for me to go, if I didn't it will cause more havoc and I could do without the bloodshed, not unless we get the first blood.

My feet wandered behind him as the people were stood firmly in front of the hut's. They weren't moving from their spot as Thorn ordered,

"don't move a muscle, we can't have the impure wanderers stain you, brothers and sisters be patient, the rituals are coming soon, and when it starts we will convert them to our eyes",

with fear in my eyes I looked at the walls of the hut, the dark murky stone wall looked as though it could fall apart but it was holding up by his sheer beliefs, this whole place was starting to make me feel powerless.

I bit my lip as he opened the door, looking past him seeing the large hall inside, there were a set of stairs going up to the next floor to my left as there was a basement staircase tucked underneath it, they were large as a double door, it was large enough for three people to walk up and down the steps together. To the right was a ring of cubed shaped stone squares, they were hand-sized, there were a dozen of them that were space out to form the ring, it was large enough for a human to lay inside of it with an extra two-foot of space around them, just by looking at the bloodstains on the floor I knew exactly what it was used for.

He moved to the stone circle as he welcomed,

"this sector is the ritual chamber, the sign is drawn here as the wanderer can be cleansed",

he had me in his line of sight, ensuring I stood to his right as we looked down to the bloodied circle as I questioned,

"why do you do this? Cleansing them this way",

I turned to him as he challenged,

"what other way do you suggest I cleanse the impurities of a human being?",

I said with sharpness,

"you don't cleanse people, they cleanse themselves. We all have flaws, we all have impurities but draining them of their blood? Hanging them like they are sack of meat isn't going to cleanse them",

he put his hand up as he defended,

"oh quite the contrary. You see the marks have a power to each, they resemble what humans should be",

he firmly took my right hand, making me look at it as he stated,

"the triangle is the shield that protects their heart, it creates the boundaries between the life and death, it prevents humans from dying so easily",

he didn't allow me to free my hand as he continued,

"the circles represent the four horsemen of the apocalypses, the very thing that destroyed this world but in the end it will protect us in the world of today, they have done their job and will serve us in the world of today",

he gently brushed his fingers up the line going down the palm of my hand as he went on,

"the line is the road we take, from our end to the new beginning, the endless road that you carry yourself down, leading a heard of clueless sheep's",

I moved my hand, causing him to put his hand on my throat as he clenched his teeth as he threatened,

"you try to fight me, but it's no use, Merider",

he put his hand away, clenching his hands slightly as he apologised,

"sorry about that, sometimes when people don't let me help them, it gets me a little angry",
his eyes shimmered a neon red as his words finished.
He lowered his hand as he questioned,
"now did you need me to answer your questions? After all, you said you were here for answers",
I rubbed my neck, as my right hand was feeling sore and warm from the burn mark, I don't know what he was or how he did it but his powers are corrupted, I know a corrupted K.I.L.O when I see one, he just isn't letting it change his form, but I don't want him to change, I've been into too many fights with a K.I.L.O to know that's never a good idea when a simple human, not infected. My words were jittering as I was trying to find a different question to ask him, one to not insult him but still needing some understanding to all this madness, perhaps if he tells me more about this place I can figure out what to do, so far purifying the springs might be a lost cause.
I questioned,
"what are you? Who are you people? We came here knowing about The Cursed Village",
he corrected,
"we don't like that term. Look I can tell you about our cause and what we stand for, but to tell you about us? No, you are not wanting to know for the right reasons, you wish to figure us out, and we can't let you do that without you wanting to know us, you don't wish to know us, not yet",
he continued firmly,
"you never thought of us like family and we may not be blood-related, but they are my brothers and sisters, daughters and sons. They will never want anyone else to be like a father, husband or ruler like me. I am the one that will help cleanse them, heal them, they came here as broken people, but I fixed them into tranquillity",
he looked to the basement stairs as he informed,
"Merider, come with me",

362

he moved to the edge of the hall wall to his left, letting us watch them move Marella out of the basement.

The room was filling with smog, as the ground was shielded with it. They dragged Marella to the circle.

I couldn't move from my place as Thorn stated,

"you will be the star of the show, Merider, you get to see how the process goes, we have my trusted wife to do the job for me, Ariala, as you know from earlier",

Marella was unconscious, I don't know what they did to her but she was completely stone-cold, for all I know they could have deactivated her powers, if they worship Artell and he wanted her to pay he would have told them how to deactivate her powers.

With anger, I raged,

"you can't hurt her",

he smirked wondering,

"you think she will feel this? She's out cold but I guess when she wakes up she will feel it, you're fortunate that we aren't the barbaric people you think we are and have her awake during this process",

they had her wear nothing but her undergarments, my eyes wanted to look away, but he was watching me, ensuring I looked at her as Ariala cut Marella's bra as she laid in the centre of the circle.

She had her knees next to each side of Marella's waist, mounting on top of her as she held a dagger made of glass in her hands.

The dagger had a cylinder-shaped to it as the blade's edge was pointed and sharper than ever, the hilt of the dagger was too made of glass but ravelled in a strip of black leather, the transparent glass blade allowed me to see Marella's bare body as Ariala started to engrave the symbol on her chest.

The triangle was carved carefully above her breasts, the point facing down to her feet was between each breast, bleeding drizzles of blood down her chest, as the top left and right side of the triangles were getting the circles carved next to them.

Ariala carved a circle ring to the left side of the point of the triangle, along with the right just below the collar bone, it was making me cringe, hearing the tear of the flesh and the squelching of the blood as the flesh rubbed against each other, only to expose the thick red blood underneath the skin.

I looked to Thorn as he admired,

"Ariala does such a careful and tender job, she makes sure every person is respected for the preparation of the gallows",

my throat swallowed as I brought myself to question,

"what are you going to do to Deago? What are you going to do to my team",

he didn't answer me, he was watching Ariala as she carved a circle below the triangle point, soon making a line going vertically down the stomach, she ended the line only to create a small circle above the belly button as Thorn stated,

"Artell said to leave her pride, he merely wanted her to pay, so we shall put the sacrificial wear on, the thorns",

I said with a snarl,

"you make me sick, you think this is going to do anything? You're just going to kill her, he doesn't want her to suffer, he wants her to die, and that's what you want too",

he smirked coldly as he looked at me as he ordered,

"Ariala, get Marella dressed and place her to the left of the ritual ring as Deago needs to be cared to"

she did what he said, moving Marella to the left of the ring as she used her powers to make thorn undergarments, it looked painful, but it was layered over her previous undergarments, the bra on the other hand what removed by Ariala before she continued to coat her body in thorns.

As she finished up she moved away from her body as she placed her dagger to the left of the ring as she informed,

"I will get Deago, my love, Frayus will help me, not to worry",

Thorn reassured,

"I'm certain you will get the job done, Deago won't need the sacrificial clothing nor the symbol, he will be hung",

Ariala brushed her hand on his shoulder before kissing his cheek as she walked past him, they were psychopaths, they thought they were in some sort of happy ending world, the world of green and the towering mountains in the horizon. They were in the world of the dead and burned lands, they saw the ashy ground as the greenery, but they were in hell, they were going to be sent to it when I get through to them; this magic, this power they are using will be the end of them, they don't need it but they feel like they do, perhaps the side effect to drinking the tainted spring water is that it's addictive, just like a drug.

Thorn snapped his fingers as he stated,

"We better get Marella out there",

the fog ate her body, taking her into the smoke, soon disappearing as she was teleported outside, alive or unconscious I don't know but there must be a way to stop this.

With a thought, I pleaded,

"please, I will do anything, just let my team go, please",

he wondered,

"you say team, why not call them your friends? After all, you claim they are wolves in sheep clothing",

he observed me as I stated,

"they are my friends, but they are my team, they are my people and they are survivors. No matter what label I give them their lives don't belong to you, they belong to me and you don't get to take them like a coward",

he challenged,

"so you want them to fight for their death? You have a weird sense of words Merider, you want them to die",

I stated, "we are all facing death but this isn't the way;,we need a compromise you can't kill my team, you can't take us like this",

he took my pleads, my words, perhaps they convince him to change his mind or I made things worse, either way, there's a way out but I know that it can't be blood-free, we're too deep into it to not shed blood on the way out of this prison.

My helpless pleads for mercy were no use, perhaps something else for him, do something else.

With firmness I questioned,

"what do you want from me? and don't say cleansing because it's more than that, I know when I see revenge, I can see it in your eyes",

he had a sly smile on his face as he remarked,

"what can you possibly give me? you have already given me everything I needed, you are pure and",

I cut in,

"I don't fucking care what you think of me, pure or not, what the hell do you want? I'm not messing around",

his amused face was like thunder, as he weren't happy with my words, I wanted him to listen to me and he certainly did, he stated,

"you say you want to help me but you use that tongue of yours, something about you is pure but the language you speak is not",

I head-butted him, trying to agitate him, his nose was busted as the blood streamed down his nose, his already wonky nose snapped and crunch back into place, as the blood streamed down his nose was wondering back into his eyes, staining the whites of it red, to soon returning into his red glow as he stated,

"you try to fight me, but it never works, you see the spring is what makes you who we are, you ask about what we are and we are the spring, we belong to the springs, we take it into our systems and merge it into the world of today",

he let the fog clear, allowing me to move freely as he persisted, "come, lets see how your team are doing",

my eyes glared at him, seeing him open the door as he let me go first.

When leaving the hut my team was rounded to face the gallows ahead of us, from left to right stood Abby, Aries with Fuel on her shoulder, Alis, Marcella, Xharlot, Qorin, and

Rhax.

When moving to the left side of the line I stood firmly by Abby as Thorn ensured,

"not to worry, the child will be dealt with later, seems as though we have our target, for now, our main objective", even though the fog covered our feet, this time it allowed us to move, he didn't see any reason why he would need to restrict us, even though we were going to be watching one of our friends be hanged...strange, I just called Marella my friend. Abby was looking up to me as she worried,

"Merider what happened in there?",

she could see I was upset inside, something that no one could tell, not unless they looked into my eyes to see the tears irritating it.

I bit my lip before I said firmly,

"Abby, I need you to close your eyes",

she puzzled,

"Merider",

I repeated, "

I need you to do this Abby, I don't want you to watch this", Thorn remarked,

"you think that will help her? She needs to see this, if she doesn't, then she will be weak forever, you believe she is weak, you want her to close her eyes, not see the face of death, the greatest honour to us",

I looked left to him as I snapped,

"there's no honour in seeing a dead body",

my lips sealed itself when facing ahead at the gallows as he stated,

"if you think this is dishonourable, then you might not be as pure as I predicted",

Marella was stood on the wooden platform of the gallows ahead of us, she faced us as she stood firmly where she was, she was looking to us, like she she was saying with her eyes not to worry, but I couldn't help but worry, her powers are gone, she can't get it back.

There was a cloud of fog forming to her left, it was shaping Deago as he stood firmly with his helmet on his head, they had him in his clothes, they didn't see him pure, but I don't know if it's going to be a fifty-fifty thing, what even is this suppose to prove?

They can't live this, they both can't, perhaps one of them goes and the other one lives but who? They want Marella dead just as much as they want Deago dead, they marked him with the Thorn band, that must mean something, or was that all for show? These people were crazy, I couldn't watch this, but I had no choice, if I don't he will have less trust in me, he won't see me fit to be near him, I need to be near this man, the time will come when I can strike but so far with all the eyes of his minions and people, I don't think now is going to cut it, there must be a way where I can end him for good.

Deago looked around only to freeze when feeling the barbed wire tuck under his neck, it prevented him from speaking a word as they were tightening it, just enough so Thorn could stand in front of the platform with ease.

He snapped his fingers, making the fog lock on our feet's as he remarked,

"almost slipped my mind, wouldn't want a hero to try and save the day",

the people were lurking behind us, crowding just a few feet leaving a large arched gap as they were watching Thorn as he announced,

"my brothers, my sisters. We stand here to watch these impure mortals go through the trial of Artell, live or die they will choose, but even a death can be a good sign, they will be apart of us, be one of us",

he moved his right arm out to motion Marella as he went on,

"Marella has been to us once but she came back, returned for our help and guidance",

when lowering his arm he moved his left arm to Deago as he expanded,

"as for Deago he is but a wondered, a lost and helpless

wonderer, he could be our brother, or like Marace in the woods who hands in the forest, she takes the pledge to protect us but she has failed us, lets hope he will not", Marace? That couldn't be the person we found earlier? I think it might be, how the hell do they live with themselves.
He looked to me as he stated,
"we have Merider who is willing to change, make the first step to her pure life. To watch the two souls collide or perhaps one leave and the other will stay, either way, their resurrected souls might turn them to us, or turn them to the dead, our judgement is with the gallows, we can tell who will be ours and who are not fit to be within our presence",
my words were frozen, I couldn't bring myself to scorn him, tell him what I thought of a sick human being he and the others were, they didn't deserve to be alive, they took lives for no reason, no motives, nothing to fight for, they were just taking things that didn't belong to them, the only thing we belong to is death and this isn't his work.
My words shook as I begged,
"don't do this, this isn't deaths work, you know full well he wouldn't want this unless deserved",
he tried to be smart as he stated,
"ah but they deserve this, you see Merider death is everywhere, he watched us, he is us, but you out of all people he cares for the most, or tries to kill you off first but you never gave him the chance, now I am handing him a gift, to spare you, the gift of death is the best gift of all",
he said it with a cold grin as he was persistent to do this, him wanted me to suffer this wasn't what he was believing in, he wanted us to suffer and he enjoyed it, he enjoyed every moment as he strolled to the left side of the gallows to where the leaver was that lowered the floor of the platform.
The rugged iron made leaver was to the left of the crank that raised the barbed wire rope.
He stood with pride as he looked to the crowd as he announced,

"we hold our brother and sister in the wires of Artell, the very thing that will tell us who dies, and who lives, a door will lower and it shall tell us who our next member will be, but the one that dies will not be singled out, I can assure you", as his words were muffling I said firmly,

"Abby, do what I say",

I glanced down seeing her screwed face as she tightly closed her eyes, she was clenching her fists as she was fearing the gallows noises, and the sound of the people as they cheered.

My eyes were watering with as the team was forcing themselves to watch the suffering wait, the horrible pause as Thorn was getting carried away with his roars and speech of pride, the one he had practised over and over, to think that we weren't the first people to be here.

With my left hand I firmly held my necklace, un-tucking it as my mutters for mercy repeated as I said with a whisper,

"The heart of the moon, please don't fail us, show us the night is merciful, please help us and show us the way, we need your help, we need guidance, we need this to stop before we lose ourselves forever. The bad, the good, we just need the silence to be thick, the people need your help, we need your help",

my words to the moonstone might help, but it may not, yet what Byzer's mother told me was that he was the protector of the moon, healer, he healed people, so perhaps Khonsu can heal them or help us find a way to stop this from happening again, I just can't deal with this anymore, the pain, the hurt, it's killing me and cutting me into pieces.

When Thorn's words were stopping I knew what was going to happen next, I pulled Abby closer to my side, letting her hold it tighter as the sounds of the gallows crackled.

What has the world come to?

Printed in Great Britain
by Amazon

41202789R00205